THE ROMA SEVEN

RICHARD L. ROSS

ISBN-13: 978-1541297869
ISBN-10: 1541297865

Richard L. Ross
rich.ross79@gmail.com
theromaseven.com

Dedicated to my wife Lori, who was patient enough to watch me sit at my computer putting this together for those many hours. And also for granting me my two little reasons for being, my children, Aliyah and Dylan Ross.

Be careful fighting someone else's demons—it may awaken your own.

- Bryant McGill

PART 1

CHAPTER 1

Christian Xavier Solomon

August, 1995

Black Pillar Island: his mother's solution to their lifetime of problems. Christian's mother had raised him to deal with life by burying all that was wrong and turning his back on it. But Christian didn't believe such a quick fix would cure years of poison. His life, and everything that surrounded it, was a quagmire of pain and disillusionment. Everything . . . except one thing. That one thing had come and gone, but it was something he would never let go of.

The life he had lived back home in Stoneminster Falls, since birth was rotten to the core. It was all he'd ever really known. He could only conclude that everything he would touch, even if it was a new city, would all end with the same result.

He found it almost comical that his mother thought simply living in a different place while working another dead-end job would make things different. Could they have been? It was such a frustrating question when the answer always remained the same. Maybe it wasn't so comical after all.

It was a new start, though. He could take it by the hand and see where it led him. Maybe he could be proactive and make things different, instead of continuing to lock himself in the dark shell that had always been his prison.

He lay on the floor amongst scattered, unpacked boxes and bags. This small, cluttered space was now his room. His thoughts flowed through his head like a river raging towards a waterfall that eventually just hurls itself into a misty pool of oblivion. Some would supposedly find this darkly beautiful, but Christian found it empty. Yet this is where he chose to remain as he stared at the yellow, cigarette-stained ceiling. *What am I doing here?*

His mother had asked him at least three times to put everything away, but he didn't know where to start. He didn't want to start. His self-justified defiance made him question why he even should. He didn't choose any of this. That bitch should be the one to do it if she wanted it done. It was the least she could do.

His hand protected an unopened envelope pressed firmly against his chest. He held it up towards the bedroom light, hesitant to open it. Everything he had ever thought was good and had cared about was tucked neatly inside that little package. He feared that by reading its contents the one positive thing he once had would come crumbling down like everything else in the first seventeen years of his life. On the other hand, if it remained untouched, nothing bad could come of it. Ignorance of reality can never disappoint a person.

What did it matter anyway? Opening the envelope wasn't going to change anything. It was already a loss with no sense of closure. The words on that piece of paper were irrelevant now that goodbye had already come and gone.

"Fuck it," he whispered.

He got up off the floor and reached into his duffel bag, pulling out a pocket knife. He gently sliced open the top of the envelope, taking care not to disturb the area where her saliva had sealed it. That was the one and only thing he could preserve. His chest pounded as he slid his fingers in, gripping the thin slip of paper.

"Christian! What the hell?"

Christian quickly dropped the envelope. Still clutching the pocket knife, he looked at his mother with disgust, and discreetly nudged the envelope behind a box with his foot.

His mother, cigarette in hand, pushed a stack of boxes to the side, easing her way into his room. "You haven't even touched one single thing in here. What have you been doing?"

"I've been doing whatever I'm doing."

"What is that supposed to mean?" She walked towards him, noticeably trying to peer around the box where he was hiding the letter. "Chrissy, what's in that envelope?"

He put his head down, avoiding eye contact.

Her irritable excitement quickly calmed, "Christian baby, is that from her?"

"It's none of your business."

"This is a fresh start, Chrissy. Let's try to keep looking forward and—"

"Chrissy is a girl's name. Don't call me that anymore."

She sighed, disappointment and sadness replacing the sternness and concern on her face.

"You need to start leaving the past behind you and let those things go. Including her."

"I know Mom, she's gone. Permanently. I get it. I wish you would do the same thing sometimes. And could you quit smoking that in my room?"

His mother's eyes moistened. She took the cigarette in her right hand and butted it in an ash tray she held in her left. She wiped her eyes quickly and turned to leave, but paused at the doorway and turned around.

Before she could speak another word, Christian continued.

"What? Don't look at me like that."

"You aren't the only one that hurts, Christian. I'm trying really hard here. What have I done that's so wrong?"

"Good question. What *haven't* you done wrong?"

"I've done this all for you!"

"Running here? You've done nothing for me."

"That's not true, Chrissy."

"You think by running here things will be different?"

"You've only been here for three days!"

"Things will never be different! Shit happens, over and over and over! And don't lie to me and tell me you care. You've only ever showed that you don't."

"How can you say that?"

"Don't think these so-called changes you've made suddenly makes you mother of the year. It doesn't."

She stepped out of the room and Christian quickly slammed the door behind her, leaning his back against it and sliding down to the floor. He hugged his knees to his chest. His eyes brimmed with tears; not of remorse, but of hatred. It was the only emotion he ever felt. So strong, so dominating. Hatred birthed by years of unforgiveable pain.

If only he could inflict this pain on everybody who had ever hurt him or let him down. Even though he got the blame for standing up to that fat bastard back home, for once in his life, it felt good to finally stand up for himself. If he had to do it again, he would. He wouldn't get knocked down anymore. Not this time around.

Although he didn't fully believe he had what it took to follow through with his new thought process, he might as well try to speak it into existence. Besides, there was only one thing back home that could ease his pain.

He glared at the half-open envelope on the floor. He retrieved it on the way to the bare mattress and pillow he called his bed. Lying down, he took a pack of cigarettes and matches out from under the mattress. Despite telling his mother to put hers out, he lit up, then slipped the paper out of the envelope. After a deep drag, he unfolded it.

August 19, 1995

Hey Christian,

This is really hard for me to write. I wish I could have had the chance to speak to you in person, but you couldn't even find it in yourself to say good-bye. Rightfully so, I guess.

I'm starting the communications program at South Stony in a week; you know, for the whole journalism thing? Writing is my passion, and I write about anything and everything all the time. But despite it all, I can't figure out why I find it so difficult to write you this letter. Even though I'm at a loss for words, I think of you every single day...and my heart breaks more and more.

Do you remember that fall 10 years ago? Do you ever think about that? I do all the time. It seems so long ago. You were eight and I was ten. I thought you were so cute, with your pudgy cheeks that still had all their baby fat. Should I even mention your lisp? I cannot forget that cute little lisp you used to have. And I still laugh inside at how you didn't even want to acknowledge me when I approached you at the park. You acknowledged me once I let you play with my Gameboy, though. You told me, "Girls aren't supposed to play video games." That was so typical of you, even to this day.

But most importantly, that was the day I met who I still consider my best friend.

I really wish things didn't turn out the way they did, Chris. It just makes me so sad that when you came to me, I turned you away. You just don't know how truly sorry I am for that. I didn't know how far you were willing to go to escape your life; if I did, I wouldn't have told you to leave that night.

I just want you to know how much you really mean to me, Chris. You were my first real friend, my first kiss and my first love. Yes, I said it: my first love. I always wanted to tell you that, but you push away any positive feelings anybody, including me, tries to show you. I understand that you hate yourself, and I also understand why you're so bitter towards the world. But you need to know that you're such a good person underneath all that sadness, anger and pain.

I know that for many years people have treated you very badly; but you can't let people, especially those people, define who you are. Sometimes I think I know you more than you know yourself. From the outside looking in, I see so many wonderful aspects of your character that you never let out. At least you were able to sometimes show that side to me, and I feel privileged to know what a remarkable person you really are.

I know all you want in life is to know what real happiness is, and I only wish I could turn back time and be the one to show you.

Remember, none of these things in your life are your fault. You are not to blame.

Anyway, I just wanted you to know how much I care for you. This is the only way I could tell you. I admire you for everything you are—and don't ever forget that. It just shouldn't have ended the way it did. And I wish, wish, wish you just stayed with me that night. I thank God every day that you are ok, and I hope you can find happiness and inner peace, because you deserve it.

Just so you know, I will always be here for you...no matter what.

Victoria
xoxo

CHAPTER 2

Diana Solomon

Diana, just out of the shower, retrieved a towel off the rack. She thought back to the conversation with Christian and sighed. *Why must everything be a fight?*

Did she fail him so severely that all their communication had to be a confrontation? It wasn't like she was overly strict with him; in fact, Christian was always given his space. Maybe that was the problem. It was hard to love someone who seemed to hate her so much.

Getting ready to wait tables at the strip club till odd hours of the morning only added to her gloom. She sat at her dresser mirror staring at her makeup. Before picking up her lipstick she studied her face; once beautiful, was now worn out, tired and too aged for being thirty-six. Her tired look was permanent.

She softly ran her fingers down her cheek, feeling a mask hiding something that no one but her knew was there. She slightly turned her head right and left, exposing her teeth, lamenting over their discoloration. They were yellow and seemed on the verge of rotting away. She picked up her brush and vigorously dragged through the knots in her wet, stiff, bleach-blonde hair.

The phone rang and there was only one person with her number.

"Dammit Mom."

She put her brush down and half-heartedly walked over and picked up the phone.

"Hi Mom."

"Hi Di, it's me."

"Miranda?"

"Yeah, I got your number from your mother."

Diana grabbed her hair as if to pull it out. "I was planning on calling you but I've had so much—"

"Save it, Di. Why didn't you at least tell me you were leaving?"

"Well, shit, all you would have done was talk me out of it as usual."

"You could have at least told me."

"It's all for Christian." Diana fiddled with the phone cord and leaned her back against the wall.

"How are you going to fix your son when you've hardly been able to fix yourself?"

"You know what, Miranda, this is why I left without getting your fricken permission."

"Ok, what's done is done, I'm just concerned. I need to know, have you had any cravings?"

"What the hell, Miranda? You know I haven't touched ice in twenty-six months."

"I wasn't talking about meth. Anyways, have you told him yet?"

"He wouldn't care in the least." Diana looked at the floor and massaged her temples with her middle finger and thumb.

"Did you find a new doctor?"

"I'm not going to chemo, if that's what you mean."

"It sounds like you're giving up."

"Just because you're my sponsor doesn't mean you know what's best for me." Diana took the phone away from her ear, held it in front of her and glanced at the receiver.

"I *was* your sponsor, you mean. I'm here as your friend, as I've always been."

"Look, I have to go to work," Diana said.

"Have you had a drink?"

"I'm a meth addict, not an alcoholic. Why does it feel like you are interrogating me?"

"That concerns me right—"

"I'm not your concern. If I had a drink or not, it's all over for me now, anyway."

"Don't say that, you have options. Don't—"

"Give up?" Diana said, "well, I give up!" Diana slammed the phone down. She reached for it again, but pulled her hand back.

She walked over to her night table, sat on the edge of the bed and opened the drawer. There lay an unopened bottle of Jack Daniels. Staring at the amber liquid in the bottle was as if she were locking eyes with her greatest enemy or best friend, depending on which day it was. She grasped the bottle with both hands, closed her eyes and took a deep breath.

When it was cracked open she was calmed by the comforting aroma of numbness. She put the bottle to her mouth and tilted her head back quickly, longing for that lingering burn in her throat.

However, as soon as the soothing, warm liquid filled her mouth, she jumped up and ran to the bathroom, bottle in hand. She spit the whiskey into the sink. Befriending her worst enemy again was too close for comfort.

The bottle now sat on the counter as she wiped her mouth in a hand towel and began to cry. Turning back to the sink, she looked at the bottle and then the drain.

She wiped the tears from her eyes, picked up the bottle and returned to her night table to put it back in the drawer and resume her position in front of the dresser mirror. Frustrated, she began to rip through her knotted hair with her brush again, whispering, "I'm not an alcoholic."

CHAPTER 3

Greener Grass

It was a long, dreaded walk up to the entrance of Christian's new school. Despite chaffing at having to make this walk with his mom, he was determined to make something out of this undesired fresh start.

The courtyard and the school itself were a lot larger than he thought they would be. The area was scattered with benches and perfectly trimmed random trees. The lawn was so green and well-kept, quite unlike the run down schools he had attended back home. Could this be a sign that things would be different?

He and Diana walked past dozens of chattering students laughing and yelling. Christian couldn't help but feel that it was all at his expense. That all-too-familiar tightening anxiety overtook his body, giving him a knot in his chest. He had felt this too many times before, and it made him want to turn around, run away and not look back.

Entering the school, Christian was blasted with the institutional smell somehow common to every public school. He was amazed at how the smell was always the same; if torment had a scent, this would be it.

They approached the front desk in the office where a receptionist and two other secretaries sat typing at their keyboards. The receptionist, who appeared to be in her sixties, glared up above the rims of her bifocals.

"Good morning, how can I help you?"

"It's my son's first day of school," Diana said, placing her purse on the reception desk.

Those were very familiar words to Christian. How many *first days* of school was a kid supposed to have? In almost thirteen years, he had probably been to about seven or eight different schools. He should have been getting better at this, but he only seemed to be getting worse.

The secretary motioned toward another lady, Mrs. Wallace, to escort Christian to his home room. As Christian began to leave the office, his mother gently grabbed him by the shoulder. Christian stopped and only looked at her from the corner of his eye.

"Chrissy, please do your best to make things work here."

Christian squinted his eyes and shook his head. He was in disbelief that she would even say that; but at the same time, not surprised.

"Look, I know you weren't the instigator of a lot of those fights. But if someone makes you angry, instead of beating them senseless, how about trying to use your words. You might be pleasantly surprised."

His mother was so clueless and insensitive when it came to what he had to endure at school. It was more important for her to save face and not have to be the embarrassment of the town, rather than caring an ounce about his own well-being. He turned and walked out of the office with Mrs. Wallace following behind him.

Classes had begun. Most of the students were already in their classrooms with the exception of a few stragglers who were rushing to beat the bell.

Christian did not want any part of the small talk that Mrs. Wallace attempted to engage in and kept his responses limited to *yes* and *no* answers. He was just anxious to get to class, find a seat—preferably one in the back—and experience the relative relief provided by someone else taking center stage, such as a teacher.

Outside of Christian's new classroom, he felt that gnawing tightening in his chest again. He hated the idea of walking in and being introduced to his new classmates. At the very last minute before opening the door Christian said, "Miss, where is the closest washroom?"

"Just around the corner to the left. But can it wait? Class has already started."

"No, I really have to go."

"Ok then," Mrs. Wallace said, "I'll wait right here."

Christian didn't really have to use the washroom, but just needed a little time to collect himself. The first thing he saw when he walked in was a kid who was visibly upset standing at the first sink along the washroom wall, staring blankly into the mirror. He was no larger than Christian's small-for-his-age stature and looked to be in the same grade.

Christian went to the sink farthest away from him and turned on the tap, proceeding to wet down his face. He dampened his hair and combed through it with his fingers, pushing his bangs back out of his eyes, all the while forcing himself not to look in the kid's direction.

"I'm not gonna take this shit anymore," the kid said as he continued to stare himself down in the mirror.

"What?" Christian said. The last thing he wanted was to have a conversation with this kid.

"It's hardly the first class and they've started with me again. I can't handle this. I need to do something."

"Why are you telling me this?" Christian was still not looking in the kid's direction.

The kid blew out a deep breath as though readying himself for battle, and turned to walk out of the washroom. "Forget it."

Christian finally took his eyes away from his reflection and watched as the kid reached the entrance. For one second he put his own feelings aside. "Hey, what's your name?"

"Liam."

"How old are you?"

"Seventeen."

"One word of advice, Liam. Stand up to them or you'll always find yourself in some washroom, staring at a mirror."

Liam pushed through the door and left, not saying a word. Christian felt satisfied that he did his part. Fricken kid. Last thing Christian needed was some stranger dishing out their personal problems on him. At least it was brief and he was finally gone.

Although, just like Liam, Christian had found himself staring at many a mirror, hoping to find answers deep in his own soul, answers that never came. For Christian, the searching always ended in disappointment. Hopefully Liam would have it better.

CHAPTER 4

Liam Malachi

Liam never went to his first class. He successfully ducked teachers and other school staff who were roaming the hallways. He just didn't have the energy. He waited outside his brother's home room for his class to end.

The bell rang and the students rushed out of the classroom. His brother walked right by not noticing him.

"Sammy! Wait up," Liam said, stopping Sammy in his tracks.

"Oh hey, Li."

"Get your stuff, we're going home."

"But Li, schools not over." Sammy kept on walking in front of Liam.

Liam grabbed Sammy's back pack, stopping him. "It is for us."

"Ok." Sammy shrugged and walked behind Liam as he always did. Sammy never really questioned his brother; he'd always follow his lead.

Liam and Sammy went through hard times in and outside of school on a regular basis. The difference was that when something happened to Sammy it was almost like he could just forget about it by the next day. But in Liam, it got buried and slowly built up. Liam wanted to be a source of stability and protection for his brother, but how could he be when he was such a mess himself?

He sometimes thought that being simple like Sammy would make things easier. He didn't know for sure, but he believed Sammy didn't fully understand everything that went on. It was sad; but at the same time, it was an antidote that kept his brother from the poison that destroys innocence.

They successfully made it outside and walked over to the bike rack to unlock Sammy's bike. The courtyard was empty and everything was clear for their escape.

Liam, who was walking, watched Sammy ride his prized possession. Sammy sped away from him and then back towards him, over and over again. It was just like he was a little kid. On paper he wasn't, but in every other way he was. Liam longed for that childhood that was cut short.

"Are we going to the Creek?" Sammy said.

"In a bit."

The two entered an open area with a bike path surrounding a man-made pond. Sammy leaned his bike up against a bench and they sat down looking out at ducks being fed by an old lady a few benches away.

This scene of people walking and riding by brought up bitter sweet memories for Liam. Memories of a time when things were normal. When he was an everyday kid with not a worry in the world.

"Why we stopping here, Li?"

"Just killing time."

"Mama used to bring me here all the time."

"Yeah, me too." Liam picked up a rock and skipped it in the water.

"You know when we can see her again? She's been sick for so long."

"Dunno, Sammy."

This was a story he had to tell for years, and was one of the many crosses he had to bear because his father was too scared to tell

Sammy the truth—or maybe his father was scared to face the truth himself.

"Why did Mama never let us feed the ducks?" Sammy said.

"I don't know."

"She always told me I could only look at them."

Liam stood up and brushed off the back of his pants. "Who cares, Sammy? Let's go."

Sammy looked up at Liam with confusion. It hurt Liam to see that his brother just didn't know any better, and his dismissiveness quickly evaporated, and he sat back down.

"You want to sit a while?" Liam rubbed Sammy's shoulder.

Sammy nodded his head.

"You really miss her, don't ya?"

"I do, Li. Don't you?"

Liam grabbed his backpack and pulled out the sandwich he had packed for lunch. He pulled the pieces of bread apart and let the meat drop on the ground next to the bench.

"I don't know why mom would never let us feed'em." Liam ripped off a piece of bread and threw it towards the ducks. He handed Sammy the other slice.

"Forget what Mom said. Go feed them damn ducks."

CHAPTER 5

Stand Up

With two classes down, there was only lunch and two more classes to go. Christian managed to get through the morning without incident. There were kids whispering behind his back, but he made a conscious effort to tune out everything around him. Unfortunately, because of that, he tuned out the teachers too.

The lunch room was full with all the cliques gathered at their tables cracking jokes and laughing. Christian stood holding his food tray of dried up shepherd's pie and half-cooked vegetables, along with whatever the hell the mushy stuff was for dessert.

He scanned the room to figure out what category of clique he would fit into. There was the jock table, with the meat-head freaks. They were probably discussing their good times at the gym and what muscle group they planned to work next.

The closest table in proximity was the skater and grunge crew, who smelled so strongly of pot that Christian imagined he could see smoke wafting from their bodies.

In the far corner of the cafeteria however, there was a table that was completely empty, so that was where he headed. Christian put his tray down and pulled out a chair.

"Hey, small fry, that seat is taken," said a guy from two tables away.

Christian looked at eight empty chairs and then moved to the next one.

"That one's taken too," the same guy said again.

This time Christian shook his head and sat down. The guy in question stood up from his seat and made his way towards him. He was a blubbery mass of a man. He had a shaved head, with his eyebrow and both ears pierced. He sat directly across from Christian and stared at him with a smug half-smile. Christian remained silent without taking his eyes off the fork he was using to play with his food and trying his best to ignore the confrontational presence that sat in front of him.

"Maybe you didn't hear me, small fry. This one's taken, that one's taken, and so are the rest of'em."

Christian still didn't acknowledge him. He did not want any problems. But the chances of that were starting to look slim. So much for going through the day without incident.

Christian was ready this time around. He even knew he could hold his own against this guy if he had to. He had proved in the past that his size didn't matter.

One thing Christian knew how to do was fight. This asshole stood about six feet tall and probably weighed a good two-hundred and fifty pounds. That was nothing.

Christian didn't want any part of that though. He just wanted to be left in peace and not embarrassed in front of the school. But he would act on instinct if it came down to it. This guy's larger size did not intimidate him. Christian sat on the edge of his seat, ready to pounce.

"You don't listen, you don't speak. Doesn't that make you . . ." The guy paused and turned back towards his table. "Who's that retarded poet we were laughing about in English class, Kirt?"

"Helen Keller."

"Yeah. You're like that Helen Keller bitch."

While Christian tried to make sense of the Helen Keller comment, he still remained true to his decision to ignore this guy. It was only his first day. The last thing he needed was for things to escalate.

"Fine. Let me do the talking for both of us. I'm Jordy, last name Baxter. I make the rules in this school . . . fuck that . . . I make the rules in this city. Rule number one, no mainlanders allowed. You a mainlander, right?"

Christian tossed his fork onto his plate and leaned back in his seat. He made eye contact with Jordy for the first time. His impassive expression matched his relaxed, careless posture.

Jordy placed his elbows on the table, easing his way closer. "This is how my people see mainlanders. Y'all either get fed with a silver spoon or you're street-rat scum who eat their own shit off the street to survive. Which one are you, small fry?"

Christian broke his silence. "I don't want a problem."

"You already got one, you little bitch, by sitting in my chair. Get it?"

Christian remained silent again.

"See that table over there." Jordy pointed to the table where he had been sitting and six of his friends were sitting there, apparently greatly entertained by the harassment Jordy was inflicting on Christian. "That table is all white, pure blood, islanders. Born and raised here. We all belong here. I don't see no mat saying, *mainlander scum invited.* Did you see a welcome mat, fucktard?"

If history spoke for itself, this was going to turn into a do-or-die situation. If Christian stood down, he would follow the same pattern he always did. He would allow the Jordy's of the world to bring him down. There was nowhere lower he could go. It was all up from here. He was not going to let this cycle continue and only take action when it was too late. Not this time. Not today. As the saying went: *If you do what you've always done, you'll get what you've always got.*

Christian placed his elbows on the table mirroring Jordy. He said in a softer voice, only loud enough for Jordy to hear. "You know, I may not speak, I may not listen. But Helen Keller, she was also blind. I'm damn sure not blind."

"Oh the mainland scum speaks," Jordy said.

"I see you, right now, sitting in front of me. You're just a fat-ass that even Helen Keller couldn't miss." Christian pointed to Jordy's table. "Do those guys take turns on you? Top or bottom, fucktard?"

Christian was surprised as his mother said he would be, when she told him to *use his words* this morning.

"The hell you say to me?" Jordy stood up and slammed his hands down on the table. His eyes were bulged and his face flushed.

Christian also stood up. "Go fuck your mother, asshole."

A choir of *oohs* and *aahs*, with some laughter resounded through the lunchroom. This time Christian's words were loud enough for the surrounding audience to hear. Christian stared down Jordy with his right fist clenched; his left hand was gripping his chair. He wouldn't think twice about using it as a weapon if need be.

The lunchroom supervisors took notice of the commotion and started rushing the table.

"You *must* be one of them street-rat mainlanders," Jordy said.

Jordy picked up Christian's tray and held it over his head, as if to slam it down on Christian. Christian put his hands up anticipating whatever was coming his way.

"Jordy! Put that down now!" One of the supervisors said.

Jordy looked at the supervisor and hesitated with the tray still up in the air. Another supervisor came from behind and restrained him while trying to remove the tray from his hands. Instead, the tray flipped in the air and crashed to the ground leaving a pile of mangled shepherd's pie and vegetables on the floor.

"What is wrong with you, Jordy? Come with me to the office—now!" The supervisor grabbed Jordy by the arm and pulled him away.

Before he was led from the lunch room, Jordy turned to get the last word. "Must feel like home now that you gotta eat that shit off the floor."

Christian turned back to the table and sat back down. The other supervisor approached him. "You're Christian Solomon, right?"

"Yeah."

"I'm Mr. Berry, Mercfield High's guidance counselor. I was going to catch up with you later to make an appointment."

"Appointment? For what?"

"Just some preliminary formalities. It's protocol for new students."

"You do this with every student? You must be busy."

"Let's talk at 2:15. Just go to the main office, they'll tell you where to go."

Christian would have liked to tell this guy where to go. He wasn't about to subject himself to someone attempting to pick his brain apart.

There was only one person that could have been behind this *introductory* session. His mother. Why couldn't people just leave him alone? She was the one that needed counseling, not him.

***

Christian decided to cut the day short. His blood was boiling and he meant to have some choice words with his mother. After leaving the lunchroom, Christian headed to his locker to grab his things. He'd hardly slammed his locker door and headed for the entrance when he heard a voice behind him. "Excuse me."

Ignoring the voice, Christian pushed his way through the school's front doors and could hear the person speed walking behind him, right on his tail.

"Hey! Don't you have a class to get to?"

Christian stopped in his tracks and turned towards the man. "Who the fuck is asking?"

"Pardon me?"

"You heard me." Christian took a pack of cigarettes out of his jacket pocket, stuck one in his mouth and lit it.

"I'm Mr. Stewart, the industrial arts teacher. I think you should come with me."

"And who the fuck are you to tell me what to do?"

"What's your name, boy?"

Christian rushed up and stood face-to-face with the teacher. "Give me a fucking reason, old man."

Mr. Stewart, who was in shock at Christian's sudden reaction, backed off. "You wait right here. Let's see what Principal Molzan has to say about this."

Mr. Stewart retreated into the school and Christian didn't stick around to find out what the principal's reaction would be.

***

Christian had a lot of time to kill and didn't want to go home so early so he found a bench just off school grounds that was shielded by a large tree. He sat down and pulled out his pack of cigarettes. Might as well chain smoke for the next few hours until it's time to actually go home.

After a couple hours of sitting on the bench mulling things over, he finally heard the school bell ring which was his cue to start the long walk home. He took in the sites which were new to him. It was actually a pretty nice town. The street was lined on either side by trees whose branches arched over empty road. A light, cool breeze, ushered the fragrance of nature to his nose. He much preferred those smells to the foul odor of sewage that dominated the street he used to walk on, to and from school. In the distance he heard people yelling.

"Hey you, kikes!"

Christian squinted and tried to make out what was going on, but from this distance, it wasn't clear. He crossed to the side of the street furthest from the commotion so he could avoid it altogether, but the voices were still loud enough that he could still hear what was being said.

There was one large figure standing in the middle of the street and another tall and skinny male who was standing on the sidewalk beside a wire fence. There were two other individuals, one of which were on their elbows and knees, nursing their stomach; the other mounted a bike that was close to the oversized male.

"Look, Jess, a retarded kike on a bike!" The guy then body checked the kid off the bike causing him to roll on the cement that was partially covered by gravel.

As Christian drew closer, he quickly realized that the instigator of the disturbance was none other than Jordy Baxter. Seeing Jordy ignited a desire in Christian to quickly diffuse the situation.

He rushed toward the commotion. The male on the side of the road spotted him before Jordy did. "Yo Jord," the guy said and was pointing at Christian.

Jordy glanced back at Christian approaching and smirked. He picked up a stick at the side of the road. The friend that was with him was not taking part, but at the same time not taking any action other than a half-hearted attempt to convince Jordy to leave them be.

Jordy, with the stick in hand, turned towards Christian. "Looky here, Jess. It's the mainland scum."

"Back off, Jordy," Christian said.

"Looks like the mainer is also a Jew lover. Why am I not surprised? Same shit different pile, eh Jess?" Jordy laughed as he looked at his buddy, who shook his head and looked away.

Christian glanced over at the other two who were dusting themselves off. To his astonishment, one of them turned out to be Liam who he'd met in the bathroom earlier that morning.

Christian stepped around Jordy towards Liam. Jordy threw the stick between Christian's legs as he walked past, causing him to stumble. He turned back around and faced Jordy.

"What the hell is your problem?"

Jordy, without answering, pushed Christian to the ground. Christian sprang back up and got within inches of Jordy's face.

Other students walking home from school were now gathering around to watch what would become of this slim, defiant kid who dared to stick his face so close to the school bully's. Christian, staring up into Jordy's face, felt overshadowed, but he was determined not to back down. The engulfing stench of whatever Jordy had last eaten didn't make it any easier.

"Come on, mainer. You got one free shot. Hit me. I dare you."

Christian continued to stare him down. His body shaking and blood pulsing through his veins. His jaw was clenched and his fists were squeezed so hard it felt like his finger nails were breaking the skin of his palms. Everything surrounding him was a complete blur. All he saw was this mass of a boy-man in front of him who wanted to crush him like a grape.

Jordy grabbed Christian by the scruff of his shirt. Immediately, with all of his might, Christian punched Jordy directly in the throat. Christian's unyielding knuckles connected so hard with Jordy's windpipe that he stumbled back, holding his throat and lowering himself to one knee.

Jordy coughed and gasped for air. Liam and the other boy just stood there gawking. Jordy's friend Jess also stood there looking like he didn't know what to do.

Christian decided to capitalize on Jordy's vulnerable position. As Jordy was still struggling to breath, Christian kicked him in the chest, causing Jordy to fall on his side. Taking the opportunity, Christian jumped on Jordy and started raining down blows. Most were body punches, with very few connecting with Jordy's face or head. Jordy covered himself up well. Nevertheless, Christian felt taken over and would not relent in his vicious attack on Jordy.

Jess finally acted and rushed to pull Christian off of Jordy. Christian yanked himself out of Jess's grasp and turned to face him with a maniacal look in his eyes. Jess put his hand in front of him as he slowly backed away toward Jordy, who was on his feet again. Jordy touched his broken lip and pulled his hand away to see blood on his fingertips.

As the hushed onlookers watched, a silver Camaro crept past the weary threesome standing their guard, the male driver making eye contact with Jordy, and then abruptly speeding off.

"Jess, let's get outta here." Jordy and Jess retreated under cover of the dispersing spectators.

Christian turned to look at Liam. "You ok?"

"Dude, thanks for that, but you must be crazy." Liam said.

"Why?"

"That's Jordy Baxter. You can't mess with the Baxter's."

"Whatever." Christian walked past Liam and continued on his way.

Liam called out, "Wait. I didn't get your name this morning."

"It's Christian."

"Well this is my brother Sammy. What are you up to right now?"

"I'm heading home."

"Well, do you want to hang out? My brother and I are meeting up with our buddy, Davie Boy, at a place we call the Creek."

Christian turned and briefly pondered the invitation. "No. I'm going to pass. Maybe another time."

As Christian turned to walk away, he said, "Don't forget what I said to you today in the washroom. It's always going to be this way, if you don't one day choose to stand up."

CHAPTER 6

The Creek

If there was an escape, it was that place. The little piece of land portioned off on their friend Davie Boy's property felt like home. The Creek was Liam and Sammy's domain, where they could let loose without worrying about anything or anybody intruding on them. It was a place of solace where their childhood resided.

"You okay, Sammy?" Liam said.

Sammy didn't respond. He just silently pushed his red bike along the road as they approached a forest trail. They entered a wide gravel walkway that was surrounded by bushes and trees which eventually narrowed as it went along. Although they were no more than fifty feet from the road, the atmosphere of these woods gave the perception of being engulfed in a vast wilderness.

They entered an opening through the bushes into a clearing. A fire pit burned a few feet away from a tall treehouse fastened high up to a thick tree that had to be hundreds of years old. There was the sound of a river flowing in the distance, but the water that eventually met the rapids, about ten yards away was completely calm; the sky reflected on its surface proving a perfect match of tranquility.

Davie Boy sat leaning towards the fire, stirring the embers with a stick. His disheveled dirty blond hair, flowed down the side of his mucky cheeks. He wore a plaid jacket, with torn, brown-stained jeans.

"It's about time. What took you so long?" Davie Boy said, without looking away from the fire.

Sammy rolled his bike up and placed it on its side next to a tree that stood between the treehouse and fire pit.

"Jordy Baxter. Need I say more?" Liam said.

Davie Boy stood up to retrieve some logs that were beside Sammy and threw them in front of the fire pit. He dislodged an ax that was imbedded in a stump that was next to the flames. After placing one of the logs on the stump, he raised the ax and said, "I'll talk to Jess and Kirt." He brought the ax down, instantly splitting the log in two.

"Jess?" Liam said, "He was there, man. He did nothing."

Davie Boy swiftly swung the ax down, splitting another log in two. He looked at Liam and shook his head.

"One kid did something though," Liam said.

"Who?"

"This Christian kid."

"Who's that?"

"New kid, from the mainland. He took down Baxter in seconds. And he's like half his size."

"Mainlander? No shit?"

"I shit you not. It was nuts."

"Shit's gonna hit the fan for that there kid now," Davie Boy said.

"I dunno, man. There's something about him." Liam joined Davie Boy by the fire pit and started poking the fire with a stick.

"You know, Liam. I think you gotta stop having other people fightin' your battles."

"What was I supposed to do?"

"I was thinkin'. We all should consider gettin' in on some of Jess and Kirt's action."

"Dealing drugs? How the hell does that solve anything? Not to mention they're both Jordy's boys."

"Money, power, respect. Problem solved. Ain't nobody fuck with you then." Davie Boy took a couple of the split logs and through them on the fire.

The bushes at the entrance started to shake. Davie Boy and Liam turned to see the tall and scrawny form of Jordy's friend, Jess Olson, enter the clearing.

"You got some balls showing up here." Liam said.

"I had nothing to do with that."

Davie Boy stood up from the fire pit. "What the hell happened, Jess?"

"The same shit that always happens," Liam piped in.

Jess walked towards Davie Boy and pulled a backpack from his shoulders and sat down on a log. He opened his bag and pulled out a bag of weed that he threw towards Davie Boy. "This one's on me."

Liam shook his head and stood up. "Sammy let's go."

"What's your problem, man?" Jess said.

"My problem? Don't pretend you're innocent, dude. When you're with Baxter, you take part."

"Quit being a pussy. He hardly even touched you. He's gonna rip that other kids heart out though."

Sammy got up and joined Liam who was walking towards the exit.

"You know. I'd expect that shit from Kirt, not you. You're nothing more than Jordy's lackey now."

Liam stormed out with Sammy rolling his bike behind him.

***

It was hard to picture Jess as a childhood friend anymore. There was a time they were all inseparable. Now Jess was like two different people. He had fallen into the wrong crowd and now was constantly trying to prove something.

Night had fallen, and Liam and Sammy were facing a twenty minute walk home. As they walked along, Liam felt lost. Above everything else he was facing, Davie Boy, someone he deemed his own brother, was proposing that they become drug dealers just to gain some sort of power over their lives. It was against everything he believed. But maybe that was his problem. Maybe everything he believed had always been wrong. More importantly, he couldn't expose his brother to that way of life. But what was that way of life? Liam's mind swirled with questions and possibilities. If he gave in, would he be giving up, or starting an actual life?

"Li, what's a lackey?" Sammy said, pushing his bike beside Liam.

"Don't worry about it."

"You mind if I ride up ahead?"

"Go for it Sammy. I'll see you at home."

As Liam continued to walk, he reflected on how Sammy was all he had at school since Davie Boy had quit. Without Davie Boy there to stick up for them, it became a source of frustration to see Sammy being subjected to humiliation without him being able to stop it. He knew Davie Boy was on the verge of deciding to sell drugs. If Liam didn't follow him down that route, maybe he would lose him too. Is this what that kid Christian meant when he said *stand up*? Christian was just a stranger that knew nothing about him; yet he couldn't stop thinking about his previous interactions with him. Like he said to Davie Boy, there was just something about him.

Liam was walking through the neighborhood near his house when he heard someone holler his name. He turned towards the house he was passing and saw Christian standing on its front deck. He was leaning over its rail smoking a cigarette.

"Christian? You live here? I live like two blocks away."

"What're the odds of that?" Christian said.

Liam approached the deck and walked its stairs. He looked at Christian's cigarette. "You got another one of those?"

Christian handed Liam a cigarette and lit it.

"Good thing you didn't come to the Creek. Jess, the guy that was with Jordy, showed up," Liam said.

"Serious? Did he start shit?"

"Nah man. Me, Davie Boy and Sammy were diaper friends with this kid."

"Diaper friends?"

"Friends since birth. Now he hangs with Jordy and deals drugs and shit."

There were two deck chairs separated by a glass table against the wall of the house. Christian sat down, gesturing for Liam to sit down on the other one.

When Liam sat there and conversed with this stranger, the change in scenery was refreshing. He got the feeling that there was more of a story to Christian and this mystery was intriguing to Liam. He tried his best not to pry or fish for information; he just enjoyed a new face for once, rather than the same ones he saw every day.

"Your brother doesn't really say much." Christian said.

"My brother has his issues."

"He's younger than you right?"

"Actually he's nineteen."

"He's your older brother? Didn't seem that way."

"Yeah. People always think he's younger." Liam helped himself to another smoke from Christian's pack. "Sammy is . . . you know . . . special."

Liam didn't like talking about Sammy, or any of his family for that matter. He preferred shovelling his family's history under the rug. They were a disgrace. But that shame he felt only fell on his parents shoulders and not Sammy's whom he loved deeply.

He envied Christian's courage earlier that day. He wished he could have done what Christian did for him and Sammy, instead of a newcomer he had hardly met.

"Where'd you learn to fight like that?" Liam said.

Christian shrugged. "Didn't learn. Just life experience."

Christian's dismissiveness prompted Liam to change the subject. "Why'd you move here?"

Christian shook his head and let out a deep sigh. He stood up and leaned over the balcony, looking at the street. Was Liam asking him too many questions? Liam wanted to know more without getting under Christian's skin.

"What happened this morning?" Christian said with his back to Liam.

"Was nothing, man."

Christian turned around and faced Liam. "I was never taught how to fight. But I had to learn. I had no other choice. I've been beat down more times than a kid my age should have. Not just at school either."

"Your Dad?"

"Don't know him. Anyways, it won't happen to me no more. Won't happen to you either if you make up your mind to not back down," Christian said.

"I can't fight."

"It's not just about fighting and it's not just about those kids at school. It's about saying fuck the world and then backing it up by standing your ground against anybody or anything."

"Easier said than done." Liam stood up and butted his cigarette. "I gotta go, thanks for the cigs. Wanna do this again?"

"How about you show me that Creek of yours?"

"Friday?" Liam said.

"Sure. Talk to you tomorrow at school."

CHAPTER 7

Cancerous Bond

Diana stood up holding onto a bar above her head on a packed bus trying to see the street signs so she wouldn't miss her stop. The droplets of rain that had collected on the bus's windows weren't making it any easier. To make matters worse, there was a grossly obese man next to her clad in a leather vest sans undershirt. His armpit was inches from her face and the smell was nauseating.

She had saw her new doctor on Black Pillar Island a few hours ago, and he had confirmed the bad news of her previous doctor back in Stoneminster Falls. She needed to tell Christian. Where would she find the strength to tell her little boy this harrowing news? He had been through enough and this wasn't what he needed right now. But she didn't have a choice because time was a factor now.

She saw her stop approaching and quickly pulled the wire to bring the bus to a halt.

She stood at the front door of her home, dread posing a road block to turning the knob. With a deep breath, she entered. Christian was tying one of his sneakers.

"Chrissy, where are you going?"

Christian continued what he was doing without acknowledging her. He got up and crossed over to the coat rack by the door, grabbing his gray hoodie and putting it on.

Diana waved both her hands in the air. "Hello? Christian? I'm talking to you."

Christian put his hand on the doorknob without looking back at his mom.

"Chrissy, we have to talk. There's something I need to tell you."

Christian finally turned towards her, the irritation on his face more than evident.

"I went to the doctor today . . ."

"Story of your life." Christian said, "I don't want to hear about the new drugs you're getting to get you off the old drugs."

"Christian, that's not what this is about. Can you just listen?"

"No, you listen. You opened your big mouth to the counselor."

"I had to. It's for the best, baby."

"To start over by opening old wounds? That makes sense." Christian turned and opened the door.

"Chrissy . . ."

"Don't Chrissy me! Why don't you just go to the bar and get drunk, or some shit."

Christian left, slamming the door. A picture of Diana and Christian fell from the wall near the door, smashing the glass in the frame.

Diana ran to the door and opened it. "Christian!" She paused, watching her son walk away. "Christian!"

Diana went back in and gently closed the door. Placing her hands in the small of her back which was leaning against the door, she let out a deep breath. "Your mama's dying, baby."

CHAPTER 8

Acrimonious Glory

Christian's blaring alarm clock startled him out of a restless sleep. While putting up one hand to block the sunlight peaking in through his curtains, he used his other to slam the clock's snooze button.

Besides grogginess, Christian was fatigued from a long walk he'd taken the previous night. He didn't have the energy to go to school. Not only was he dreading the forty minute walk ahead of him, but also the prospect of dealing with the fallout left over from his confrontations with Jordy Baxter the previous day. He wondered how many more people would be zeroing in on the target on his back. It left him anxious, and as a result, he intentionally slept through his first class. However, he was surprised his mother didn't wake him. Maybe he could skip the tedious walk and get her to drive him. No doubt she would jump on any opportunity to share some quality time with him, and he could find a way to put up with her if it meant avoiding the trek.

After getting ready for school, Christian went to his mother's room, finding it empty. He yelled for her from the top of the stairs, but there was no answer, nor could he hear any movement. He searched the rest of the house finding nothing but the couch in the front room having recently been slept in, and his mother's obsessively clean kitchen left in disarray. Puzzled and frustrated, Christian grabbed his bag and left for school.

***

When Christian finally made it to school, he was just in time for lunch. As he walked through the halls, he couldn't help but notice that there were students doing double-takes in his direction. Some smiled and seemed to nod their approval. Was this his imagination? Either way, his uneasiness began to subside.

"Yo!" A loud voice hollered above the din of chattering teenagers.

"Yo, mainlander!"

He knew the shout was intended for him. Expecting the worst and not wanting to be confronted, he picked up his pace.

He felt a tug on his backpack; stopping him in his tracks.

"Stop, brah. Damn you walk fast."

Christian turned to see a guy about his age who was overweight and freckled, and who stood a little taller than him.

"Christian, right?" The guy asked, slightly out of breath.

"Yeah, I'm Christian."

"Brah, where'd you get the balls to take down Baxter?"

Before Christian could answer, the guy said, "I'm Braeden." He reached out to shake Christian's hand. "Dude, everybody is talking about that craziness yesterday. Nobody fucks with them boys."

"Them boys?"

"You headed to lunch? I'll walk with ya."

Braeden continued walking alongside Christian, not giving him a choice in the matter.

"Look, you gotta watch your back. I know Jord and he's crazy, you hear me? He's gonna wanna have retaliation."

Braeden turned to slap the hand of someone passing by.

"I'm not too worried about it," Christian said.

Braeden turned to Christian again. "What do you mean? You know what that dude's capable of? He'll gut you."

Christian rolled his eyes.

"Brah, you gotta take this shit seriously. You know who his brother is? If Jordy don't do it, his bro will mess you up, no questions asked. I do a little work for his bro from time to time. I know this."

They both approached the lunch counter. Christian grabbed a tray and took his place in line, Braeden not leaving his side.

Braeden continued, "Look man, I ain't tryin' to scare you, just being a good samaritan, ya know?"

Braeden was abruptly cut off by Mr. Berry who placed his hand on Christian's shoulder. "Christian, you need to come with me."

Christian frowned. "What for? I don't do counseling sessions."

"That's not what this is about."

Everyone stared as Mr. Berry took Christian by the arm and started leading him out of the lunch room.

"Alright Christian, I'll catch up with you later," Braeden called out in the background.

***

Mr. Berry was silent as they walked towards the office. When Christian asked what was going on, Mr. Berry just kept walking, continuing to hold on to his arm.

When they arrived at the office, Mr. Berry directed Christian to take a seat in front of the secretary's desk. "Wait here."

Mr. Berry stepped into the principal's office nearby and announced Christian's presence.

"Bring him in."

Christian entered the principal's office with Mr. Berry walking behind him. Christian immediately saw sitting in a semi-circle around the desk was Jordy Baxter in one chair and a man and a woman beside him. Jordy's face looked like a swollen bag of mush with two black eyes; one being almost shut. His lower lip looked like a sizzling piece of sausage about to burst.

The man who sat beside Jordy was very large, wearing a plaid shirt opened to reveal a stained t-shirt underneath. His unkempt black beard added a stormy darkness to his stone-cold face.

Next to him, the woman sat with a blank stare. Her long brown hair, which looked like it hadn't been washed in weeks, was draped over either side of her cheeks, partially covering her empty eyes.

Mr. Berry stood beside the principal who sat at his desk fiddling with a pen. Everyone but Jordy looked in Christian's direction.

"Mr. Solomon, I'm Principal Molzan. You must know why you are here, correct?"

"You little shit, look at my son!" The man sitting next to Jordy said.

Principal Molzan spoke, "Mr. Baxter, please let me handle this."

Jordy's father sighed and slouched into his seat.

"Mr. Solomon, I was hoping your mother could have been here. But nevertheless, I'm going to make this quick. You are not here to tell your side of the story. You are not here to make any sort of excuses, and quite frankly, I have no desire to hear them. Mercfield Secondary has zero tolerance for bullying or violence of any sort."

Christian was dumbfounded. "Bullying? Really?"

"Don't feign innocence with me, Mr. Solomon." Principal Molzan turned toward Jordy and his parents. "While it is indisputable who the aggressor was, I do have to acknowledge that you, Jordy Baxter, are partially responsible, and thus have to punish you accordingly."

Christian couldn't bite his tongue. "Aggressor? You haven't even heard what—"

"Quiet! Jordy you are suspended for the remainder of the day and may return tomorrow. You can leave with your parents now. Thank you for coming in, Mr. and Mrs. Baxter."

Jordy's father slammed his palm on the principal's desk. "And what is this little punk gonna get?"

"I assure you Mr. Baxter, the punishment will fit the crime. Good day."

The Baxter's sullenly got up to leave the office. Jordy avoided eye contact with Christian as his parents ushered him out the door.

Principal Molzan glared at Christian through his thick square bifocals. Disgust evident on his face. He turned his attention to a clipboard on his desk and began to write, pressing down on the pen so hard a scratching sound resonated throughout the room. Christian sat in silence, knowing that this couldn't be good.

Principal Molzan finished by dramatically signing his name at the bottom of the page. He proceeded to rip a white copy from a pink carbon copy and rose from his seat. Principal Molzan stood over Christian like some scholastic, tin-pot dictator.

"Mr. Solomon, this form goes in your permanent file," Molzan stood up from his desk and placed his finger on the white sheet of paper. He slid the pink copy towards Christian. "And this is yours. Do with it as you wish. You have a suspension effective immediately—for the entirety of this week—and you may return on Monday."

Christian's jaw dropped and his eyes widened.

"This means you can't set foot on school property, not during or after school hours. No hanging around with your friends on my grounds at any time. Should you make an idiotic decision and choose to disobey these terms, it will be considered trespassing and this matter will be escalated. Do you understand?"

Christian sat looking at the pink piece of injustice laying on the desk and snatched it up. He didn't bother to read it; he just stared at it in disbelief.

"Well? Do you have anything to say for yourself?"

A defiant half-smile formed on Christian's face, and he rose to his feet and leaned over Mr. Molzan's desk, bringing himself closer to Principal Molzan's face. Not taking his eyes from Molzan's, Christian's right hand clenched into a fist, his rising anger threatening to boil over into an uncontrollable fury. Undeterred, Principal Molzan raised his eyebrow and squinted his eyes.

"If you have nothing to say, you're dismissed. Mr. Berry can escort you off the premises."

Principal Molzan sat back down. Christian carelessly crumpled the pink slip into his jacket pocket. He turned to leave with Mr. Berry following him out the door.

***

After another silent, awkward walk, the two approached the exit to the school grounds. Mr. Berry stopped and Christian continued on without acknowledging him.

"Christian. You didn't come to see me the other day." Christian began speed walking away and Mr. Berry yelled out to him. "You know, things are only as bad as you make them. It doesn't have to be like this, Christian."

***

The events of the day started to settle in. Christian's vexation over the meeting in the principal's office was now placed on the back burner, and he couldn't help but think about the moments before that, when he first entered the school. He felt a sense of accomplishment and acceptance which was so rare for him.

This suspension, as unjust as it was, exemplified the change that he was prompting. He stood up for people and what he believed was right; even if that meant being made an example by the powers that be. Instead of only being angry, he now also embraced a sense of pride.

His internal pat on the back was interrupted. Jordy Baxter stepped out from behind a nearby tree. Christian looked at him, without saying a word and walked past him.

"Mainer, hold up."

Christian continued to ignore him.

"Mainer . . . I mean Christian . . . I'm not here for trouble."

Against his better judgment, Christian stopped and faced Jordy. He didn't know what kind of trap he was stepping into. But he waited to hear Jordy out.

They stood several feet apart. Much as earlier in the principal's office, Jordy continued to avoid looking Christian in the eyes. This didn't seem like the bully who came off so strong in the lunch room the other day.

"Christian, I didn't rat on you." Jordy said.

"That's why you stopped me?"

"Shit dude. You can't go around saying this to people, alright? I didn't rat on you. At least I didn't mean to."

"Whatever, man." Christian turned to continue walking home.

"Don't walk away from me, you miserable fuckin' punk." Jordy quickly calmed and changed his tone. "Shit, sorry. I didn't mean that. Just hear me, man."

Christian abruptly turned around and walked toward Jordy. "What really happened to your face, Jordy? You know I didn't do that shit."

Jordy put his hands in the air and took a step back. "Shit is what it is, mainer. Don't worry about it."

Christian shook his head and began to walk away again.

"I didn't have a choice, Christian. You don't know how it is."

Christian stuck his middle finger in the air and yelled, "Go fuck yourself, Jordy."

CHAPTER 9

My One Son…My One Love

Diana set her coffee mug down. The slight tap on the table gave off a little echo in the large, mostly empty kitchen. The window over the sink was open a crack, and beyond it, gray clouds like wadded up balls of lint were rolling in. It didn't rain in Stoneminster Falls as it did on Black Pillar Island, but the damp smell of rain was still familiar to her.

The days she had spent in BPI as a child were some of her fondest memories. Consequently she thought coming home to the place she grew up would be a rebirth of sorts. To the contrary, it just might be where she came to a bitter end.

She stood up from the kitchen table, picking up a bottle cap and throwing it in the garbage under the sink. She resumed her seat in front of the now half-empty bottle that used to reside in the drawer of her night table.

Diana's hand trembled as she raised the black, chipped coffee mug to her mouth to take a sip of its welcoming contents. As the anesthetizing warmth flushed through her body, she couldn't discern why her eyes were filled with tears; at this point she didn't care.

She brought the cup to her lips again, but was interrupted by the rattle of the front door lock. She sat her cup down and concealed the bottle under her chair, which her robe hung over. Christian entered the kitchen and threw his backpack on the floor.

"Where were you this morning? I needed a ride."

Diana's chest ached from Christian's constant disdain of her.

"I got suspended today," Christian said.

Diana tried to mask her slurring. "I know, Chrissy."

"You know? How?"

"It's your life, honey."

"Do you know for what?" Christian studied her face intently. "What the hell? Have you been crying again?"

"What does it matter? We're safe now," Diana said.

"What do you mean?" Christian stood over her scowling. "You know what? Forget it."

Diana watched Christian cross over to the kitchen sink. Her son was a personification of his father. It didn't make her love Christian less, but it did remind her of him. She was amazed at how she could ever say her little boy was beautiful, when it was his father that she saw.

Christian pulled a pink piece of paper out of his jacket pocket and opened the cupboard doors to the garbage. He paused, then reached in his hand to pull out the bottle cap.

"What the hell is this?"

He tossed the bottle cap and pink slip to the floor. "You couldn't do it, could you? I thought we were starting over here. Isn't that what you called it?"

"Chrissy, please . . ."

Christian stood over her on the edge of a blind rage. For the first time, Diana feared her son, rather than fearing for him.

"What, Chrissy? What is it that you want?"

"I dunno. Maybe a mom?" Christian picked up his bag and walked towards the stairs.

Those words sliced through her heart and seeped into her soul. Not only did she see a child she had failed, but she now also saw the result: a young man that had a growing distaste for life.

"Christian, stop!"

"Yes, Mother Dearest?"

"I know you didn't like when I dated Dan. I know he wasn't good for us. Your hatred toward him and . . . you know . . . I'm just really sorry for that."

"But you guys were picture perfect. He was a drunk just like you, right?"

"That's not fair!"

"Oh, fuck off. Just go whore yourself out with some other winner. It's only a matter of time."

"You selfish little child!"

"You selfish fucking bitch!"

"You ungrateful little . . . little—"

"Little what, Mom? You think you're gonna scar me for life? Go ahead and say it." Christian laughed. "Too late for that now, isn't it?"

"You know nothing! You don't know what I've sacrificed!" Diana picked up the whiskey bottle from under the chair, and put it to her mouth for a swig, but instead slammed it down on the table splashing whiskey out of the top.

She got up and staggered a few steps from the table, staring at Christian with glazed over eyes.

"God, you're a disgrace," Christian said.

"You wanna talk about scarring someone for life, my dear son." Diana lifted her shirt and pulled her sweats down enough to expose her abdomen. Her voice softened and her eyes swam from side to side, failing to keep focus. "Do you see this?" The scar on Diana's lower abdomen shocked Christian into silence.

"This is what you did to me. This is my reminder, every day of my life. This is my reminder of the piece of shit son I've raised. You weren't even worthy enough to come out of my . . ." Diana stopped herself. She was lost somewhere between her drunken state and the level head she thought she normally had.

Christian's eyes welled up. "What are you saying?"

Diana shook her head and closed her eyes, reaching toward Christian, but only grasped at empty air. "Wait, Chrissy, I didn't mean that."

Christian turned and rushed toward the front door.

Diana followed after Christian, "Chrissy, wait! I didn't mean it. I'm sorry, I'm sorry, I'm sorry!"

Her words were interrupted by the slamming of the front door. Diana collapsed on a chair in the front room and put her head between her legs, sobbing.

CHAPTER 10

Braeden Cunningham

A broken home. Not by choice or bad decision, but broken and empty, nonetheless. It had been four years since his parents' car accident, but it was something that he relived every day.

Braeden stood in front of the stove, mixing the ground beef in with his special tomato sauce; it was his own recipe. He loved to cook, even if it was a responsibility he had been forced into.

As the water gurgled from the pasta boiling on the back burner and the sauce simmered, Braeden scrubbed the last dish in the sink and placed it in the draining board. He then began to wipe down the counter.

"Chloe!" Braeden yelled.

He dipped a wooden spoon into the pot and tasted the spicy, sour thickness that was his creation. "Damn, I'm good."

He walked over to the hallway. "Chloe!"

"What?"

"Come eat. Bring Nana."

Upon entering the kitchen, Chloe looked at the table that was only set for two. "You're not eating?" Chloe said.

"No, I gotta work. Where's Nana?"

"She didn't want to leave her room. She just mumbled something."

Braeden shook his head and grabbed Nana's plate heading down the hall towards her room. When he found her, she was sitting in her wheelchair, facing away from him and looking out the window.

"Nana, you gotta eat."

"I know what you're doing, Arthur," Nana said.

"Nana, it's Braeden." He walked over to the dresser beside her and placed the food down. "Can you please eat something?"

"You're going to put me in a home!"

"What? I never even—"

"Don't you love me anymore, Arthur?"

Braeden walked over to her and leaned down, gently planting kiss on her forehead. "Of course I love you. Try to eat, Norma."

Braeden returned to the kitchen and couldn't help but smile as he watched his little sister eating. She was such a cutie with her dark hair that she always weaved into a French braid and big blue eyes that would most likely one day steal the hearts of many. More than that, cooking for his family wasn't a chore, it was a labor of love, and seeing them enjoy something he made brought him joy that he could never adequately express. He walked over to her and kissed her on the top of the head.

"I gotta go. The nurse will be here later to check in. You need anything, call Becky next door."

He walked over to the door that led to the basement suite where he resided.

"You're hardly ever here," Chloe said.

"You know I gotta to work."

"I know. I just miss you sometimes."

"Tell you what. This Saturday. You, me and Ed's Bowling. I'll kick your ass again."

Chloe smiled and shoveled some more pasta in her mouth.

"You're on," she said with her mouth full.

Braeden closed the basement door and locked it behind him.

His space was typical of a young male and completely lacking the attention to spotlessness he gave the upstairs. Here, in his private domain, the smell of dirty socks and sweat were the main players on the stage, while the scent of cheap drugstore aftershave provided the background.

The primary smell at that moment however was from Jordy, Jess and Kirt who sat at the coffee table dividing a large quantity of marijuana. Braeden took a seat on a lazy boy recliner next to the couch.

"Spoke to that mainer kid today," Braeden picked up a rolling paper and a pinch of weed.

Jordy looked up at him and shook his head. "I can see it on your face already, asshole."

"What?" Braeden said.

Jordy snickered. "You like him, don't you?"

"Well no—"

"You better not tell me to leave him be," Jordy said.

"Well yeah. I think you should leave him be, brah."

"Like hell I will. You need to stop being soft."

"Soft? I ain't soft." Braeden ran his tongue along his newly rolled joint.

"Why are you two so silent?" Braeden nodded his head upward toward Jess and Kirt.

They both looked up but didn't say anything. Braeden got up and walked towards the entrance door to go outside.

"Where you going?" Jordy said.

Braeden held up the joint. "To smoke this."

"You know why my brother only has us peddling a little pot, instead of the real shit?"

Braeden turned around, his joint flopping in his mouth.

"Because we have no balls. My bro feeds off of that shit." Jordy threw a bag of weed down on the table and walked towards Braeden. "There's this kid named Hans, or Gonz, or whatever his name is. He's our age, ya know? Know why he pushes ACB? It's cause he took a swing at my brother. Russ beat him down and all, but he got right back up. Now he makes mad coin 'cause he showed my brother he can cut it. Only thing we cut is this shit."

"What's wrong with weed?" Braeden said.

Jordy shook his head. "ACB is the most lucrative high on the street. The pink powder. It's a gold mine my own brother monopolized. Yet he's got his own flesh and blood sittin' here portioning pot."

"Aright brah, whatever. I won't be soft."

"Nah, you *won't* be soft. That's why you gonna help us fuck this kid up."

"Who?"

"The mainlander, dumbass." Jordy returned to his position on the couch.

"Whatcha gonna do, brah? Jump him at school?"

"No. But you know Jess' friend, Davie Boy? Jess got word the mainer is gonna be there at Davie's little playground Friday night." Jordy turned to Jess. "Whatcha gonna do?" Jordy laughed.

"Become friends with the little mainland shit. Then invite him to Jord's brother's party on Saturday," Jess said.

Jordy grinned, "We'll show my brother we're soldiers then."

CHAPTER 11

Stolen Dreams

Liam was choking down stale cereal that tasted like cardboard as he kept a watchful eye on the living room from his place at the kitchen table. It looked like a bomb had gone off, and his father, who sat snoring in his recliner, was in the middle of ground zero. He wore only a sleeveless undershirt and boxers. The TV was blaring and empty beer bottles were scattered on the floor beside him. There was no question he'd slept there all night.

Liam did his best to rush through breakfast hoping that he and Sammy could leave for school before his father woke up. However, the sound of the front door slamming most likely foiled those plans.

"Liam! Liam!" Sammy was hysterical. He rushed into the kitchen in tears.

Liam got out of his chair and put his hand on Sammy's shoulder. "Calm down, what's wrong?"

"My bike . . ." Sammy couldn't even put the words together to finish his sentence. His voice quivered as he tried to hold back his tears.

"Your bike?" Liam shook his head. "What about your bike?"

"It's gone."

"Gone? What do you mean . . . gone?"

"It's just gone, Li."

"Stolen? Did you lock it?"

"Yes, I locked it. I locked it! I swear I did."

Their father shambled into the kitchen. He was disheveled and the strong odor of stale cigarettes and booze rolled into the kitchen with him like a storm front.

"What are you boys on about now?" He walked straight to the fridge and pulled out a carton of orange juice.

Liam tried to console Sammy, who was now seated at the kitchen table with his hands over his face.

Their dad took a large swig out of the carton and sat down with them. "You crying, boy?"

Sammy looked up, his eyes were blood shot and brimming with tears. In a soft voice he said, "Dad, someone *stoled* my bike."

"You're crying about a goddamn bike? No one stole your bike."

Sammy's face lit up and he took a sigh of relief. "For real? Did you move it?"

"Well don't get too excited. I sold it."

"No, no, no!" Sammy rocketed from the table and ran into the living room."

"Oh, be a fucking man and quit your crying."

"How could you do that?" Liam said.

"This is not your concern, boy. That one hundred and fifty bucks will put food on the table."

"That bike was worth over eight hundred dollars. Gramps bought it for him. It wasn't yours to sell." Liam slammed his hand down on the table.

His father rose to his feet and stood directly in front of Liam, the pungent odor of spent alcohol and bad breath flooding over him.

"Don't you ever raise your voice to me."

Liam froze. His father grabbed him by the scruff of his neck and pulled Liam towards him, bringing him to his tippy toes.

"Anything else to say, boy?"

Liam only looked at his father with hunted eyes.

"That's what I thought." He pushed Liam back and he stumbled to the floor. "Get your ass to school."

Liam gathered his and Sammy's bags. "Come on, Sammy."

***

Liam walked ahead of Sammy on the way to school, brooding in silence.

"Liam, I can't do this."

Liam stopped and turned around. "Sammy, don't worry, I'll find a way to get you another bike."

"No, I mean I don't wanna go to school."

Liam thought a moment. "Then don't. Why don't you just go to the Creek? Davie Boy will be there."

"You think I should?"

"Yeah. Just go and read his comics and I'll come meet you after."

As they both turned to walk in their separate directions, Liam turned again. "Hey Sammy." Sammy looked back. "I hate your face."

Sammy smiled and waved.

***

As Liam walked, he couldn't help thinking about what Christian had said to him about taking a stand. But really, what could a kid like himself do about the many injustices he had experienced in his young life?

When he was younger, he remembered dreaming that once he became a teenager, things would just work themselves out. He always heard that the teenage years were the best years of a person's life. How naive he had been.

Feelings of envy started clouding his mind as he passed houses on the way to school, watching other families piling into their mini vans, laughing, consumed by bliss; wives kissing their husbands as they left for work; mother's hugging their children as they sent them off to school.

Did these places actually exist? As wonderful as it all seemed, he also couldn't help but feel a little sick. This had to be fake. These people were simply painting over what was truly there. They must have all been hiding something underneath all this pretentious joy.

Liam stopped and turned at the sound of a father scolding his son near the edge of the street. The kid couldn't have been more than six-years-old. This was more familiar to him. He got a dark satisfaction out of this, which was unusual for him. This was real . . . this was home.

The father dragged his son by the arm. The boy stumbled as he tried to keep up.

"What the hell were you thinking?"

"Daddy, I'm sorry."

"I know you know better, Danny. You could have been killed by that car."

"I'm sorry."

"Daddy loves you so much. Promise me you will be more careful."

"I promise."

The man hugged his son and kissed him on the head. He took notice of Liam staring, so Liam abruptly continued on his way, feeling awkward and ashamed.

For some reason, even though he should have been happy that the child had a father that loved and cared for him, he just couldn't shake his disappointment.

CHAPTER 12

That There Creek...Again

Christian sat on the porch, pen and pad in hand; the only word written on the page was *Victoria.*

He spent the past three days of this involuntary vacation trying to figure out what to say to her, or if he should say anything at all. Maybe it was better to let things lie and not open up old wounds—or create new ones.

Maybe he could have gotten away with writing something as simple as, *I love you,* and leave it at that. Why dig deeper? He never said or wrote anything of the sort to her before, even though he felt it. Being just on the verge of eighteen, did he really know what those three words meant?

He regretted not letting himself tell her how he felt about her. On so many occasions he had the chance to let those emotions flow. He could only wonder, if that night she turned him away from her home, would he have in fact told her how he felt? Among plenty of other things, that rejection, no doubt was what pushed him over the edge that night.

He put the pen and pad down, and stood up and lit a cigarette as he leaned over the porch railing.

He closed his eyes and started tracing the features of her profile to gain some inspiration to write more than just her name.

He pictured her alluring face. He immediately relaxed at the thought of her eyes which were always accompanied by her bright smile that would tease one cute dimple in her left cheek. He took a deep breath as if he was actually inhaling her. And her hair. He was always secretly enraptured when her long, dark brown hair would get blown and tossed in the wind. And when she hugged, it was with her whole being. But that kiss, he would never forget that one kiss. Her soft, moist lips fit his so perfectly. He could almost taste the strawberry lip gloss that she religiously coated them with.

He was momentarily joyed by his conjured memories, but ultimately, strangely, it left him feeling emptier than before. It was at this moment that he fully understood the word *bittersweet.*

"You're gonna burn the shit outta your fingers."

Startled, Christian tossed away his cigarette that was burning at the butt. Liam stood at the bottom of the porch stairs.

"You often sleep standing up?" Liam said.

"Not sleeping. What's up?"

Liam walked up the stairs and sat on one of the lawn chairs. He picked up Christian's pack of cigarettes and held it in the air.

"Go for it," Christian said.

Liam pulled out a cigarette and lit it. "I gotta tell ya, man. That shit that happened on Monday with Jordy . . . It's still being talked about."

"All that's done now."

"I'm about to head to my house and cop a couple brews off my pops. And then, the Creek. You still in?"

"Your friends won't mind?"

"Nah, they're cool."

***

Christian and Liam made their way to Liam's house. Christian did in fact have a sense of pride being the talk of the school. He would never have admitted it, but he was doing back flips on the inside.

They approached Liam's driveway. A rusty old blue truck sat on the uncut grass. Dandelions poked out through the soil. The garage door was half-open.

"My pops has a stash of brews in here, c'mon."

They ducked under the door. The garage was piled high with junk with boxes lining the wooden slats of the walls. The smell of old oil and gasoline hung heavily in the air. There was another vehicle inside, looking like a project that was now being left to rot away.

While Liam walked to the back corner of the garage, Christian noticed a box with a picture on top and picked it up.

"That is one big ass fish," Christian said.

"What?" Liam who was bending down said from the other end of the garage.

"This picture with Sammy, and I guess this is your dad . . . and you . . . kind of?" Christian laughed. "Did Sammy out fish you that day?"

Liam walked around the corner abruptly, putting two six packs that were in his hand on the ground. "Put that back! Where'd you get that from?"

"Chill," Christian said, "I'm just messin' with ya."

Liam took the picture out of Christian's hands and threw it into another box a few feet away.

"What's wrong? It's just a picture," Christian said.

"That was one of the last times my brother was sick. Or I should say, one of the first times he wasn't sick."

"Sick?"

"I just met you. I don't know why I am telling you this."

"Telling me what?"

"That picture. It was the week my mom went away, and Dad took us on a fishing trip."

"So?"

“I shouldn’t be saying this.” Liam leaned up against the car, looking at the beer he put on the ground.

“Saying what? Did something happen to your Mom?”

“She’s in Jail.”

“What the hell?”

“Christian. Know how I said Sammy’s special?”

“Yeah?”

“He wasn’t born that way. And I’m not about to talk about it. So let’s just go.”

***

Christian was intrigued by what Liam had said about Sammy, but it was apparent that Liam did not want to go into detail about Sammy’s disability. So, he decided to not pry. Consequently, their walk to the Creek was punctuated by long silences between awkward attempts at shooting the breeze.

They soon came upon the gravel trail that led up to the Creek’s entrance. Christian inhaled the pristine smells of the woods that flowed through the rustling leaves. It brought Christian back to all the times he had spent with Victoria. They used to spend hours in the forest. Those times, and only those times, brought a smile to his face; yet there was an undercurrent of sadness in those memories that followed him everywhere. It had the immediate effect of dulling the vivid colors of the trees and the pungent smells of the forest just a bit.

When Christian and Liam entered the Creek’s opening, they found Davie Boy sitting on a wooden stump in front of a fire. There were three empty beer bottles in view and he was sipping on a forth. Sammy sat in the distance against a tree with a small stick in his hand, toying with the dirt.

“Davie Boy, this is Christian.”

“How you doin, Davie Boy?” Christian said.

Davie Boy rose and eyed Christian up and down. "So you're that there hero I've been hearing about."

Christian looked at Liam and then back at Davie Boy. Liam sat down on a log and Christian followed his lead.

Looking at the surroundings, Christian couldn't help but wonder what the hell he just walked into.

"So, what is this place?" Christian said.

Liam pointed to the house in the distance that was visible through the trees. "That's Davie Boy's folks' place. All this is on their property. Goes out to the creek over there."

"Davie Boy has the biggest comic book collection ever," Sammy piped in, "he keeps it here. It's gonna be worth something someday."

Liam pulled out two beers from his bag and cracked them open, handing one to Christian.

Christian took a healthy swig of beer and lit a cigarette. He stared up at the tree house and snickered. "This looks like a little boys club or something."

"Used to be," Davie Boy said.

"All three of you?" Christian said.

"Four. Jess grew up with us too, I told ya," Liam said.

"Five!" Sammy yelled out.

"Sammy, not now." Liam threw some dirt on the ground at him.

Davie Boy stood up and grabbed more logs beside the fire and tossed them in. "No, Sammy's right. He was his best friend and all. There was five."

"Was?" Christian said.

"Christian man, just let it go." Liam said.

"No. There was five," Davie Boy said, "Pete, my dead brother was the fifth."

A strained silence settled over the Creek. Christian and Liam took several sips of their beer while Davie Boy crouched in his usual spot near the fire. Christian regretted pushing for more information, and he felt like he put his foot in his mouth.

Christian stared at Sammy for a moment, watching him continue to prod the dirt with a twig. He turned to Liam, "Your brother doesn't look too happy."

"Yeah. My pop's went and sold his bike without him knowing."

"What for?"

Liam ignored Christian's query, "Sammy loved that damn bike. Woke up every morning shining it up all nice."

"Never mind all that," Davie Boy said, "Heard you been telling my boys here to stand up for themselves." Davie Boy stood up and walked a little closer to Christian and Liam.

"Yeah, so?" Christian glared at Davie Boy in the eye.

"You lookin' to get 'em hurt?" Davie Boy eased his way closer. Christian didn't like being looked down on so he rose to his feet and cocked his head up. "What would you do, Davie Boy? Run away?"

Davie Boy took a swig of his beer. "There wasn't a day I didn't fight some punk in that there school, to protect myself and these boys."

"So you should and so should they."

"You're fuckin' clueless, mainer."

"Is there gonna be a problem here?" Christian said, "if there is, I'll just leave."

"No problem." Davie Boy said and he backed off slightly.

"Instead of letting people control you and drive you out of school, you all need to stand up to them," Christian said.

Davie Boy shook his head and turned towards the fire but immediately turned back around. "How do you think we're gonna do that? You think it's just them kids? We're outcasts in this city and we take the heat. It ain't just them kids at school. It's the cops, parents, teachers . . . you name it. All we got is us."

"Then stand up to them, too." Christian said, not really knowing himself how that was possible.

Davie Boy gave a partial smile, rolled his eyes and returned to his spot by the fire. "Where'd you find this guy, Li?"

"Davie Boy is right in a way," Liam said, "we've always been the outcasts. You know, like misfits."

"What's your point?" Christian said.

Davie Boy stood up again and walked towards Christian. "I ain't got the energy for this shit." Davie Boy held out his hand to Christian and shook it. "I'm Davie Boy. You're Christian. There, we met. Done like dinner. Now let's drink." Davie Boy headed up towards his house.

"What's his problem?" Christian said to Liam.

"Nothin. Just takes a while for him to warm up, is all."

CHAPTER 13

David Fisher

All the constant echoes in his head, never ceased to exist. The voices of the kids chanting, *murderer, murderer, murderer.*

There were only two people who knew the whole truth about the last time he saw his brother, Pete. One was dead—and the other was him.

Davie Boy walked to his father's liquor cabinet and grabbed a twenty-six ounce bottle of Crown Royal. He went to his room and pulled a box out from under his bed.

In the box were a couple of bags of weed, some newspaper cuttings and a small bag of pink powder which he proceeded to take out.

ACB was, in its purest form, one of the most potent drugs that could be had. With an X-Acto knife, he divvied up two lines, quickly sniffing them up with a dollar bill and then took in a swallow of the Crown Royal. He closed his eyes and cocked his head back. The sensation was calming, yet also awakening.

As he placed the dollar bill inside the box, he saw the article. He knew he shouldn't read it again, but he picked it up anyway. He just read the headline; *The Drowning of Peter Fisher: Hidden Secrets.*

How was that ever allowed to be published? Even though his name was never mentioned, the implications were clear. Guilty before proven innocent. At least the courts ruled it an accident. That meant nothing in the eyes of society, though. The damage was done. Even before the incident and its fall out, Davie Boy could have described himself as a misanthrope; but after, his feelings of societal separation were only deepened.

Davie Boy pushed the box back under the bed. As he pulled his hand out, it hit a heavy object. His first hammer; a birthday gift his dad gave him when he couldn't even read. His hand glided over its hard, smooth contours, and he smiled. He slid it out and held it up, closer to the light. As he held it in his grip, his smile widened.

***

Davie hammered a nail into the tree. Their work-in-progress was coming along quicker than anticipated.

"You're a natural, son. I'm proud of ya."

"Thanks, Dad." Davie admired the now-standing frame of the tree house. Now, picturing the end result was easy. His vision was coming to life, and there was no better feeling.

"Where's your brother?" His father said.

Pete came walking out of the bushes with a shameless grin. "I was takin' a wiz."

"Ya know, Pete, you could learn a thing or two from your little brother."

Pete shook his head and sat down on a stump.

"You boys wait here, I got something for ya." Their father lightly jogged back up to the house.

A pebble hit Davie in the back of the head.

"What the hell, Pete!" Davie said.

"A little suck up, that's what you are."

"Screw you."

Pete stood up and came over to Davie. "Dad always does that. Oh David this *and* oh David that."

"Quit being a pussy," Davie said.

"You're the pussy!"

"Get out of my face!" Davie pushed Pete but he came forward. He grabbed Davie by the shirt and they both fell to the ground. They were wrestling in a tangled mess, none of them able to get their hands free to throw punches.

Their father returned, finding them in a writhing ball on the ground.

"Again?" Their father pulled Pete off of Davie.

"What's the matter with you?" He yelled at Pete.

"Me? He started it." Pete said.

"I did not. You did."

"I don't care who started it. But you two are going to resolve it."

They both stood looking at each other, out of breath.

"Pete, you can forget about taking the boat out this evening." Their father said.

"That's not fair!"

"Ok. Here's what's fair. You can take the boat, but you're going to bring your brother."

"That's bullshit!" Pete kicked the ground sending up a cloud of dust. "Then I'm not going."

"Damn right, you're going. The both of ya. And you stay out there till you work this out."

Their dad turned to leave. He threw a sign down on the ground that must have been the surprise he had for them. It was carved with the words: 'The Fisher Men's Creek'.

CHAPTER 14

Actions Speak

Christian stood at the water's edge pondering the hilly, wooded landscape on the other side of the Creek; it appeared to go for miles. Feeling so immersed in these surroundings, it amazed Christian that the main road was only a short walk away. Even the sound of passing cars was muffled to the point that it completed the illusion of being cut off from civilization.

On the muddy ground, close to the water, a rectangular piece of wood stuck out. It looked like it had writing carved into it. Christian walked over to it and began pushing it back and forth, trying to loosen it from the mud's stingy grip.

He finally pulled it loose and held it in front of him, scrapping the caked mud on its surface.

"Having fun exploring?"

Christian looked up and turned his head. Davie Boy stood with a big back pack draped over his shoulder.

"*The Fisher Men's Creek*?" Christian read.

Davie Boy walked over to Christian and pulled the sign out of his hand, throwing it back on the ground. "C'mon, I gotta surprise for you boys."

They returned to the fire and each took a seat on a log. Liam was sitting beside Sammy who was quietly chattering about something.

Davie put the bag down and unzipped it. He pulled out a box and two big bottles of alcohol; one rye and one vodka.

Liam's eyes widened. "What the hell! We ain't gonna drink all that."

"Time to party, boys," Davie Boy said.

Liam left Sammy and stood beside Christian who was opening a beer and pulling a cigarette out of his pack.

"This ain't all for us," Davie Boy said, "I just spoke to Jess. Him and Kirt will be here any minute."

"You nuts, man? They bringing Baxter, too?" Liam said.

"Liam, brotha, shit's cool. And negative on the Baxter."

"You must be fricken drunk." Liam turned and walked towards the bushes.

Christian stared at Davie Boy. He was trying to figure out if there was something more in play here. Davie Boy cracked open the bottle of rye and took the first swig.

"What's in the box?" Christian said.

"Ah, that's my stash of that there sweet green. Want some?"

A voice coming out of the bushes cut them off. "I do."

"Jess," Davie Boy said, "I got enough for an army."

Another guy was walking right behind Jess. "

What up, Kirt? Long-time no see." Davie Boy lifted the bottle of rye and winked.

"Sup, Davie Boy." Kirt glanced back at Liam who was standing, facing away in the bushes. "Shouldn't you be squattin'?"

"Leave him be." Jess chuckled.

Jess and Kirt sat on the log beside Christian. Liam returned with a stick and began poking at the logs in the fire pit.

"Sup mainer? Remember me?" Jess said around the cigarette hanging from his mouth.

"Yep."

"You know I had nothin' to do with all that shit, right?"

Christian looked at him and squinted. He was trying to figure out what Jess' intentions really were. Trust was something that was always in short supply in Christian's life. Why start now? With this guy? Not to mention he hung around with Jordy Baxter, who wanted to potentially take his head off.

Jess stood up and flicked his cigarette into the fire. "Stand up, mainer."

Christian's brows furrowed and he got up, standing a little less than an arm's length away.

"Now, now boys, let's play nice," Davie Boy said, taking another swig of the rye.

"So, mainer, your name's Christian? What you go by for short, Chris or Chin?" Jess snickered and turned his head toward Davie Boy. "Davie Boy, light up a spliff."

Christian still said nothing. He only stared at Jess, anticipating what his next move might be.

"What kinda name is that, anyway," Jess said, "you a bible thumper or somethin'?"

"Chris." Christian said.

"What?" Jess scrunched up his face and turned his head to the side.

"You asked me what I go by."

"That shit ain't original. I'mma call you Chin." Jess laughed. "Nah, how about Chinny." Jess held his hand out. Christian didn't acknowledge the handshake.

"Chinny, brotha, I'm messin' with ya. I ain't here to start nothin'. Just wanna make peace, is all."

"I like the sound of Chinny," Davie Boy said as he was finishing rolling a fresh joint.

Jess lowered his hand and took the joint from Davie Boy. "You first, Chinny." Jess held the joint in front of Christian.

"I don't smoke that shit." Christian sat back down on the log.

They passed the joint around, all of them partaking except Christian and Sammy, who was now nursing a beer beside Liam.

They also passed around the bottle of rye, which Christian did partake in.

***

As darkness crept in, so did the clouds that concealed what should have been a full moon. The mixture of booze and marijuana seemed to have diffused the tense situation that had infiltrated the surroundings of the Creek.

Christian nicely buzzed, slowed down on the rye and laid on his back. He looked up at the clouds that slowly devoured the stars, smoking cigarette after cigarette, ignoring the laughter and juvenile jokes that filled the background. He wasn't used to any of that. He had spent most of his life alone and never built bonds with a group of guys, or a single guy for that matter.

The fire that was being fueled by Davie Boy, with a bottle of lighter fluid, continued to rise ever higher.

"Sammy, why you wearing a devil symbol?" Jess said, pointing to Sammy's necklace.

"Are you stupid?" Liam said, "that's a Jewish symbol. Or as you would call it, a kike symbol."

"Alright, alright, chill out. I was just asking."

"My mom gave me this. It's the Star of David." Sammy said.

"Jew, Christian, Muslim . . . It's all bullshit," Davie Boy said, "my parents tried all my life to push that there bible shit on me."

"I hate being a Jew," Sammy said, "It's all bullshit."

Davie Boy laughed. "That's right, Sammy, me and you are apostates."

"Apostate? What's that?" Liam said.

"You know, folks that say fuck it to their religions and shit."

"How do you even know big ass words like that? Dude, you don't even go to school," Liam said.

"Fuck you, I still read . . . pass me that fuckin' bottle." Davie Boy gestured toward Kirt.

"Yeah, cause comics are *real* educational." Liam laughed and asked Christian for a cigarette.

"I don't read comics, I collect them. So fuck you again."

Christian handed Liam a cigarette and said, "My mom did all that born again crap for a while and tried to put that on me too. I pissed on that real quick."

"So you're an apostate too." Davie Boy lit up another joint. He took a toke and coughed out. "Speaking of rebelling. You were saying today you wanna stand up to people who fucks with us wrong. You know, when we were talking about being misfits and outcasts."

"Yeah, so?" Christian put a smoke in his mouth.

"When're you gonna stand up to Molzan, hero?"

"Don't start this shit again," Liam said.

Jess turned to Liam. "Dude, can you shut the fuck up for a second. My boy here has a point. This kid takes down my boy Jordy and everyone has love for him. I think he's a one hit wonder."

"What do you say, Chinny? I know where Molzan lives," Davie Boy said.

Liam lightly threw an empty can at Davie Boy. "Just let it go."

"Nah, he's right." Christian stood up and walked to the bushes to relieve himself and turned his head to yell in their direction. "Davie Boy, get some toilet paper and eggs."

CHAPTER 15

Degeneration

Liam approached Christian as he was walking back towards the fire. "Chris, you don't need to do this."

"Yeah, I do. You don't gotta come."

"No, I'm coming." Liam said. He pondered for a second and then looked back in Sammy's direction. "You gonna be ok here for a while, Sammy?"

Sammy stood carving something into the tree he normally sat against.

"Let him come. Quit babying him all the time." Christian said.

Sammy turned to face Liam and Christian. "Yeah, Liam, quit babying me all the time."

"Whatever," Liam said. But if things go sideways, it's on you . . . Chinny."

The three approached the others who were standing around the fire. Davie Boy had just returned with a back pack and was crookedly walking.

"Let's go," Christian said.

"Dude, I think I'm too high," Jess said, "Maybe another night."

"Yeah man, I was kinda just messin' with ya," Davie Boy said.

"You guys can talk the talk, but you tuck tails when it's time to walk the walk, huh?" Christian walked over and picked up Davie Boys bag. He lightly bumped his shoulder into Jess as he walked passed him to the entrance.

Liam and Sammy were right behind Christian.

They were hardly ten feet outside the forest when they heard a voice.

"Yo, wait up!"

Davie Boy, Jess and Kirt caught up and joined them on their march.

***

A light drizzle started to coat the street as the boys made their way to Principal Molzan's house. Christian walked a few feet in front of everyone else, with his head down. He was taking in the fact that he was going to practice exactly what he had preached.

The sound of a beer bottle smashing against the pavement did not jar his focus. He tuned out the banter behind him and concentrated on the task at hand.

He couldn't decide whether this was something he wanted to do, or if it was something that he just had to prove. Really, was a little toilet paper and eggs going to prove his point?

"Chinny, this way!"

They approached a street where one side had houses that were generously spaced out, while the other was a field with a large hill.

"That's our escape route," Davie Boy said.

The six of them finally stood in front of Molzan's home, scoping out the best places to hit. There were trees that were not only perfect to wrap with toilet paper, but that also made for excellent cover from the front windows of the house. And, best of all, a blue Porsche sat in the driveway.

"How does a teacher afford that?" Jess said, "That has to be a brand new ninety-five."

Christian stepped away from the group and sat on a rock close to a fence on the side of the driveway.

"You backing out, Chinny?" Jess said.

Christian remained lost in his own thoughts.

"I knew *one-hit* over there was a pussy." Jess said.

"It's ok Chris, you had my back, now I got yours. You can sit this one out," Liam said.

Liam picked up an egg and the rest of the boys followed. Jess and Kirt started rolling toilet paper around trees trunks and looping it around their limbs. Liam threw the first egg and it landed right beside the front window.

"Minute someone wakes up, we run," Davie Boy said as he picked up another egg.

When the toilet paper had run out, everyone except Christian continued to pellet the house with eggs. The nearly continuous sound of them breaking against the house was sure to wake someone sooner or later.

The shenanigans were interrupted when the boys heard a large crashing noise echoing through the street, followed by the blaring of a car alarm. The five of them saw Christian standing on the hood of the Porsche, looking down at a massive rock that now rested on its dashboard among the glittering chips of glass that once made up the Porsche's windshield. He looked possessed and was now holding Davie Boy's bottle of lighter fluid in his hand.

"Fuck! Let's get outta here!" One of them yelled.

The windows on the top story of the house lit up and all the boys ran. Christian remained where he was. He was far from finished. He poured lighter fluid on the dashboard and the front seats.

Liam stopped in the distance and turned. "Don't do it dude . . . Come on!"

Christian stood in a trance. He pulled a pack of matches out of the back pocket of his jeans. The soft drizzle picked up as if a power from above was urging Christian to stop.

Christian looked up as the lights from the lower part of the house turned on. He lit a match, then used it to light the rest of the matchbook. He held his hand over the burning matchbook to protect it from the rain. The burning light from the matches revealed a complacent grin the second before he tossed them into the car. Immediately, the front dash went up in flames and quickly spread to engulf the front seats.

Christian watched as the fire first began to dance and then to rage. A man opened the front door and ran out on the porch. He quickly ran back inside. Christian held up both his middle fingers and spat on the ground. Jumping off the hood of the burning car, he escaped into the darkness.

CHAPTER 16

The Star of David

The whistling birds brought life to the peacefulness of the early morning. The sun defeated the night clouds, and its rays began to slowly warm the street.

John Molzan stood at the edge of his driveway staring at the burnt mess that was being lifted onto a tow truck.

"Daddy, what happened to Mommy's car?" A little voice behind John said.

"Just a little accident. Go inside honey."

"Can I get my bear out of there before they take it away?"

"Go inside, Ali!"

They both turned to walk away and John hardly took two steps when the sun reflected off of something on the grass in front of one of the trees covered in the pulpy residue of wet toilet paper. He picked it up to take a closer look. In his hand he held the Star of David.

CHAPTER 17

Fearless Defiance

Christian had no regrets about what he'd done the previous night. Molzan had asked for it when he didn't give Christian a chance to explain his side of what had happened between him and Jordy. Besides, it was important to Christian that all the guys at the Creek who questioned him, saw what he was capable of.

There was a markedly different atmosphere when they all met up at the Creek again that same night. He was praised for his actions. Jess even invited him to a party that he'd wanted to go to.

Christian was mulling all this over when there was a knock at the door. When Christian answered it, he was caught off guard to see Jess standing there. The door was only a quarter of the way open and Christian stepped out on the balcony and closed it behind him. The two of them pulled out a couple lawn chairs and lit up cigarettes.

"That shit you did last night, Chin, was awesome."

Christian sat back in his chair and took a long drag from his smoke.

"Sorry if I was a dick," Jess said.

"It's whatever man. How'd you know where I live?"

"Liam. Would you consider running with us? I think you know what me and Kirt do."

"I bust up a car and you want me to deal drugs with you?"

"It ain't about the car, it's the balls it took to do it. We could use guys like you."

Christian stood up and leaned his back against the railing, flicking his ashes. "It's not what I stand for. I'm the solution, not the problem. Besides, you run with Jordy."

"I can smooth things over with him."

"Forget him, Jess. That's done."

"That's something else I needed to talk to you about. It's not done." Jess joined Christian on the railing of the porch.

"What do you mean?"

"Don't go to the party tonight."

"Why not?"

Jess took in a deep breath and exhaled heavily. "I invited you 'cause Jord asked me to. He wants to fuck you up, bro."

Christian tossed his smoke over the balcony. He looked away from Jess. "So you were setting me up?"

"I was. But now I don't want to no more."

"I'm going," Christian said.

"That's not a good idea."

"What the hell do you know? I told you what I don't stand for. Well this *is* what I do stand for."

"Dude…"

"I'll see you there."

***

Christian decided to go to the Creek to see what he could find out in order to be prepared for the party that night and to find out who else knew he was being set up. Christian didn't know who he could trust. And though he sensed that Liam and Sammy were harmless, Davie Boy was still an enigma.

While they sat around the fire Christian was pretty silent at first. He was going over in his head what could possible happen at the party and what he could do about it.

"Who's Jordy's brother?" Christian said.

Davie Boy was pouring water on the fire and put the canister down. "That there dude is the biggest gangster in this city."

"Why would he care what happens in a high school fight, if he's so big time? Makes no sense," Christian said.

"It's his last name. You fucked with his brother, Chinny. But who knows? Maybe he don't care," Davie Boy said.

"What's he . . . like thirty?" Christian said.

"Don't matter, Chin," Davie Boy said, "half the people he recruits is our age or younger. Gets them to do the dirty work."

"We don't gotta go to the party," Liam said.

Christian tossed his cigarette butt into the steaming remnants of the fire. "You boys need to understand. A last name isn't gonna stop me from standing my ground."

"That's Jordy's territory you wanna piss on," Liam said.

"Don't care. If you wanna cower away for the rest of your life, Liam, then don't come. Or come, and we can show them us four stand strong and won't be intimidated."

"Us four?" Davie Boy said, "This ain't my fight."

"Fine. Choose your side. I don't care if it's just me."

CHAPTER 18

Blind Side

It was early and the night was young, but the music was already thumping. One of the best DJ's in the city was the M.C. that night. There was a large crowd of people gathered in the huge yard that looked more like a greenbelt, but it still didn't have half the people it would have later. Jordy and Kirt were in the distance laughing it up with some of the other party goers. Meanwhile, Braeden and Jess shared a joint and sipped on some booze.

Braeden was uneasy about Jordy's plan to make an example of the new kid. He knew that Jordy just had something to prove and that the mainlander was his main ticket to further ingratiate himself to his brother.

"Yo brah, you sure he's comin?" Braeden said.

"Yeah, he was pretty set on it." Jess took a swig of his beer.

"This shit ain't right," Braeden said.

"Truth Braed? I ain't sure it's right neither. Kid seems ok. He's a crazy motherfucker though." Jess chuckled.

"Whatcha mean?"

"Shoulda seen what he did to Molzan's car last night. Kids cool."

Jordy and Kirt were walking towards the two, drinks in hand. Braeden gestured toward Jess to cut the conversation short.

"Boys! This party's gonna be killer. When's our friend getting here?" Jordy said.

"Ya know, brah, maybe we should just let it be."

Jordy shook his head and looked at Kirt. "This is exactly what I'm talking about."

"I gotta agree man," Jess said, "we should let this one go." Jess pointed behind Jordy. A group of guys were walking in their direction and Jordy turned around.

Jordy's brother Russ was leading the pack. He wore a tank top with a large gold chain hanging down to his chest and was carrying an open bottle of scotch with an unlit joint hanging from his mouth.

"What's this shit I hear about some of your little friends comin' here?"

"Russ, it ain't like that," Jordy said.

"Whatever this high school drama is, keep it out of here," Russ said.

"You don't get it, the mainer is—"

"Keep it outta here, Jordy." Russ turned and his boys followed.

Braeden couldn't help but feel a little relieved that this pointless situation seemed to have been averted. Braeden knew Jordy had a hard head though, and when he put his mind to something, there wasn't much that could stop him. As it happened, Jordy sat in a chair not saying a word—and that was always troubling.

Braeden spotted Davie Boy in the distance and he nudged Jess.

"Shit," Jess said.

Braeden rose to his feet and rushed over to Davie Boy. "Dude, is it just you?" Davie Boy jerked his thumb over his shoulder and trailing only a few steps behind him were Liam, Sammy and Christian.

"Brah, take these boys outta here." Braeden said.

Jess also approached, standing behind Braeden. "Look Chinny, Jordy ain't messin' around."

Christian stepped forward and stood closer to Jess.

"Neither am I. You're the one who invited me here—"

All of a sudden, Jordy came out of nowhere, decking Christian at the side of the head. Christian fell to the ground and Jordy dropped on top of him and started raining down punches square into Christian's face and head. Braeden moved forward, but Kirt grabbed his arm, stopping him.

Jess came charging, tackling Jordy and pulling him off of Christian. They both fell onto their backs as Christian crawled away, bleeding from the side of his face.

"The fuck you doing, Jess?" Jordy said as he and Jess rose to their feet.

"He had enough. You made your point," Jess said.

"Ya, brah, it's done," Braeden said.

The commotion prompted onlookers to gather. Christian, who was now standing with the help of Davie Boy, breathed heavily and held the side of his head, wiping away the blood from his temple. "Round three," Christian forced out through his panting.

"Shut up, Chinny," Davie Boy whispered.

"What did you say?" Jordy glared at Christian.

"Let's do it again, right now, when I'm not blindsided."

"Dude! Let it go." Braeden said.

Jordy smiled and nodded his head. "Okay. Let's go to the street." Jordy turned and walked away, followed by a retinue of onlookers.

"Are you crazy, Chin?" Liam said, "We need to get out of here."

Christian ignored him and started following the crowd. Braeden took Davie Boy aside. "You gotta talk some sense into your boy."

"He ain't my boy," Davie Boy said.

Braeden ran ahead and caught up with Jordy, who was walking toward the entrance like a brahma bull.

Braeden put his hand on his shoulder. "Look, we've always been like brothers. I know you wanna prove somethin' to Russ, who probably don't give a fuck about this crap anyway. Not tonight, brah. Not with some nothing kid."

Jordy jerked his shoulder away and kept walking. Braeden couldn't stop him. Nothing was going to stop him. For all Braeden new, he was out to kill Christian.

CHAPTER 19

Brotherly Love

The crowd was gathered on the street. The cheers and drunken yelling wouldn't disturb the neighborhood because the next house was blocks away. Jordy stood a few paces from Christian, with Braeden and Jess standing hesitantly behind him, alongside Kirt, who seemed indifferent.

Davie Boy, Liam and Sammy stood directly behind Christian.

Sammy, who had looked lost in the overwhelming shuffle since they'd gotten there, tugged at Liam's hand. "Li, I wanna go home."

Christian pulled off his hoodie and threw it on the ground. For his part, he had no fear of throwing down with Jordy again. Whether this was good or bad, he didn't know, nor did he care.

Christian and Jordy advanced towards each other with their eyes locked.

"You ain't gonna get up from this, mainer," Jordy said.

Jordy lunged and grabbed Christian by the shirt. Christian tried to swing, but Jordy was too powerful and he threw Christian to the ground. Jordy charged Christian to keep him down but he didn't get far. He was stopped in his tracks by a gunshot that pierced the night and silenced the crowd.

Russ Baxter stood there lowering a gun. Two other men walked with him toward the commotion.

"Well, well, now. Is this him, Jord?" Russ said.

Jordy nodded and stepped back.

"And these three must be your boys?" Russ said to Christian as he pointed to Davie Boy, Liam and Sammy.

Christian rose to his feet and Russ approached him and they stood face to face, with his two friends hanging by his side like shadows.

"Let me introduce myself. I'm Russ Baxter. This here is my boy, Dax, and that there is my boy, Fiend." Russ's friends were both deeply tanned and looked to be juiced up on steroids.

"I been hearing some things going on with my brother. Normally, I got bigger fish to fry then some playground bullshit. But when I hear my name being dragged through the dirt over and over, I gotta take a stand, you hear me?"

"Li, that's Jordy's gangster brother" Sammy said.

"Shut up, Sammy," Liam whispered.

Russ glanced toward Sammy and then looked back at Dax and Fiend. He smirked and shook his head. "Anyways, the last thing I need is some mainer coming to my town—"

Sammy interrupted Russ again. "His name is Chinny."

Russ didn't ignore the interruption this time. "Is your boy there a retard or something?"

On hearing this, Christian's face quickly darkened. His fists clenched and he immediately advanced toward Russ. Liam tried to latch on to the lower part of Christian's shirt.

Russ pulled the gun from the front of his jeans instantly and cocked it, placing it against Christian's forehead. "Nuh-uh, cupcake. You best stand down. I ain't Jordy."

Christian stood his ground. He glared past the barrel that was creating an indentation on his forehead. He looked deep into Russ' eyes as if there were no gun. His legs shook, not out of fear, but of rage. He didn't care if Russ pulled the trigger. He would rather choose death than submit to intimidation.

"Ok, you got a few choices, mainer. You ready?" Russ said, "Jordy come here."

Jordy came and stood beside his brother. "Russ, I ain't sure you gotta shoot no one. You're taking this too far."

"Am I, brother?" Russ laughed. "Here are your choices, mainer. Tell me to pull the trigger and I splatter your brains over the asphalt. Or choose one of those boys standing with you and I'll cap them. Make your choice, and we walk away with three of you going home to snuggle and cuddle in your beds. But one of you is dying tonight."

Davie Boy took half a step forward. "Whoa . . . I ain't got nothin' to do—"

Russ caught eyes with Davie Boy without swaying his gun away from his current target. "Shut up, peon."

Christian closed his eyes for a second and took a deep breath. He opened them, resuming his stare down.

"Speak up, mainer. You got the floor now."

Christian pushed his head harder against the barrel. "If you pull that trigger, that bullet's for me."

Russ's stern look loosened and he eased up slightly. "Wow. Damn, boy . . ."

Christian shook his head. "But you ain't gonna do it, are ya, Russ?"

Russ turned back to Dax and Fiend again. He lowered his gun as he stepped back and grinned. "My man . . . this boy's got balls . . . damn, Jord, how's it you fucked with him?" Russ laughed, carelessly waving his gun around and then putting his arm around Jordy. "You know brother, I got love for you. That's why I'm sorry."

Russ took the gun and flipped it around in his hand, butt end facing forward. He squeezed tighter with the arm that was around Jordy and smashed the gun into his temple. Jordy dropped to his knees. Russ leaned forward and struck Jordy in the head a second time. He fell face first on to the cement. Russ motioned Fiend to continue the assault.

Fiend pounced on the motionless body of Jordy Baxter and began inflicting swift, solid blows, repeatedly to his face with his fists.

Christian watched in disbelief. No one was doing anything to stop it. He could see all these people feared this man and he could feel Russ's eyes settle on him and only him. Russ paid no attention to his battered brother or anyone else in the crowd. Christian shook his head and rushed Fiend, kicking him in the face. Fiend fell backwards and Christian immediately mounted him and began furiously raining down blows on Fiend's face and head. The sound of Fiend's head repeatedly bouncing off and banging against the hard asphalt turned many of the spectators' stomachs. Fiend quickly covered up, revealing that all those steroids were just money down the drain.

Dax made a half-hearted attempt to help Fiend, but Russ easily restrained him, letting the beating prolong. When Russ was satisfied, he finally pushed Dax forward, giving him permission to stop the attack.

Dax grabbed Christian from behind and threw him off. "Yo, that's enough."

"Yeah, that's enough," Russ said as Christian got back to his feet.

"Let me tell you something, mainer." Russ approached him with an ear-to-ear grin. "What did your boy call you? Chinny?" Russ put his arm around Christian. "Let me tell ya . . . you ain't the one who tarnished my name. It's that fat chump who wears my name that's a fuckin' disgrace. Good on you for not backing down. How old are you?"

"Seventeen."

Russ released Christian and took a step back. "My man. That's prime time age. You got something, boy. How about you come to my club next Friday night. Drinks, drugs and bitches on the house, and we can have a chat. Bring your little friends too."

CHAPTER 20

Lost and Found

Christian was finishing his last few bites of cereal in front of the blaring TV, which he was paying no attention to.

Like most people, Christian never had a gun held to his head before. And though this past weekend had been a dangerous one, it made him feel like he was performing a high wire act, and it gave him a rush.

His mother had been missing in action over the past week since their last encounter, and it was refreshing having the house to himself. It wasn't the first time she performed a disappearing act.

Christian had mixed emotions about going back to school after all that had happened in the interim. On the one hand, he looked forward to seeing the reaction of his peers; and on the other, he knew he would have to face Molzan at some point during the day, and he would have to keep a solid poker face.

There was a knock at the door, and when he answered it he was greeted by Liam and Sammy.

"You ready, Chinny?" Liam said.

***

Walking with Liam and Sammy gave Christian a sense of belonging. It was the fruit of something that he had initially cultivated, and he found it tremendously satisfying.

As they approached the entrance doors to the school, a girl's voice called out to him.

"You're Christian, right?"

She leaned against the brick wall near the entrance smoking a cigarette and curling a strand of dyed, fire engine red hair behind her ear, getting it out of her emerald eyes. A plaid shirt was tied around the waist of her jeans which were torn at the knees. However, none of this took anything away from her allure.

Liam nodded in acknowledgment that Christian was being drawn into this fine female's orbit and he and Sammy made themselves scarce.

Christian consciously sauntered over to the girl.

"Yeah, I'm Christian. You can call me Chinny." The name started to grow on him.

The girl laughed and gave him a heart penetrating smile. "Chinny, eh? Well, Chinny, I'm Heather."

"You can call me Chris if you want."

"No, I like Chinny. So, you're the mainer kid from the weekend, right?"

"The weekend?"

"Oh, come on, Chinny. Everybody knows." Heather lightly brushed her hand against his chest.

Christian went silent. He knew what she was talking about but wanted to pretend otherwise.

"So, I was thinking about ditching today. But I have no one to hang out with." She smiled and winked.

Christian awkwardly returned the smile and then turned his head toward the school doors. "I would join you, but this is my first day back in a week."

Liam ran out of the school looking alarmed. "Chinny! Come here."

"What's wrong?" Christian said.

Liam ran up to Christian holding a piece of paper. "Dude, look at this."

Christian took the paper from Liam and read it.

FOUND. PENDANT. If you are the rightful owner OR you know someone who is the rightful owner, please report directly to Principle Molzan's office.

The pendant in the picture was the Star of David.

Liam grabbed Christian by the shoulders. "If Sammy sees this, he will go straight to Molzan."

"Well, let's talk to him." Christian said.

Liam released Christian and leaned against the wall beside Heather who was looking away, but most likely listening intently.

"Man, there's no time. He's in the washroom. Can you just grab him and go back to the Creek. I need to get these posters down somehow."

"Why me? Why don't—"

Christian was interrupted as they spotted Sammy walking out of the entrance doors. Christian took the poster and shoved it into his jacket pocket.

"What you guys doin'?" Sammy said.

Liam whispered to Christian, "Please just take him away." Liam scurried back into the school.

"Sammy, we gotta go to the Creek." Christian said.

"Why? I got math. Mrs. Dunn says I'm the top of the class."

"Just come with me, buddy."

Sammy looked back at the entrance doors. "Liam, what about—"

"Don't worry, he'll catch up with us."

Christian took Sammy by the arm and started walking towards the courtyard. He stopped and turned around to Heather. "You still ditchin'?"

"Sure am, Chinny-Chin-Chin."

"Well let's go," Christian said.

***

Christian and Heather walked a few steps in front of Sammy on the way to the Creek. Christian thought the whole thing with the pendant was ridiculous and that Liam was making a mountain out of a mole hill.

"What was that all about?" Heather said.

"Don't worry. So you grew up in BPI?" Christian said, anxious to change the subject.

"Born and raised. You born a mainer?"

"Yep. I only been here for a few weeks."

"Wow. You sure know how to make quite the impact in a few weeks."

Christian's hands were tucked into his pockets and he gave a half-smile as he kicked a pebble to the side of the road. "I wouldn't call it an impact."

"Oh, you don't know, do you? If you're in with the Baxter's, you're set."

"I'm not *in* with the Baxter's."

The street they walked along was lined with stores. There seemed to be a payday loan shop on every corner.

"MY BIKE!" Sammy yelled.

"Shit. What now?" Christian turned and saw Sammy running towards a pawn shop. There were multiple bicycles on display in the window surrounded by second hand junk. Sammy burst through the door and Christian and Heather followed him.

"This is my bike!"

"You sure, Sammy?" Christian said.

An Asian man stood behind the front counter. He closely watched his three new potential customers. He took his glasses off and set them on the counter in front of him.

"Can I help you?"

"Apparently, this is his bike," Christian said.

"Well, no. It's my bike. But five-hundred dollar, then it's his bike."

"Five-hundred? Didn't you buy this for less than two?"

"Okay. How's six-hundred, then?"

Christian approached the counter and placed his hands on it. He stared the man up and down. "Why are you being a prick?"

"Do you have money? If no, then no welcome here."

"Christian! I want my bike." Sammy kneeled down and rested his head on the seat.

Christian looked back at Sammy and Heather and wished there was something he could do about this injustice.

The man chuckled, "Is your friend retard?"

The compassion on Christian's face drained. His eyes widened and became glossy. His hand snapped forward before the man could blink. He grabbed the man by the collar and pulled his head almost over the counter.

"What the fuck did you just say?"

"Back off, little boy."

"What did you just say about my friend?"

"Let me tell you. My right hand that you no see, is on pistol. I give one opportunity for you to go now."

Christian released him, but not without a shove. He walked towards Sammy and Heather who both had shocked looks on their faces.

"Sammy, let go of the bike. Let's get out of here."

Christian pushed through the front door so hard that it slammed against the pawn shop's outer wall.

Heather gently escorted Sammy out of the store with her hand on his back.

Christian was rapidly walking away from the pawn shop. He was clenching and grinding his teeth so hard that his jaw muscles were beginning to cramp.

After Heather and Sammy caught up to Christian, Sammy asked, "Christian, am I retarded?"

Christian stopped in his tracks. He lifted his head, looking up at the sky. "No, Sammy, you're not. Come on."

"Why do people always tell me that then? I think people are embarrassed to be with me 'cause I'm not smart like all you."

Christian turned and walked back toward Sammy. Standing directly in front of him, Christian placed his hand on the side of Sammy's face. "Let me tell you something, Sammy. You are no different than anyone else. You're the top of your math class, remember? Only the smartest kids are at the top. Liam is lucky to have you as a brother, and I'm proud to call you my friend. You're top notch, buddy."

"What's top notch?" Sammy said.

"It means you're the shit."

CHAPTER 21

Renegade

When Christian, Sammy and Heather arrived at the Creek, they saw Davie Boy in his normal position, while Jess and Kirt, who apparently were also ditching, were sitting on a log drinking and smoking.

Before anyone took notice of them, Heather whispered to Christian, "What the hell are they doing here?"

"Who?" Christian said.

"Kirt and Jess."

"They're friends of ours, why?"

Kirt spotted them and stood up. "What the hell, Heather?"

"Let's get out of here, Chinny," Heather said.

Kirt approached them. "What the fuck are you doing with them?"

"None of your business," Heather said.

"You slut."

"Don't talk to her like that, asshole," Christian said.

Kirt charged Christian and went nose-to-nose with him. Jess and Davie Boy rushed to pull them apart.

"Shit doesn't end, does it?" Jess said. "Can't we all just get along?"

Kirt turned and grabbed his bag. "Fuck this shit, I'm outta here." He charged out of the Creek, and Christian turned to Heather.

"What the hell was that about?"

Jess answered for her, laughing. "She's Kirt's ex-bitch."

"Why do you have to call her that?" Christian said.

"No, I am a bitch. That makes these assholes douche bags." Heather plunked herself down and grabbed a beer.

"Yeah, help yourself," Jess said.

Sammy went back to the tree he always sat beside when he was at the Creek and sat with his back against it. The other four sat around the fire. Christian sat close to Heather.

God she was beautiful. She was the complete opposite of Victoria, yet so sexy in her own way. Which made him wonder what she could have possibly seen in Kirt, whose large pointy nose and long, raggedy hair that was shaved at both sides made him look like a sideshow.

Christian grabbed himself a beer and was now playing the waiting game for Liam to return with the posters.

***

Dusk had finally settled on the Creek and Liam was still nowhere in sight. Heather began to cuddle closer to Christian as the temperature fell. The booze must have been taking over because she was in and out of sleep. Jess looked to be almost passed out on the ground, while Davie Boy sat silent sipping on what had to have been his tenth beer.

At last, Liam appeared, pushing his way through the bushes. Christian made eye contact with him and gently nudged Heather. He got up and walked towards Liam.

"What took you so long?" Christian said, "did you get the posters?"

"No, it was way too hard. We gotta talk about this."

From the distance they heard Sammy yell. "Li! Christian says I'm a top notch shit."

Liam tilted his head and looked at Christian.

"I'll tell you later," Christian said.

Sammy got up and sat beside Heather while Christian and Liam walked deeper into the bushes.

"Chin, Sammy don't understand simple logic or consequences. He can't find out Molzan has his stupid pendant. He *will* go straight to him. This is bad."

"You gonna keep him away from school forever?"

"I dunno man. But you don't get it—"

"What's this?" Sammy again yelled from the distance, interrupting Christian and Liam.

Christian and Liam turned and saw Sammy running towards them. He was squeezing the now pendantless chain around his neck and holding a piece of paper in his hand. Christian quickly searched his pocket and found nothing.

"Shit," Christian said, "the poster must have fell out of my pocket."

"Li, my star!"

"Sammy . . . Listen," Liam said.

"We need to go to talk to Principle Molzan."

"Sammy, school is closed," Liam said.

"I remember where he lives. I need to go there."

Christian and Liam looked at each other. It now began to dawn on Christian how serious the situation was. Sammy ran past them through the woods and Christian and Liam followed.

Liam looked at Christian, exasperated. "See why I didn't want him to come that night? Sammy!"

Christian and Liam struggled to catch up with him. Sammy may have been a little slow upstairs, but he was quick on his feet. They followed Sammy out of the woods surrounding the Creek and onto the main road leading up to some blinking red street lights.

"Sammy, stop!" Liam yelled.

Sammy stopped dead in his tracks and turned around.

Liam was out of breath and tried to push out his words. "You gotta listen to me, ok?"

"What, Li?"

Liam looked over at Christian who just shrugged. "Hold on one sec, ok Sammy?"

Liam walked over to Christian and leaned into his ear. "We're in shit. I gotta tell him."

"Tell him what?"

"About my mom."

"I'm going Li," Sammy said.

"Sammy, wait! Who gave you that pendant?"

"Mom did. You know she did before she got sick."

"Sammy . . ." Liam looked in Christian's direction again and Christian gave a nod. "Mom isn't sick."

"She's better?"

"Mom was never sick. Our mother's in jail, Sammy."

Sammy just stood there, clearly puzzled. "Why are you saying this, Li?"

"You deserve to know the truth. When you were younger, Mom used to make you sick on purpose."

"Shut up, Li!"

"She did it so she could get sympathy. She used you to do that."

"I don't understand."

Liam walked up to Sammy and put his arm around him. "Remember you used to puke a lot? You remember all that time you spent in the hospital?"

"Kind of. Mom said it was—"

Liam cut Sammy off before he could hear the lies again. "She poisoned you."

"No she didn't. I had that—"

"Fuck! She almost killed you Sammy. She drugged you every day and then she pushed you down a flight of stairs. You hit your head so hard and you almost died. You were unconscious for over a week."

"A lie!"

"You're my brother. I love you. I would never make this up. She never loved us. She hated us. I was too young to understand why my big brother was always sick."

"I don't remember, Li. What are you saying? I don't understand!" Sammy wiped tears from his face. He slowly backed away from Liam who was acting out of desperation.

"Try to understand." Liam's eyes started to well up. "She hated us, she hated Dad. She was never good to you, Sammy."

"Dad's not good to me. He calls me retard!"

"He has his shit, but he never hurt us like she did."

Sammy sat down on the cement and put his head between his knees. Christian simply stood there, a dumbfounded witness of an innocent kid's heart being obliterated. He'd had an idea that their mother had done something horrible, but nothing like this. He gazed at Liam and could easily see the pain cut into his face. He'd had a hard time with his own mother, but quickly realized that some had it so much worse. What could he possibly do to make all of this go away for his new found brothers?

Christian and Liam helped Sammy up from the street. "Let's go back to the Creek, Sammy."

Christian was convinced that, that intense moment had to have brought Sammy into the real world, even if it was just a second. Christian felt sorry for him because it was apparent that he didn't understand the potential cruelty that this world could offer. Consequently, Christian respected Liam for stepping into the place Sammy was forced to vacate at the hands of his mother, and taking on the mantle and burden of older brother.

At the Creek, everyone was still fixed to their same spots with the exception of Braeden who must have arrived while they were gone. Kirt, who also returned, was trying to put his hands on Heather.

Christian turned a blind eye having something more important on his mind. He walked to the tree where Sammy normally sat, ignoring Braeden who stood up trying to get his attention.

He studied the tree and observed Sammy's carving that read *OMA*.

Heather came up behind him. "Hey you."

Christian looked at her and then focused his attention on the group just over her shoulder.

"Sammy," Christian said, "what does *OMA* mean?"

Sammy, in a broken voice, said, "It's what you guys argue about."

"What do we argue about?"

Sammy sniffed and wiped the moisture from his nose. "You keep talking about what we are. Outcasts, misfits and apost . . . apos—"

"Apostates." Davie Boy finished.

Christian gave a rueful smile and cocked his head. "You know? That is what we are. I don't know all you that well, but I do see we have lots in common. I think we got the short end of the stick in life. We were never given a chance."

"With due respect, brah, you don't know me," Braeden said.

"Does it matter? I know more than you think. Speaking for myself, I refuse to take shit anymore."

Christian picked up a knife that lay on the ground near the tree. He turned to the group again. "I *am* these things. But I refuse to let these be the only things that define me anymore."

Christian carved an 'R' in front of the three letters. He picked up a bat that leaned against the same tree and walked with a purpose towards the entrance.

"Seriously, Chin," Davie Boy said, "What is it you think you can do here?"

"I'm doing what you're too scared to do most of the time, Davie Boy."

"What's with the 'R'?" Braeden said.

"Renegade."

Christian walked to the exit to the Creek. Liam ran and caught up with him.

"Where are you going with the bat?"

"I'm gonna get your brother's bike back."

CHAPTER 22

The Root

Christian lay in bed staring at his alarm clock that read 2:14pm. On the ground beside him there was a busted-open safe that he hadn't touched since earlier that week. He should have felt guilty, but he didn't. That prick deserved it.

It was a much bigger score than he initially intended. Something just came over him when he smashed through the pawnshop's window and came face-to-face with all the merchandise owned by the man who so egregiously disrespected Sammy and him.

He was lucky that Braeden had caught up with him that night after looting the pawn shop and that he ended up getting a ride from him in his truck. Besides Braeden being the only one that night who actually gave him positive feedback about what he'd said to the group, he was also an accomplice to Christian's little escapade.

He turned over towards the center of the bed. His eyes met hers which were now wide open.

"Good morning, Sunshine," Heather said.

"I guess another day's written off."

Heather turned over on her side and held her head up with her hand. "Yeah, we should consider showing up to school onc of these days."

"Let's go on Monday." Christian sat up and swung his legs over the side of his bed clothed in only his underwear. After retrieving his jeans from the pile of clothes on the floor and pulling them on, he put a cigarette in his mouth.

"Yeah, but what about today?" Heather gestured toward the half-open safe. "I say we should spend some of that. You can buy me something real nice," she said with a sly smile.

"Not yet."

"Ok, well there's a party tonight at my friend Amanda's house," Heather said, "wanna go?"

"Can't tonight. I gotta be somewhere else."

"Okay, I'll go with you then."

"Sorry. Can't bring you to this one."

"Why not?"

"Don't ask. Just can't."

"Fine." Heather turned onto her back and folded her arms over the blanket.

Christian crouched down and sat on the floor with his now-lit cigarette. He glanced at the safe. The money spilling out of its gaping maw called out to him seductively. He still couldn't quite believe it was sitting right here in his room, just a couple of feet away, within reach and there for the taking.

Heather got up from the bed and threw her clothes on. "I'm leaving."

Christian remained mesmerized by his new riches.

"Did you hear me?" Heather said.

The spell was temporarily broken. "What?"

"I'm going home."

"Cool. Call me later if you want."

Heather shook her head and walked out of the bedroom slamming the door behind her. Christian picked up one of the stacks of cash that was bundled in plastic. He could take this money and start over in a place of his own if he wanted to. But with no other income, it would eventually run out.

If there was only a way he could use the money to make more. Russ Baxter would likely have a proposition for him at the club later that night. A couple jobs here and there couldn't hurt, could it? But he was on the fence because it would contradict everything he wanted to stand for. But what if it was just temporary? And if he did make money in a questionable way, he couldn't be a lone ranger. He had to get the guys on his side. If his words couldn't convince them, maybe the contents of the safe would.

***

As usual, the crackling fire was the center piece at the Creek, and Liam, Davie Boy, Jess, Kirt and Braeden, sat around it drinking and smoking up a storm. Sammy, however, was off sitting against the tree which was now engraved with the word ROMA, along with his bike which also leaned against it.

As Christian approached the entrance to the Creek, he heard his name come up. Curious to see what was being said about him in his absence, he stopped and peered through the bushes.

He heard Davie Boy's voice first. "I like'em and all, but that there kid's all talk."

"All talk?" How do you figure?" Jess said and started counting on his fingers. "He busted up Molzan's car, kicked the shit outta Jord, stood up to Russ, beat the fuck outta Fiend and busted up the pawnshop for a fucking bike . . . How is he all talk again?"

"He went and took a bike, big deal," Kirt said. "And what's with that shit on the tree?"

"Was more than a bike, brah," Braeden said.

"What else?" Davie Boy said.

"Not my place to say. Just ask him."

"Whatever. A bike and a couple of trinkets ain't gonna impress me," Davie Boy said.

They were interrupted by a duffel bag landing in front of them. Christian heard enough and was undecided if he wanted to let on that he was eavesdropping. While he was impressed with Braeden closing his mouth about the night at the pawn shop and Jess for sticking up for him, he was disappointed that he was being talked about behind his back, not to mention it probably wasn't the first time.

He had little time to rethink what he wanted to do. He didn't feel he could trust most of these guys. But he needed them. He didn't know how yet, but he knew that he did.

"Chinny, what took you so long? Beer?" Davie Boy said.

"If you guys don't want me here, say it, and I'll be out."

"It's not like that, Chin," Liam said, "You're just freakin some of us out."

"Freakin you out? Look, I didn't choose the shit storm of a life I have, as you guys didn't choose yours."

"Oh, fuck. Is this gonna turn into a support group," Kirt cracked open a beer bottle and threw the cap into the fire.

"Shut up, Kirt," Liam said, "It's important to talk about this."

"Dude, seriously, are you gay? This ain't fucking Doctor Phil" Kirt said.

"What if he was gay?" Christian looked down at Kirt, and then at the rest of the guys. "Has a gay person ever hurt you, Kirt?"

"Well . . . no."

"Then choose your battles, choose who you hate and choose wisely."

"Fags creep me out, is all," Kirt said.

"You bully to make up for shit. I see right through you," Christian said.

Kirt stood up and pulled a pack of cigarettes out of his pocket. "I took my hits, man. Me and Jess here don't got family and bullshit. I got a story, too. But fine, I won't piss on Liam for being gay, if that makes you happy."

"Good." Christian sat down on one of the logs.

"Can I just clarify I'm not fricken gay?" Liam said.

Christian slapped his hand down on the log. "You guys are missing the fucking point. We need to stop fighting. At least amongst ourselves. Every one of us are pissed off at the world. Let's piss on those people who make us that way."

"Don't know 'bout anyone else, but only one pissed at the world is you. Us here, we've been just fine," Davie Boy said.

Christian stood, scooping up the duffel bag and throwing it around his shoulder. "Forget it." He looked up at Sammy being his normal silent self. "Enjoy your bike, Sammy."

Sammy nodded and Christian turned to leave.

"What's in the bag?" Liam said.

"Don't matter, Li," Christian said. He didn't even turn to look at Liam because he was spent. He had no energy to deal with cowards who cried about life and then took it out on people weaker than themselves to feel better. That was exactly what he wanted to stand against.

Braeden stood up and yelled out to Christian, "Tell'em, Chin. Tell'em whatcha got."

Christian turned and walked back to the fire. He threw the bag back down. He figured he might as well give it one more shot. He glared at all of them, slowly making eye contact with each one. He locked eyes with Davie Boy.

"You think this is about high school drama? If we had power and respect, no one would fuck with us."

"I've been saying that all along," Davie Boy said, "But I ain't sure what you're proposing."

"Neither am I."

He wasn't. He didn't know what he wanted to accomplish. He looked at the tree with ROMA scored into its bark; everyone was confused as to why he'd carved the letter 'R' with such ceremony that night.

He *was* a renegade, or at least he was going to be one. Christian being the new kid in town presented an extra obstacle to convincing the group that they should band together to fight for a mutual goal. They all, in their own way, had broken homes just like him. They all had their own battles that people their age should never have to face.

So why not come together to form a bond under those mutual conflicts and challenges?

"We all need to talk. I'm gonna make this quick, and I'm starting with you, Sammy. You got your bike now. I want to make sure you understand you keep that under one condition."

Sammy simply looked at Christian.

"Promise me you'll never try to get that pendant back."

Sammy looked back down at the ground.

"Sammy!" Christian said, "Look, I know your mom gave—"

"I have no mom."

Christian, satisfied with that response directed his attention to the group again. "If any of you guys have any problems, speak right now, and I will take my shit and leave. But if you want a better life, I think we got something here. Fuck the world. It's just us against it. Your choice."

Jess spoke up. "I ain't got no problem with you, Chinny. I know you're for real." Jess motioned towards Braeden, "My boy here also spots something in you, too. I dig that. Only thing I got to say is, my business with Kirt, Braed, and even Jordy, is our shit. I asked you the other day if you wanted to run with us, but I hope you ain't tryin to get a piece of the pie without putting the work in."

Christian knelt down on one knee and started to unzip the duffel bag. "Nope, I'm not. But you can have a piece of mine . . . without putting work in." Christian dumped out the contents of the duffel bag.

"This is twenty thousand." The group stared in disbelief at the pile of cash in front of them. "I'm taking ten thousand and splitting it with Braeden, fifty-fifty."

"Holy shit, brah, you serious?" Braeden said.

"Yeah, you were with me when I got this shit. You five get the rest. Two thousand each." Christian began to throw the pre-apportioned money out to each of them. He walked up to Sammy and held out his share, but Sammy looked away.

"It's ok, Sammy. I'll hold on to this for you."

Christian turned to walk back to the group and Sammy stopped him. "How'd you get my bike back?"

Christian looked back at Sammy. "It isn't how I got your bike back that matters, Sammy. What matters is, I took back what's yours."

Christian joined the group again and sat down on one of the logs.

"Why so generous?" Kirt said, "You know what they say when something is too good to be true."

"A part of standing up for what's right is taking care of the ones you wanna bring with you. It's not about building a pyramid. It's about building a square. It's all about equality and not a hierarchy."

CHAPTER 23

The G's Spot

Bright purple lights emanating from the sign above the club, that read *The G's Spot* reflected off of the wet pavement. There was a light drizzle and the line of people that extended around the building was not moving. The three bouncers who stood at the club's entrance lost in conversation had long since given up paying attention to the restless patrons.

Christian and Braeden had hung back to relax a bit at the Creek while the rest went ahead to the club. When Christian and Braeden arrived, they split up, with Braeden approaching the bouncers and Christian getting in near the end of the line with Liam, Davie Boy and Sammy. Jess and Kirt were nowhere in sight.

"Why you guys standing back here," Christian said.

"Those muscle head twats say they don't know us and shit. They ain't letting no one in," Davie Boy said.

Braeden was shaking his head as he walked towards them. "Those boys ain't letting us in."

"I thought you knew them," Christian said.

"I do, but they don't like me much. They said the only tits they let in are bitches. They were making fun of my man boobs, brah." Braeden, seemingly unconsciously, pulled the front of his shirt away from his chest, somewhat alleviating the expression of his ample cleavage.

"That's bullshit," Christian said, "I'm not standing in this line."

Christian walked up to the bouncers. After attempting to get their attention a few times, one turned around. "What?"

"I'm here on an invite."

"By who? Your girlfriend over there?" The bouncer pointed towards Braeden and laughed. "What's your name?"

"Christian. Russ Baxter told me to come down."

The bouncer looked Christian up and down and smirked. "Yeah? Russ Baxter? I don't know no Russ Baxter. There ain't no Christian on this list either."

Christian went back to Liam, Sammy, Davie Boy and Braeden. "Come on, guys. We might as well get out of here.

As they were about to leave, a disheveled looking black man approached the head of the line and began to ask people for change, starting at the front of the line and working his way to the back.

A man who stood in the line a few feet away from Christian yelled out, "I didn't know there's fuckin' niggers in BPI." He laughed and fist bumped one of his friends.

The beggar lifted his head and then looked back down, but it didn't dissuade his soliciting for change.

Christian turned and locked eyes with the man in line.

"You gotta problem?" The man said.

"Maybe I do," Christian said. Disgust and anger resonated through his body and was portrayed on his face.

Christian turned to the beggar. "Come here, man."

He walked up to Christian. "Good evening, sir."

"Apologize to him," Christian said to the man in line.

"Fuck you," The man said.

The people in line took notice but watched without getting involved. Christian pulled a hundred dollar bill out of his pocket and gave it to the beggar. "Take it and don't listen to douche bags like that."

"God bless you sir, God bless you." The beggar opened his arms for an embrace and Christian awkwardly extended one arm to reciprocate.

"Aww, looks like you found a date tonight," the man in line said.

Christian walked toward the man very quickly and grabbed him with his fist hovering in front of the man's face, ready to strike. Suddenly a bouncer came from behind and wrapped his arms around Christian's body and threw him to the cement.

The sound of one person clapping was heard coming out the front door. "My man."

Christian looked up to see the grinning Russ Baxter. He extended his hand and helped Christian to his feet. He fixed the bouncer with an icy stare, "Don't you ever put your hands on my guest again." Russ jerked his head toward the front door and the bouncer returned to his post.

Russ turned his attention to the man Christian was having words with, pulled him out of the line and pushed him in front of the beggar. "Apologize."

The beggar looked down at the pavement, clearly uncomfortable.

"I'm sorry," the man said.

"What was that?" Russ grabbed the man by the back of the neck and jerked him to the ground. He fell at the beggar's feet. "Lick the dirt off his shoes."

The man crawled closer to the beggar's legs but did nothing. Russ pulled a gun from his pants and placed it against the back of the man's head. "You got ten seconds."

Christian glanced back at Liam and the guys; they looked speechless. Christian didn't know what to do and could only assume the boys felt the same.

The man complied. He licked the shoes. The beggar, who seemingly didn't want any part of this, bowed and hurried away.

Russ signaled for a bouncer to come over. "Get this piece of shit off my sidewalk."

"C'mon," Russ said to Christian. Christian motioned for Liam and the guys to follow.

Russ wasn't finished dominating his territory. When they walked past the front door he grabbed the face of the bouncer who gave Christian a hard time.

"Whatcha think, Chinny? Should I fire this chump?" Russ was holding the bouncer's cheeks tightly with his thumb and middle finger; Christian remained silent. With a push of the bouncers head, Russ released his face from his grasp.

The club was packed and the bass was pumping. People were piled on the dance floor, and amid the flashing pink and purple lights, dancers writhed rhythmically in cages suspended above the crowd.

Russ gestured for the group to sit down at one of the open corner booths. When Christian and the boys were about to take their seats, Russ grabbed Christian by the arm. "Not you."

Russ snapped his fingers at a waitress and pointed at the booth. "You make sure all these boys are taken care of."

Russ led Christian through a door next to the main bar and down a hallway. At the end of the hallway, Russ opened an unmarked steel door that revealed an exquisitely appointed room with its own bar, lit with a soothing red light. There were fewer tables and less people here, and the music from the club's main floor was dulled to a greatly muffled roar. They walked to the back corner where there was a circular booth. Russ instructed the guys that were sitting there to leave, and put his hand out directing Christian to sit down. They both sat and Russ lit a joint.

"Welcome to the G's Spot. This room here is for VIP. I like to call it the Red Room."

Russ sucked back on the joint and put his hand forward, offering Christian a toke, but Christian shook his head.

"You know, Chinny, in my biz, there's dudes that are over fifty and then some your age. Most youngins just fake shit and think they got what it takes. They try to be all gangster. When shit gets real, they tuck their tails and run." Russ waved down one of the waitresses.

"Then there's some old dogs. Been searching for their place for years. Just 'cause they partake in some of the game, they think they're players."

The waitress arrived at the table. Christian thought her short dress resembled a painted-on bodysuit—until he realized it *was* painted on.

"What can I get you, honey?"

"Get me and my boy here a bottle of absinthe," Russ said. "Let's get this started right."

The waitress winked and walked toward the bar. The supple yet well-defined movement of the waitresses' buttocks confirmed for Christian the only thing separating her skin from the air was a layer of body paint. Christian couldn't help being temporarily mesmerized.

Russ noticed Christian's wide-eyed stare and gestured toward the waitress. "You roll with me, and you'll be swimmin' in women like that. They'll be everywhere so often they'll be like wallpaper." Russ winked at Christian.

"Like I was sayin'," Russ continued, "I saw something in you that night with Jordy. There's many a time I stared down a barrel of a gun when I was comin' up. It takes a man to pull that trigger, boy, but it takes a bigger man to call his bluff. You called mine. You think my brother could do that? And I saw how you handled your shit with that dude outside, just a few minutes ago."

"I was just doin the right thing."

Russ chuckled, "The right thing. My man. Anyways, I saw how you handled my own damn boy, Fiend, at the party. I also heard how you dealt with that useless motherfucker who bleeds my blood and wears my name."

"Your brother."

"No, my unchosen liability."

The waitress returned with the drinks. She put two glasses on the table and placed an absinthe spoon with sugar cubes on the rim of the glass. She carefully poured water into it. She rubbed Christian's head. "Enjoy cutie."

Russ held up his glass, "Cheers brotha, to a new found friendship." Christian smiled and they clinked their glasses together.

Russ stuck two hundred dollars in a lace garter that was wrapped around the waitresses' thigh, and smacked her on the butt as she walked away. "Always treat them ladies with respect." He nodded his head in a downward motion, directing Christian to take a drink.

Christian choked down the first sip and pulled his head back, screwing up his face.

"Aw, shit. I forgot. You got virgin lips." Russ laughed.

The two sat there while Christian nursed his drink; he was only pretending to take sips. Russ was already on his second glass.

Christian was people watching as they temporarily ceased conversation. Out of the corner of his eye he noticed that Russ continued to stare at him. It was uncomfortable and borderline creepy.

"You don't gotta pops, do you?" Russ said.

"Nope."

"Your mother's still around, but you hate her. You came to BPI with a purpose. In your own way, you're trying to help them boys of yours sittin' out there. You ain't trying to lead, but that just comes naturally to you, and you can't help it. They all see something in you that they look up to."

"Where are you getting all this from?" Christian said.

"Let me finish. Your biggest weakness is that hint of softness you got in your eyes, boy. You got yourself a girl, right?"

"Not really."

"Careful of that love shit. It's a man's greatest weakness."

Christian was caught off guard. How was this stranger spelling out his life? He raised his drink to his lips. Without taking a sip, he placed it right back down.

"You're also pretending to drink your fricken drink." Russ waved down the waitress again. "Sweetie, bring this boy here a beer."

"How did you know all that?" Christian said.

"Chinny, my man, to sit this seat, to wear these shoes, you got to know how to read people. The last place I would ever look, when I wanna know something about someone, is in what they say. I never listen to their words. Ninety percent of communication is non-verbal. Bet you didn't know that, youngin. The other ten percent is all lies and bullshit, you hear me?"

The waitress brought over a beer and Russ motioned her down towards his face. He whispered something in her ear and she nodded. He put his hand behind her head and pulled her in for a kiss.

"What was I saying?" Russ said.

"Communication."

"Right. It's in their actions and reactions. How they walk, how they sit, how they smile. Mostly though, everyone's story lies right in there fuckin' eyes."

"I gotta ask. What is it that you're wanting from me?"

"That right there is what I'm talking about. My man—you wanna skip the bullshit and get straight to the point. That *is* my point. You see shit. You remind me of me when I was your age. See, my boy Dax, he's my best friend since kids. He'd take a bullet for me in a second. He's a soldier, but he could never be a leader. None of these boys are leaders like you and I."

"I don't lead nothin', Russ."

"Not yet, you don't. I said you're prime time age. This is when the best of the best start to build empires. You got guts that none of these chumps have. That's why you will start ahead of the rest."

"Start what?"

"I want you on my payroll."

"Like, deal drugs?"

"Forget that shit. We can talk details later. I got some ideas for you."

Christian knew this was coming. He wasn't invited there as a friend. He had something that Russ liked. It was a lot easier contemplating his answer in his bedroom and weighing out the options. Now he didn't even feel torn about it. The decision was very easy now that it had become real. "I gotta say no, Russ."

"I ain't looking for an answer now. If you're not down, no harm done, youngin. We can still kick back and shoot the shit over drinks. You're my friend, it's all good. All I ask is that you think about it."

Two girls were approaching the table. They both appeared to be in their early twenties; one blonde and one brunette. What they had in common were killer curves and perfect breasts that bulged out of their low-cut, tight dresses.

"Ladies, come have a seat," Russ said.

"Hey Russ, how's it hanging?" The blonde said.

Russ smiled, "This is my boy, Chinny. He's new to the city."

The brunette said, "Hi Chinny, I'm Dixie. My girl here Sandy's been eyeing you up all night."

Christian flushed.

"Actually, so have I." Dixie giggled.

"You've what?" Christian said.

"Been eyeing you up, silly."

"We even played paper, rock, scissors." Sandy moved closer to Christian, "Trying to decide which one of us would approach you."

Russ laughed, sat back in his seat and took another healthy sip of his drink. "And who won?"

"It was a tie," Dixie said through a vivacious laugh.

Christian was immediately dazzled.

"My man, it's your lucky day. Why don't you lovely ladies show him the upper levels of the club?"

***

Five minutes later, Christian, Dixie and Sandy were walking down the upstairs halls of the club. There were some people standing around partying in the hallways that were lined with multiple doors. They opened a door to one of the rooms and entered. There was a bed, nicely made, and on the dresser there was a bucket of ice with a bottle of champagne chilling in the middle.

The giggling girls approached the bed and immediately pulled their dresses over their heads, wearing nothing but bare skin underneath. They jumped onto the bed while Christian just stood there stunned.

"Oh, he's so shy," Dixie said.

Sandy started caressing Dixie's breasts with unrehearsed familiarity. "Don't be shy. We're naked, now it's your turn."

Christian awkwardly sat on the edge of the bed and started taking off a shoe. Was this really happening? Christian wasn't so naïve to think that Russ wasn't behind this, but he wasn't complaining. The girls started making out with each other behind him and Christian started working on his other shoe, which was taking abnormally long.

"My God, Chinny, you're so slow," Dixie said.

They both pounced on him from behind and pulled him onto his back. Sandy and Dixie pulled up his shirt, almost ripping it. Dixie then started undoing Christian's belt buckle while Sandy repositioned herself down by his legs and pulled his pants down; Dixie and Sandy worked with the practiced efficiency of a Daytona pit crew.

"Just lie back and enjoy," Dixie said.

He did.

CHAPTER 24

Eighteen

It was an interesting night, to say the least. What better way to end it than with a nightcap after their first time at a club? Christian and Davie Boy sat at the kitchen table at Christian's house, and in front of them were two half-empty glasses and less than a quarter bottle of whiskey. Davie Boy was attempting to stave off the promise of a vicious hangover, while Christian simply needed to flatten out the wrinkles after being put through what felt like a heavy-duty tumble dry cycle.

Christian knew his mother still hadn't been home, since the bottle still had booze in it. It was the very bottle she was pounding back the last time he had seen or even spoke to her. Even for her, she'd been gone an abnormally long time. So long that actual concern began to nibble at the edges of his mind.

"You tuck Li and Sammy into your bed all nice?" Davie Boy said.

Christian didn't answer, rather he pulled the bottle towards him.

Davie Boy tried again, "You get some from them girls tonight or what?"

Christian looked up at him and poured whiskey into his glass. He took Davie Boy's glass and poured almost the remainder into it, leaving about a shot and a half in the bottle.

"Well? Was that your first time?" Davie Boy laughed.

Christian sipped his whiskey and lit a cigarette.

"Oh wait. You're banging Kirt's girl, aren't ya? You know them two is on-and-off, right?"

A few fruit flies started swarming around their heads. Annoyed, Christian batted them away, and it began to dawn on him that the kitchen was in the same state of disarray as it was the last time he'd seen his mother.

Christian picked up the near-empty bottle of whiskey and chugged what was left. Afterwards, he continued holding the bottle, looking closely at it.

"Something's not right," Christian said. He placed the bottle back on the table.

"You trippin' out, or what?" Davie Boy said.

"What's the date today?"

"I dunno. September . . . um . . . somewhere in the teens."

"I moved here three weeks ago, yesterday."

"So?"

"That means today is September 15th." Christian turned his head to the side, rubbing the back of it. "Dude, I turned eighteen yesterday. I totally forgot it was my birthday."

"Well that there sucks." Davie Boy held his glass in the air, slurring. "Oh well, happy fuckin' birthday! Let's drink."

"You don't get it. Something isn't right. If there is one thing my mom doesn't miss, it's my birthday."

The two were interrupted by a heavy knock at the door.

Christian jumped to his feet and ran to the window beside the entrance, peering through the curtains. He saw two looming, uniformed figures before being temporarily blinded by the glare of a flashlight. He turned back to Davie Boy. "Shit! It's the cops."

Davie Boy quickly retreated and ran up the stairs.

They knocked again, this time louder. Christian had no choice. He took a deep breath and unlocked the deadbolt. He couldn't figure out if this was about Molzan or the pawn shop. It had to be Molzan because of Sammy's stupid chain.

He opened the door and was met by a female and male cop.

"Are you Christian Solomon?" The female cop said.

"Yeah."

"Is there an adult home?"

"Just me."

"Well you need to come with us."

"What for?"

The male cop said, "You're not in trouble. But please come with us."

CHAPTER 25

I Love You…I Hate You

Her soft voice soothed him as she sang the last line of their bedtime song. "If there's one thing I hope I show you, just give love to all, let's give love to all."

"Mama, when you sing you sound like Snow White."

"Oh I do, do I?"

"Mama?"

"Yes, Chrissy baby."

"Can you sing, 'You are My Sunshine' one more time?"

"Enough songs tonight, my love. It's way past your bedtime."

Diana turned off the lamp, flicked on the night light that was plugged into the wall with her toe, and got up from the side of Christian's bed to leave.

"Mama?"

Diana stopped and turned in the doorway, her face draped in shadow from the light beyond. "Yes my love."

"Sometimes I can't sleep."

"Why, Chrissy?"

"I don't like it when your friends come over."

"What friends, love?"

"Those men. They use the 'B' word a lot. Gran told me that word is a bad word and I should never tell a girl that."

"Go to sleep now, baby."

The afternoon sunlight was struggling to penetrate the forest canopy overhead as Christian stood in front of what he came to think of as the ROMA tree, staring at the four letters carved into its surface. He reached out and rubbed some of the errant flecks of bark away from the letters.

Davie Boy sat behind him, beer in hand and glanced in his direction. "So, it's been a couple weeks. Did you see her yet?"

Christian came over and sat on the ground, leaning his back against one of the logs stationed around the fire and lit a cigarette.

"You know, Chin. My Daddy and I built that there tree house. Well my brother too, kind of. He started it with me, but I finished it on my own. I added the extra level on by myself, too. I was only eight or nine." Davie Boy cracked opened another beer and threw the bottle cap towards the unlit fire pit.

"My pops, he been teaching me to swing a hammer since I be like four years old. He owns the biggest construction company in this here city."

Christian listened silently, as he often did. He spent a lot of time at the Creek alone with Davie Boy since that night after the club, and this was the most he had ever really spoken.

"You would think I had it good with two working parents still together and well off and shit. My mom is one of the top realtors, too. But what good is that if you ain't see them ever? They been outta the country for months. How often did you see your mom, Chin?"

"I saw her enough."

"My pop's always says I won't get nothing from him. Not a dime. Not even in his will and shit. He says, anything I want, I'll have to earn. They don't give a shit about nothing but money. They don't even know I exist no more. We all got fucked up families. But love'em or hate'em, I wouldn't turn my back if they laid up in that there hospital."

"What's your point, Davie Boy?"

Davie Boy glared at Christian for a second. "I ever tell you how I got the name Davie Boy? Well my name's David and all, that's obvious. You ever hear of *The Outsiders*?"

"That movie? I might've seen it, don't remember."

"If I wasn't readin' the book over and over, I was watchin' the movie, day after day. Jess and Li started calling me Davie Boy. One dude's name in the story was Pony Boy Curtis. Them boys in that story was just like us. No guidance, shitty parents. They *were* outsiders."

"Stay gold, Davie Boy," Christian said.

Davie Boy chuckled, "You *do* know the story."

"I'm gonna see my mom today. I just got a hard time with hospitals," Christian said.

"Suck it up. She's your mom."

Christian stood up and dusted off the back of his pants. "Hey, thanks for this."

"You're a good man, Chin. Forget shit I said in the past. You *are* good for us."

***

Christian felt a knot in his chest that made it hard to breathe as the entrance doors to the hospital slid open.

He approached a set of elevator doors with a sign above them that said *ICU*. Below it, another sign with an arrow pointing to his left read *Psychiatric Ward*. Those two words caused his heart to speed up as they flashed over and over in his mind. At one time it had been a home away from home, of sorts. Anxious, Christian pushed the button going up to the ICU.

Christian saw his gran at the edge of the bed when he walked in his mother's hospital room. She was sobbing with her head down near his mother's shoulder. Standing at the end of the bed was his mother's friend, Miranda. As soon as Miranda noticed Christian she came over to him.

"I'm so glad you decided to come, Chrissy. This would've meant a lot to her."

"Would have?" Christian said.

"Let's just sit down for a sec and talk."

Miranda and Christian left and sat on two seats just outside his mother's room. Miranda took Christian's hand between both of hers.

"You have to listen to me now, ok Chrissy?"

Christian looked at her numbly.

"Your mother's condition hasn't changed. She's in what they call a persistent vegetative state."

"English please," Christian said.

"She isn't going to come back to us, Chrissy."

Christian stared off into space over Miranda's shoulder.

"Your grandma and I had to make a difficult decision. We had to get a DNR order from the court with the Doctor's recommendation. What that means is, we will have the permission to take your mother off her life support."

"How long?"

"It will take a few days."

"Was she high?" Christian said.

"What do you mean, Chrissy?"

"When she jumped. Was she on drugs?"

Miranda looked at Christian, tilting her head. Tears filled her eyes and she put her arm around him.

"Can she hear us?" Christian said.

"We like to think so."

"I want to see her."

Christian and Miranda entered the room. His gran, who was now sitting on a chair, stood up and approached Christian.

"Hi Gran."

His gran immediately grabbed him, hugging him tightly, crying on his shoulder.

"Gran, I'm sorry it took me so long."

His gran moved her hands to his cheeks. "It's better late than never, Chrissy. I'm happy you're here now." She planted a big kiss on Christian's lips.

"Do you think I can have a second alone with her?"

"Of course lovey, we'll be right outside."

He carried a large weight on his chest. A portion of it was lifted by being there and finally acknowledging his gran. She and Miranda were staying at the house and since they arrived, he had only seen them once. He either stayed at Davie Boy's or Braeden's. He knew it broke his gran's heart, but he didn't want to face the mixed emotions he was feeling.

The room his dying mother was in was lit only by a lamp that sat on her bedside table. The rhythmic beeping of the heart monitor and the huffing of the ventilator she was attached to gave Christian the creeps.

She lay there motionless. Despite the tubes and her bandaged head, it looked like she was just sleeping and could wake up at any moment.

He leaned against the foot of her bed. He had the floor with no interruptions; it was his time to say all that he could before she took her last breath.

"Is this where I'm supposed to say I forgive you, Mom?" Christian bit his quivering bottom lip. He shook his head, attempting to shake away the tears welling in his eyes. And when he did, he spotted a tiny framed picture of his mother holding him when he was a baby on the nightstand.

He went over to the nightstand and picked up the picture. "I don't hate you. I never actually hated you. But it sure as hell felt like you hated me at times. When I was a kid, I just didn't understand why. And as I got older, I just stopped caring." Christian placed the picture back down and took his place at the foot of the bed again.

He breathed in and out heavily. "I try so hard to think about a time, that just maybe I saw spurts of a good mother. Sometimes I think I did. I don't know if those are thoughts I made up in my head, or if they're actually real. I just don't remember, Mom.

"You always left me alone. I was a little boy, I should have *never* been left all alone." Christian sat on the end of the bed, focusing on the floor. Tears quietly streaming from his eyes.

"There were so many nights I cried myself to sleep after tucking myself in. I spoke to you and pretended you were there. I was so scared and I wanted to be cuddled. It was all I knew. I thought it was normal and I hated being normal. 'Cause normal hurt. I know now I was just abandoned. Now I'm about to be abandoned for good. I guess, in a way, I should thank you for preparing me for this, but you didn't even say goodbye or leave a note. All I'm left with are the words you said to me in the kitchen that day."

Christian paused and placed his hand on her feet that were covered by a sheet. "I'm letting you know, Mom, *this* is goodbye, and I won't be at your funeral. I hope you've found your peace."

Christian stood and walked toward the door. As he reached for the door handle, he grabbed his chest; the pain and reality hitting him with the force of a hammer blow. He shook his head and struggled to suppress the turmoil in his soul. He turned back and went to the head of his mother's bed.

He looked down at her helpless state. "I know there's more to our story."

He bent down and a single tear fell from his eye. It landed on her cheek and streamed to the corner of her mouth. He pressed his cheek against hers as he pictured the bedtime songs she religiously sang to him at one time, and whispered in her ear. "I *do* remember, Mama." He closed his eyes and gently kissed her forehead.

***

"…as I drift off to your world, I'll rest in peaceful sleep. Goodnight, my beautiful baby boy." Diana bent down and kissed Christian gently on his forehead.

CHAPTER 26

New Light

December, 1995

Most people fear darkness. Christian didn't; it hid him from all that could hurt him. Instead, he embraced it.

The shades had been shut in his room for a couple months. The alarm clock blinked 12 o'clock, over and over. When he woke up he sometimes didn't even know if he slept through the day, or if it was actually morning. Either way, he didn't care.

He sat up in his bed and rubbed the sleep out of his eyes. A half empty-glass of water sat on the dresser beside a few dirty plates. He silently cursed at himself for leaving the glass so far away. He forced himself out of bed and navigated his way through the clothes strewn on the floor. He picked up the glass and chugged every last drop. His stomach grumbled, but he ignored it and went back to bed. He had hardly put his earphones on when he was interrupted by a knock at his bedroom door.

"Yes?" Christian said.

Christian's gran opened the door and shook her head when she looked at the mess of his room.

"Chrissy, this is not healthy." She walked over to the shades and opened them, letting the daylight in.

Christian squinted, putting his hand up to block the invasive glare. "C'mon Gran!"

"I've been trying to give you your space, Chrissy, but we really need to talk now." His gran sat at the foot of the bed and placed her hand on his leg that was covered by a bed sheet. "I know it's hard, now that your mother—"

"This isn't about Mom. I don't want to talk about her."

"Lovey, you need to stop with this resentment. What's it about then?"

Christian slipped out from under the covers and stood up, wearing only his boxers. He picked up a pair of jeans and quickly put them on.

"Is this about moving back to Stoney?"

Christian grabbed a shirt and made his way towards the door.

"Christian . . . talk to me. I am at a loss here. I don't know what to do to help you."

Christian paused and turned around. "Did you make anything to eat?"

His gran put her hand on her forehead and peered down at the floor.

"Guess not. I'm going for a walk, I need some air," Christian said.

"Wait, Chrissy. You need to be home for dinner. Miranda is coming to town. She's going to help us organize things for the move over the next few days."

"Why do I have to be here?"

"For God sakes! Out of courtesy, maybe? And Chrissy, this isn't a request."

***

After all the progress he felt he'd made in BPI, Christian thought going back to Stoneminster was such a step down. The respect he'd gained and the group he became a part of was a positive step forward. After all these months, the group of friends became like family. He hadn't felt that sense of belonging before in his whole life, and the last thing he wanted to do now was relinquish it.

Being eighteen years old, he didn't have to go with his gran, but what choice did he have. After all, he couldn't afford the rent for the house they were in. The only way that could happen was if he went back to Russ; but he knew a dark road lay in that direction.

He had to tell someone of the plan that he had no choice but to follow. So he decided the best person to speak about this with first was Davie Boy.

He entered the Creek and saw Davie Boy lounging on his new hammock. He nudged him and Davie Boy came to.

"Oh hey, what's up?" Davie Boy sat up and rolled off the hammock to his feet.

"I'm leaving."

"What do you mean? You just got here."

"I mean, I'm leaving BPI."

"For good?"

Christian lit a cigarette and went over to sit down on a log. "I dunno man. For a good amount of time."

"Let me get this straight, Chin. You come here to the island and start talking your shit. You bring all of us together. We become almost like brothers. Then you fuck off?"

"I don't gotta choice, man."

"Course you do."

"How you think I can take care of myself? Work at McDonalds?"

"Russ."

"Ain't gonna lie. I thought about that. But I can't."

Davie Boy stood up and spread his arms in the air, looking down at Christian. "Why? You don't wanna be the bad guy? Tell me this—who *isn't* the bad guy?"

"I just came here to say goodbye. At least for now."

"Look at Liam and Sammy, Chin. You changed their lives."

Christian shook his head and snickered. "Changed their lives? That's a little extreme."

"Since you been here, no one has fucked with them at school, 'cause people know they're tight with you."

"You can take that role, Davie Boy. You had that role before I was even a thought in your mind."

"You got an offer from one of the most powerful businessmen that our little world of BPI can offer. And you are going to run away."

"I'm not running."

"Like fuck you're not. You ran here and now you're gonna run back. Which grass is greener, Chin?"

"Davie Boy . . . you don't think this hurts me?"

"Just go then, Christian."

Christian got up and began to walk away when Davie Boy called out.

"I thought you were all talk when you first came here, and then I *thought* you proved me wrong. We all thought that."

Christian stopped at the bushes and turned before leaving. He took a breath and didn't waste it with anymore words.

***

Christian walked aimlessly, with no thought of where his destination was. He thought about going to Liam's but didn't want to face him with the news.

He wasn't sure that Russ's offer was even still on the table. Liam would do anything to be out of the living situation he was in, but had the same mentality as Christian. If they did work for Russ it would only be temporary. That was the last conversation they had about it before they let it lie.

He wasn't ready to go home just yet and see his gran and Miranda. He wanted to breathe in this place that he'd grown so fond of, one more time.

He thought a lot about his mother since her passing. He never really let anyone know that though. These thoughts weren't about him coming to grips, it was about never knowing the answers to so many questions. His mother was always so secretive about her past. Their past. Now, more than likely, he will never really know what plagued her. People don't just choose to be as messed up as she was. Something had to have caused it.

The clouds started moving in and he felt a light drizzle sprinkle on his face. The streets seemed so empty. It was almost like everything but him, was frozen in time and he was the only moving being on the planet. There didn't seem to be a car or a person in sight. Being lost in his thoughts, as he often was, brought on this illusion.

He stood outside the graveyard where his mother was buried, beside a taxi cab that was running, with the driver leaning against it smoking a cigar. Looking up at the tall black gates, he fought with himself. *Why are you here? What's the point of this?* Something was pulling him in, even though he was urging himself to move on. He didn't intend on going there, but his subconscious led him there, so it seemed.

He entered. He was in a battle with himself and he lost. He didn't even know where his mother was buried. He caught a glimpse of the only being in sight. A man wearing a trench coat and a rain hat was standing at a grave in the distance.

The first gravestone Christian saw read:

Edgar Bradley
January 10th 1959 – April 8th 1977

This guy died the year Christian was born, not to mention he was the same age as he was now. There was a gold plate with a quote attached to the tombstone.

Death is nothing. But to live defeated and inglorious is to die daily.
-Napoleon Bonaparte-

Christian looked at the rows and rows of graves and realized that they had been there for years, with the freshest ones in the back.

Tombstone after tombstone, he saw many a sad story, but none of which was his mother's.

The newer the grave he approached, the closer he got to the man who was down on one knee with his hand on the gravestone in front of him.

As Christian drew near, the man's face came into sharper focus. He had a large salt and pepper beard and a suit under his opened trench coat. He looked like a hobo wearing a rent-a-suit. When Christian got closer to him, the man looked up. He abruptly rose to his feet and casually walked away.

Christian thought it was strange that his presence startled this man so much that he had to leave. While the man retreated into the distance, Christian skipped over the gravestones to the one the man was kneeling at.

Diana Christine Solomon
February 28 1958 – September 28, 1995

The rain grew icy and started pelting Christian's hood.

"Hey!" Christian began running towards the departing man.

The stranger was now rushing to the exit.

Christian never got close. The man jumped in the parked cab, and sped away.

***

It was evening, and Christian sat on his front porch, content to simply watch the street being flooded by a mixture of sleet and freezing rain.

The front door abruptly opened and Miranda rushed out. "Christian, I was about to go looking for you. What are you doing?"

"Honestly, Miranda, I don't want to see anyone right now. I promise I'm not tryin' to be rude."

"Honey, what's wrong?"

Christian got up, walked past Miranda through the front door and saw his gran. The house smelled strongly of a freshly cooked meal, but Christian had no appetite.

"Chrissy, baby . . ."

"Not now, Gran, I just want to go to my room."

"Lovey, wait."

Christian turned and pointed his finger. "For Christ sakes . . . I just want to be left alone."

Christian entered the kitchen and headed toward the stairs on a mission to get to his room. He caught a glimpse of someone else at the corner of his eye and did a double-take. All the rage and sadness drained from his body in an instant. He was in shock.

"Hi, Chris."

"Victoria."

CHAPTER 27

The Eighth Pillar

"Been here this long, and this is the first time I saw this. The Seven Pillars of BPI. Seems kinda overrated."

"I think it's beautiful," Victoria said.

"Do you though? Really? They just look like big black rocks in random places. They don't even look like pillars. They look more like arches."

Christian and Victoria sat on a large rock overlooking a straight drop. They watched as unforgiving waves violently crashed against the cliff. The tall, obscure rock structures were an enigma. The jet black colour and the random placement of the seven pillars were yet to be fully explained.

"Seriously though, Vic, who was the genius that came up with the name of this city?" Christian lit a cigarette. "Oh look, there's some weird rocks sticking out of the water. Let's call it Black Pillar Island. How stupid is that?"

Victoria laughed and put her arm around Christian. "You haven't changed a bit."

They looked at each other for a moment and Christian awkwardly looked away.

"I've really missed you, Chris."

"Me too."

"I didn't know how it was going to be . . . you know . . . with me coming here and seeing you again." Victoria tightened her jacket collar and pulled her hands into her sleeves.

"I didn't know what to say . . . or if you would even want to see me." Victoria gave an awkward smile and looked into his eyes.

Christian's eyes turned toward the ground and he flicked the ashes from his cigarette. An enormous wave hit the side of the cliff and splashed them both. They both laughed and stood up.

"Well I guess the ocean is telling us to go." Christian flicked the his soaked cigarette out by the water.

"Come here," Victoria said.

With a half-smile, Christian hesitated as his eyes met hers and then looked away.

"Come here and hug me, dummy," Victoria said.

Christian wrapped his arms around her petite body, firmly holding her close. The comfort and warmth of the fulfilling hug put him in that one place that was safe, where only happiness resided. Content, he breathed her in deeply.

Victoria pulled her head away from Christian's shoulder. She looked at him with sparkling eyes. Her eyelids, extended by her long dark lashes, blinked in slow motion. Her gentle, soft face that wore a partial smile—and some uncertainty—melted him.

She closed her eyes and Christian submitted to her cue. He moved his head closer. His lips connected with hers.

They kept their lips pressed together. It wasn't a dramatic kiss. But it was passion nonetheless. Their energy and feelings were transferring back and forth between them.

They separated and Christian stepped back. "Thank you," he said.

"For what? You ok?"

Christian's eyes were watery. "Don't worry, Vic. Just . . . thank you."

"There's that sensitivity that I've always admired."

CHAPTER 28

No Sunshine without Clouds

Victoria's presence for those few days were very uplifting. Going back to Stoneminster Falls was something that didn't seem so bad anymore. It excited him to actually tell his gran that he looked forward to the move. In fact, he wasn't even saddened that Victoria had to go back home very soon. He was going to be back in Stoneminster Falls within the next week or so, anyway. But the fact he would have to end what he had with the guys in BPI still saddened him.

The clock said 8:58am, and the welcoming light breaking through his curtains was a sure sign a nice sunny day was in the forecast. He got out of bed, picked up the glass of water on his dresser that was half-full and slammed it back. He threw on some sweats and a t-shirt and rushed downstairs. Hopefully he could sneak to the couch and wake Victoria up with a little kiss. He quietly tippy-toed toward it, but the couch was empty and had been tidied up.

"Good morning," Gran said from the kitchen table.

Gran and Victoria, both in their robes were sitting there sipping coffee. Miranda was in the kitchen washing some dishes.

"This is the earliest I've seen you up since I've been here," Gran said.

"Yeah, I couldn't sleep. I've actually been awake since 7:30, thank you very much. What's for breakfast?"

Gran looked at Victoria. "This boy, I tell you. That is all he ever says to me."

"Sorry, Gran. But fine. Today you can sit down and relax and I'll make breakfast."

"Oh lovey, won't that be nice."

"Eggs?" Christian said.

"There are no eggs, hon," Miranda said from the kitchen.

"No problem, I'll run to the store."

***

Christian's gran let him borrow her car. When he walked out of the grocery store he threw the bags in the back seat and slammed the door. On opening the driver's side door, he noticed a familiar man entering a coffee shop across the street. He had to be sure if this was who he thought it was so he crossed the street to check it out.

He entered the coffee shop and looked around. He had to get to the bottom of who this man was—assuming this was the man who'd been in front of his mother's grave.

Christian spotted him in a booth. He was looking down at a newspaper sipping a cup of coffee. The distinguishable salt and pepper beard confirmed it was him. Christian approached the table and stood a couple of feet away, staring down at the man and he looked up at Christian.

"Can I help you?"

"I saw you at the graveyard the other day."

"And?"

"Who were you visiting?" Christian knew the answer but wanted to hear the man say it.

The man looked up at Christian and frowned. "None of your business. Now, if you don't mind, I would like to get back to my paper."

Christian continued to stare at him. He was at a loss for words and contemplated just walking away and forgetting the whole thing. Something just didn't sit right, though. If this man knew his mother, what else did he know?

"Son, you're making me nervous. I asked nicely, please go on your way now."

"Who are you?" Christian said.

"Look, kid," The man stood up pointing at other empty tables. "Go choose one of those tables or someone else to bother. Are you looking for money? If so, I don't have any." The man sat back down.

"Diana Solomon." Christian said.

The man's eyes flickered up and right back down.

"How do you know Diana Solomon?" Christian said.

"Who's asking?"

"Her son."

The man's head darted up; that clearly caught his attention. He stood up again and studied Christian's face. "You're Diana's son?"

Christian, who was now a little creeped out, took a step back.

"I didn't know she had a son. What's your name?"

"Christian."

"I'm sorry kid, I didn't know. Please, have a seat."

Christian and the man sat across from each other. The man continued to study Christian.

"Can I get you a coffee or something?"

"No. I'm good." Christian said, "Did you see her before she died?"

"Your mom? No, I haven't seen her in . . ." He looked up scanning the ceiling. "It's probably been about twenty years. How old are you Christian?"

"Turned eighteen a couple months ago."

"Seventy-seven baby then. How are you holding up?"

"I'm fine."

"Your mom was a good girl. I wish we never lost touch."

"Actually, she was a fuck up. Maybe you knew a different person than I did."

The man shook his head and looked down at the table. He ran his hand through his beard. "She was troubled? How?"

"Sorry. I never caught your name?" Christian said.

"Edwin. Edwin Steed."

"Ok Edwin, I have lots of questions, but I have to get back home. Can I see you again?"

"Of course, son. I come here quite a bit."

"Friday . . . around one?" Christian said.

"Deal."

***

Gran, Victoria and Miranda sat at the kitchen table while Christian tossed the last egg on the plate. He hadn't cooked a single thing from scratch in his life. He can't remember fried eggs smelling so horribly pungent. He carried the plate of eggs over to the table, along with a plate of bacon and toast.

"Bon appétit," Miranda said.

Christian took his seat and his gran took the first bite. She grimaced and her head darted back. "Lovey, what did you put in these eggs?"

"Nothing special, why?" Christian took a bite of the egg and had a similar reaction. "This is nasty!"

Miranda looked over at the stove before she took a bite. There was a bottle with a yellow liquid in it that had no label. She walked over to it and picked it up. "Chrissy, what were you doing with this?"

"Well I thought you had to use oil on non-stick pans," Christian said.

Miranda's snicker turned into a laugh. "Hon, this isn't oil. It's dish soap."

Gran and Victoria joined in with Miranda's hearty laughter. Christian simply sat, not looking amused.

"Oh, cheer up," his gran said, "It's an honest mistake." She broke out into laughter again.

Christian, who had a partial smirk, said, "I was wondering why it was all foamy when I was cooking it."

"No harm done. I'll whip up some scrambled eggs," Miranda said.

Christian got up from the table and went out the front door to sit on the porch and have a cigarette.

He was going to miss this place. He needed to meet up with Liam and the boys at some point pretty soon. He didn't know about Davie Boy, though. After the reaction he had, Christian wasn't sure how receptive Davie Boy would be to him now. Apart from that, his heart was still heavy knowing he had to walk away from them.

What was he going to say to Heather? Maybe it would be best if he didn't say anything at all.

In truth, he had completely forgotten about her, apart from the fact she had unknowingly taken his virginity. Victoria, on the other hand, was a big distraction; it was very easy to forget everything else.

The door opened behind him. "Hey," Victoria sat beside him on the step.

"Sorry about the eggs," Christian said.

"Oh god, don't be. That was hilarious." Victoria put her hand on Christian's thigh and leaned her head on his shoulder. "We need to talk."

He hated those four words. It always meant something negative was going to come after them.

Victoria lifted her head off his shoulder and looked at Christian, who was staring ahead at the street. "Miranda never told me that you were moving back to Stoney. I think she wanted it all to be a surprise. I only found out when you mentioned it the other day."

"Yeah, it's going to be weird. But I'll adjust," Christian said.

"I've been wanting to tell you something. I was looking forward to telling you, but now not so much, since you're moving home."

Christian shook his head. "Let me guess, you have a boyfriend."

"No, no, nothing like that. Chris . . . I quit school."

"Why?"

"I just didn't like it. I'm a writer and I have a job opportunity."

"What job?"

"Just office admin. But it's for a major paper. I found it through my cousin and I can freelance on the side. If they like anything I write, they could pick it up and publish it."

"Well that's fricken awesome. What's wrong with that?" Christian put his arm around Victoria and snuggled her.

"Well the paper I am working for is The Stoneminster Mett."

"Well congrats, that's huge."

"Chris, I'm working for the head office, which is here in BPI."

Christian's arm dropped down by his side. "What? You're moving *here*?"

"Within the next two weeks."

Christian placed his elbows on his knees, his hands supporting his face. All the positive emotions he'd been feeling the past few days were rapidly draining from his body. Things just could not be perfect. Why was he constantly being punished like this?

He thought about the simple philosophy he adopted when he moved to BPI, and how he vowed to himself to destroy the obstacles that stood in his way—by any means necessary. He had to stand up, even if it meant standing up against the one authority figure he loved deeply. His gran.

"Chris, talk to me. We can still make this work."

In that moment Christian came to a decision. "Yeah, I know. This is going to work. I'm not leaving, Vic."

"Christian. You have to. You need to finish school, and then—"

Christian got up from the step and walked towards the street.

"Christian!"

Christian ignored her and kept on walking.

CHAPTER 29

Gainfully Employed

Another long walk to gather his thoughts. He was eighteen-years-old after all, and he could legally make his own choices in life without anyone doing anything about it. Heck, he was cooking his own TV dinners and putting himself to bed since he was eight. And ten years later he was forced to be a man while other teenagers were being molded into what society said was acceptable.

Russ, in a way, was right about love. As much as Christian avoided being controlled, his decisions were based on someone he loved. Was it really a weakness? Was he contradicting himself by letting it control his choices?

Maybe it was more of a strength. Isn't that how the movies portrayed it? Fight for being with the one you love, no matter what you have to do to hold onto the eternal fire that fueled this emotion.

It was looking like he wasn't going to have to say bye to the boys after all. This could remain the new beginning he was creating, with an added motivation: Victoria.

New beginnings. There was only one person that could give him a stepping stone to obtaining a more stable life. Russ Baxter; so to the G's Spot was where he was headed.

By the time he finally mustered up the courage to actually go to the G's Spot, it was evening. He walked up to the bouncer who unhooked the rope with no questions asked. Christian ignored the loud music and dancing crowd as he made his way to the Red Room. As he walked into the Red Room, he saw the same table that he shared with Russ the first night he was in the club.

Russ sat with two unknown men and four girls. Christian stationed himself directly in front of the table and Russ stared back at him. Russ's grin spoke volumes. Without words, his acknowledgement gave Christian the unspoken message saying, *I knew you'd be back.*

"Chinny, what's up?"

Christian looked around at the others seated at the table. He wondered if he should bite his tongue or speak.

"Russ . . . I need a Job."

Russ laughed as he sat back, inhaling a puff of his joint. "My man."

CHAPTER 30

ROMA

Christian had convinced himself that this was going to be a temporary solution for a long term problem. He would make money and then he would have the means of making a difference in his and his friend's lives; maybe even other people's lives. This was important to him. Over and above anything, his priority was Victoria. If it meant getting all he wanted by getting his hands a little dirty, then so be it.

He knew he needed Russ and his guidance to be able to pull any of this off. Before bringing this in front of the guys, he went over the conversation with Russ over and over in his head:

"If you're going to do this, you're going to need to put some guys together," Russ said.

"I have some guys."

"You're not talking about those three weak ass dudes you run with, are you?"

"They're not weak," Christian said. "But I had a few others in mind."

"Who?"

"Your brother and his crew."

Russ pondered for a second. "That could work."

"I know nothing about this life, Russ."

"Well yours truly is the best in the biz. No one better to learn from, youngin."

"Why are you willing to do this for me?" Christian said.

"First off, I ain't doing this for you. I recruit many. I know within the first ten seconds of meeting someone if they can cut it. You've exceeded my expectations. My gut's rarely wrong. You just gotta learn."

"You know this is just temporary, right?"

Russ snickered. "It's up to you to make peace with Jordy. Shouldn't be hard. He owes you."

"I can do that."

"All my crews have names. By the time you get your territory, you're going to need one."

***

Liam and Davie Boy were the only ones at the Creek with Christian for the time being. The absence of Sammy was intentional. He just couldn't be a part of this plan because it was too risky. Davie Boy didn't have any objections; in fact this was what he wanted to look at doing for quite some time. Liam on the other hand, had a lot of questions.

"You've talked a lot about standing up against this and that, Chin. How does dealing drugs help that cause?" Liam said.

"It's not about dealing drugs. This is just a push forward so we can take control of everything around us.

"Still don't make sense to me."

"You wanna make money, Li?"

"Yeah."

"You want to get out of your father's house and take ownership of your life?"

"I do but—"

"Then trust me. This is the means to do that."

"Look, I already agreed, but ain't like I won't have questions. There's only three of us. How's that gonna work?"

The second half of the conversation was going to be harder to convince Liam of. The others were going to be there any minute and he still hadn't warned him. Davie Boy was pretty nonchalant and agreeable, unlike Liam.

The bushes rustled and Christian realized he had waited too long.

"Who's that?" Liam said.

Braeden, Jess and Kirt emerged from the bushes. Right behind them Jordy Baxter also appeared.

"Look, Li, before you say anything—"

Liam jumped to his feet. "What the hell is *he* doing here?"

"Li, it's cool," Christian said.

"No, it's not cool. Why the fuck's he here?"

"This is our ticket, man," Christian said. "Jord knows this life. So now we're working together."

Jordy approached Liam and stood in front of him. He held out his hand. "Malachi, this is bigger than high school shit. You don't gotta like me, but Chinny here wants you along for the ride. So let's bury this."

"Fuck you." Liam retreated and sat down on a log. "I don't trust him and neither should you, Chinny."

"Li, all that is the past. You gotta move forward." Christian said.

"Whatever. I ain't shaking his hand."

"Li, listen to me—"

Liam cut Christian off. "Chin, I'll do it 'cause I trust you. Once I had enough, I'm out."

The seven of them sat around the fire. This place that was once a little boys club to a few of them, had evolved. This life to some of them was completely new, whereas it wasn't to others. Christian stood up and walked towards the tree with ROMA carved into its bark.

"Russ said we have to have a name." He looked at the tree, then turned back to the guys. "*This* is our name." Christian pointed towards the four letters engraved on the tree.

"We are ROMA."

CHAPTER 31

Stepping Stone

Braeden, Jordy, Jess and Kirt were all seated around Braeden's coffee table in the basement. It was the last time they were going to be cutting up and portioning weed.

"Well Jord," Braeden said, "This is what you've been waiting for."

"I've been waiting for? Let me tell you boys something. I ain't gonna question my brother's decisions. But we're just piggy backing off this bullshit. Second, when we're established, I'm putting a bullet in the mainland scum's head."

PART 2

CHAPTER 32

Molded

June, 1996

It was surprising how life could change so drastically in only six months. The second Christian felt he was about to take ten step backwards, by losing Victoria again and going back to Stoneminster Falls, he made up his mind to do something about it. He refused to let life defeat him, yet again, and fall into the dark pit of which was his former self.

He found a way to stay on Black Pillar Island. It was a challenge for Christian to convince his gran that it was the best decision, but at eighteen years old there was not much she could do about it. His gran struggled with it and that did bother Christian, but he was determined to be his own man.

He explained to his gran how he was able to get a job and that he would be able to fend for himself. The only problem was he couldn't stay in his mother's house—renting to a teenager, was something the landlord didn't want any part of. Luckily, his meeting with Edwin Steed that day couldn't have come at a better time.

They met quite a few times after that day in the coffee shop and Edwin sure did take a liking to Christian; as a result it didn't take very long for Edwin to open his doors to him.

The partially furnished suite in the basement of Edwin's house was all Christian needed. And now that Christian was starting to earn some real money, he was easily able to afford rent, but felt that Edwin wouldn't have cared either way.

Edwin genuinely liked Christian, and he also seemed very lonely. Christian felt that Edwin was appreciating the company. Christian never pried, and only asked Edwin minimal questions about his personal life. Christian made his own assumptions that probably weren't even accurate, but decided to just leave it be, unless Edwin chose to open up to him.

Christian looked up to him, because his advice about life proved that he was wise and been around the block. He was turning out to be a major influence on Christian, almost as much as Russ Baxter—another man who had taken an active role in Christian's molding.

"You do the job, and I'll take care of you youngin."

Russ lived up to that. The amount of cash flow Christian was seeing was rapidly growing. It was more money than he had dreamed of ever making, though he had always dreamt small, it was still significant.

"You ever hear of ACB?" Russ said.

"Nope."

"The pink powder. It is a high that no other drug can come close to. It picks you up—every sight, every thought, every smell—it all becomes heightened. The world becomes more beautiful. Each person experiences something different, but for all it's pure pleasure. It's my baby and I control it."

"Sounds like any other drug to me." Christian said.

"No, it's not. It's the most lucrative cash game on the street. I'm talking huge."

"What do I do?"

"Simple drops. You take the package and transport it to various locations."

It all seemed so simple—at least Russ made it sound that way. Christian never heard of ACB before he started *droppin' it.* Russ was extremely secretive about his sources, because it could be detrimental if his connections were known by his enemies. A lot of Russ's dealings were on or close to enemy territories, which prompted him to give Christian one of a few major warnings. He told Christian to take extreme caution when setting foot on an area called Deer Park. Deer Park was dominated by two groups who shed more blood amongst themselves than anyone else. There were the Hindu's, who were known as the Indo Nation and the Sikh's who proclaimed themselves as the GN Soldiers; the GN standing for Guru Nanak, the founding prophet of Sikhism.

"If they don't shoot you on sight, they will try to tax you—or both."

Christian should have feared the danger involved, but for whatever reason it didn't faze him. He was up for the challenge.

The payoff for taking this on was a lot more than just making a quick buck, in fact, the money making motivation didn't compare to building a future with the love of his life, Victoria. Greater the risk, greater the reward. He would do this on a temporary basis till he was grounded. The money he was making and the life he was living to get it wouldn't change his end goals—he was convinced of that.

On the other hand, while he lived the life, he might as well bask in it, embrace it and reap the benefits as well. There was no need to turn that leaf just yet.

CHAPTER 33

Samuel Malachi

Sammy sat on his bed flipping through albums containing photos upon photos of what he thought defined happiness and came to a vexing conclusion: he led a confusing life.

Memories was the only thing he had to live for, until Liam abruptly confronted him months ago with the news that none of it was real. How could his belief in what he perceived as reality be so different than the supposed truth that Liam informed him of? He never did come to terms with that and he secretly questioned if it was actually the truth. Could Liam have lied about all of this over a necklace?

Sammy had always been underestimated but he wasn't completely stupid. He knew that Christian did some things that weren't right in order to get his bike back those months ago. He also knew there was more to the story when it came to the money Christian handed out that night. But what about the money they were all making all of a sudden? The money he wasn't supposed to know about.

He didn't say much, because he was always second-guessing himself. And at the end of the day, he didn't completely understand; so who was he to say anything?

He pulled one of his favorite pictures out of an album. He and his mom were on a water slide. She wore a blue, flowery full-body swim suit while she held him on her lap. Her arms were draped around him, their laughter frozen in time.

Laughter. That was something he didn't really know anymore. He placed the picture under his mattress.

He pushed all the remaining photo albums under his bed, retrieved a sweater from his closet and made his way downstairs.

Once outside, he stood beside his bike that he hadn't ridden for quite some time. His gramps had given it to him, but when it was stripped from him by his father, it destroyed all of that meaning. And when it was placed in his possession again, it just sat as a broken memory trying to regain shape.

He ran his hand across the cross bar, unlocked it and mounted it. He decided to take it out for one last ride.

Every push of the pedal, caused his guilt of riding this stolen merchandise to become more intense. He made up his mind and decided that he was going to confront this guilt; he just needed to build up the courage to get there.

He had to make one stop before he reached his final destination—Christian's house. It was the first time he had ridden there, and it was quite a bit further than when Christian had lived at his mother's.

He just stared at Christian's place when he stopped his bike. He felt this kid he met about a year ago was stealing his brother away. He didn't know for sure, but Liam had seemed a lot more distant.

Sammy ascended the stairs leading up to the front porch and rang the doorbell.

A man whom he had never seen before answered.

"Hi, my name is Sammy. I'm looking for Christian."

"You're a friend?"

"Yes sir, I am."

"Well Sammy, I'm Edwin," he said, shaking Sammy's hand. "He lives in the basement. The door is just around the corner." Edwin pointed to the side of the house.

Sammy was greeted at the side door by Christian after a couple knocks. Christian, who was still in his boxers, looked like he had slept away a good portion of the day.

"Sammy. What's up?"

"I want my money, Chinny."

"Your what?"

"My money. Long time ago at the Creek, you gave everyone their money. You said you'd hold on to mine."

"What are you talking about?"

"The same time you got my bike."

"Oh right. Why now? What for?"

Sammy looked away. He didn't want to explain himself. He just wanted what Christian promised him.

"Forget it Sammy, don't explain. It's yours. Wait right here." Christian ran back into the house and within minutes returned with an envelope and handed it to Sammy.

"You going to the Creek tonight?" Christian said.

"Nah. I ain't feelin' good."

"Well, if you change your mind, Li's meeting me here first. You should come and let loose a little."

"Maybe . . . I might."

As Sammy walked back to his bike, Christian yelled out to him. "Hey. If anyone asks you where you got that, you say nothing till you talk to me, okay?"

Sammy nodded and waved.

***

He left doing what he loved most, which was riding. He loved the wind hitting his face, especially when he went down steep hills. It was like he was flying. It was peaceful; just him and his bike, with no one else to bother him. Simple pleasures, for a simple person.

Simple or not, he did know right from wrong. Weren't Christian, his brother, and the other guys supposed to be doing the right thing?

He often thought about what Christian said to him at the Creek that night.

It isn't how I got your bike back that matters, Sammy. What matters is, I took back what's yours.

What's his? The bike was in fact his. But it was his own father that took it from him. The pawnshop guy was just making a living.

Sammy stopped in front of the pawnshop. He hesitated, staring at the entrance.

He walked his bike up to the door and opened it. The door chimes rang and he rolled it in.

It was time to do the right thing.

CHAPTER 34

Innocent Guilt

The basement suite was a pretty comfortable space for Christian, even though everything was in just one big room. The hot plate on the counter and mini fridge was all he needed. The double bed was a little much, seeing as he slept on the couch most nights. However, it was nice to have when Victoria occasionally stayed at his place.

He was vegging on the couch, flicking through endless channels when the phone rang.

"Hello?"

"Hey babe, whatcha doing?"

"Hey Vic, just waiting to head out to the Creek."

"So when are you going to finally invite me to the famous Creek?"

"Soon babe, very soon. What you up to?"

There was an awkward pause and Victoria exhaled into the phone.

"What's wrong?" Christian said.

"You just seem so secretive all the time."

"I don't mean to be. There's no secrets. There's not much to show you at the Creek."

"Alright."

"Anyways, Liam will be here any second and I'm still in my boxers. Can I call you later?"

"I guess, if it's not too late."

"Cool. It won't be."

"Actually wait, Chris. I have a question."

"What's up?"

"Was I your first?"

"Like, love or sex?"

"Sex."

"Why are you asking? We talked about this before. Of course you were."

"I know, I know. But I just wanted to hear it from you again."

"Vic, c'mon. There was no other girl I wanted to be with other than you."

"Are you sure?"

"I promise you . . . I was never with any other girl. You were my first, and I hope to god my last. You're all I need."

"Aw, that is so sweet. Ok, I will let you get ready then. Call me later."

He hated having to lie to her, but it would only complicate things otherwise.

There was a heavy knock at the door and Liam stormed in before Christian had a chance to answer.

"Chin, we gotta big problem." Liam was pacing back and forth.

"Story of my life. Can you stop moving around you're making me dizzy."

Liam stopped in his tracks. "Sammy got arrested."

"For what?"

"Did you give him that two thousand?"

"Yeah."

Liam slapped his forehead and fell back against the door. "Dude, he went to that pawnshop and tried to return his bike and the money."

Christian walked over to the couch and flopped down on it. "Shit. But that was like almost a year ago."

"Don't matter, Chin. Anyways, he called me and they're holding him there now. This is really bad."

"You tell him not to say shit?"

"Of course. But you know, it's Sammy. Good thing I answered the phone instead of my pops when he called."

"Do the guys know?"

"No, I came straight here."

"We need to get to the Creek to get our stories straight," Christian said.

Christian threw on some jeans and hoody, then gathered up his bag. As Liam and him were exiting, the phone rang. They both turned around and made eye contact with each other. Christian sighed and rushed to the phone before the answering machine picked up.

"Hello?"

"It's Braeden."

Christian said nothing. He ran his hand through his hair, anticipating bad news. He knew Braeden was supposed to be at the Creek.

"Brah, I've been arrested. Coppers are gonna come for you too, I'm guessin'."

"Don't say anything, Braed. Tell them you're waiting for your lawyer."

When Christian hung up with Braeden, he looked pale and leaned with both his hands on the table his phone was sitting on. "Go to the Creek without me, Li."

"Why? We gotta—"

Christian stood up straight and opened his arms in the air. "Do you wanna get arrested, too? Just go!"

Liam shook his head and without further protest he left.

Christian wasn't running. None of the other guys needed to be arrested along with him. They weren't even at the pawnshop that night. This was on him, and they should be protected from the decision he made when he got Sammy's bike back and the money.

He dreaded what Sammy had already said. He was going into this blind not knowing what the cops knew. They sure wouldn't disclose their knowledge; they would want to trap him.

He sat on the doorstep waiting, and saw a car in the distance. It was a police cruiser. No lights, but it slowed in front of his house. Christian stood up and walked towards the sidewalk that the car was now parked in front of.

A plain clothes officer stepped out of the passenger side of the vehicle. His shoulder holster was in clear view along with a badge hanging around his neck. His hand reached down for a pair of handcuffs that were clipped to his belt. "Christian Solomon?"

"Yes sir."

"You're under arrest. Please turn around."

CHAPTER 35

Bringing on the Heat

Christian sat face-to-face with the cop in a little room with his hands still cuffed behind his back.

"So Christian, you had your phone call. Time for some questions."

"Ask away," Christian said.

"Your record goes back a little bit, doesn't it?" The cop held a folder in front of him that only his eyes could see.

"Dunno."

"Robbery was a little more extreme, even for you, don't you think?" He closed the folder and placed it down in front of him on the table.

"Didn't say I was gonna answer your questions," Christian said with a smirk.

"Here's something off-topic. How about we have a chat about Russell Baxter, or Dexter Maxwell?"

Christian's heart temporarily picked up its pace as he denied any knowledge of the two.

"Oh, I'm sorry. Maxwell goes by Dax Max. Ring any bells?"

The door opened behind Christian. A man in a suit with a briefcase entered and took a seat.

"I'm Jay Peterson. Is my client being charged with something?"

"Not yet. We're just having a chat," the officer said.

"That's nice. Anyways, if he is not being charged, I'm going to escort him home."

"Oh you are now, are you?"

"I sure am. Along with Braeden Cunningham."

The officer paused and looked out the window at another man in a suit. "Malachi is being released without bond, you can take him. I'm not done with these boys yet though."

"What grounds are you holding them on again?"

"Well Peterson, we're trying to establish—"

The man the officer was looking at outside the window pushed the door open. He shook his head and walked towards the table. "Mr. Solomon, I want to make this clear. This is far from over. Detective Steeves, remove his cuffs."

Christian and Peterson proceeded to leave the interview room. The Detective who interrupted the interview placed his hand on Christian's shoulder as he walked past and whispered in his ear. "My name is Detective Ross Williams. Remember that name."

He let go of Christian but quickly grabbed his shoulder again. "Oh, and Chinny." The detective winked at Christian, who was caught off guard by the fact the officer new his nickname. "Give them boys Russ and Dax a big wet kiss for me."

CHAPTER 36

The Other Side of the Tracks

After a long night at the police station, the last thing Christian wanted was to be woken up the next morning, but Edwin didn't give him much of a choice.

Christian was riding in Edwin's pick-up truck. For a man that loved to talk, he was unusually silent. He seemed thoroughly intent on the road ahead of him.

"Thanks for doing that for me last night," Christian said, "You gonna tell me where we're going?"

Edwin looked at Christian and then looked away. They pulled up to a stop light. Christian hadn't been in this area of town before. The grass and trees sure weren't trimmed to perfection here. There were abandoned buildings and garbage strewn on the street. The people looked like zombies as they randomly wandered around. The houses didn't appear to have been lived in for years; at least not by the rightful owners. Every inch of the walls on most of the buildings were coated with graffiti. Anything that seemed like it was actively being used had bars in the windows. This was a mirror image of the downtown east side back in Stoneminster Falls. Christian didn't think BPI had anything comparable to that.

"Why are we here?" Christian attempted to get Edwin's attention again.

"Just take it all in and keep quiet."

They continued to drive and Christian was repulsed by the hideous area embedded in such a beautiful city.

There was a large building with cement stairs leading up to the entrance. A large clock was fastened to the steeple. Many people, all seemingly homeless, were scattered on the stairs and against the walls. Some were just lying in their sleeping bags looking passed out.

Christian was weary. The inhabitants were just walking freely on the road with no regard to the passing cars. Christian rolled up his window and tried to refrain from making eye contact.

Edwin pulled the truck over and parked.

"Why are we stopping here?" Christian said.

Edwin opened the door and sat halfway out of the truck and turned to Christian. "You comin' or what?"

"Hell no. I'm fine right here."

"Suit yourself." Edwin walked to the rear of his vehicle and opened the tailgate on the truck bed that was covered by a canopy.

He pulled out two large boxes and walked up to the entrance through the sea of vagabonds.

A large black lady met him at the door. Christian couldn't hear what they were saying, but he could see that the boxes were filled with food products, among other things.

Edwin left the boxes at the door and the lady hugged him; he also handed her an envelope.

When he returned to the truck, Edwin still hardly said two words and they sped off.

"You drove me there so I can watch you make a donation?"

"I didn't say speak."

They drove towards the ocean and Edwin approached a look-out point that oversaw the seven pillars and he parked the truck again.

He looked over at Christian and finally spoke. "I told you a lot of surface stuff about your mom."

"Yeah."

"I don't know what led her down the path she took. I would love to give you answers to that, son, but I lost touch with her. I tried to help her, Christian."

"You tried to save her. I can only guess what your point is here."

"What's that?"

You are trying to do for me what you couldn't do for my mother. Let me tell ya, Edwin, you ain't my pops and I don't need no saving."

"That's what you think this is about, kid? Christian I know who you work for. That scuzzy club up in the hills. It's run by drug dealers. You think I don't know that?"

"I just do odd jobs and—"

"Cut the crap, son. I wasn't born yesterday. Anyways, I'm not here to stop you from doing whatever you do. Just don't be bringing that crap around my house or you'll be gone. And I mean that."

Christian rolled down the window and put a cigarette in his mouth. Edwin quickly grabbed it and scrunched it up in his hand. "You listening to me, boy?" Edwin tossed the crushed cigarette out his window and dusted off his hands.

"Yeah, I hear you. I get it." Christian turned away and looked at the ocean in front of them.

"You have to listen, son." Edwin put his hand on Christian's shoulder. "Whatever choices you make in life, be it running with the bad or not. No matter what, always leave room for the good. Be good to people, even if it contradicts what you stand for."

"I am good to people. Have been since I moved here."

"If that's the case, then don't stop. Stick to always doing right."

Christian stared ahead, getting a little irritated by the lecture. He didn't need to be told how to do right. He *was* doing the right thing. But he also had to survive.

"This club you work for. You and your friends are those people's delivery boys, aren't you?"

Christian didn't respond.

"What happens when they tell you to go to the area we were just at, to do one of your drops? You gonna go back and tell those boys you were too scared to get out of the car? Thought you were a tough guy."

Christian abruptly turned toward Edwin. "Again, why are we here?"

"To show you that," Edwin pointed towards the pillars.

"Yeah, the seven pillars. I've seen them already."

Edwin reached under his seat and pulled out a pair of binoculars and handed them to Christian. "Look closer, son, past the pillars."

Through the binoculars, Christian could only see water and some open land where there appeared to be some construction going on.

"It looks a lot closer than it actually is, but do you see that island?" Edwin said.

"Yeah."

"I own it."

"How do you own a fricken' island?"

"It's my life's project. Its purpose is to help get people off the street. I'm going to clean this city up."

"Crazy. Can we go there?"

Edwin chuckled. "Yeah, we can. Just not today. I wanted to ask you something, Christian." Edwin ran his hand through his beard. "Would you like to be a part of it?"

"Like, help build it?"

"I guess, build it per se. But I mean run it with me and I will teach you."

"I appreciate the offer, I really do. But you know, being only nineteen—"

"All I'm asking is that you think about it."

"One question. If you are doing this for the city and you apparently have a kajillion dollars, why didn't I ever hear of you—before I met you?"

"I keep a low profile. I have people that act as my face. I prefer it that way."

The drive back home was long. Christian thought about Edwin's proposal. He felt he might have been a little too quick to dismiss Edwin's idea. It could be something right up his alley. At that moment however, he wasn't ready for such a commitment. He didn't want to give his word and then not follow through.

Maybe after he was done with the gig he currently had, he could consider it. Cleaning up the streets and standing up for the people who were just the ghosts of society sounded good to him. They needed voices too. Christian could be their voice by recognizing them and making people aware they exist. Some were never given a chance, just like him. Edwin was his ticket to push him to the level he originally planned to be on.

When they arrived at the house, there was a black SUV with tinted windows sitting across the street. To Christian's dismay, the man leaning up against the front of the hood was Russ and not too far away from him was Dax Max. This was exactly what Edwin forbade not even an hour ago.

Edwin pulled the truck up into the drive way and got out while Christian stayed where he was.

"You coming?" Edwin said.

Christian could see Russ and Dax in the side mirror creeping toward the driveway, peering into the passenger side of the truck where Christian was sitting.

"You know these guys, Chris?" Edwin said.

Christian opened the door and slammed it behind him. "Yeah, I know 'em."

Christian walked in their direction to cut them off before they walked up the drive way and stopped them on the street. "I'll catch you later, Edwin."

Dax wrapped his arm around Christian's neck and flexed his muscle. He forcefully ushered him towards the SUV.

Russ remained standing there in the middle of the street, glaring at Edwin, urging his head forward and squinting. Edwin returned the stare and nonchalantly turned around and headed for his front door.

CHAPTER 37

Little Boys Club

Christian sat in the back of the SUV with Russ, while Dax drove and Fiend rode shotgun.

"What's that dude's name that was at your house?" Russ said.

"Edwin. You know him?"

"Nope. But the man has a familiar lookin' face."

"Well you can't miss that beard," Christian said.

"It's the face behind the beard which is familiar."

Christian stared out the dark tinted window. "You can't just show up like that, Russ."

Russ leaned forward, waving his finger at Christian. "Shut the fuck up and listen. You got arrested yesterday?"

"Yeah."

"By robbing that place, you realize you put us all in a bad position?"

"That all happened way before we met."

Russ grabbed Christian by the shoulder. "Dumb fuck. I don't care if shit happened ten years ago. This poses a problem 'cause these damn pigs are gonna be watchin' you now. What did you say to them?"

"Nothing." Christian pulled his shoulder away from Russ' hand.

"Did they mention me?"

"Why would they?" Christian turned to stare out the window again.

Russ quickly grabbed him by the shoulder again, forcing him to look in his direction. "Don't lie to me, Chinny."

"I'm not."

Russ eased off and sat back, shaking his head. "You have now made yourself a liability."

"Where are we going, Russ?"

"To the place you ROMA boys call the Creek. I gotta check on my merchandise and talk with your crew."

"They're not there."

"They are. I made sure of that."

As the four drove to the Creek, Christian couldn't help but feel nervous. Russ Baxter was unpredictable. Hopefully Davie Boy had everything in order or it was going to be Christian's head.

***

All the boys, as Russ said, were gathered at the Creek with the exception of Jordy. They all simultaneously looked in Russ's direction when they came through the entrance and Davie Boy stood up. "Russ. You wanna beer?"

Russ walked past all of them towards a newly built shed. It was fairly large and was made from solid wood and steel. He glanced up at the treehouse and shook his head. "What the hell is that?"

Nobody answered.

He approached the shed which had a padlock on it. He grabbed the lock and turned towards Davie Boy. "Don't be tellin' me you're locking up my shit with this."

"Well I was tryin' not to be obvious. You know, I thought—"

Russ charged Davie Boy. "You thought? I don't give a fuck what you thought. That's not what I'm paying you for." Russ picked up an ax that was embedded in a tree stump. "Let me show you what your thoughts are worth to me." Russ held up the ax with the blade facing Davie Boy's face. Davie Boy took a step back.

Russ returned to the shed; with one, weak swing the lock busted open. "It's that fuckin' easy."

Russ opened the shed door and went inside as Davie Boy stood at the entrance. Russ looked around at the empty space.

"I still gotta fill it up with stuff, to make it look like a real shed," Davie Boy said.

"Yeah, yeah, where's my shit."

Davie walked over to a rug and lifted it up. Under it was a handle and he snapped it up. There was a ladder that led below ground.

Russ proceeded to step onto the ladder and descended a few feet. He looked up at Davie Boy. "You built this yourself, kid?"

"Mostly. These guys helped a bit."

"Holy shit . . . my man. This is what I'm talkin' about. It's perfect." Russ came back up the trap door entrance and exited the shed. He pointed toward the damaged lock. "Fix that shit. Otherwise, this storage is stellar."

Russ started pacing around the rest of the group, staring each of them down. "Where's my brother?"

"He's out on a drop," Jess said.

"Yeah? Where?"

"Deer Park."

"Indo territory? Why'd he go alone?"

"You said you wanted us all here," Jess said.

Russ took the ax and raised it above his head. He plunged it into a tree stump and turned toward the group again. "You guys need to get your shit together. You don't send one guy into the Punjab neighborhood. What if something happened to him? You know how much money that would cost me?"

Christian stood there shaking his head. He sat down on a log and lit a cigarette.

"You got a problem there, Chinny?" Russ said.

"Nope. No problem."

"Well you're sleeping here till that lock gets fixed. No drops till shit's cleared with the pigs. Hear me?"

"Loud and clear," Christian said.

Russ turned towards Davie Boy. He tossed him a stack of cash. "Keep up the good work and fix that lock."

Davie Boy caught the cash. "You want me to rip down that there tree house?"

"*That there tree house, that there tree house.* Speak English, motherfucker. Anyways, keep it. It's a good cover. Makes this place look like a little boys club."

CHAPTER 38

Silenced

Evening was approaching and the businesses in the area began to close, including the pawnshop. A vehicle pulled up in the front and came to a screeching stop.

Three men in masks exited the vehicle. Two of them held shot guns while one had a hand gun.

They burst into the pawnshop. The same man Christian had words with was standing at his post behind the cash register. He put one hand in the air but reached with his other hand below the counter.

One of the men holding a shot gun raised it to the pawnshop owners head. "Don't even think about it, chink."

"I got money, I got money, take what you want."

One of the men pulled out a piece of paper from his jacket pocket. "You're Huang Fu Chow and live at 562 Maple Street. Your English name is Stephen Chow. Your wife is Daiyu Chow. She runs an in-house daycare with eight children. You have a four year old daughter named Lian Chow. Your wife's parents also live in your basement and I'm not going to even attempt to pronounce their fuckin' names."

"What you want? Money?" Stephen said.

"You're going to make the situation with Christian Solomon, Braeden Cunningham and Samuel Malachi go away. They didn't rob you, did they, chink?"

"I never heard of them . . . I swear . . . please."

"Also, you're not going to report this incident to the police. If you don't comply, we will tie you up and let you watch us give your wife and little daughter a slow painful death. We will take an extra-long time with your little girl. Then we will shove a stake up your ass and burn you alive."

Stephen Chow, now sweating profusely, nodded his head.

"Good choice. Now open the fuckin' safe, immigrant."

Stephen didn't move, but his body trembled. The man pointed his shot gun right in his face and pushed the barrel hard against his head, breaking the skin. Stephen turned and opened the safe. He pulled out every last dollar and placed it in a bag.

The man lowered his gun and grabbed the bag. "You're still that dumb to keep money up in here, huh?" The man laughed. "It was a pleasure doing business with you."

He and the other man with a shotgun rushed towards the exit. The man with the hand gun pointed it at Stephen's head.

"You're horrible at negotiating, you stupid fuck."

"Please sir. My daughter—"

"Your daughter?" The man laughed, "Love that fresh meat." He lowered the gun and fired a bullet into Stephen's knee. Stephen fell to the ground screaming.

"The next bullet's a head shot, with your little girl's name on it, if you don't comply." The man strutted out of the store.

CHAPTER 39

Movin' on Up

"Do you think I can talk to Edwin about his project on the island?" Victoria said.

It was morning, and Christian was spooning with the love of his life in bed. They were procrastinating getting up to start the day.

"What for?"

"Well I think it could be a brilliant story."

"Not a chance, Vic. He don't like being in the spotlight for some reason."

Victoria shifted her body around to face Christian and curled his hair behind his ear, smiling. "He *doesn't* like, you mean."

"What?"

"It's not he *don't* like—it's he *doesn't* like. Anyways, can you at least ask him, babe?"

"I guess so."

They continued staring into each other's eyes. Christian licked his lips. He knew that look—he was about to get lucky.

"Well?" Victoria said.

"Well what? Sexy lady."

"Are you going to ask him?"

"Right now?"

"Come on, Chris. I don't ask you for much. Can you just go up and ask him? These are the kinds of stories that can be my big break."

Christian read those signals completely wrong. He got up and threw on some clothes. He knew Edwin would not want any part of Victoria's proposal. There was a reason nobody really knew what was being built on the island or who was building it. But for his girl, he might as well put in the effort to try to get her the break she needed.

Christian knocked on Edwin's front door. There were a few sealed boxes piled up on the patio. He figured it was another donation.

Edwin opened the door and Christian walked inside where everything was also packed in boxes.

"I was just about to come talk to you," Edwin said.

"What's all this?"

Edwin walked to the kitchen to pour a cup of coffee and raised his voice to Christian who was still standing just inside the doorway. "I'm going to move to the island. I've built a place there. Now that the construction is coming along, I thought it would be a good time."

"Permanently?"

"That's what I wanted to talk to you about." Edwin returned to the entrance and pulled up two stools. "Kitchen's a mess. Have a seat."

"You selling this place?" Christian said.

"Nope. Keepin' it. I have a proposition for you."

"I'm not moving there, Edwin."

"Kid, I know that. How'd you like to keep this place, though?"

"Nah . . . too expensive."

"That's why you'll pay me rent by working for me on the island three or four times a week."

"How would I get there?"

"I have two boats at the dock, one's yours to use."

Christian thought for a minute. A whole house to himself in exchange for some labor a few times a week. The idea of the island itself was pretty appealing. "You know, I think I'm down with that."

"Good. I will get all my things in order and I'll call you and let you know when to come."

Christian felt pretty good about this arrangement. A home, a steady income, his girl. What more did he need. He made his way back down to the suite.

"So what did he say?" Victoria said.

Christian, who was distracted by Edwin's proposition, completely forgot. "Oh, right. Sorry, Vic . . . he said no."

CHAPTER 40

Student and Teacher

It was expected that the G's Spot would be hopping that night. Christian grabbed a bag and went over to his closet. He stuffed stacks of cash into it and zipped it up.

It was hard lying to Victoria about where he went and what he did some nights. He wasn't ready to expose this part of his life and wasn't sure if he would ever be ready. He didn't think she would understand why he did what he did. For some people, it wasn't easy to see beyond certain things and look at the big picture.

Braeden picked him up and they drove down to the club. The line, as always, extended around the corner. As they were walking to the door, a vehicle slowed down in front of them. Christian realized that it was an unmarked police car. The man driving it was Detective Ross Williams, the cop he encountered at the station.

The detective rolled down his window. "Got a second, Christian?"

"Braed, go inside. I'll meet you in a bit."

"You sure, brah?"

"Don't worry, just go inside."

The detective asked Christian to take a seat on the passenger side. Christian complied and clutched the bag of money tightly. It gave

Christian sort of a high having dirty money so close to the man that could bring him down for it.

The officer glanced out his rear view mirror and then pulled away from the curb. "So how'd you do it?"

Christian had no clue what he was talking about. "How'd I do what?"

The detective glanced at Christian raising his eyebrows and shook his head.

"Where are we going, Detective?"

"The pawnshop owner, Mr. Chow—he recanted his entire statement."

Christian was in silent disbelief.

"Kind of lucky for you, isn't it, Chinny?"

"Well, I suppose he wanted to do the right thing," Christian said.

"Did he? I guess that bullet to the knee must've knocked some sense into him, huh? Know anything about that?"

"Nope."

"He told us he accidentally did it when he was loading his gun."

"He shot himself?" Christian laughed, "Guess karma's a bitch, hey Detective?"

Detective Williams pulled over a block away from the club. "Get the fuck out of my car."

Christian opened the door and gladly exited. The detective rolled down the window. "If you want to play on the side you are playing on, Christian, I assure you, I will take you down."

Christian looked him in the eye, spat on the sidewalk beside the car, and winked at him.

The cops had always been the enemy. *To serve and protect*, that was all a bunch of bullshit. They found answers which weren't always the correct ones just to close cases, and didn't care whether innocent people were hurt in the process. Then there was the famous words of every pig: *I was just doing my job*. What a joke.

It enraged Christian that now he was being threatened by one of these guys. The pawnshop owner got what was coming to him. So bring it on Detective Williams.

The only thing that Christian was weary about was the fact that someone had retaliated without him knowing. He knew there was only one person behind that shooting, and he had to have taken action to shut the mouth of the man who brought on the heat.

When Christian was finally in the club, he walked straight to the Red Room and Braeden caught up with him.

"We gotta talk, Chin."

Christian walked straight past Braeden on a mission towards Russ's table.

"Chinny!" Braeden yelled.

"What?"

"Liam fricken' brought Sammy here."

"I'll talk to you in a sec."

Christian stormed away and stood in front of Russ's table. As usual there were multiple girls surrounding him.

"Russ, what the fuck did you do?"

Russ looked up at Christian with a stone cold look on his face. He motioned to the girls to leave.

"Sit down," Russ said.

Christian sat down and placed the bag on top of the table.

Russ scowled and pointed his finger at Christian. "Don't you ever walk into my club and disrespect me like that."

Christian didn't flinch, with one hand grasping onto the bag of money. What did you do, Russ?"

"What are you talking about?" Russ said.

"The Chinese guy at the pawnshop, he changed his story. He isn't trying to press charges anymore."

"Well that's fuckin' great, ain't it?" Russ said. "What does that have to do with me?"

"He changed his story courtesy of a gunshot wound to his leg," Christian said.

"You think I had something to do with that?"

"Who else, Russ? I do my job for you. I never asked for this kind of bullshit."

"Don't you ever call me a fuckin' liar, youngin. I had nothing to do with that shit. Last person who questioned me like that ended up in a body bag, kid."

Christian sat back in his chair and pulled out a cigarette. He was frustrated because he just didn't know what was what. If Russ did it, he would have probably taken pride in it and bragged about it.

"Look, Chin, I didn't mean that. Relax and have a drink. But I didn't have nothin' to do with the pawnshop."

Christian accepted that and pulled a drink towards him. Maybe it was a coincidence. Maybe the pawnshop owner pissed someone else off. Christian could only speculate.

"Please tell me that bag ain't my shit," Russ said.

"Sorry. I'll bring it upstairs."

Christian picked up the bag and left the table. Braeden caught up to Christian walking up the stairs. "We gotta talk to Liam about bringing Sammy everywhere."

"I know. That's kinda my fault," Christian said, "I pushed Liam sometime back to include his brother in more things."

"He was the one that got us arrested, dude. I know he never meant to rat or nothin'. But the kid will spill his guts to anybody who asks . . . and you know . . . with our thing now, it's—"

"I get it. I'll talk to Liam."

Christian and Braeden approached two doors side by side. Christian reached out for one, but hesitated and looked at the other. "I forget which one it is."

Christian opened one of the doors and they both stepped back in shock. They saw a man on top of a woman and there were two other men around the bed, drinking beers and watching.

"Please stop, you're hurting me." The woman was crying.

"Shut up bitch!" The man struck the woman in the face.

One of the men turned around and noticed the intrusion. "Get the fuck outta here!"

Christian slammed the door. "What was that?"

"Brah, that girl's being raped, I think."

Christian opened the other door and rushed towards a safe and stuffed the bag in. He quickly ran down the stairs, with Braeden following. He rushed over to Russ's table. "Three of your boys are raping someone up there."

"My boys? What the hell do you want me to do?"

"You serious?" Christian said.

"Bitch ain't getting raped, youngin, she's probably likin' it." Russ laughed.

Christian stormed away joining the ROMA boys at their table. The blood rushed from his face; he was as pale as a ghost. He grabbed a bottle of whiskey on the table and took a big swig of it.

"Chinny, what's wrong?" Liam said.

Christian took another drink, emptying it into his mouth. All the other guys were silent with a look of confusion on their faces. Christian slammed the bottle down on the table. "Since this ROMA thing started, I have taken care of all you. Your pockets have been lined and it was all because of me." Christian rose to his feet and scanned the table. "What we stand for, we haven't even touched. It's like we just forgot. Today, we are going to stand up like we were supposed to do from the beginning."

"I'm too baked to stand up." Kirt laughed.

"This isn't a fuckin' joke. If you think it is, then walk away." Christian said. "And Sammy, go home."

"Why?" Sammy said.

Christian knocked a glass from the table with his hand and it shattered against the wall. "Sammy get the fuck out of here!"

Liam stood up and faced Christian, "What the hell's your problem?"

"Now's not the time, Liam. Tell your brother to go home."

Liam instructed Sammy to leave, and he complied. Christian remained standing. Half of the guys were drunk and stoned to the max as usual. That was another thing that was getting to him.

"We came together with a common goal. Some of us friends, some of us enemies." Christian looked at Jordy. "But we came together, did we not?"

"Your goal," Jordy said.

"I don't see you complain about the money you're making because of me."

"I don't need handouts. I'd have got mine eventually." Jordy poured himself a drink.

"How about we talk to your brother and see what he says about that?"

"Fuck him." Jordy held up a middle finger to Christian.

"Yo, Russ!" Christian shouted.

"Okay, okay, shut up," Jordy said.

Two of the men from the room that Christian and Braeden had witnessed upstairs walked down the stairs and headed towards the bar; Christian followed their every movement and nudged Braeden. "That's two of 'em."

"Brah, I'm with you on this. I'll follow your lead."

Christian glanced up the stairway and saw no signs of the third. He turned back to the boys. "You're either with me or against me. Stand up now, or don't stand up at all. You choose the latter, I don't wanna see your face again."

Christian ran up the stairs, and as he reached the top he came face to face with the man who was on top of the girl. He stopped and glared into his eyes. The man returned the stare down.

"You gotta problem, partner?"

Christian ignored him and returned to the room he and Braeden had unintentionally entered. He opened the door and rushed to the bedside.

The girl was lying on her back and her face was swollen and bruised. She was still partially awake. The combination of black mascara and tears flooded her temples and her cheeks. Blood was drying around her nostrils.

Christian placed his hand on her head and gently ran his fingers through her hair. "Are you ok?"

She whispered in a soft, broken voice, "Please, no more."

"I'm not here to hurt you. What's your name?"

"Krissy."

"That's a coincidence. My name is Christian and some people call me Chrissy. How old are you?"

"Sixteen." She started to quiver and suck air back with the attempt to hold in her cry.

Christian's jaws clenched and his chest tightened. For her sake he was keeping calm. "Listen, I have to step out for a sec, but I'll make sure the door is locked. Take a rest and I will be back in a bit."

Christian returned to the table and picked up the whiskey bottle he had emptied earlier. His head pounded with rage. He took one last look at the boys. "With me . . . or against me."

He approached the man he came face to face with on the stairs. Without hesitation he swung with all he had and smashed the bottle over the man's head, and he instantly fell to the floor. Christian immediately jumped on top of him. He repeatedly punched him in the face and as his head bounced back up off the floor, meeting the unforgiving fist of Christian to repeat the same process.

The volume of blood on the ground was increasing. His skull cracked from hitting the ground multiple times.

From the corner, Dax tried to make his way to the commotion. Russ Baxter held him back as he sucked on his cigar and smirked. "Let this shit go. Just go lock the Red Room doors."

The two other guys pounced on Christian, but within a second, the rest of ROMA pulled them off and held them down.

With a signal from Russ, Dax Max pulled Christian off and neutralized the situation.

Russ walked towards Christian, who was now standing, "Go upstairs for a few minutes. Dax will come get you. Everybody out!" Russ yelled and then gestured towards ROMA. "You guys too."

Christian went back upstairs. He stopped at the washroom to wash his hands. Before leaving he grabbed a bundle of paper towels and wetted them down. He returned to the room where Krissy was fast asleep. He gently placed his hand on her ankle.

"Hey, it's me."

Krissy barely lifted her head, briefly making eye contact with him.

He sat down beside her on the bed. He took the wet paper towels and started cleaning her face. She was fully nude from the waist down. There was blood on the side of her inner thigh, close to her groin. He quickly wiped it off, trying his best not to violate the poor girl any further. He took a sheet that was on the ground and covered her nakedness. He cleaned her nose, softly dabbed the corners of her eyes and then her mouth.

"Thank you," Krissy said.

"Where do you live?"

Krissy paused. Her eyes started to brim with tears again.

"You do have somewhere to go, right?" Christian said.

The door abruptly opened behind Christian. Dax walked in. "Chinny, come."

Christian stood up from the bed and looked down at Krissy. "You're gonna be okay for a couple more minutes?"

Krissy nodded. Christian covered her up with another blanket that was on the floor and then followed Dax.

Once they made it to the main floor, Dax opened another door that Christian had never been in. There was a set of stairs leading down to a lower level.

"That girl needs a hospital, Dax."

"She'll get there, don't worry."

In the basement, the man that Christian beat to a pulp was laid out on the floor. Christian couldn't tell if he was unconscious or not.

His other two friends were tied to chairs and gagged.

"What's goin' on, Russ?" Christian said.

"Chinny, my man, you know who you just fucked up?"

Christian shook his head.

"He's one of my top earners. A true gangster." Russ chuckled. "And these other two are his brothers. I don't think he's gonna be able to earn no more, Chin. So I'm going to be throwing some more business your way."

Russ walked over to the man who was lying on the floor and pulled out a gun from the front of his pants. "This motherfucker is as good as dead now." Russ pointed the weapon and pulled the trigger. The point-blank gunshot penetrated the man's skull like a watermelon. His brains spewed out onto the floor.

The other two men were starting to squirm in their chairs. One of them was trying to speak. The muffled words couldn't be deciphered.

Christian put his hand on his head and stepped back. "What the hell, Russ. You can't just . . . you can't just—"

"Finish what you started?" Russ said.

Russ stood in front of one of the other men who were tied up. "Ya know, their mom made the best fricken spaghetti. They didn't eat turkey on thanksgiving. They ate lasagna. Man those were some good times, hey Johnny?"

Russ stood above the man he called Johnny, looking down at him with pitiless eyes. He leaned down placing his face directly in front of Johnny's and whispered, "I never liked you anyway."

He raised the gun and placed it against his head. He cocked the hammer and pulled the trigger. There was a mini explosion of blood spatter that erupted from the back of Johnny's head. He violently snapped back and then forward. His head hung low and his body was motionless.

"At least I know what motivates you, Chin. C'mon, take the gun. Finish this."

Christian backed away even further. He slowly approached the stairs and grabbed onto the railing.

"My man, you got to learn at some point."

Russ put the gun back into his pants and faced the last man alive. "So, you get off on raping little girls?" The man's muffled screams made no impact on Russ.

"You remember that camping trip when we were kids? Was me, you and your dead brothers. We were only eight or nine or somethin'. We stayed up for seventy-two hours straight, pretending to get drunk off pop. We played with them cap guns in the woods. Childhood memories. Ya gotta love 'em. Shit . . . that was one of my best memories." Russ pulled out a knife that was strapped to his belt. He looked at Christian with a half-smile.

"You gotta be a soldier, Chin. I believe there's one in you. "Russ plunged the knife into the man's throat. He rushed to remove the gag while Christian stood in horror.

"This is my favorite part," Russ said.

The man coughed and gurgled as blood was pumping out of his mouth and dripping down his neck. Within seconds, he completely bled out.

CHAPTER 41

Bloody Endings

Krissy was lying on the bed still. A congested snoring flowed through her nose. Dax entered the room and approached her bed.

"Hey little lady," Dax grabbed her shoulder, nudging her body.

Krissy woke up, glanced at Dax, and then closed her eyes again.

"You're a mess, I'm gonna take you outta here."

Dax helped her to her feet, picked her up and brought her to the washroom.

"Where's my pants?" Krissy's phlegm-filled voice muttered.

"Don't worry, I'll go grab them."

Dax helped her lean against the edge of the tub. He draped the front half of her body inside as she knelt down on the outside. He turned on the tap and brought the shower head toward her.

"Here, rinse your hair. Holler at me when you're done."

She took the shower head, propped herself up and leaned even further into the tub. Dax stood up, walked towards the door and closed it, but he stayed on the inside.

He removed the gun from his belt and quietly placed it on the counter. He pulled his belt off slowly, and gently placed it on the floor. Krissy remained in that position letting the water pour over her head, which was impairing her hearing. Her exposed naked bottom was pointing in the air.

Dax removed his pants and picked up his pistol. He crept toward Krissy and stood directly above her. "Damn bitch, those boys made your shit raw."

Krissy dropped the shower head and tried to look up, but Dax grabbed her head by the hair and pushed it into the tub.

She started wailing. "Please, no!"

"One more scream bitch and I'll blow your brains out."

He pulled the trigger anyway and her blood coated the bathroom tub like dark red, dripping paint.

"Oops, sorry." Dax thrust himself inside of her and continued his work on her limp, lifeless body.

CHAPTER 42

GN or Die

August, 1996

Drop after drop, Jordy and Liam always rode in silence. Christian paired them up to force them into situations where they had to be civil with each other in order to survive and make money. The bitterness was always going to be there, but Liam was getting over it. They only spoke about things they had to. It was better that way. Get the job done and get paid. Then kick the cash up to Christian who'd been MIA most of the time since the last night they were all at the club.

While Liam didn't care about having to pay Christian, he knew it was getting under the skin of some of the others.

"We don't need'em," Jordy said.

"Chin?"

Jordy screeched around the corner making an aggressive right turn. "What does he actually do, besides bark out orders that we could just take from my brother directly. I don't get it."

Jordy pulled over in front of Liam's house. "I wanna have a meet with everybody," Jordy said, "Something needs to be done about this."

"I don't want a part of your beef, Jord."

"You're in this deep now. You don't got a choice."

Liam quickly exited and slammed the door to the truck as Jordy sped off, shaking his head.

Liam walked up the driveway toward the front door. All he wanted to do was lie in bed and rest. He had been up all night and all morning yet again, and it was taking a toll on him.

A car pulled up in front of the house and caught Liam's attention. Two men with turbans and full beards exited the vehicle and yelled out, coming towards him. Liam picked up his pace.

"Hold up for a sec, kid."

Liam stopped. He didn't want these guys following him up to the front door.

"Just wanna talk to you." They both walked up the driveway and Liam slowly walked back meeting them half-way.

"What's your name?"

Liam's heart began to pound rapidly. He had an idea who these guys were, but couldn't be sure.

One of the men leaned into Liam, putting his hand on his shoulder and whispering in his ear said, "You tell them Baxter brothers, the next time any of your crew crosses the GN's territory, there will be a blood bath." He deftly kneed Liam in the groin and pushed him to the ground.

The two men went back to their vehicle and drove away. Sammy came running out of the house. "Li! Are you ok?" He reached down and helped Liam to his feet. "Who was that? Should we call the police?"

"Nobody." Liam wheezed. "Don't call the police. Is Dad home?"

"No."

They both went into the house and Liam grabbed the phone. "Sammy, give me a sec."

While Sammy left the room, Liam called Davie Boy.

"Davie Boy, we got a problem."

"I know. Guess you heard about Braed."

"No. What happened?"

"His truck's messed up."

"How?"

"Them boys took bats or somethin' to it. *GN OR DIE* was spray painted all over it."

"Shit man. We gotta talk to Chin. We've caught the attention of the wrong people."

CHAPTER 43

Unmasked

Christian's time on Edwin's island, gave him the opportunity to clear his head. It was very unsettling for him to witness the murders at the club.

Since the night of the killings, Christian had spent most of his days working for Edwin. Everything seemed to be coming along well and he was learning a lot. He was currently erecting the frame of a huge building that would be able to house quite a few people. He didn't really know of Edwin's full plan for this place, but he did know it was for a good cause. His back ached from shovelling dirt for hours and he stopped for a moment to scan the huge open space, picturing what the building would look like once everything was finished.

"Christian." Edwin walked up to him from behind. "Take a break."

They both started walking to Edwin's house. "I'm proud of you, kid."

"Why?"

"I've never seen a kid work as hard as you do."

Christian put a cigarette in his mouth and stopped momentarily to light it.

"All this work you're putting in will pay off when you help me run this place."

"Yeah, I've been thinking about that," Christian said.

"And?"

"I wanna do it." Christian was serious. Combined with that he fully intended to get out of the business he was currently in.

They arrived at Edwin's house. The yard was expansive and looked like a putting green with a white picket fence surrounding it. There was a huge deck that started at the front and went all the way around to the back. The swimming pool in the backyard was calling Christian's name. The two sat on the front deck.

"Can I ask you something, Edwin?"

Edwin gave Christian a nod.

"Why are you doing this all for me?"

"Why not?"

"I mean over the past year or so, you've been pretty good to me."

"I like you, kid. Is that not enough?"

"I guess." Christian flicked his ashes and watched Edwin sip his coffee.

"You've never told me about your son." Christian knew very little about Edwin's life.

Edwin put his cup down and looked at Christian then looked away. The awkward pause told Christian that there was a story there.

"Sorry, I shouldn't have said that." Christian retreated back in his seat and crossed his arms.

"No, it's OK. And it's two sons."

"Two? I thought you said one."

"It was a long time ago. I don't know where they are now." Edwin got up and walked down the stairs. "Come help me with this crate."

The quick change of subject intrigued Christian even more, but he knew Edwin avoided the conversation for a reason, so he let it rest for the time being. He followed Edwin down the stairs and the two of them lifted the large, heavy crate up the stairs onto the deck.

"My Grandma is coming to visit for a few days. Mind if I go back for a week or so?"

"Sure son, no problem."

***

Christian and Victoria did some last minute finishing touches to Christian's house. Victoria had a pot of chili simmering on the stove. It smelled great. This was what married life must feel like.

Victoria lit a few candles at the dinner table and cracked open a bottle of wine. "You want some wine, Chris?"

"No, thanks. You know I hate wine."

"I know. But there isn't any beer or anything, thought I'd offer."

The doorbell rang and Christian answered it. His gran stood in the doorway, her pearly whites spread from ear to ear as he looked into her eyes that were identical to his mothers. "Gran." They hugged and Christian helped her in with her luggage.

"This place is very nice, Chrissy. Do you have the whole place to yourself?"

"Yeah, Gran. I work two jobs now."

"Well, can't say I'm happy about you dropping out of school. But I'm quite proud that you're working hard to provide for yourself."

That was a far cry from what she thought the last time she was in town.

The three sat at the dining table and Victoria served up the chili with some garlic bread. They ate and talked. Christian felt a warm feeling; he could get used to family life. The conversations were just so simple and innocent. There was no fighting. It was just people who wanted to spend time with each other. It was rare that Christian was exposed to this kind of environment. The only fly in the ointment was Christian anticipating questions from Gran about his work, and he had to ponder what he would say when Gran eventually asked him.

The empty plates from the dinner rested in front of them. Victoria and Gran were sipping on their glasses of wine and Christian quickly stood up and started clearing the table. Christian, hoping that the subject of work wouldn't come up, took a deep breath and returned to the table.

"So, Chrissy, tell your gran, what is it that you do at your two jobs?"

"Well . . . I'm a food runner at the bar. It's a pretty easy gig."

"And the other?" Gran said.

"I work at a construction site."

"Well that's fantastic. Must be very busy."

Christian wiped his moist brow with his forearm. "It is busy, Gran. I was actually going to head over to the club tonight and quit. It's really draining me."

"Do you have to go tonight? Can't it wait till tomorrow?" Gran said.

"It could, but I want to give them some notice. Plus, I'd rather get it over with."

"Ok then, why don't you take your car?"

"My car? I don't have one."

"Your gran's eyes aren't like they used to be. My doctor said I should start refraining from driving. I was going to wait for your birthday later this year, but I thought you could have mine."

Christian cringed a little. That big blue seventy-nine Chevy was a boat. An overly ugly one at that. But he didn't want to hurt her feelings.

"Really, Gran? How will you get around?"

Gran pushed the keys over to him, her face proudly beaming. "Public transportation, lovey. Your gran needs her exercise."

***

Christian drove his new ride to The G's Spot and was nervous about confronting Russ. He was serious about quitting, especially after being exposed to what he witnessed the last time he was at the club. He knew Russ wasn't going to like the fact that he wanted out.

He didn't want to dismantle ROMA though. He was hoping that he could convince Edwin to let them get involved in the project. This kind of thing was his original intention in the first place. Edwin would be good for all of them.

Being Monday night, the club wasn't busy and Christian headed straight to Russ' office.

Russ, who was sitting at his desk, looked up. "Chinny, long time no see."

"Hey, Russ."

"You've been laying low. That concerns me."

Christian got straight to the point. "I want out."

"Out?"

"I can't work for you no more, Russ."

"You want out?" Russ laughed. "You can't just go out. Your boys are pushing cash up to you and you want out?"

Christian shrugged.

"Listen to me." Russ leaned forward and placed his elbows on his desk. "I have a big job. I am choosing you to pull it off, 'cause you got the brains."

"Russ . . ."

"Shut up and listen." He motioned for Christian to take a seat in front of him and Christian complied.

"I'll make this quick. There's this guy. He embezzled a bunch of cash from a company he worked for. I'm talking a large chunk of change. Most of it's offshore. The dumb ass keeps a shitload of it in his house. Not even in a damn safe. Put a crew together and you know the rest."

"Russ, you gotta listen—"

"There's more. I know how much you hate rapists. Well this guy is a registered sex offender. A pedophile."

"Bullshit." Christian said.

"I can prove it. Shit's all public record anyway. Find out for yourself if you think I'm lying."

"Still, I gotta decline. Things are getting too risky for me and the guys. I'm fine doing my construction thing."

"With that Edwin Steed dude? That's bullshit man. Listen, this guy we wanna hit, stores about two-hundred-and-fifty thousand up in his crib. You take sixty points and I'll take forty. That's me being generous."

"Nice payday. I'm still out."

Russ stood up from his seat and slammed his hand down. "You stubborn fuck." He reached into his desk drawer and pulled out a bottle of Johnnie Walker and two glasses. "I was gonna hold off on something for a bit. I want to tell you a little story."

Christian was on the edge of his seat, anxiously wanting to get up and leave. He knew this wasn't going to be as easy as coming and going. So he decided to give Russ the floor one last time.

"Listen to me, then decide if you wanna quit." Russ poured both glasses half full.

Christian lit up a cigarette, grabbed the drink and reluctantly leaned back in his chair.

"Before my time, I had an older cousin who ran the streets. He ran it with this guy named Anthony Carter Brooklyn. Most knew him as A.C Brooklyn. But when his name got thrown around on the street, you usually heard A.C.B."

"ACB? You mean the powder we're peddling? Christian said.

"Chin, the pink powder is named after him. He was the smartest hustler around. I talk about owning this city. This guy owned this province and who knows what else. He bought shit direct, with no middle men. He had a piece of every gang in this province. You ever hear of a gangster named Frank Lucas?"

"No."

"He did the same thing. Shit, that's who A.C. looked up to. Anyways A.C. Brooklyn ended up murdering my cousin. I was just a teenaged kid, younger than you. He never got caught for nothing. Then one day, poof! He disappeared."

"He ran? Was he some sort of rat?"

Russ poured himself another drink and pulled out a cigar from his drawer. "Nope. As far as I know he has only been arrested once. Otherwise he had a clean record. There was some kind of assault or rape charge that got him in trouble. He used to like to lay low and this publicity was detrimental to him, I guess. He did get them charges dropped and then never returned to the game."

"I thought you couldn't quit."

"Chin, he *is* the game. This man hides among us and is still active in the biz. I'm sure the cops even know this, but they can't and won't touch 'em. He controls lots of shit. Damn, I indirectly work for him and have been wanting his crown for a long time. To be the king, you gotta kill the king, if ya know what I mean." Russ winked at Christian.

"If he was who you say he was, it's kinda weird he would rape someone and get caught. I thought police didn't touch him." Christian said.

"They won't now."

"Why are you telling me this, anyways?"

Russ pulled out a picture. He placed it on the table in front of Christian. In the picture there were two men. Russ pointed to one of them. "This one here, this is my cousin he killed. This other guy—that's A.C. Brooklyn."

Christian pulled the picture towards him. He shook his head and looked up at Russ. "I'm still missing your point."

"Look closely at A.C. and age him twenty years."

Christian pulled the picture closer and squinted.

"Now put a big ass grey beard on 'em," Russ said.

"What are you saying, Russ?"

"Your boy, that day Dax and I pulled up at your house, the one with the familiar face—your other employer. That's Anthony Carter Brooklyn."

"Edwin?"

"Bingo!"

Christian stared blankly at the picture, trying to see the resemblance. There was a slight one, but maybe it was just that Russ was implanting it in his head. Was he being manipulated into seeing a resemblance? There was no way the good man he knew was the biggest drug lord in the surrounding areas.

"Chinny, let's talk biz once it sinks in. Having a connection like this is huge for our business."

"This can't be him."

"We can own these streets, Chinny. Either get him onside, or take his crown. Like I said, king for king, youngin. I'll take his crown and I'll take you with me. Think about it."

CHAPTER 44

Recognition

Christian was suffering from mental indigestion, unable to absorb the claims Russ made about a man he looked up to almost like a father. What if it were true? If it wasn't, what game was Russ playing?

One thing this man didn't lie about was money. He may lie about the risk, but definitely not the reward. Maybe Christian could do this one last thing, then focus on taking ROMA where he wanted to in the first place.

The guy whose house he had to hit was supposedly a registered pedophile. If he could confirm it, that alone would be worth it.

Christian's decision about being in or out was going to be decided that very moment, as he sat around with all the guys at the Creek.

"It's been a while since all eight of us been around this here fire," Davie Boy said.

Sammy was sitting against the tree, nursing one beer and the rest were drinking hard liquor straight from the bottles and smoking weed.

Christian leaned over to Liam and whispered, "I need to talk to you."

"What the fuck, man." Kirt stood up. "I sit here smashed and high all the time and never say shit. What did you just whisper to'em, Chinny?"

"I just need to talk to him. What's your problem?"

"That right there is my problem. You carved that shit on that tree and then we line your pockets. Anything you need to say to him, you can say to us."

"Oh, here we go again." Jess said.

Jordy stood up. "I'm with Kirt. Mainer there always hides shit. Say what you gotta say to all of us."

Christian's need to talk drained out of him. He only wanted to talk to someone who he could fully trust. He never intended to lead all of them down a dark criminal path. What these guys had been doing was the result of the decisions he made. He didn't think *they* even realized that. Even the guys who had peddled a little weed here and there, before ROMA, were never in this deep as they were now because of him.

This was his moment to stand up to all that he had created and make it all right—by destroying it. Maybe they wouldn't all want to do this with him, but the ones who would follow would be the only ones who mattered.

Christian stood up and lit a cigarette.

"Every time this boy stands and lights a dart, you know he got something to say," Jess said.

"You guys are right." Christian sat down beside Davie Boy. He puffed his cigarette as he slowly looked at each of their faces in turn.

"I'm sorry. This is not what I intended. There are no secrets. What happened at the club, you all know about. I stood up for a girl, but didn't mean for it to go down like it did."

"You didn't intend to play with the big boys you mean," Jordy said.

"I didn't intend for all this. That shed Davie Boy built, the drugs, the threats. I should've been here when the GN's started sending their messages."

Jess chuckled. "I have no complaints."

"That night when I wrote that 'R' on that tree. I had a goal." Christian paused to regain his thoughts. He flicked his half-finished cigarette into the fire.

"I don't want this all to go to shit. I think it's time that we all realize what ROMA stands for and tell Russ . . . tell him we're . . ." Christian stopped and focused on the ground.

"You're gonna say we're out, aren't you? Love to see what my brother would say about who he put in charge," Jordy laughed.

"Shut your fucking mouth, Jordy. You know nothing."

Christian knew Jordy actually hit the nail on the head. He didn't know what stopped him. He could have ended it all right there. Just like that, he made a last second change in plan. "Russ has a job for us. It pays well."

He explained everything Russ had told him and they mentally inhaled every word. The only sounds were Christian's voice and the crackling of the fire.

"The only reason I've considered this is because embezzlement isn't this guy's only problem. The guy's a pedophile."

"Why'd Russ choose you to mastermind it?" Jess said.

"It's 'cause my brother don't want to risk no one important, that's why," Jordy said.

Christian's blood pressure rose from yet another smart ass remark from Jordy. "Why don't you just walk then, Jord?"

"Chill out mainer, I'm messin with ya."

Christian stared hard at Jordy.

Jordy waved his hand at Christian. "Mainer. This is getting weird."

"Let me ask you something, Jordy." Christian pulled the picture Russ gave him out of his back pocket. "You know who this guy is?"

Jordy looked at the picture and then back up at Christian. "Why are you carrying around a picture of my cousin?"

"He *is* your cousin then. Where is he?"

"Been dead since I was like two, or some shit. Only know him from pictures. Who's the other guy?"

Do any of you recognize the other guy?" Christian took back the picture and passed it around.

None of them recognized him or even mentioned a resemblance to Edwin. Davie Boy put the picture on the log beside him and Sammy got up and walked towards it.

"Why you asking, brah?" Braeden said.

"When I met with Russ—" Christian was cut off by Sammy.

"This is that man that was at your house that day when you gave me my money."

Christian's eyes widened. "Why do you say that, Sammy?"

"Because, it looks like him is all. He don't got a beard in this picture, but sure looks like him."

"Give me that." Davie Boy took the picture from Sammy. "Holy shit, dude. Look at his eyes and shit, this *does* look like Edwin . . . I mean, that there boy's younger, but I see it."

The others gathered around Davie Boy and they all started to see the resemblance.

Jordy looked up at Christian. "So let me get this straight. The man you rent from and work for, used to be friends with my dead cousin?"

"Something like that. Give me the picture, I gotta go." Christian abruptly left the Creek. As Christian pulled open his car door he heard someone running up behind him. He turned and saw that it was Braeden.

"What do you want, Braed?"

"Why'd you say that shit about the job in front of Sammy?"

"My mistake. Heat of the moment, I guess."

"That's not good man. He will get us all busted. Anyway, can I ask you something?"

Christian closed the car door and leaned up against it.

"What happened in the basement at the club that night?" Braeden said.

"You know what happened."

"Yeah, but—"

"Russ killed those boys. Cold blood. No questions asked." Christian lit a cigarette and stared at the ground. After a few seconds he looked up at Braeden. "You know what, Braed?"

"What?"

"I've been trying to deny it, but I don't feel any sort of guilt or remorse. I feel almost glad it happened." It was the first time Christian even admitted it to himself, let alone someone else.

"Well them boys got what was comin'. All us guys agree."

"Did they, though?"

"Sometimes, brah, the only real justice, is street justice."

CHAPTER 45

A Softer Source

Gran sure liked to stay up late. Christian walked in the door, paused and looked at her; she didn't even know he'd come in. She was watching an old Western. He approached the living room and she finally unglued herself from the black-and-white justice being dealt out on the television.

"Chrissy, how was your night?"

"Hey Gran. Can I ask you something?"

"I'm just about ready for bed, but sure, lovey." Gran lightly patted the cushion beside her.

Christian sat down while his gran muted the TV.

"Gran, you were pretty involved in Mom's life. Did you know a lot of her friends?"

"Oh yes. Well I knew most of them. Why?"

"Have you ever heard of a man named Edwin Steed? He was older than Mom."

Gran slowly picked up the remote and turned off the television, then looked up at the ceiling and back at Christian. "No, lovey, I can't say I have ever heard that name."

"Well, I mean it's possible that you didn't know *all* her friends right?"`

"Of course. I only really knew the ones fairly close to her." Christian's gran yawned and pulled Christian close to kiss him on the cheek. "The sandman is calling your gran now."

She stood up and walked slowly toward her room. She stretched her arms in the air as she approached the door.

"What about Anthony Carter Brooklyn?" Christian said.

Gran's arms immediately fell to her sides, interrupting her stretch and stopping her in her tracks. She didn't turn to face Christian. "Where did you hear that name, Christian?"

"Gran, I'm just—"

"No. The answer is no. Your mother, nor I, have ever associated with anybody by that name. Good night." Gran opened the door to her room and quickly shut it.

CHAPTER 46

Droppin' the Ball

Christian, Liam and Braeden were driving in Braeden's newly fixed truck to the Punjab territory, Deer Park. It was just a simple drop most of the time. But it was always an extra risk when the drop was in this area because it was the Indo's turf.

The drop was just on the border of Deer Park. They supplied to a white supremacy group which on the most part laid low. The whites and the browns were always at war over something. It would be disastrous if Christian and the guys showed up at the wrong time. The brown and white turfs were too close for comfort.

"Braed, you said you're packin' right?" Christian said.

"Of course, brah. I ain't walkin' into this shit without being strapped. These towel wearing bastards will shoot first and leave no chance for questioning."

"They just shoot at anybody?" Christian said.

"Second you set foot in this game. These dudes know who you are. Trust me, you ain't just anybody, Chin."

"Got another gun?" Christian said.

Braeden pointed over to the glove box. "Check out what I got in there."

Christian pulled out a revolver from the glove box. He popped out the cylinder looking to see if it was loaded, then snapped it back in place.

They pulled up to the drop spot and exited the vehicle. Liam got out of the backseat and pulled out two large bags with him, allowing them to fall onto the unpaved ground, kicking up dust.

The man they were supposed to meet was nowhere in sight. He was supposed to be waiting at the entrance. An eerie silence settled over the area

"We'll give him five minutes." Christian said.

The approaching sounds of vehicles began to grow rapidly in the distance.

"Who's that?" Liam said as three black SUV's and six motorcycles ground to a stop right in front of them half a minute later, filling the air with dust.

A number of men wearing turbans exited the vehicles and got off their bikes. The men on the bikes had full face masks to match their head attire. They were heavily armed and approached the three of them.

"Them boys are the GN Soldiers, brah."

Christian and Braeden were armed with two little hand guns. These guys were carrying AK's.

The men surrounded the three and commanded them to drop their weapons. Braeden and Christian complied and put their hands in the air. A GN approached and kicked the guns aside.

"I'll take this." He picked up the bags and carried them back to the group.

One of the men came forward and glared at them. He paced with his gun leaning against his shoulder, barrel to the sky. "You are just little boys," the man laughed. "Nevertheless, my name is Jag Sidhu, maybe you've heard of me. Which one of you are in charge?"

Christian, Braeden and Liam all looked at each other.

"I am," Christian said.

"And you are?"

"Chinny."

"Well, Mr. Chinny. I got a message for your employer. I've warned your boys there'd be bloodshed if you set foot on my territory. But as a businessman, how about we just start taxing you eighty percent. This drop is Russ Baxter's first installment."

"You can't just take it," Christian said. "You sure you wanna go to war with Russ Baxter?"

"You are just a little boy. That's the only reason why I'm not putting a bullet in your head . . . this time. You tell him there is a new alliance. The GN soldiers are aligned with the Indo Nation as of yesterday. Then ask me, who doesn't want to go to war with who?" Jag put two of his fingers in his mouth and whistled loudly.

A group of men came out of some nearby bushes pulling a trailer behind them. They were brown but did not wear turbans. There were five white men tied up on it and they were all naked, badly beaten and clearly dazed. Their bodies were covered in tattoos which were of swastikas among other white power symbols.

"I'd like to introduce you to our Hindu brothers, the Indo Nation." Jag pointed to the men pulling the trailer. Two of the Hindus started pouring gasoline on the men on the trailer.

"These Neo-Nazi motherfuckers are a dying breed, Mr. Chinny," Jag said. "The first of many."

"Don't do it," Liam broke his silence.

"What did you say?" Jag said. "Do you want to join them?"

"Shut up, Li," Braeden said.

"Shut up? Do you not see what they're gonna do?" Liam said.

Jag walked toward Liam and stared at him. He looked back at Christian. "Maybe you boys need to learn how to keep quiet. I was just about to let you go." Jag struck Liam in the head with his gun, knocking him to the ground.

"Yo, Lakh," Jag said as he turned to one of the men in his crew. "I wanted to send a message, but maybe my communication skills are lacking. You thinking the same thing?"

"Sure am," Lakh said.

Jag picked Liam up off the ground and threw him towards three of his guys. "Strap him up with the whiteys," Jag said.

They dragged Liam along the dirt toward the platform with the other men. "Christian!" Liam yelled.

"No, no, no, don't do this," Christian found himself going against everything that made up his defiant, rebellious nature and pleaded with the GN's.

One of the GN's struck Christian with the butt of his rifle and he fell to the ground. The three men lifted Liam onto the trailer and tied him up. They forced Braeden and Christian toward the trailer and pushed them down to their knees, placing guns against the backs of their heads.

One of the Hindus stepped up on the trailer and poured the remainder of the gasoline on Liam. He retrieved a zippo lighter from his pocket.

"I'm humane," Jag said, "Have any last words for your boy, before you hear his screams."

"Jag, please don't do this. I'm begging you." Christian said.

Jag punched Christian in the face causing him to fall to the ground again. Jag gestured towards his men who came forward and started kicking Christian.

Christian was trying to catch his breath. "Please don't."

"What? I can't hear you!" Jag said.

"P-please . . ."

Jag turned toward the man with the zippo. "Light'em up!"

The man sparked up the zippo and held it in the air.

"No!" Christian yelled, "put me up there instead."

Jag put his hand in the air and the man that was about to do the unthinkable, paused.

"You serious?" Jag said.

Christian started to cough as he was down on his hands and knees at Jags feet. He spit out the dry dirt that he had sucked in after the beating. A long string of saliva fell from his mouth onto the ground and a lone tear streamed down the side of his face. Braeden was kneeling as still as a statue.

Jag lifted Christian to his feet. He pulled out a large knife from his side pocket and handed it to Lakh and muttered something in Punjabi.

Lakh walked up to the trailer and put the knife to Liam's throat. The sinister grin on his face revealed pure enjoyment.

Lakh looked back at Jag who nodded his head. He lowered the knife down to Liam's hand and cut the rope. He lifted Liam to his feet and threw him off the trailer. Liam was barely able to brace himself when he landed face first into the dirt.

"Alright, light'em up." Jag said.

The man with the zippo fired it up and threw it on the five men who were tied up on the trailer. He quickly jumped off as the trailer and the men engulfed in flames.

Screams of agony echoed in Christian's ears as the men were cooked alive. The blazing heat, the smell, the sizzling and spattering of roasting human flesh, the collapsing wood, all gave Christian his first glimpse of hell. The hell he had created.

CHAPTER 47

Crossroads

Liam lived in a nightmare since the day of the last drop. It was the first time he had faced imminent death, and the harsh reality triggered his gag reflexes, causing him to try and block out the memory.

Christian's balls of steel seemed to have saved them once again that day, but Liam didn't understand why Christian's heroic gesture would even have changed the GNs' minds in the first place. These gangsters seemed to be impressed by men with no fear. Maybe it was a respect thing, but whatever it was, Liam was still alive because of it.

Liam entered the Creek. To his surprise, there were no signs of Davie Boy, who was always there. He heard a noise coming from the shed. He discovered it was unlocked, so he opened the door. Davie Boy stood on the other side, simultaneously reaching out to open it.

"What the fuck, Li. You scared the shit outta me."

"What are you doing?"

"Just organizing the inventory." Davie Boy quickly walked past Liam and turned his head away from him.

"What's on your face?" Liam said.

Davie Boy rubbed his hands across his lips and nose, and sniffed. "Nothing. Probably just dirt."

"That wasn't just dirt."

"Don't tell Chin, man."

"Fuck, Davie Boy. It ain't Chinny you gotta worry about," Liam slammed the shed door, locked it and approached Davie Boy.

"I'm covering the costs," Davie Boy said.

"That's not the point. Anyways, I haven't spoken to Chinny in a while." Liam planted himself on a stump. "I'm done with all this crap, man."

"You know Chin is gonna be here any minute, right?" Davie Boy said.

"For real? I'm gonna leave then." Liam shook his head and walked toward the ROMA tree.

"What was this all supposed to be about? This whole ROMA thing. What was it supposed to stand for?"

Liam stood in the very same spot Christian had stood the night he carved the 'R' into the bark. The letter that completed the words his brother started. The word that complicated their once simple lives.

"I think Chin likes the shit storm this life brings. He ain't right in the head no more. Honestly, I'm scared of what he's capable of."

"Whatcha getting at, Li?"

The conversation was interrupted by Christian entering the Creek "Yeah, Li. What're you getting at?"

"Chin . . . forget it, I'm outta here." Liam turned to walk away.

"Why, Li? I heard everything you were saying. Now say it to my face."

"Talk to you? You've turned into a power hungry asshole. Is that what you want to hear?"

"You got to be fucking kidding me? You're calling me an asshole?" Christian kicked the dirt up as he took a few steps closer to Liam.

"What *is* all this, Chin? Answer me that then. We were supposed to be standing up to the powers that be. Or all them peeps that wrong people. Not become one of them."

"You're an ingrate." Christian kicked a small rock that bounced off the fire pit. "If it wasn't for me you'd be a burnt corpse."

"If it wasn't for you, I wouldn't have been strapped up there in the first place."

Christian charged Liam and went face-to-face with him. Liam saw someone different. This wasn't the kid he had vouched for many a time when everyone else doubted him. Now he was staring down the beast that he took part in creating. Everyone let this guy get his own way. Now it seemed that no one could stop him.

"You think he was bluffin', Li?" Christian said, "Those fucking sand niggers. You think they were bluffing?"

Liam took a step back and shook his head. "Look how you talk man. You would've never said shit like that before."

"When life throws you shit, you become shit, so get over it." Christian said.

"You're a fricken sell out, Chinny. That's the only shit being thrown at me."

"Sellout!?" Christian advance and swung and connected with the side of Liam's face; the force made Liam do a double-step backward. He held the side of his head and looked up at Christian. Davie Boy started forward, but didn't intervene. Liam looked down and walked towards the entrance. "I'm out, don't ever fucking contact me again."

"Good!" Christian yelled in the background, "You fucking pussy!"

CHAPTER 48

A Third Wheel

The fast and furious motions of Christian's tooth brush was making his gums bleed. He glared into his own eyes and tried to bring to the surface the fearlessness that came to him when he faced dark times. Dangerous times.

He had to face the music later. Russ was away for a while, so Christian didn't have a chance to talk to him about the drugs he lost at Deer Park. Russ would surely pop a blood vessel in his head when Christian told him about it. The man was impulsive and might just put a bullet in his skull right then and there.

The phone rang. Christian quickly rinsed his mouth and ran to answer it.

"Hello?"

"Chris, where are you? I been here for a half hour."

"Oh shit! Vic, I'm so sorry, I slept in. I'll be there in fifteen."

Victoria sighed. "Maybe quit staying up so late with your friends that I met like once."

Christian hung up and ran back to the bathroom, kicking himself for forgetting about his meet-up with Victoria. He picked up a pair of jeans from the floor and rushed back to his bedroom as he buttoned and belted them up.

"You gotta go," Christian said.

"Good morning to you too, Chinny-chin-chin." Heather sat on the bed, topless, with her back against the head board reading a magazine.

"I got no time for this. You gotta go."

"You're meeting her, aren't you?"

"Fuck, Heather. Yes I'm meeting her. She's my girlfriend." Christian quickly gathered his keys and wallet and put on his hoodie.

"What am I? Merchandise?"

"Just go, I'm late."

"You're such an asshole. Can I at least use the washroom first?"

"I gotta go. Use the washroom then let yourself out."

***

After a hardy meal, Christian and Victoria walked down a path that was surrounded by a man-made body of water. There wasn't a cloud in sight. It was such a clear day and the water was so still that the slightest breeze caused it to ripple across the whole pond.

Other people walking, bikers and skaters also shared the path with them.

Victoria's arm was intertwined with Christian's and they walked in silence. They took in the soft breeze that was cooled by the water, relieving them from the scorching heat of the day.

"You seemed quiet at breakfast, Vic. Is everything alright?"

"You mean lunch?"

They sat down on a bench in front of a family of ducks swimming near the water's edge.

"I was actually going to say the same thing about you," Victoria said.

"Just lots on my mind. I don't really wanna talk about it."

"You never want to talk about it. Anyways, I have to get to the office soon. Can we talk tonight? Maybe at your place?"

"Vic. I don't wanna talk."

"Well I have to talk."

"Fine," Christian said. "I have some things to do. Can you meet me at mine around ten?"

"Things to do, eh?"

"There's a spare set of keys on the wood sticking out beside my entrance. Just in case I'm a little late. Let yourself in."

CHAPTER 49

Unnecessary Paranoia

His heart was pounding as he stood in the alley beside the G's Spot, waiting to meet with Russ. Christian patted his loaded gun that was stuffed in his jeans at the small of his back. He breathed in deeply. The warmth of the day still lingered in the late evening. He closed his eyes and turned the corner to enter the club. He walked past the doorman, the same one who gave him a hard time the first time he ever came to this spot. They acknowledged each other with a nod.

Russ sat in his office doing what he did best; smoking a cigar and having a drink. He took notice of Christian and gave a silent signal to the man he was having a drink with to leave. The man stood up and walked past Christian, eyeing him up and down. Christian reciprocated.

Christian sat in the seat at Russ' desk, facing him.

"I know why you're here, Chinny."

Christian's head cocked to the side. "You know what?"

"I know what happened. It's OK."

"At Deer Park?"

"Chinny, my man, biz is biz. Shit like this happens. Ain't your fault."

Christian had worked himself up for nothing. How long did Russ know? He was being more reasonable than expected.

Russ grabbed an empty glass from his drawer and poured Christian a drink. "Whatcha think youngin? This kinda shit hasn't happened before? Like I said, it's the nature of the business. You always gotta be cutting losses here and there."

Russ took a sip of his drink. "So you ready for the job tomorrow night?"

"It's good to go."

"Who you got? The ROMA crew?"

"Most of them."

"OK, well this job'll easily make up for what you lost." Russ held out his glass and they clanked them together.

"We gonna retaliate on the GNs anytime soon?" Christian said.

"We? No, not we. I will handle them and their little alliance. You just get this job done."

Christian stood up and put his half-finished glass on the desk. "Okay, well I'm glad that's settled . . ."

"Whoa, whoa, whoa." Russ also stood up, stopping Christian from leaving. "One other thing. Dax went to go check on our merchandise about an hour or two ago. He says it's light."

"Light? Well he accounted for the GN loss, right?"

"Yep. Go handle shit with your crew for the job tomorrow. I'm letting this go for now. But you need to deal with that shit once the job's done, hear me?"

"I don't know how it could be short."

"Forget it for now."

Christian turned to leave and Russ stopped him again. "You talk to our boy A.C. Brooklyn yet?"

"Give me some time. I'll let you know."

"My man." Russ chuckled.

CHAPTER 50

In and Out

Liam sat on his bed against the wall throwing paper clips into a plastic cup on the ground. His heart was heavy, but he needed to do exactly what Christian always preached—stand up.

His brother was the only thing that was important. Forget his father and fuck his mother. As for Christian, he could drop dead for all he cared. Liam was his own leader now.

He had two goals: one was to get him and Sammy out of his father's house one day; and two, get into college. He didn't plan on leaving the house anytime soon, however, because he couldn't. He just didn't have the means to take care of him and his brother on an honest salary. He had some money put away, but it wouldn't be enough in the long run.

Davie Boy's first instinct was that Christian was bad news, and he should have just stuck to his guns when Liam first brought Christian around. But then again, who was he to blame Davie Boy. Liam had made his own choices and it was he who had contaminated their lives with Christian's influence.

Liam walked out of his room and headed towards the washroom. He was met at the door by Sammy coming out.

"You going out tonight?" Sammy said.

"Not tonight."

Liam walked past him into the washroom and locked the door. He stood doing his business and looking into the mirror just above the toilet. He did do the right thing. No more risking his life for the almighty dollar. Those boys were going to plan a robbery that night and he was content knowing that he'd forfeited that unnecessary risk.

Once out of the washroom he walked into the living room where his dad sat on the couch with a beer in his hand and his head down. Sammy must have gone to his room because he was nowhere in sight.

"Dad?"

He didn't answer. He wasn't sleeping though. He was looking down at a piece of paper that was ripped in half on the ground among tipped over beer bottles.

"Dad!"

His father lifted his head. "Go pack."

"What?"

"We got seven days."

"What are you talking about?" Liam said.

Liam's father was completely drunk again and was not making sense. He reached down, picked up the papers and attempted to throw the halves of paper towards Liam, but they dropped down pretty much in the same place.

Liam walked over and picked them up. He looked at his father who now put his legs up on the couch to pass out and forget his life again.

He put the two halves of paper together and established that it was from a mortgage company. The big, black, boldfaced letters that spelled *Foreclosure Notice* was all Liam needed to read.

"We're losing the house?"

"Go pack your things, Sammy."

"I'm not Sammy. What's going on?"

Liam's father, whose eyes were now closed, loosened up and sunk into the couch as the drunkenness took over his body. The hand holding the beer collapsed as his arm fell to the floor beside the couch. The beer tipped over and spilled.

"Dad . . . wake up!"

"I . . . mortgage."

"Dad!"

Liam's father lifted his head ever so slightly. "My Dad . . . your grandpa . . ." He closed his eyes. He was trying to explain something, but he couldn't snap out of his drunken stupor.

"Dad, talk to me! Please!"

He woke for a second. "Son, your grandpa gave me this place."

"Yeah, I know. So?"

"I borrowed off of it . . ."

"How could you lose the fucking house? Fuck! This shit doesn't end." Liam stormed out of the house and slammed the door.

He walked down the street at a fast pace, still tightly grasping onto the foreclosure papers. How could his father do this? Gramps gave him that house and it was free and clear. All along he was drinking and gambling it all away. He drained everything out of a home built with the love and hard work of his grandfather.

Liam heard footsteps rushing up from behind.

"Li, wait up!"

Liam turned and saw Sammy running toward him. "Sammy what are you doing? I need to be alone."

"Why, Li? I'm bored."

"Go home, Sammy. I don't need this right now."

"No I won't go home. Stop ordering me around all the time."

"Do what you want, then. Just don't follow me." Liam walked away, leaving Sammy standing in the middle of the street.

Liam had to find a way to save his house. He knew of only one possible way, so that's where he headed.

CHAPTER 51

Pre Job

Christian hated what had happened with Liam. He sat with the guys around the fire pit bothered by Liam's absence. It wasn't the way he wanted to part ways with him and he regretted hitting Liam. In this type of business, however, there couldn't be regrets. But Liam was his friend before he was a business associate. He didn't deny that his way of thinking had evolved a little, but it had to. The robbery was likely the one big stepping stone toward his end goal.

"The six of us have sat around this fire many times. You guys have become like brothers to me," Christian said.

"Right back at ya, Chin," Braeden said.

"I'm not your leader, I know some of you resent that it looks like I am. But there's nothing to resent."

"Dude, you are," Jess said. "We don't got no beef with that no more. Tell'em, Jord."

"Mainer, past is the past. This score tomorrow's 'cause of you," Jordy said.

"That's good to hear. The six of us . . ." Christian paused, he heard the snapping of twigs coming from the entrance of the Creek. Liam appeared through the bushes.

The guys watched Liam as he slowly walked past them, stationing himself in front of Christian. He leaned over and wrapped one arm around Christian's shoulder and whispered in his ear. "Let's bury this. I want back in. Just for one night."

Christian directed Liam to have a seat.

"The *seven* of us," Christian winked at Liam, "We need to stand strong. We can pocket a shitload of money tomorrow. I said before we got lots in common. I know when I speak for myself, I speak for all of you." Christian stood up and put cigarette in his mouth. "All my life I've been robbed. I've been robbed of acceptance, justice, friends and most importantly, family. But I found a family . . . of a different kind."

Everyone but Christian sat down while he went over how everything would go down the next day. Every last detail was finely combed over. Once they wrapped everything up, Christian finalized it. All that was left was to have a drink and a few last words before parting ways with them to go meet Victoria.

"One last thing—no guns."

"Why not?" Jordy said.

"We ain't there to kill no one, that's why."

"That's the wrong call, mainer," Jordy said.

"I'm calling the shots on this one, Jord. You bring a gun, you won't get paid."

"No guns, just funds," Jess said. "Cheers to ROMA." Jess held up his bottle.

They all held their drinks up.

"How much is our cuts, Chin?" Liam said.

"After Russ' cut, I'd say thirty to forty each."

There was noise at the entrance of the Creek again. All of them turned to spot Sammy.

"You guys are robbin' someone?"

"What the fuck, brah? Why'd you bring your brother?" Braeden yelled at Liam.

"I didn't. Sammy, what are you doing here?"

"You guys gonna hurt someone?" Sammy said.

"Christian, what'd I tell ya?" Braeden said.

Liam shot a glance at Braeden.

"Shut up, Braed. Sammy, what did you hear?" Christian said.

Liam got up and walked toward Sammy. "Let me take him home, Chin. Sammy, come on."

Liam rushed Sammy out of the Creek and all but Christian and Braeden sat down. Christian said he had to go, but Braeden followed and grabbed him by the shoulder. "What the hell, brah? This is exactly what I'm talkin about. He's gonna fuck us now."

"Get your hand off of me and calm down. Focus. We can talk about this later."

"Later? This could change everything."

"It won't change shit, Braed. Liam will smooth things out," Christian said.

"I hope you're right, because I *won't* go to jail."

CHAPTER 52

Betrayed

Planning the job that night had been promising. After so many struggles, it seemed they were finally all on the same page—with the exception of a few hiccups. But overall, Christian was confident they wouldn't have too much of a problem pulling the off the robbery.

Christian was happy to be home to see his girl. He was much later than expected, and Victoria lay peacefully on the couch with the TV still blaring. What an angel. Watching her breathe heavy as she was lost in a dream, he saw his future. He was pretty sure he would marry her and see this sight every day for the rest of his life. He was elated with this idea.

He did fear she would find out about what he actually did for a living, though. She had no clue how much money he actually had stashed away. Also, lately, he really hadn't been thinking straight about a lot of things, and the pressures of life had led him to make some poor decisions, like Heather, for instance. That needed to stop. Based on how he and Heather had parted ways, it was probably over already—which was relieving. He waited for the day that there were no more secrets.

He picked up the remote and turned the TV off. He put his hand on Victoria's head, combed his fingers through her hair, and leaned down and planted a soft kiss on her forehead.

Victoria took a deep breath, lightly moved her body and nuzzled her head deeper into the cushion.

"You're so late," she said.

"Sorry, Vic. Let's go to bed."

"What took so long?"

"My boss wants me to start bartending, so he was showing me the ropes. Got paid for a full shift though, and all I had to do was watch." Lying was becoming a lot easier.

"Bartending? That's good." Victoria sat up on the couch, yawning. "You'll make a lot of tips that way."

"I know."

"Chris, I still want to talk."

"Can we save it for another time?"

Victoria went silent and stared at the ceiling. She suddenly broke into tears.

"What's wrong? Okay, okay let's talk." Christian sat beside her on the couch.

"I'm so scared, Chris. I don't know what to do or how to tell you."

"Are you sick?"

"No."

"Your parents?"

"They're fine . . . Chris, do you love me?"

"Yes, I love you. Why? Is there someone else?"

"Of course not." Victoria pushed Christian's leg. She sobbed and struggled to get out the words. She sniffled and brushed the tears away from her eyes. "This is ridiculous, I'm sorry. Can we go to bed and talk? I have something I need to show you."

"Sure, Vic. You have me worried."

Victoria picked up her purse which was laying at their feet and they both got up from the couch and walked toward the bedroom.

"You go ahead, I just have to use the washroom real quick." Christian said.

Victoria went into the bedroom and Christian went to the washroom. After using the toilet he stood in front of the sink washing his hands. There were so many things in his life that he should have been scared of, but wasn't; he *did* fear talking about stuff. What was Victoria so wound up about? He was soon going to find out, but was apprehensive. He pleaded with God, just in case he existed. *Please don't let her be sick*. She said she wasn't, but what else could it be?

After wetting his face down, he exited the bathroom, turned off the light and walked toward his bedroom door. It was partially opened and he stood there for a second as a base drum pounded in his chest.

He pushed the door open and the room was lit by his bedside lamp. Victoria stood with a piece of paper in her hand and something scrunched up tightly in her fist. The look of shock on her face replaced the former look of dread. Her cheeks were flooded by tears and her nose was running down to her upper lip.

"Vic?"

"What is this?" Her shaking fist opened. A pink thong hung from her fingertips.

Christian squinted his eyes and moved his head forward.

"What the fuck is this!" Victoria shook the piece of paper she was holding in her other hand.

"Vic," Christian eased closer having no idea what was happening. "Talk to me, Victoria, what's going on?"

Victoria threw the underwear and the paper to the ground. "Fuck you!" Victoria picked up her opened purse and pushed past Christian.

Christian recognized the pink thong. "Vic, it's not what it looks like." Christian picked up the piece of paper.

Thanks for the wonderful night, Chinny-Chin-Chin. Here's a little something for your lonely nights without me.
Love Heather

Christian sprinted to the front door, and Victoria turned to him before leaving. "You fucking asshole!"

"Vic, wait! Please don't do this. It's not what it looks like."

"Fuck you!"

She turned to leave, but Christian put his hand on her shoulder. She quickly turned again and punched him straight in the nose.

Christian pulled back, putting his hand over his face and the blood freely began to flow from his nostrils.

Victoria shovelled her hand through her purse ferociously and pulled something out. She threw a small plastic stick at Christian and it landed on the floor.

"This is what I wanted to tell you."

Christian picked it up and it was a pregnancy test. "Oh my god, Vic. What are you saying?"

Victoria was standing with one foot out of the house and one foot in. "What do you think I'm saying, you idiot?"

"These lines mean…"

"Yes, I'm pregnant."

"Well we gotta . . . I mean . . . you need to get an . . ."

"Fuck you. I would never."

"How do I know if it's even mine?" Christian immediately slapped his forehead with his bloody hand.

Victoria's jaw dropped. "I can't believe you just said that." She took a small step into the house. "Unlike you, Christian Solomon—you are the only one I have ever been with. For that matter, ever wanted to be with. I am such a fool. You cheating, fucking asshole." Victoria slammed the door.

CHAPTER 53

The Job

Christian paced back and forth from his living room to his bedroom. He was an emotional wreck from the confrontation with Victoria, but he had to keep it together, for the next few hours anyway.

The clock on the microwave said 5:11pm. Less than six hours till he had to leave.

The job itself he dreaded, but the end result would be worthwhile. He needed to keep repeating in his head: *pedophile, pedophile, pedophile.* That was what this man was and so he deserved what was coming. It wasn't like they were attacking him either. They were just taking his dirty money and leaving. All that stress-relieving justification was what pushed Christian forward.

The phone rang, stopping Christian in his tracks. He was hesitant to answer. What if it was Victoria? He picked up the phone and placed it against his ear, not saying a word.

"Hello? Anyone there?" The voice on the other end said.

"Gran?"

"Hi, Chrissy. How are you?"

"What's up, Gran?"

"Well, I know it's last minute, but I'm coming tomorrow afternoon."

"Oh, Gran. I need more notice than that. I mean—"

"Chrissy, I have a surprise for you."

"Tomorrow isn't good for me. I have to work on the island."

"Can't you go the next day? I really am excited to talk to you about something. Maybe you and Victoria can pick me up at the ferry, and we can all go out for dinner."

Christian rubbed his hand over his head and took the phone away from his ear, mouthing the word, *fuck*.

"What time?"

"Two. Is that ok?"

"Yeah, Gran. I'll be there."

This was definitely not what he needed right now.

Christian sat in the living room for hours staring at the clock. The second it turned eleven o'clock, he got up and went to his bedroom and approached the dresser. He pulled out a pistol despite saying *no guns,* and quickly checked to see if it was fully loaded. He tucked it into the back of his pants, pulling his hoodie over it.

Christian drove to the meeting spot which was about ten blocks from the target's house. Before he met with the guys, he drove by slowly and scoped out the man's property. It was a like a mini-mansion. The numerous windows made Christian a little worried about finding the exact location of the money in a timely manner. None of the lights were on, which was a good sign.

The meeting spot was an empty parking lot, and when Christian arrived, the other six of them were standing around Braeden's truck.

"You guys ready?" Christian said.

"Chin. Dude ain't outta town," Jordy said.

"He's in town? When did you find this out?"

"Right before I got here. But Russ said he's still out for the evening, though."

"That changes everything. We have to make this even quicker," Christian said.

Christian went over the plan with all of them one last time and confirmed that they all knew their role.

Liam, Jess, Kirt and Davie Boy got into Christian's car and Braeden drove Jordy in his truck. Christian parked in the alley behind the house and Braeden parked a couple blocks away as instructed.

"That right there is our entrance." Christian pointed to a window on the ground level of the house.

"What happens if someone hears the break?" Liam said.

"You go in. I'll wait five minutes. Something happens, just run and I'll pick you up."

They waited till they saw Braeden and Jordy run past the alley to the front of the house and Liam exited the vehicle. He put on a ski mask that only showed his eyes and mouth and a pair of gloves, as did the rest of them.

Liam crept toward the window with a tire iron and hesitated. He looked back at Christian who gestured with his hand for him to keep going.

Liam tapped the window only hard enough to crack it. He hit it once more and the shattering glass was loud but brief. Christian scanned the area and hoped the boys in front were doing the same.

Liam place the tire iron on the ground, entered the house, and after waiting five minutes, Christian instructed the others to make their way to the front.

Christian entered the house through the shattered window, met up with Liam, and they headed up the stairs where they could hear the whispers of the other guys. He opened the door and let Jess, Kirt and Davie Boy in to guard the ground level entrance; Jordy and Braeden guarded the outside.

Christian and the others stood at the base of the staircase, and as Christian pulled a map from the pocket of his hoodie, he noticed that Jess was holding a crowbar.

"Jess, where the hell did you get that?" Christian said.

"It was on the side of the house."

"There's seven of us. Even if he came back, what's he gonna do?" Christian said.

"Better safe than sorry, Chin."

Christian shook his head and shrugged it off. He and Liam slowly walked up the spiral staircase with flashlights and an empty bag that Christian was holding. They took care by pointing their torches mainly toward the ground so that there weren't flashes of light out of the window.

The house was huge. There were eight bedrooms just on the one floor. Whatever this guy did, he must have been good at it. They both crouched down and shined the flashlight on the map. Christian counted the doors down the hallway to the seventh and pointed. "It's that one."

They entered the room. It looked like it was a guest bedroom. Right beside the double bed there was a small dresser that had a vent that was partially hidden, but visible on the side.

"That has to be it right there," Christian said.

Christian and Liam pulled the dresser away from the wall and Liam knelt down beside the vent. He tried pulling it off with just his hands, but it wouldn't budge. He retrieved a hunting knife from his pocket and started prying it off at the corner. There was a small crack from the vent coming apart from the wall, and Liam and Christian both ripped the rest of it away. The open hole in the wall was not a real vent at all. And it went back a lot further than Christian anticipated.

They flashed their lights in the opening, and there it was a large sum of cash wrapped in plastic. Christian couldn't help but smile. A part of him thought this might not have been the real deal. But it looked like it was well worth it.

Christian threw the empty bag on the ground. Liam sliced open the plastic and started shovelling the money into the bag.

"Chin, there has to be about three hundred thousand in here." Liam said.

Christian heard a car and walked over to the window. He put his back against the wall and turned his head to peak through the glass.

Liam finished gathering up the cash and flashed his light deeper into the vent. "Yo Chin, there's a big bag here."

"Fuck!" Christian yelled, "I think he's back."

"Shit! What do we do?" Liam said.

"Grab the other bag. Let's go."

Christian and Liam ran toward the stairs but stopped for a second when they heard a commotion outside. They continued down the stairs with the two large bags and found Jess, Kirt and Davie Boy just standing around at the base.

"What the hell are you guys standing here for? Go out and help them!" Christian said.

Christian looked out the window by the front door and saw an unknown man who was on top of Braeden, punching him relentlessly. Jordy was lying on his back on the sidewalk and wasn't moving. This was going to be a huge problem, considering this one man could take out Jordy *and* Braeden by himself.

Christian, Liam and Davie rushed to the back door. Jess, who was still holding the crowbar, ran out the front along with Kirt.

Christian, Liam and Davie Boy ran to Christian's car. Christian picked the tire iron up along the way and threw Liam the keys as Davie Boy jumped into the passenger seat. Christian tossed the bags and the tire iron in the trunk of the car. "You guys go ahead and bring the cash to my house."

Christian ran to the side of the house and pulled out his gun. He peered around the corner, dreading what he was going to see.

Jordy was sitting up and Braeden was lying on his back, rubbing his head with both hands. Kirt stood beside Jess, whose eyes were blank, and was slowly backing away.

As Christian got closer, he saw the man they had robbed lying on the ground motionless. Christian's eyes widened as he looked up at Jess who was staring off into space. The man's temple was impaled with the hook end of the crowbar. Christian put his gun back in his pants and rushed over to him.

He looked back at Jess. "What did you do?"

"I didn't mean to. I didn't know that side of the bar was pointing forward. Shit…I…I didn't mean to."

Christian frantically scanned the area as he thought about what to do. "Okay. We gotta keep it together and do something with this guy. Let's at least get him inside. Jess, remove that damn crowbar."

Jess, with his eyes wide, shook his head; he would have no part of it.

Christian closed his eyes and took a deep breath. He stood above the man and looked down at him. He couldn't have been more than thirty-years-old and sure didn't look like he would be capable of taking out Jordy and Braeden. He grabbed the end of the crowbar and placed his foot on his forehead; he jerked the crowbar out of his head. The boys cringed at the wet crunching sound and the blood that began to profusely flow onto the lawn.

They all picked him up, with the exception of Jess, and rushed him toward his house where they quickly opened the front door and dropped him in the entrance.

They didn't look back when they sprinted off the property. When they got to Braeden's truck, Christian hopped in the front seat and the rest jumped into the truck bed.

Braeden took side roads and drove carefully as not to alert any law enforcement. Christian glanced back at the guys in the back of the truck and saw Jess hugging his knees against his chest.

"Li and Davie Boy go back to the Creek?" Braeden said.

"Nope. My house. Drop me there. We'll catch up with you guys at the Creek after."

"Shit's fucked. What are we gonna do?"

"No clue, Braed."

"Was there a score?"

"Yep. Not sure how much yet."

Braeden pulled over in front of Christian's house. Christian got out and walked to the back of the truck where Jess, Kirt and Jordy sat. They all jumped out of the back in front of Christian and started entering the truck. Christian stopped Jess and placed both his hands on his shoulders. "Look, Jess. That man molested little girls. You did the world a favor."

Jess nodded head and got in the front seat, and Braeden sped away.

Standing at his front door, Christian was not looking forward to rehashing the details of the night again with Liam and Davie Boy. Although the man was supposedly a pedophile, one troubling thing about the situation was that he hadn't confirmed it as he had planned to after the conversation with Russ. Maybe it was better that he never really knew one way or the other. He didn't even know the guy's name. He's gone and he probably deserved it.

When Christian entered the house, he immediately saw Davie Boy sitting on the couch.

"Chinny. How's them boys?"

"Where's Liam?"

"I think he's takin' a shit," Davie Boy said. "Listen, that there payday isn't what we expected."

"Short?"

"Go see for yourself." Davie Boy was grinning.

Christian stopped abruptly when he entered his room.

Liam sat on the edge of the bed and his face painted a picture of Christian's emotion.

"I sure didn't expect this, Chin. The plastic is just over two hundred. But the other bag, I can't count it all. Looks like a few mil."

"Million?"

"I can't even breathe," Liam said.

Christian sat next to Liam on the bed. The money that now covered his mattress like a quilt was diluting the thoughts of what happened earlier that night. A murdered man and a killer score.

"Li, shit went down after you left."

"Everyone ok?"

"Let's go to the living room."

Christian followed Liam out of the bedroom but paused to look at the score again. He exhaled heavily at the surreal sight.

Liam sat on the couch with Davie Boy while Christian stood in front of them. He explained the incident while both Liam and Davie Boy silently took it in. Christian tried to instill in them who the man was and that their actions were justified. Christian felt the man had deserved to die, and now Christian was showing pride that it was at the hands of ROMA.

The three sat in silence for a while. Liam and Davie Boy were sharing a joint while Christian sat on a single chair completely sober, only smoking cigarettes.

"Liam, how much does your pops owe on your granddaddy's house?" Christian said.

"'Bout eleven grand in missed payments," he said, before exhaling a big, blue cloud of marijuana smoke. "They'll let him keep it if he pays that. So my cut will be more than enough."

"Then what?" Christian said, "He'll get behind again with no job. How much is the full amount?"

"I think about two hundred and seventy-five or so."

"Let's buy it."

Christian's wheels were always in motion. He knew how much pride Liam had in his granddad's house. The one man Liam adored was the one who put that roof over their heads, and Liam saw the house as the love his grandfather had left behind.

"I dunno, Chin. How do I pull that off?"

"Well let's put about three hundred grand aside for now. Then we'll talk about this later," Christian said.

Davie Boy, who was still sucking back on a joint said, "I'm not all that knowledgeable about this here shit. But don't we need to talk to Russ before we start portioning out shares?"

"We look out for our own before we submit to the code of this biz. He doesn't know how much we got, so he won't know the difference," Christian said.

"Ok then, what about the crew?" Davie Boy said.

"They don't gotta know everything. We'll just say a few mil. They won't know the difference either if we don't mention the extra few hundred grand. Besides, Li needs this."

"Aright. I hear ya. Stays in these walls, then," Davie Boy said.

CHAPTER 54

Blood Money

When Christian, Liam and Davie Boy arrived at the Creek, everyone but Jess were sitting around the fire pit in somber silence. Jess sat at the tree where Sammy normally sat. He was spaced out and probably reflecting on what he'd done. Christian had never taken a life, so he didn't know how it could impact a person.

It looked like all the guys had some reflecting to do. The shock of the incident was thickening the air to the point of making it hard to breath.

"How's he holding up?" Christian pointed at Jess as he looked down at Jordy and Kirt.

"Dunno." Jordy said.

"What are we gonna do, brah? If anything's found there, we're done," Braeden said.

"Nothing will be found. We were careful."

"Nothing?" Jordy said, "Are you forgetting we left the biggest piece of evidence there? You know . . . the body."

"Look, we had no time to do anything." Christian took a seat on a log and lit a cigarette. He stared back at Jess who was still sitting motionless. "The cops are probably taping off the place as we speak."

Jess broke his silence. "How much?"

Everyone turned to Christian as he flicked his cigarette ashes and glared at the fire. Jess got up from the ground and joined the rest of them around the fire pit. "How much, Chinny?"

"We didn't count it all. Looks like a few mil."

Everyone's jaws dropped.

Christian stood up and threw his cigarette butt into the fire. "Here's what we're going to do. We give Russ forty percent of, let's say . . . three hundred thousand. That's more than what he expected. Then we can sit down and talk about how we split the rest. Sound good?"

"Definitely down with that, brah."

It wasn't surprising that they had no objections to Christian's proposition. It was more money than any of them had ever dreamed of seeing. It wasn't just a score. It was a life changing pay day. All but one of them were celebrating their new riches.

Jordy was unusually quiet, which was definitely out of his character. He stood up and dusted off his pants. "Sorry to burst your bubble boys. But that shit ain't happenin'."

"What's not?" Christian said.

"That money ain't ours. It's my brother's. He gets forty points on the full amount."

"Not a chance." Christian said.

Jordy walked up to Christian and stood face-to-face with him. "You may have led us to the score. But you're a small player in my brother's game."

"You think so, eh?" Christian eased a few inches closer.

"He calls the shots, mainer."

"Let's vote," Christian said as he turned back to the crew.

"Fuck your vote," Jordy said.

"All in favor for giving Russ points on the full purse, raise your hands."

No one raised his hand. Jordy just walked away and sat back down on a log. He didn't raise his hand and refused to acknowledge the vote altogether.

"All in favor of forty points on three hundred?"

The vote was unanimous with the exception of Jordy.

"Majority speaks, Jord. We stand united. You're the odd man out."

Jordy stood up again and eyed Christian up and down. "I've been around street life since I could remember. Ya know how this works, mainer? You fuck my brother, then you are asking for a war. The top gangsters in this city don't go head-to-head with him. You ain't nothin' but his pawn."

"Your brother never touched a bankroll this big on just one job. He ain't shit. And he brings you down."

"Don't talk about my brother like that." Jordy came closer with his fists clenched.

"When are you going to realize he pisses on your existence daily?" Christian chose not to fuel the fire. Instead he took a passive stance, even though Jordy's body language was threatening.

"Fuck you, mainer."

Christian took a small step back and remained calm. "Listen to me, Jord. We don't need your brother. He'll get a cut as I said. Then let it lie. He don't gotta know."

Jordy took a deep breath and paused. Christian continued. "We took the risks. We put in the work. We earned this. You're worth more than what your brother thinks, Jord."

"Whatcha mean?"

"We'd have a hard time being ROMA without you? You're the backbone man." Christian had learned a lot about manipulation—from none other than Jordy's brother Russ.

"You think?"

Christian nodded and lit another cigarette. "So what do you say?" Instead of fueling the fight, Christian fueled Jordy's ego.

"You're asking me to screw my own brother, mainer. Would you screw your boy Liam like that?"

Christian looked back at Liam who was standing with the rest of the guys who were soaking in the dialogue, then rested his eyes on Jordy again. "Nope, I wouldn't. Liam doesn't beat me down like your brother does you."

"I need to think about it," Jordy said.

"Fine. Till there's an understanding here, no one gets anything." Christian turned to walk away and headed to the exit of the Creek.

"Whoa, Chinny," Kirt said. "We get paid for what we rightfully earned."

Christian looked at the group and shrugged his shoulders. "You want your money. Convince our boy over there to make up his mind." Christian proceeded to leave and Liam followed.

"Li, wait up!" Everyone's eyes darted in the direction of the tree house and saw Sammy climbing down the ladder.

"The fuck. This kid's like a ninja." Jess said.

"What the hell are you doing here, Sammy?" Liam said.

"Li, I fell asleep up there."

"How much you hear, brah?" Braeden said.

"Nothin'. I was sleeping."

Christian glanced over at Braeden who was looking directly back at Christian. He nodded and used his eyes to direct Braeden to sit back down. Braeden complied.

"C'mon then, Sammy." Liam said. "Let's go home."

CHAPTER 55

Villainous Hero

It was a sleepless night. Christian was lying in bed trying to process the millions of thoughts racing through his mind. What if he was wrong about the scene at the house they had robbed and the cops did knock at his door? It would be the end for him and the boys. He spoke to ROMA with such conviction and certainty, when in reality he wasn't convinced himself. What if there were mistakes made and it all pointed right back at them? Of course Jordy Baxter had to be the one to make this difficult situation even more challenging.

The phone on his bedside table rang.

"Hello?"

"Chinny. Heard you won the game."

"Yep." Christian immediately knew it was Russ.

"How many points?"

"Three Hundred."

"My man . . . when are we gonna meet so you can share the story?"

"I gotta leave for a week. I'll call you then."

"Say what? You ain't goin' without—"

"Talk then."

Christian hung up on Russ and quickly dialed Liam. If he was going to avoid Russ for a while he had to get out of the city. Christian asked Liam to pick up his car from the docks. He didn't explain much because time was now a factor. He was going to the island and he instructed Liam not to tell anyone where he was.

Christian lugged three bags that were full of cash out the front door and threw them in the trunk of his car. He walked around the entrance of the driveway and scanned the street. There was no one in sight. He got in his car and quickly sped off.

***

When he arrived at the island, he saw Edwin's truck parked not too far away. He lifted his three bags over onto the dock. One was a large backpack and the other two were suitcases that he pulled on wheels. The incline on the way to the truck was killing him. The backpack alone felt like it weighed about fifty pounds.

"Well Mister MIA, you ready to get some work done tomorrow?" Edwin grabbed one of the bags and lugged it over onto the truck bed. "What do you have packed? You planning on staying here permanently?"

Christian threw the other two over and wiped the sweat from his brow. "Not permanent, but maybe a week or two."

"Well, glad to see the luggage I left behind came in handy. I got some fresh prawns and steaks ready to grill. You'll need your energy tomorrow." Edwin laughed.

***

The two sat down and had a feast with a couple of beers to wash it down. A little too hoppy for Christian's liking, but that didn't deter him from drinking it.

Christian was pretty nervous about having those three bags of cash sitting up in the guest room. Thankfully Edwin wasn't really the snoopy kind.

"You want another beer?" Edwin got up from his seat carrying the empties and walked through the terrace doors. He returned with two beers and sat back down at the table. "What's on your mind, son?"

"Nothing."

"I know there's something. What's up?"

Christian thought a lot about what he wanted to say and how to say it. He thought about this moment for weeks. It was risky to accuse someone so close to him of being something they weren't. Edwin had been good to him. Probably better than anyone had ever been in his entire life. But he couldn't let it go. If he confirmed all that he had heard and now believed about Edwin, that would mean the man he adored as a role model had lied to him.

"Edwin. I got a question for ya?"

"Shoot kid."

"Have you ever heard of a man named A.C. Brooklyn?"

Edwin sat back in his chair. He took a sip of beer and glared at Christian without batting an eye. "Never heard of him. Why?"

"You know. When I was first told this—"

"Told what?"

Christian became hot and was nibbling at the side of his index finger. "When this first came to my attention, I spent days completely denying it. But really, the second I saw the picture of you, that's when I actually knew it was true. It's not that I didn't want to believe it, I just couldn't bring myself to admitting I believed it."

"What picture?"

"Are you A.C. Brooklyn?"

"Who fed you this? Russ Baxter?"

With that one question, it was confirmed. Christian sat back in his chair, grabbed his beer and relaxed. He smirked before he put the bottle to his lips. "So you know who Russ Baxter is, then?"

"Gonna need more than a beer for this conversation." Edwin went back into the house and returned with two glasses of scotch. He placed one in front of Christian and resumed his position in his seat. "I could prolong this and come up with some story to make it go away, but I'm not going to do that, son. I don't have the energy. You want to play the truth game? Well it's a two-way street. I'm going to need some truth from you too."

"So you *are* A.C.B."

"You gonna play?" Edwin put his drink down and leaned forward.

"I have nothing to hide."

"I'll tell you my story. But I'm kinda fond of you, kid. You're not gonna get scared away, are ya?"

"Nope. You said you know what I do and *you're* still here."

"Alright, I'll spill it."

Christian got more comfortable and put his feet up on another chair. Edwin loved to tell stories, and they were usually long—but definitely not boring.

"I was born Anthony Carter Brooklyn."

Christian gave a knowing smirk again.

Edwin continued. "What you were told about me was probably partly true and partly lies. Years of rumours usually get jumbled up, if you know what I'm saying." Edwin stood up with his drink and leaned up against the railings of his porch.

"What's true is that I started leading the same life you are leading now. I became successful at it and made a significant amount of money. So yes, I lived a questionable life, but I left that behind a long time ago. As an old man, I'm trying to right all my wrongs and do good for my community. This is why I lay low. I changed my name years back. Now, I stand here today as I am. Edwin Steed. I'll leave this world knowing I started wrong, but died doing right. And that's it."

"That's it?" Christian removed his legs from the chair and flopped them down on the ground. "That's your truth?"

"What do you want me to say, son? That I made wrong choices? Yes. Did I hurt people? Yes—"

"Did you kill anyone?"

"I can't do anything about the past now. I can't bring people back. I can only outweigh my rights to my wrongs with the last years I have left on this earth."

Christian squinted and looked up in the air. His eyes widened with revelation. "You were the one behind the pawnshop owner getting shot, weren't you?"

Edwin looked at Christian and then looked away. He didn't even acknowledge the question.

"My sources say you're still involved in all of this," Christian said.

"Forget your sources. My turn to ask some questions."

"Go ahead."

"Did I ever tell you I had a brother?"

"No."

"Well here's another piece of my past. Listen carefully now, kid." Edwin sat back down on the edge of his seat, leaning forward. His face grew more intense as he prepared to divulge another secret.

"I was an only child all my life. When I was twenty, my folks gave birth to my brother. His name was Donovan Brooklyn."

"How old are you again?" Christian said.

"I'm fifty-six. When Donny got older, he wanted to be just like me. I kept him away from anything to do with the crap I was in. He insisted though. I don't think it was even about the money, just the lifestyle. He was way too smart for that life, though."

"Just wondering, how is this a question for me?" Christian was a little weary of Edwin's demeanor.

"Be quiet and listen, kid. I have a large amount of money and you know that. I can't use banks or set up trust funds with dirty cash. I have to store it in multiple low-profile locations. One place I stored money was at Donny's house. We had this agreement for years as I do with multiple other individuals and businesses. They all get a cut, as did Donny." Edwin sucked back air and turned his head. He tried to pass it off as a hiccup, but it was apparent that he was holding something back. He composed himself and continued. "A month ago, Donny said to me that he didn't want to do it anymore. He was one step away from becoming a lawyer. Damn, I was proud of him. The kid was a fighter too, literally. He held a black belt in Brazilian jiu-jitsu and was a boxer. "

"You keep talking about him in the past tense. Did something happen to your brother?"

"For a kid, you're observant. Years of who I was and my unspeakable acts made me stone cold. I can sit here and have dinner with some beers with no sort of emotion. Even with a damn smile on my face. You learn to bury any pain and just play the game. So ask me that question again, Christian."

Christian's head darted back. He was completely confused. "Did something happen?"

"There's been many that have tried to get to me and take my crown for years. This is the closest they've come and the closest they will ever get. Now you need to tell me what you know."

Take my crown. Russ used those exact words when he spoke about getting to A.C. Brooklyn. "What are you talking about, Edwin?"

"It's your boy Russ, isn't it? Or that god damn GN Solider leader, Jag. They're the top dogs right? They want me to come out of hiding so they can make a name for themselves."

"Edwin. What's going on?"

"You need to tell me if you know anything about a robbery last night."

"No . . . what robbery?"

"My baby . . . my little brother." Edwin's eyes became watery.

This was the first time Christian had ever seen Edwin get emotional. He always had it together.

"My brother, like I said, stored some of my money. He got robbed and murdered last night."

Christian's heart sank like a stone. He could feel his body shake, and the more he tried to appear calm, the more he trembled. He couldn't tell if Edwin noticed or not, but it felt like it was causing the whole deck to rumble. He grabbed his drink and quickly sipped it. He held on to it tightly, which helped him keep his hands steady. He was about to speak, but Edwin cut him off.

"Tell me. Do you know if your friend Russ Baxter is behind it?"

"Edwin. I'm sorry. I know nothing. I can try to find out for you, though. Russ doesn't say much to me."

"Let me tell you something, Christian. I may be a fifty-six-year-old man, but I'm not dead. I don't care who they are. They want to get my attention and bring me out of hiding? They got it. The day I find out for sure who is behind this—that will be the day A.C. Brooklyn returns with a vengeance."

For the first time, Christian saw the gangster behind the generous, charitable man he looked up to. He couldn't believe Edwin was the man Russ had spoken of who killed his cousin. Now he was even more fearful because of the bags in his room. It wasn't a snoop that he needed to worry about; it was a villainous wolf who was on a war path to avenge his brother's death. The brother Christian had a hand in killing. A pedophile? Russ *did* lie to him after all. Russ lied to Christian to get A.C. out into the open so he could take his shot at him. Russ obviously knew that Christian wasn't going to deliver A.C. to him. And the unplanned killing of A.C's brother, Donovan, would put Russ over the edge with pleasure. Icing on the cake.

The phone rang, breaking the tension. Edwin's icy stare softened, and he got up to answer it.

"It's for you, kid."

The only people that had Edwin's number were Liam and Victoria. Assuming it was Liam, he took the phone and put it against his ear.

"Yeah, what?"

"Did you forget about your gran, Christian?"

"Vic? Shit! She was supposed to be there. I totally forgot."

"Well she called me. She's at my house right now."

"Dammit, I'm at Edwin's."

"I know, I just called you there. I picked her up 'cause I love your gran. I didn't do it for you."

"You know where my extra key is by my front door. Can you take her there?"

"Yep. I'll take her now."

"Thanks so much, Vic. So, how are you doing?"

"One day, you'll wake up Christian, and realize you're not the only one that exists in this world. You selfish asshole."

Victoria slammed the phone down as Christian stood just a few feet from Edwin, the dial tone buzzing in his ear. "OK, nice talking to you. Love you."

Christian turned to Edwin who just smirked and shook his head. "Need a ride?"

"My gran, I forgot—"

"Don't worry about it, kid."

It was premature and risky, but Christian had to go back. Once he dealt with his gran, he would just have to come straight back to the island. Hopefully he could successfully avoid Russ Baxter.

***

Edwin pulled up to the dock and Christian exited the vehicle. Edwin didn't help Christian with the bags at all. He instead watched Christian struggle down the slope to the boat.

"Hey, Chinny," Edwin called out. Christian turned around. "It's pretty dark. Make sure you navigate those lights properly."

"Yeah, I know."

Edwin drove off and Christian threw the bags into the boat. As he put one leg in, he paused. He looked at the rear lights of Edwin's truck disappear into the distance. He realized that Edwin called him by the name that only a select few knew him as. Did Edwin dig deeper than he let on?

CHAPTER 56

Oblivious

It was better that Christian had some warning about Edwin before the truth came out. The only thing that didn't sit easy with him was the other likely secrets behind the man he still looked up to as a father. Maybe there were secrets that were better left unspoken.

Christian didn't consider himself a gangster or a drug dealer like Edwin had once been. He still believed it was a temporary money grab to get ahead. To Christian these were all logical choices. Hell, Edwin had been a kingpin and now did charity work. Christian didn't want to be a kingpin, or anything like that. The recent score in his mind very well could have been his last job.

It wasn't just about getting out, though. He also needed to try his best to forget the horrific acts that he had witnessed. Dwelling on them would bring him to a dark place. It wasn't like these were innocent people, though. The closest thing to innocence was Edwin's brother, which was a huge problem. A scary problem. The guy had been stashing bloody money, though, which didn't make him all that innocent. Having any part of this game, a person needed to accept the risk involved, and Edwin's little brother paid with his life.

A more immediate problem Christian had to worry about was sitting right across the dinner table from him. His gran wasn't saying a word. They ate in silence, which was out of the norm. She hadn't even mentioned the good news she had; she had hardly said hello.

"Gran, I'm really sorry."

His gran ignored him and continued eating the meat loaf she had prepared.

"I didn't mean to forget. There is just so much going on with my job."

Gran placed her fork on her plate, took a sip of water and looked at him. "It wasn't even twenty-four hours, Chrissy. I don't understand how my coming could have slipped your mind."

"Stress, Gran. I'm just stressed."

"You know what, lovey? I'm not even upset about you thoughtlessly leaving me stranded anymore. I'm more upset about Victoria."

"Why? What'd she tell you?"

"That is a horrible thing you did to that girl. When she used to visit me in Stoneminster, all she spoke about was you. She loved you since she was a little girl. Do you know how hard that is to find?"

"What'd she tell you?"

"She told me you were being unfaithful. How could you do that to her?"

"She has no right to tell anyone about our business. Does everyone on this planet forget I'm nineteen? I'm not even out of my teens . . . maybe I'm not ready for commitment." Christian pushed his chair back from the table and slammed his fork onto the plate. "People forget I'm pretty much still a kid. I was forced to be a man at eight fricken years old."

"Listen to your gran now. I'm going to say this only out of love. What you just said is bullshit."

Christian was taken back. He had never heard a cuss word come from his sweet gran's mouth.

"Chrissy, I offered for you to come home with me to Stoneminster. You chose to make adult decisions. You quit school, got a job and this place. You chose to be an adult. So don't start complaining about how you're *just a teenager* when it's convenient."

"I can't listen to this."

"Doesn't work that way, lovey. You need to quit blaming other people for your poorly made decisions and victimizing yourself with every unpleasant situation that results."

Christian stood up from his seat and looked down at his gran. "Forget this. I can't talk to you."

"Sometimes it *is* your fault." Gran said.

Christian walked toward his bedroom and heard his gran say softly under her breath, "Just run away again."

He slammed the door and fell onto his bed. Who the hell was she to say that crap? She knew nothing about what he had to go through with his mother; her daughter. All of this was his mother's fault, not his.

The phone rang and Christian grabbed it, fumbling it in his hand. He wanted to get it before his gran picked it up and pried even further into his life.

"Hello?"

"It's Jordy."

"And?"

"The proposal you made the other night. I'm on board. Three hundred at forty points."

There was a knock at the door and Christian put his hand over the mouth piece. "Gran, give me a second."

"Good to hear. Set it up with your bro."

"It's already set up."

There was another knock at his bedroom door.

"I'll call you back later to get the details."

Christian hung up and plopped his head back onto the pillow. There was a third knock at the door, but this time his gran barged in.

"You may be done talking. But I'm not."

"Don't need this right now, Gran."

"Christian. Are you dealing drugs?"

"What? No. Look, Gran, you are the last person I wanna lose it with. I think it's best you go watch your shows or something."

His gran shook her head and wagged her finger at him. "Everyone walks on eggshells around you because you are a ticking time bomb. It's your greatest defense mechanism, Chrissy. Well not anymore."

"Please, just—"

"You are hateful, you're selfish, and you have lied to and manipulated everyone in your life—even me."

"You don't know fucking shit!"

"Now you are going to start with the swearing."

Dark spots in the shape of stars flashed before his eyes and a blind rage was beginning to settle in. "Get outta my room."

His gran just looked at him blankly and raised her eyebrows.

Christian got up and pushed his bedside lamp against the wall, causing it to topple over. "Get outta my room!"

Gran didn't change her soft expression. Her eyes were glazed and watery, yet she didn't budge.

"Do you think that intimidates me, lovey? Your childish, little tantrum? Are you going to strike your gran now?"

Christian was at a loss. His blood was boiling, but at the same time, disbelief was neutralizing his anger.

"You need to know the truth about your mother. You always talk about being left in the dark, Chrissy. So it's time you know."

"Truth about what? The cancer she had that no one thought I should know about?"

"Would you have cared, Christian?"

Christian just stared blankly at her.

"Anyways, you wanted the truth, now you're getting it. The only condition is that you sit down and remain calm."

Christian took a seat on the edge of his bed, rubbing his face. He tried his best to snap out of the over-the-edge anger that was consuming his body. It was now a battle against himself. *Just snap out of it! This is your gran for Christ sakes.*

"You don't think I know what you were carrying in your pants when you went to your room last night, Chrissy? God knows why you needed so many bags. Your gran is old, but not stupid."

"I pack a lot for the island, Gran."

She pulled out a folded picture from her pocket and opened it. "How do you know this man?"

"Where did you get that?"

"It was on your counter."

It was the picture of Edwin and Russ' cousin. Christian closed his eyes and tried his best to think of a way to explain this away. The night he had asked his gran about A.C. Brooklyn, he'd suspected there was a story based on her dismissive reaction.

"You need to promise me, Chrissy, when I tell you what I am going to tell you, you won't do something irrational or drastic."

"Fine."

"The other night when you asked me about Anthony Brooklyn, my greatest fear came to fruition. I didn't know if you found out the truth for yourself, or you were involved in something very dangerous. Or both. Are you in trouble?"

"No Gran, just go on."

"Your mother was a good girl, Chrissy. All her childhood and teenaged years, my little girl had so much promise. She was just so bright. She even finished high school early and all she ever wanted to do was help people. So she chose to go to college to pursue nursing. She could have been a doctor, you know. But for some reason she just wanted to be nurse since she was a little girl. She was a born nurturer."

"Coulda fooled me."

"Close your mouth and open your ears—just let me speak."

Christian laid back, propping himself up on his elbows.

"Besides doctors, there weren't many that knew the truth. Your mother confided in me a little bit, but not much. I know some, but not all of the details of what happened to her back then. But she spent many days in the hospital, and you don't know how it feels to learn of some of the horrific acts that your own daughter, who I was supposed to protect, experienced."

"Hospital?"

"Speeding up her education, in hindsight, was probably a big mistake . . ."

CHAPTER 57

Innocent Di

Twenty Years Earlier

It wasn't too long ago that between her studies and work she didn't have any time for a social life. Diana envied her friends who were graduating school at the time. Like any normal teenagers, the class of '76 partied hard with no cares in the world. She never got to experience the excitement of walking down the aisle with her friends at the ceremony, Diana Solomon was in a grad class of her own.

As it turned out, being dedicated to success did more harm than good. The night her old high school classmates were graduating, Debbie, who was her best friend for years, tried to convince Diana to come out for just the one night. If anyone deserved it, it was Diana. But she declined. Instead, she chose to engross herself in her text books.

Unfortunately, so many rejected offers to get together took their toll, and her friends eventually gave up and drifted away.

But everything changed the day she met Drew Saunders. He chatted her up on the Subway. She was impressed by his direct and engaging way of speaking. But what really made her heart flutter was his rugged, dark good looks, set off by bright blue eyes that could make any girl fall at his feet.

She should have known he was bad news when her grades started to slip. Then there was her job. There was a time she never missed a day of work, but after being with Drew, she ended up being fired for calling in sick too much.

It got to the point she dreaded seeing or even speaking to her mom. She became an unemployed, college drop out. All her time was spent drinking and partying with a questionable group of friends.

After a few months of her and Drew being together, she could tell the relationship wouldn't last.

Not only was Drew always secretive about what he did and where he went at odd hours of the night, she could tell he was growing frustrated with her. A part of her didn't care all that much, seeing how she anticipated ending things.

She sat at her dresser brushing her silky, golden hair, while Drew laid in her bed shirtless, watching her. She touched up her modest makeup and made eye contact through the reflection in the mirror.

"What? I can tell you have something to say."

"It's been months. I was thinking we should take things a little further."

Diana, who was now applying her lipstick, placed it down on her dresser and turned around. "You know how I feel about that, Drew."

"Christ, Di. There is only so much dry humping a guy can take."

"I'm sorry. That's all I can offer."

"Don't you think it would be special if I were the one to, you know . . ."

"Take my virginity? Maybe. Just not now. I'm not ready for that."

"You're so frustrating." Drew got up and put on his shirt. "Excuse me while I go jerk off in the washroom again."

"You're sick. Where are we going tonight?"

"The Showroom."

"Again? Can't we go somewhere else? That place is starting to bore me."

"Deal with it. We're going."

***

The crowded club was made more oppressive by the fact that Drew was snorting line after line of cocaine as he pounded back shot after shot of bourbon. Diana hated when he would get to this point of intoxication because this was where he would change into a different person. Despite her pessimistic feelings towards the future of their relationship, he usually was a pretty nice guy, but not when he was high and drunk.

Knowing she would end up taking care of him, she was forced to limit herself to only a of couple drinks. Even with his drunken verbal abuse, she tolerated it and managed to get him into his bed safely. She would never bring up his behaviour to him anymore because he would never remember. Besides, his apologies were not genuine because he never knew what he was actually apologizing for.

Dancing Queen began to play. "I love this song," Diana said.

Drew looked up from snorting another line, slurring. "Let's dance then."

"Like you're in any condition to dance."

Drew grabbed Diana by the arm and pulled her up.

"Drew, no. It's okay."

He forcefully led her on the dance floor. He was stumbling and banging into people, some of which nudged him away.

"Drew, you're embarrassing me."

"I am? Fine, let's find somewhere more private."

He pushed Diana against a wall close to one of the speakers and held her there. "Oh come on, baby. You know you like it." He continued forcing himself on her to the point of overpowering her. Diana struggled to push him away, but to no avail.

The last straw for her was when one of his hands made its way up her skirt. She got a hand free and hit him across the face with all her might. Her nails scraped his skin.

Drew stepped back, his eyes bulging with surprise. He ran a hand down the side of his face and observed a speck of blood on his fingertip.

"You fucking bitch." He grabbed her by her blouse and pulled his fist back. As he came forward with his arm, someone grabbed him from behind. The man pulled him back and threw him to the floor. Drew was down on one knee and the man grabbed him by the scruff of the neck, pulling him back up. Drew got a taste of the man's fist straight to the lips. The man held him up and punched him again, this time in the nose, clearly breaking it. He then threw him to the ground.

Other men that were surrounding them picked the now-bloodied Drew off of the ground and held him up. The man who was the aggressor walked up to Drew who was now restrained.

"If I ever see you here again, I will end you." The man punched him one more time in the gut. The two men who were restraining Drew dragged him out of the club.

The man turned to Diana who was leaning against the wall. "What's a pretty lady like yourself doing with BPI's finest?"

"He isn't always like that."

"That guy is bad news, hon. I've seen you here with him a lot."

Diana looked up at this man who was her savior. He was at least fifteen years her senior. His dark hair was slicked back. His white, collared shirt was unbuttoned down to the middle of his chest. The lights reflected off the flashy jewelry he wore around his neck. He definitely was quite well off. Diana couldn't help but feel secretly flattered that the man noticed her previous to that night.

"What's your name?" The man said.

"Diana."

"How old are you, Diana?"

"Eighteen. Well, almost nineteen."

"Is that all? My name is Anthony. Most people call me A.C."

"Thank you for doing that for me." Diana curled her hair behind her ear and smiled.

"Come join me at my table."

"I think it's better that I go."

"You sure?"

Diana nodded.

"Ok. Suit yourself."

A.C. escorted her to the door and invited her back to the club to join them the next time she came around.

***

Diana took A.C. up on his offer and returned many times. They would even meet for coffee. The days and nights were a lot more enjoyable with A.C. than they were with Drew. A.C. was a gentleman and was very respectable to her, at first.

Though Diana was fond of A.C., she had no romantic feelings towards him and she didn't think he had any for her. He was quite protective of her, however. He always watched like a hawk when she was on the dance floor with other men. He seemed like such a good man when she thought back to those nights. She did eventually learn that she never really knew him.

After Diana finished dancing she came back to sit at the table where A.C. was sitting. She had been drinking a lot more these days. Maybe it was because she felt she could let loose a little more, seeing as she didn't have to babysit someone after the night ended. She felt protected when she was around A.C. and his entourage. So why not have a few more drinks than usual?

Whether it was the security of her new-found friends, the increased alcohol intake or a combination of both, she never really knew why she decided to take that night of partying one step further. That last step was what sealed her fate.

The whole table were partaking in drugs along with the alcohol. Diana wasn't even really sure what they were taking. She knew nothing about street drugs.

She got the attention of A.C, who was sitting right beside her. "I would like to try some." She motioned towards the pink lines that were on the table.

A.C. didn't hesitate. "This right here, innocent Di, is brand new to the market."

He showed her how to snort up the powder. It was after that, that the night started becoming a blur.

Drew always told her cocaine was like drinking fifty cups of coffee only a hundred times better. She thought it was a pick-me-up. But the strange feelings she was experiencing was nothing like Drew described. But then again, what Drew used to snort was white.

All she remembered after taking the drugs, was the muffled voices and not being able to decipher any words. Something wasn't right. She later figured, whatever she was taking, whether it was coke or something else, it was laced. Most likely with PCP or something of the sort.

She didn't remember how she got to the room, but she vaguely remembered the bed. It felt like she was dreaming when her clothes were being ripped from her body.

The room was dark and she only saw brief flashes of light. She didn't understand why she couldn't move her arms or legs. There was a voice that said, "relax . . . everything's gonna be OK."

The voice spoke softly, yet it was followed by loud, piercing echoes. She couldn't tell who was on top of her. Whoever this person was, he was very rough. Her body was his play-toy. She could feel it being jerked back and forth uncontrollably like a rag doll while she lay paralyzed. She tried to utter the word *stop,* but she didn't know if it actually came out. The man put all the weight of his sweaty body on top of hers; it was a struggle to breathe. The jarring pain of her head being repeatedly bounced off of the headboard was compounded with the violent pounding in her midsection.

She blacked out. The next thing Diana remembered was opening her eyes to the sun beaming into this strange room. She had no idea where she was. Her first thought was being thankful she woke up from the nightmare.

She immediately notice her clothes strewn on the floor and that her wrists were burning. She looked at them and she darted up in the bed. They were raw.

She glanced over at the night table and saw two pairs of hand cuffs. Panic and confusion took control of her body as her heart rate picked up. She pulled the sheet down, and it was confirmation that her nightmare was no dream at all. Diana was facing a horrific reality.

There was blood on the sheets in the middle of the bed, and it was apparent that its source was from between her legs, where the soreness that she didn't notice at first began to throb.

"Oh my god," She whispered. Tears flooded her eyes and rolled down her face.

She got up and quickly gathered her clothes and the door opened. She immediately concealed her naked body with the ball of clothes in her hands. A.C. entered the room.

"You?" Diana said, gasping.

A.C immediately turned around to let her dress.

"Diana, you need to listen to me. We were both quite drunk and high. These things happen."

"I gotta get outta here. Oh my god, I can't . . . I gotta leave."

Diana rushed out of the room, disoriented. A.C. followed, passing her to intercept her at the front door. "I can't let you go till we talk about this."

Diana went for the door knob and A.C. lightly pushed her, forcing her to take a step back. Diana started flailing her arms and tried her best to battle her way past him. A.C. grabbed both her wrists with one hand and held her in place.

"Diana, please stop this. Just come with me and sit down. Have a coffee."

Diana continued to struggle as A.C. pulled her to the ground while still holding tightly onto her wrists. He dragged her back to the room and threw her towards the bed; her head hit the bed post. She rolled on her side, slightly dazed. He picked her up and threw her on the bed and cuffed her hand to the bed post.

"I didn't want to have to do this, Diana. Until you are willing to hear me, this is where you'll stay." A.C. slammed the door.

She screamed for help, but her cries went unanswered for five days and nights. In the meantime, the nightmare repeated itself every night. A.C. would go out and come back completely intoxicated. He would then have his way with her.

It was the last night that was the scariest. She didn't bother screaming anymore. She knew what was coming and it definitely wasn't help. She didn't know if she was going to die in that very spot as this man's sex slave.

He opened the door of her dark room. The light from outside shined through and she squinted at A.C's silhouette. This time there was something different. He was carrying his gun. He staggered over to her and she said in a weak, quivering voice, "I'm willing to talk."

"Gonna be hard with your mouth full."

A.C. climbed on the bed, unzipped his pants and straddled her chest, placing the full weight of his knees on her shoulders. He placed the gun firmly against her head. You bite or any shit like that, I will open your skull all over this bed."

There was a loud pounding at the front door. A.C. paused and looked back. "What the fuck?"

He stood up and rushed out of the room with his gun still drawn. She heard him open the door and say, "Baxter. What do you want?"

"I wanted to come to you first . . ."

"Hold on," A.C. said.

He returned to the room Diana was in and A.C. shut the door.

All Diana could here were muffled voices. She then heard A.C.'s volume rising and the voices getting easier to hear as a result. The last thing that she heard was the other man, who A.C. called Baxter, yell, "You don't gotta do this!"

There was an eerie silence for the next few seconds; it was broken by a gunshot, followed by what sounded like a body falling on the floor.

***

A.C. returned to Diana's room the next morning. He entered the room and Diana partially opened her eyes.

"I don't know what got into me," he said.

Diana remained silent. It wasn't that she didn't have any words to say, it was that she had nothing at all left. She was dead inside.

"Diana. I have never done anything like this before. Hell, I haven't even struck a woman." A.C. put his hand on his face. "In my line of work, I shouldn't be using my own stuff. I'm gonna get help though."

Diana looked up at him and then let her head fall back on the pillow. A.C. walked over to her hands, pulled out a key and unlocked the cuffs. "I'm letting you go."

He helped Diana to her feet, placed his hand on the small of her back and helped her to the entrance. He opened the door and Diana stepped out with her back still facing him, pausing for a second in a complete daze, when he said his last words to her.

"Look, Diana. I understand if you go to the cops. I'm OK with that. Just remember who I am. My name is Anthony Carter Brooklyn. I have the means of making your story go away."

Diana, without a word, walked out of his life.

CHAPTER 58

Truth and Revelations

Gran wiped a tear from her cheek and looked at Christian who was frozen with a stone-cold look on his face.

"I don't know everything that happened in the time she spent with this man. All I know is, it was sometime during those days, that my little girl died. To add insult to injury, this rapist, this gangster, walked away scot-free. They refused to prosecute him."

Christian was struggling to stay silent as his gran filled him in on the rape. His body was trembling and he couldn't hold it in anymore. He stood up and started pacing.

"Chrissy, please sit back down."

A dark mask stared back at his gran. Christian stood at the dresser, breathing heavy through his nose, on the verge of hyperventilating.

"I'm gonna kill him," Christian said softly.

"Chrissy, please. Calm yourself."

Christian swiped everything on top of his dresser onto the floor. "Calm myself? You want me to calm down?"

"There's more. But until you calm down, I won't continue."

Christian forced himself to sit on the foot of his bed, his elbows on his knees and both hands cupping his mouth and nose. He rocked back and forth.

"What more can there be?" Christian said.

"You always said you wanted answers. I'll give them to you, if you promise you won't fly off the handle."

Christian took his hands from his face. He looked over at his gran who was now seated on the side of the bed. "So she got high and he raped her. That's why she was a piece of shit mother to me?"

"Why do you always bring things back to you? This is exactly what I'm talking about when I say you victimize yourself."

"Damaged merchandise. She chose to be a bitch mother to me because she put herself in that position. Her choices punished me for my whole life."

"Shut your mouth, Christian. Think about what she went through."

"You sit here and defend her. My slut of a mother."

"Don't ever call her that! If it wasn't for her, you wouldn't be sitting here!"

"Don't feed me that crap." Christian stood up and put a cigarette in his mouth.

"When she was pregnant with you, Christian, everyone wanted her to get an abortion. She refused."

"Well she probably opened her legs to anything that walked. Were you ashamed she didn't know which of the hundred men she probably fucked after that was my daddy? Is that why you wanted her to get an abortion, Gran? Typical story of a broken girl. Turn to drugs and fuck everything under the sun."

"Christian…"

"Maybe my father never showed up 'cause your daughter scared him away. I don't blame him."

"Stop now, Christian."

"I'd shake his hand while we piss on her fucking grave…"

"Well then go call Anthony Brooklyn and piss on her grave!"

"What?"

"Call him, Christian. You can shake his hand before you kill him."

Christian just stopped himself from saying something he would further regret. His jaw dropped and his eyes widened. "No." Christian was rapidly shaking his head over and over. "He couldn't be."

"It's true, Christian."

"Edwin . . . A.C . . ."

"Is your father."

Christian knelt down beside his bed and placed his head on the mattress, the dark realization sucking the soul from his body.

"Chrissy. You were a product of . . . I mean . . ."

"Get out of my room."

"Chrissy…"

Christian's tear-filled eyes darted towards his gran. "Get. Out. Now!"

Gran backed away, turned around and walked out of the room.

Christian was in a trance. The information was registering and he was becoming drunk with hate. He put on a hoodie, a backpack and pulled his gun out of a dresser drawer.

He walked toward the front door of the house with a dark purpose, doing nothing to conceal the gun plainly visible in his hand.

"Chrissy, please!" Gran's plea fell on deaf ears. He grasped the doorknob.

"Think about what you're doing," his gran sobbed. "I lost my little girl to this man. I don't want to lose my grandson too. Please, baby. I'm begging you."

Christian paused, his back still to his gran. Her cries temporarily thawed his hardened heart. He dropped his bag and gently placed the gun on the floor beside it.

He walked toward his broken, delicate gran.

"I'm so sorry." Christian embraced and held her tightly. All the years of buried emotion surfaced. All the hate, anger and sadness were revealed as one. He placed his face on his gran's shoulder and began to bawl. It started as a whimper and then turned into a howling cry. The little lost boy that hid for so many years inside this now-hardened adult had shown his face. His tears and runny nose soaked his gran's shoulder while she tightened her grip.

Christian released her, his face was swollen and his eyes bloodshot. "I spent my life hating her."

"I don't believe that. I know you loved her."

"She didn't know though."

"Chrissy, she knew."

"The last thing I told her when she was dying was that I wasn't going be at her funeral."

"Was that really the only thing you said, Chrissy?"

"No."

"I didn't think so. Your mother died knowing you loved her. I promise you that."

Christian, who was now calmer, sat down with his gran. She handed him a tissue.

"I know there are a lot of things you've taken in tonight. And I know there is a lot going on in your life right now. Let's work it all out together. Can we do that?"

"Gran, I need to go to bed."

"Before you do, I have something to give you."

Christian's gran walked back to her room and returned with a little box that looked like a treasure chest. She placed it on the table in front of him.

"I know you felt like she never said goodbye. But she did in a sense. Over the years, since you were a baby, she wrote you letters. She always told me, *make sure Christian gets this box if anything ever happens to me*." Gran looked down at the floor and her chin began to quiver. Tears flooded her cheeks.

"I always told her that nothing was going to happen and she can give it to you herself. She was planning on giving them to you when you got older. She always intended on telling you the truth, Chrissy."

"You didn't read them, Gran?"

"No. But Chrissy, I'm sorry that all of this—"

Christian took the box and stood up, holding his hand in the air. "Don't worry, Gran. No more apologies."

He walked over to the door of his room and turned to her. "Go get some rest."

CHAPTER 59

Death of Christian

Christian spent two straight hours reading through the contents of the box his mother had left him. It still wasn't long enough to complete the endless words she put on paper. Words of love that he never knew. He understood her more now. He felt so sorry for all the lost years that he had spent blaming her for everything. For the first time in his life he realized that all the things he had deemed as wrong with her, were not actually her fault. She did the best she could with what she had and the circumstances she had to deal with.

There was no way that he could have known that Edwin, this man who was now a stranger, was the one who stood between him and her. It was this man that was the destruction of their relationship. Ironically, however, without Edwin, none of this would even exist.

It was two in the morning and he stood against the bathroom counter facing himself in the mirror. He held electric clippers firmly in his right hand. He turned them on and hoped the buzzing wouldn't wake his gran. He scowled at himself as he brought the straight edge of the clippers to his head. With one long stroke across his skull, he watched as his hair dropped into the sink.

After completing his new look, Christian gathered up his things, placing his gun in his bag. He walked toward the front door as quietly as he could. While trying to turn the doorknob without making a sound, he was startled by the lights turning on. His gran stood right behind him.

"Gran, what are you doing up?"

"I know what you're doing. As much as it breaks my heart, I have to say this. If you walk out that door, then you are walking out of my life forever. I will not see you again."

Christian stood looking up and down at her, absorbing the moment. It was heart wrenching, being on the verge of losing the one person in the world who genuinely loved him. He walked up to her and gently placed his hand on her face.

"I love you, Gran."

His gran partially smiled and exhaled. "I love you too."

"This is for the best. I mean, the best for you. I need to handle things the only way I know how."

Christian pulled the hood over his newly-shaved head. He placed her car keys on the table.

"Take your car. It's yours. I won't be back for a while, so take your time leaving."

After he closed the door, he could hear his gran scream out to him. Christian did what he felt was best, and ignored it.

***

Christian took a cab to bring him to the docks. The overcast sky invaded the night and the air flowing off the water became ice cold. Rain began to fall, pelting Christian and soaking him to the bone. He reached into his bag sitting beside him and pulled out a bottle of whiskey, taking three huge sips as he sped across the rougher than normal waves.

He reached the island and tied up the boat. Before leaving it behind, he turned and looked out over the water. Feeling overwhelmed with a new found love that was birthed by bitter hate. He raised his head and stared up at the sky. Tears mingled with rain began to stream down his face. He held the whiskey bottle up in the air, closed his eyes and mouthed the words: *This is for you.*

He took one last swig and capped the bottle, tossing it back into the boat where it made a hard landing, but didn't shatter.

The half-hour walk to the man's house he once knew as Edwin didn't feel as long as he expected. Being lost in endless thought had killed a lot of the time. He finally stood in front of the porch and rested his bag on the ground. He pulled out the gun, placed it in the back of his pants, and without hesitation, walked up the stairs. He gently opened the front door without making a peep.

When he entered the house, he crept as silently as he could toward A.C.'s room. The sound his soaked sneakers were making sounded almost deafening to him. He gently pushed open the door of A.C.'s room and flicked on the light. He saw that his empty bed was still made. That was unlike him. Something didn't seem right. It was almost five in the morning and A.C., or at least the man he knew as Edwin, wasn't one to be up at odd hours. Christian walked to the living room where the lamp and TV were on, but the TV was on mute.

The floor creaked directly behind him and Christian spun around. He made eye contact with A.C. who was lowering a baseball bat to his side upon realizing it was Christian.

"Dammit kid, what are you doing?"

A.C. walked past Christian toward the couch, turning his back. He threw the bat down and grabbed the remote to turn off the TV. Christian pulled the gun out from the back of his jeans and pointed it directly at A.C.'s head.

"Now tell me, what possessed you . . ." A.C. turned mid-speech, stopping abruptly when he faced the barrel of the gun.

"Who are you?" Christian said.

"What's going on, kid? Put the gun away. We just spoke about this the other night."

"Who are you? I'm not asking again." Christian raised the gun higher and gripped it tighter. His hand was shaking.

"Put it down, son. Just calm down. I don't know what you're—"

"Don't. Fucking. Lie to me!"

A.C. slowly stepped back with his hands partially in the air. He cautiously sat down on the couch at the edge of the seat. "I'm just sitting. I'm not sure what's up. But we can talk."

"I know who you are."

"What did Russ Baxter say about me now?"

"You wanted to do right by mother. You always told me that. It was all just fucking lies."

"I wasn't lying to you, son."

"Tell me who you are . . . Pops!"

"What?"

"You want to right your wrongs? Before I put this bullet in your head, you got one chance."

Christian needed to hear the truth come out of A.C.'s mouth.

"Since the day I met you Christian, I saw a lot of me in you—"

"Fuck off! Is that what all you hustlers say? Russ said the same shit. Is that the manipulation? Make a person see themselves in you, so you can own them?"

"You have the gun. You're the one in control. So can you please just sit down?"

Christian contemplated it for a second, but didn't take the gun off of A.C. He sidestepped to a single chair that was perpendicular to the couch.

"OK, I'm sitting."

A.C. looked past the gun right into Christian's eyes and Christian reciprocated. His weapon wavered a bit, but he caught himself and brought it back up.

"Christian, if you're going to do this, then all I ask is that you let me explain. Can you give me a moment to speak?"

"Speak."

"It was a long time ago. I did lie about almost everything when it came to the relationship I had with your mom. I don't know what you heard. But I can tell you know the truth about what happened. It was twenty years ago and I am a different man now. I was heavy into drugs. The stuff warped me. It's no excuse, but I never hurt a single woman before or after that."

"You done? Cause I honestly don't give a fuck." Christian sat forward and continued to point the weapon.

"Fine, Christian. What do you want to hear? That I'm your father? Fine . . . I'm your father."

Christian's head tilted to the side and he did his best to hold back any sort of emotion. He took a deep breath, but didn't exhale. He knew the answer to the question, but hearing it from A.C. brought up something a whole lot different than when his gran told him.

That brief second those words were spoken, Christian's gun wavered again and A.C. capitalized on it and quickly drew a weapon from behind him. It must have been buried in the couch cushions. A.C. was obviously prepared for a confrontation with God knows who.

"Drop it, son. Put it on the table."

Christian was caught dead to rights. His weapon was not aimed at A.C. anymore; rather, there was one now pointing at his head. He had no chance, so he placed his gun on the table.

A.C. retrieved Christian's gun and placed it down next to him. Christian seethed, mentally kicking himself for not taking care of A.C. when he had the chance.

"You wanna play in this game, son, you can't let your guard down. This is why you would be dead on the street if you played with the big boys. Not Russ Baxter, mind you, I mean the real big boys."

"If you're going to do it, then get it over with," Christian said.

"Kill you? Do you think I would be capable of killing my own son?"

"You're my blood. But you're not my father."

"Fair enough. But I'm the closest thing you ever had to one."

"Fuck you. You think death scares me, Anthony? You never left this trade of ours did you?"

"Nope. Not only did I not leave, I'm going to take things to a different level. I'm going to kill your boy Russ Baxter and anyone else I even *think* was associated with that robbery the other night."

Christian sat accepting that he was in a lost position.

"Since it's confession time, I got one for you, Anthony."

A.C. stood waiting, still pointing the gun at his estranged son.

"Russ wasn't behind the killing of your little brother. I was. I was able to witness him begging for his pathetic life."

"Oh son of mine, son of mine, son of mine. I got one for you, too. A doozy. I never knew my parents and never had any siblings. Remember I said I had two sons? Well, you're one. The man you killed the other night, he was the other."

Christian thought he had the upper hand in this battle of wits, but A.C. managed to pull another one over him.

"You mean my mother—"

"Not your mother. He was your half-brother. You know what my name is kid? You don't think I knew what was in those goddamn bags you carried off the boat the other night? I knew exactly what it was. There's a reason I own every gang on this side of the country. Some of them don't even know they're my property. Now get on your knees."

It all hit Christian hard. The tough non-caring exterior that he wore like armor had finally been penetrated. Fear, an emotion that usually eluded him, set in. And though he had received many answers this night, yet more questions had been raised. He would die never knowing the full story.

Christian knelt down, facing away from A.C.

"Any last words, kid?"

Christian bowed his head and tried his best to hold back his tears.

"You robbed me of my life, Edwin. I looked up to you. I gained a love for you that I never knew. You robbed my mother of her life, too. She loved me and I only showed her hate. Take my life as you did hers . . . Anthony Carter Brooklyn."

"You done?"

Christian didn't say another word.

"I'll take that as a yes. Now turn around."

Christian hesitated but slowly turned his head. He looked up and A.C wasn't standing there, rather he had resumed his position on the couch and wasn't even holding onto the weapon anymore. The two guns were sitting on the table.

Christian stood up, bewildered. This man, his father, was very complicated.

"You wanna survive in this game, son? You have tons to learn, and you won't learn from Russ Baxter or any of those boys."

A.C. picked up his gun again. This time he tossed it to Christian who caught it.

"Check it."

Christian popped the cylinder; A.C.'s gun wasn't even loaded.

"Hear me out now. This is important. I am sorry for what I did to your mother. I've done a lot of things in my life. But I don't know who that man was. That's the truth, Christian. There isn't a day that passes that I don't think about those five nights. I'm not a man of remorse. I'm not a man of regrets. But I do and have always regretted what happened with your mother. I was fond of her, believe it or not. Son, believe me when I say, I'm just so sorry."

Christian stood still, his lip quivering. A.C. rose to his feet, and this time he grabbed Christian's loaded gun. He held it in his hands and stared at it.

"If I were around longer, Christian, I would dedicate everything I do to helping you in your mother's name."

Christian absorbed the words that meant nothing, when it came from the devil standing in front of him.

"I'll teach you one lesson before you do what you gotta do. You ever pull a gun on anyone with a purpose, make sure the goddamn safety is off." A.C. took the safety off and walked over to Christian's side of the coffee table; he placed the gun down, directly in front of Christian.

Christian picked it up and pointed it at his father. He put his finger on the trigger and put partial pressure on it; it moved back very slightly.

"One last thing," A.C. said. "Get that hate outta your heart, son. You pull that trigger, boy, don't do it out of hate for me. Do it out of love for your mother."

Christian slowly lowered the gun. His eyes were flooded again with tears. He successfully held them back from streaming down his cheeks. He engaged the gun's safety and tucked the weapon back in his pants.

"I'll be out of your house in the next month. I don't want to see or hear from you ever again. And I'm keeping every cent of the money I took. When I do hit the street, I want you to open the ways for me silently. I know your name, now remember mine. I am Christian Xavier Solomon. I was born 'cause my mother was raped and tortured by my father. You can call me Chinny."

"Chinny. I hated that name since the day I heard it. I don't care about the money. And keep the house, Chinny. It's owned by Edwin Steed. He doesn't even exist."

CHAPTER 60

Turning up the Heat

The day was long as the night was rough. Christian was exhausted and in a daze from the past twenty-four hours, and the twenty-six ounce bottle of Jack he had slammed during that time didn't help. Christian was now riding over to Braeden's house in a cab because Braeden told Christian that he urgently needed to talk to him.

Christian had the cab stop over at his place because he needed to get the money for the meeting with Russ Baxter. His gran's car was still in the driveway. He did not want to run into her, but he had to get in his house. So he decided to run in and out and not say a word to her if she was there.

He opened his door and to his immediate right he saw his answering machine blinking frantically. He ignored it and ran to his room to retrieve a bag. He realized it couldn't have been better timing when he heard the shower running.

He ran back to the cab and threw the bag into the trunk. He looked back at his house and he could see the crack of the curtain move to the side. He quickly looked away and instructed the cab driver to move on.

Christian arrived at Braeden's house and didn't get an answer at the basement door, so he went around to the front where Braeden's little sister answered.

"Hey Chloe, is your brother around? He didn't answer his door."

"I think he's in the shower. You can just go through this way."

Chloe directed Christian to the stairway in the kitchen. Braeden's nan sat in her wheelchair in the living room with the TV blaring; she looked like a zombie.

"Hey, what's that?" Christian pointed to a structure that was sitting on the kitchen table. "Did you make that yourself?" It was a struggle for Christian to force himself to act friendly and normal.

"It's my science fair project. My brother helped with most of it. He says it's a sure fire winner."

"No doubt it is. I'll see ya, Chloe."

Christian made his way down to the basement as Braeden was in a towel stepping out of the bathroom.

"What's up, Chin?"

"What did you need to talk to me about?

"Sit down. You want anything?"

"No." Christian sat on the couch while he waited for Braeden to put on some clothes.

Braeden sat on the couch beside him and lit up a joint. "I shouldn't be smokin' this in here . . ." He paused and looked at the ground, shaking his head. "Anyway, shit's fucked, brah."

"Ya, I know."

"You don't know. That detective that's been on us, brought me in for questioning yesterday."

"For what?"

"He knows shit."

"How?"

Braeden stood up as he was puffing on his joint and started pacing.

"Fucking Sammy. He's spilling shit to the cops. He spoke to them."

"What did he say?"

"Not exactly sure. The copper wasn't even specific to who's saying shit. Has to be Sammy, though. That kid knows more than we think."

Christian leaned back on the couch and pulled out a crumpled pack of cigarettes; they were empty. "Fuck!" Christian threw the empty pack on the ground. "Did you talk to Liam?"

"How many times we gonna talk to Liam about this shit, man? I can't go to jail. He was talking like life in prison and shit like that. I got my sis and nan, yo." Braeden started to tear up.

"Calm down. What did you tell them?"

"I didn't tell them shit. But they don't believe me."

"Let's deal with tonight first. We'll figure this out tomorrow. You mind if I crash for a couple hours before we go."

"Go for it. I'll be upstairs." Before Braeden closed the door behind him, he said, "Chinny. I *won't* go to jail."

CHAPTER 61

Lightened Baggage

Christian and Braeden drove to the Creek. When they pulled up in front of the trail, Christian said, "I gotta a lot of shit on my plate right now. But I gotta try hard to keep it together. You need to do the same. Get that shit off your mind for now."

"I'll try," Braeden said.

"You won't just try. You'll do it."

They started down the trail and Christian carried the bag of money on his back. As they got closer, Christian heard female voices and laughter. He looked back at Braeden with his eyebrows furrowed.

The first thing that they saw when they entered was Sammy, who was the last person that should have been there. He was standing with two girls who were sitting on a log.

"What the fuck, brah? How you figure I ain't gonna lose my shit."

It took a lot for Braeden to be pushed to the point of losing it. Christian shook his head and looked around at the other guys standing around with drinks in hand. They were all conversing like there was nothing happening.

He walked up to Davie Boy, Jess and Kirt. "What's all this?"

"What?" Davie Boy said.

Christian walked away, exasperated. He threw his bag down in front of the fire and turned, throwing his hands in the air. "You think this is a fucking party?" Christian yelled loud enough for everyone to go silent.

Sammy backed away, and Kirt and Jess stood a few feet away from the two girls; one of which was Heather.

Heather stood up and staggered towards Christian.

"Hey, Chinny-Chin-Chin. Long time no see."

"Go home, Heather."

"Why? I heard you and your precious Victoria are on the rocks."

"Get out of here, Heather. Now!" Christian pulled Heather by the arm with the intent to direct her to the exit, and he released her.

She looked at him and gave a smile with her head swaying from side to side. "What's wrong, Chinny? Did your little girlfriend not like the surprise I left behind?" Heather giggled.

Christian took a step back. The ridge of his nose wrinkled and his brows furrowed. "What are you talking about, Heather?"

"Pink not her colour?"

"You fucking bitch. You did that on purpose?" Christian rushed her and grabbed her by the throat. With every ounce of strength in his body, he threw her by the neck and she hit the ground hard. She had no time to break her fall and her head bounced off the dirt.

Heather sat up dazed, and immediately the waterworks started to flow. "You asshole!"

Everything that he had been facing in the last several days was coming to a head and he was ready to snap.

Kirt, who everyone knew still had a thing for Heather, came out of nowhere, barreling toward Christian, but Christian side stepped and grabbed him by the collar of his shirt. Kirt tried to spit out some words, but Christian swung; his right hook instantly neutralized Kirt who dropped to one knee. He tried to rise to his feet, but Christian instantly grabbed the gun in the back of his pants and pointed it at him. Kirt quickly submitted and dropped to the ground, slipping onto his back.

Christian crouched down to his level and placed the gun in his mouth. This time the safety was off and he cocked it. "I will end you right now."

Kirt was shaking and avoiding eye contact. Everyone there was dead silent. *Pop!* Went the fire and a large piece of ember landed near Kirt's arm.

"Beg for your life," Christian said.

Kirt continued to look up at the sky, breathing heavy and tears started running down the sides of his temples.

"That there is right fucked, Chinny," Davie Boy said. "Just let it go."

Christian lifted his head and looked in the direction of Davie Boy, the only one out of all of them that had the courage to say something to stop what as potentially going to happen.

"Let it go?" Christian removed the gun from Kirt's mouth and stood up.

He circled the area and looked directly at Davie Boy. "If any of you so much as even touch the unopened merch in that shed again, without my permission, you will take Kirt's place." Christian didn't take his eyes off Davie Boy, who clearly got the message.

Christian shook his head and rubbed his nose. He turned and scanned the area around him. He caught eyes with Heather again. "Take your whore ass along with your friend there and get outta here." Christian for good measure, lifted his gun again, pointing it at her.

Heather and her friend rushed towards the entrance and disappeared into the bushes.

Liam cautiously approached Christian. "Chin, put the gun away."

Christian hesitantly put the gun in the back of his jeans. "Your brother needs to leave, Liam."

Christian looked at the rest of them and realized that he had to regain his composure. He walked over to Kirt who was sitting on the ground and reached his hand out. Kirt looked up at him and slowly reached his trembling hand towards Christian's and grabbed it. Christian pulled him to his feet.

"I need to get it together. I'm sorry." Christian rubbed his eyes with both of his hands, and with a shake of his head he said, "Where's Jordy?"

"Right here." Jordy walked through the entrance of the Creek.

"Where've you been?" Christian said.

"Got a little tied up."

"Okay. What's the plan? Where are we going to meet them?"

"We ain't goin' nowhere."

"He canceled?"

"He's coming here . . . he'll be here any minute."

"Why here and not the club? This makes no sense."

"I don't question my brother, mainer. I'm just the messenger."

That didn't sit well with Christian at all. Out of all the places they could do this, Russ chose the Creek. He had no time to prepare and they were going to be here any minute. Being unprepared—while Russ obviously had it perfectly planned out—was unsettling. Even if it was just a meeting to pay Russ his share, Christian needed to be ready for anything, because anything could happen; especially after he hung up on Russ and disappeared for a couple days.

They heard rustling in the bushes, and out from the trees walked Dax, Fiend, and right behind them, Russ Baxter.

Sammy, who had no time to leave, walked back to the tree while the rest of them watched these gangsters invading their domain. The rest of them were spread out, with Jordy right behind Christian who was anticipating that this confrontation was going to become heated.

Christian retrieved his bag from the ground and came face to face with Russ.

"You leavin' like that with my shit, Chinny, ain't a good thing," Russ said.

Christian tossed the bag at Russ' feet. Dax Max and Fiend stood on the outskirts of the group and watched the exchange closely.

Russ looked down at the bag and then, without even touching it, looked back up at Christian. "That shit's light."

"Forty points. It's all there."

"Yeah, forty points. You're short."

Christian looked back around at everyone else. Some of them slowly shook their heads and shrugged their shoulders. He didn't know what Russ was getting at. Christian caught eyes with Jordy, who looked away.

This psycho was trying to play him again, somehow. He really wished he had had more time to prepare. Instead of being one step ahead of Russ, he was ten steps behind.

Russ picked up the bag and pumped it up and down. He threw it to the side. "This bag of yours is over a mil short, Chinny. Where's. My. Money?"

"What are you talking about, Russ?" Christian was realizing that Russ knew more than he thought.

"Don't play me for a fool."

"Fuck this." Christian turned and walked toward the bag.

He stood in front of it facing Russ. He tried to discreetly reach around his back for the butt end of his gun. No sooner did he do that that, another weapon was drawn a lot quicker. Christian didn't have a chance.

"I wouldn't do that, mainer." Jordy stood pointing a gun at Christian. Dax Max and Fiend also pulled their weapons and trained them on the rest of ROMA.

Christian's eyes widened and he spread his hands away from his body. Jordy walked over to him and they stood face to face for a brief second. Christian's face was painted with disappointment and betrayal.

While Jordy pointed the gun at Christian, he also reached around and grabbed a hold of Christian's gun. "I'm sorry, mainer. He's my brother."

"How touching," Russ said, "Jord, I'll take it from here."

Jordy walked back and pointed his gun at the rest of ROMA, alongside Dax and Fiend.

"You're a fucking sellout, brah." Braeden said to Jordy.

Russ pulled a weapon of his own and forced Christian to stand in the middle of everyone who was standing in a half circle. He pushed the gun into Christian's forehead. "Now let's start over. Where's my fucking money?"

"This is now the second time you pulled a gun on me. Better pull the trigger this time, Russ," Christian said

"You got ten seconds. Where's my money?"

"Dax . . . Fiend, what kind of cut do you get? What about you, Jord?" Christian said.

None of them moved a muscle or acknowledged Christian.

"Shut your mouth." Russ said.

"How long you gonna get beat down by your brother, Jord? We just talked about this shit. You gonna be his bitch forever?"

"This is your *last* warning, Chinny." Russ said.

"You probably get, like what? Two points each?"

"Don't make me do this, Chinny," Russ pushed the gun harder into Christian's head.

"Forget Russ. I'll split it all nine ways. Almost four-hundred-thousand each."

"Chin man. Just give up the money," Liam said. "It's over. These guys aren't playing around."

"Listen to your boy, *Chin man,*" Russ said.

Christian's face remained emotionless and he wasn't budging. They stood in silence that felt like an eternity.

"I can give all you boys more than this fake gangster can. You let him pull that trigger, you will be owned by this bitch till you die." Christian attempted onc last effort to put an end to this, in his favor.

"Fuck this. Time's up." Russ grabbed Christian by the scruff of his shirt and pushed the gun into his cranium. "Say goodnight."

Liam ran toward Christian despite having guns pointed at him. He barreled towards Russ, but was too late. Almost simultaneously the blast of gunfire erupted. The splatter of blood flew through the air and soaked the dirt. The echo from what sounded like an explosion, hardly resonated, when a second shot was fired at the motionless body on the ground.

An eerie smoky mist from the combination of gun smoke and dust from the ground surrounded them. The burning smell of gun powder and the copper smell of blood invaded the air as the reverberation of shots faded. Finally, there was only silence.

CHAPTER 62

Aftermath

Clouds with the faces of demons crept in and out of Christian's view as he lay on his back looking up at the sky. He couldn't hear anything and could feel water drizzling on his face.

He turned his head and could see two legs running. This person was yelling something. Even though he was only a few steps from him, it sounded like he was miles away.

"Liam!" He deciphered the word being yelled as his temporary hearing loss began to subside.

Three bodies were on the ground. Sammy pounced on his brother and cradled him in his arms.

"Please, wake up."

"Sammy. I'm ok, I'm awake," Liam said.

"You're bleeding, Li."

Liam searched his body for wounds. There was blood on his body, but after examining himself he established that none of the blood was his.

Everything seemed to be going in slow motion. Christian could see Sammy holding Liam like he was a fallen solider. Christian pushed himself up to his feet with a half-hearted attempt to dust himself off. He turned to his right and saw the man who minutes earlier betrayed him. Time finally started to speed up.

"Jordy! What the fuck did you do?" Dax charged Jordy who was on his knees mumbling something and holding his gun by his side. Jess and Kirt rushed toward Dax and tackled him. Jess wrenched the gun out of his hand.

Before Fiend had a chance to react, Davie Boy and Braeden both grabbed him from behind; they all fell to the ground. Fiend's gun flew from his hands and slid a few feet away. Fiend wasn't putting up much of a fight. He was clearly still digesting what had happened. Davie Boy crawled over his body and retrieved the gun.

ROMA was now in control.

Christian looked down at the now lifeless body of Russ Baxter. He glanced back at Jordy who was on the verge of breaking down. "Was that bullet meant for me?"

Jordy didn't respond. He collapsed into a sitting position, cradling his legs.

"Answer me, Jordy!"

Davie Boy answered for Jordy who was in no condition to speak. "Chin, them bullets were meant for Russ. Jord put one in him, then a second one for good measure. He saved your life."

Everyone, with the exception of Jordy, were on their feet now. Fiend and Dax, who were now disarmed, looked only at Christian as he stared back at them.

Dax Max, who showed no regard to the guns that were pointing at him, walked over to the bag of money and picked it up off the ground. He stood there wearing the look of a man who just took over the throne.

"Aright. So this is what's up. I'm taking this to the club. Chinny, you're gonna bring the rest. You want protection after what you boys did tonight? All of you come down to the club, so we can talk this shit out . . . and quit pointing your guns at me."

Christian looked at the man who was Russ' lackey. He was holding onto what was once Russ' money; now that Russ was gone, Christian deemed it as his own.

"Go to your club? So you can lead us to the slaughter?" Christian said.

"You've done some damage tonight. Takin' out my boy and all. If it's not me or Fiend, you're going to be facing the rest of our crew. Join us and I can help you. Or go to war with us and you'll lose."

"I'll take my chances with the latter." Christian said.

You honestly think you gotta chance?" Dax laughed and shook his head.

"I own you, Dax." Christian's voice was monotone.

Dax rolled his eyes and looked over at the tree house.

"Nice. Do I gotta be initiated into your little girls club?" Dax laughed again and walked towards the entrance with Fiend following him.

Christian walked towards Jordy, who was now in the weakest state that he had ever seen him. He looked down at him as he sat beside his dead brother. He put a comforting hand on his shoulder and leaned down further to slip the gun out of his hand.

He raised it and pointed it at Dax Max. "One more step. That's all it's gonna take, Dax."

Dax turned around. "Look kid. That gun means nothing to me. Because without me—"

"Shut the fuck up. You don't call the shots. You ain't runnin' this shit."

Dax smiled and looked at the group who were standing like useless props. "Little boys. That is all you are. Yo Fiend, let's jet."

"One more step it's over, Dax." Christian tightened his grip on the gun and raised it a little higher.

Dax turned around again. He dropped the bag right beside Fiend. He took a few steps forward and stopped.

"Put a bullet in my head then, Chinny. You can't 'cause you know the stakes. Stop pretending cause we both know you won't do shit."

Christian turned the gun towards Fiend. He immediately fired the gun twice. One bullet hit Fiend in the chest and as he was falling back, the second penetrated his skull. A lucky shot, but he made his point. Fiend fell to the ground and the dirt around him was splattered in red.

Dax stood with widened eyes as he saw his comrade twitching on the ground.

"You wanna go to war . . . I'll take you to war. The next bullet's for you," Christian said.

Dax held up his arms and glanced down at the money. The bag dictated their lives in more ways than one. "Okay, okay . . . I get it. Just calm down."

Sammy, who was on the ground, started rocking back and forth, squealing. Christian turned towards Liam. "Control that shit, Li."

The split second he turned, Dax took off and ran out of the Creek, empty handed.

"Everybody is dying!" Sammy said, and Liam walked over to try and comfort him. Sammy pushed Liam away.

Christian walked back to Liam who was trying to gain control of Sammy's hysterics, but Sammy would not let anyone near him.

"We need help," Sammy said. "We need the police."

Christian looked over at Braeden who was looking back at him. They exchanged silent words with their perturbed faces. The conversation that they had earlier was surfacing.

"Sammy, don't even think about the police," Liam said.

"You're all murderers!" Sammy stood up as he yelled at the top of his lungs. "I'm not helping you murderers. I'm going to the police."

"Calm down, Sammy," Christian said.

"Shut up, Chinny. You're a murderer. So fuck you!"

Liam walked up to Sammy again and grabbed him by the shirt. "You know what happens if you tell the cops, Sammy? We will all go to jail for the rest of our lives. Even you."

"I did nothing!"

"Are you that stupid?" Liam pushed Sammy hard and he stumbled backwards. "You *are* a fucking retard, aren't you?"

Sammy's flooded eyes looked back at Liam in disbelief. The one person on this earth that always protected him just stabbed him in the heart with those words. He turned and ran into the woods and disappeared down a trail. "I hate you, Liam!"

"Ain't you gonna stop him?" Davie Boy said.

Liam plunked himself down on a log. "Let him go. He's just going to his stupid little spot."

"Brah, what about the cops?"

"Trust me Braed, he won't be doing that tonight. I'll talk to him tomorrow," Liam said.

Davie Boy was circling Russ' Body as he looked back at Fiend. "We gotta do something about them bodies. I can't have this here."

Christian walked toward Davie Boy and put his arm around him. "We'll cover them for now. Russ' crew will be in the area, I'm guessing. Your folks still gone?"

"Yeah."

Christian picked a gun off the ground and walked over to Braeden. "Take this. Drive around, and if everything's clear, call us at Davie Boy's house." Christian put his hand on Braeden's shoulder and whispered, "You got this. Just be careful."

They shared a silent stare and Braeden took off down the trail.

***

They all sat around one of the living rooms in Davie Boy's house. Christian and Jordy made eye contact. Christian nodded his head in a downward motion and Jordy reciprocated.

Davie Boy was right, though. They needed to do something about those bodies very quickly. Christian had no experience with this, so he felt that he was forced to make a call for help to someone who did, but he had no desire to associate with that someone.

CHAPTER 63

Flash of Light

It was really dark in the forest. Running into the woods wasn't the best choice Sammy could have made. It wasn't easy finding his spot in the middle of the night. He wished he just ran home instead.

The sounds of the forest were scary. Why does fear make everything seem so much louder? Sammy walked along the water where the creek turned into a rapid flowing river. It was probably safer that way. At the very least, there was less of a chance that he would get even more lost.

Who were these people he hung around with? Christian had turned into a monster and the rest of them were following him down this dark path. More importantly, though, what had his brother become?

Sammy wasn't ignorant of the fact he was the slow one. But if that was the case, then why was it only him that seemed to question the actions of the group? Aren't they supposed to be the good guys that help people? Instead, they're dealing drugs and murdering people. Why does this not affect anyone else? It was to the point that they treated it like a normal everyday occurrence. People were dying for this cause that Christian Solomon created.

Sammy heard a twig snap and quickly stopped in his tracks. He looked around and saw nothing. He didn't even have a flashlight. He tried to hide himself behind a tree, which wasn't much good, considering he didn't know what he was hiding from.

He heard another snap. His heart picked up its pace. There were wild animals in these woods that would love to make him their main course.

A third time he heard the sound; this time it was closer and louder and finally showed its face. It came sprinting out of the bushes and ran right past him.

Damn raccoon. Sammy took a sigh of relief.

He started to walk again with the intent to get the hell out of the woods as soon as possible. He just wanted to be back home safe in his bed.

Sammy's eyes suddenly met a bright flashlight, blinding him. He froze and squinted. He put his hand in front of his face, trying to block out the light.

"Hello?"

Sammy's attempt at communication was answered by a loud pop, which was followed by the sounds of birds flapping their wings and flying away from wherever they were nesting.

Sammy dropped to his knees holding his shoulder that now throbbed with excruciating pain. The pain was so severe that he couldn't breathe. He looked down at the ground and saw a light shine on a pair of boots that stood directly in front of him.

"Help," his cracked, weak voice whispered.

He struggled to lift his head to look up. His face met the barrel of a gun.

"I'm so sorry, brah."

He heard a click and saw a flash of light . . .

CHAPTER 64

Broken

The Creek was eerily silent. It was late afternoon and there was plenty of daylight. Despite that, there was a shadow that was cast around the whole area and it wasn't from the trees. Once an innocent spot that was filled with the laughter of little boys, it had now been invaded by a malignancy that was rapidly spreading.

Davie Boy looked at the ground where the bodies previously rested. There wasn't even a blood stain; no one would ever suspect that there were two dead bodies there about twelve hours ago.

He glanced over at the tree house, with a cheap bottle of rye in hand.

The day that his dad started building it with him felt like almost yesterday. But that wasn't what was burned in his memory. What lingered in his head was the day he finished it all by himself.

"Hey, dad!" Davie ran into the house. "Dad!"

Davie's mom stood at the kitchen counter chopping vegetables. "David, don't bother your father. He's busy."

"But Mom, I gotta surprise for him."

"Now's not the time."

Davie ignored her and ran through the kitchen into his dad's office. He burst through his father's door. "Dad, you gotta come check it out."

"What the hell did I tell you about knocking?"

"I know. But dad, the tree house…"

"I have no time. Can you not see I'm busy? Get out of here and close the door."

Davie turned around, bowed his head and closed the door. He walked past his mother again in the kitchen.

"I told you not to bug him. I don't know if you are deaf or dumb, boy."

Ever since Pete died, the conversations always seemed to go like that, finally to the point of not communicating at all. He knew his parents never forgave him for his brother's death. They blamed him, even though they never said it.

He looked over at the ax. The very same ax that Russ Baxter held in his face, quite some time ago. He grabbed it and walked over to the tree house and climbed the ladder. This place wasn't what it used to be. He wasn't a kid anymore. The wooden box that held all his comics, among other things he collected over the years, was a useless fixture collecting dust.

He dragged it to the entrance above the ladder and pushed it over the edge. It crashed loudly to the ground and the lid flew open.

He gathered up all the comics that were strewn upon the ground at the foot of the ladder and began stacking them in the fire pit. Back and forth he walked until he gathered every last comic, along with other trinkets and old toys from when he was a kid.

One of the first things he ever built was the wooden box these items had been stored in. He viciously took his ax and smashed the box and his belongings to pieces and added it to the fire pit.

He poured his lighter fluid over everything that was once his childhood. He lined some rolling paper with marijuana. He shoveled through his pocket and retrieved a little vial that contained pink powder and poured it carefully into his joint.

He lit the joint that was pressed firmly between his lips. Like Christian did to that car way back when, he lit the rest of the matches and threw them into the fire pit, which immediately went up in flames. He looked at the ax, and then back up at the treehouse. He nodded his head, picked up the ax and walked toward the treehouse to complete what he started.

***

Later, Davie Boy was passed out with a sleeping bag over him. He abruptly woke up but couldn't breathe. He was winded. He looked up to see a group of men surrounding him. His open eyes were welcomed by a swift boot to the head.

"Get him up."

Davie Boy was pulled to his feet and supported by three of the men.

"We're here to take back what's ours."

Davie Boy received another blow to the head with a tire iron and fell to the ground. The men swarmed him and laid the boots to him.

The men let up and Davie Boy rolled to his side, then to his stomach. Davie Boy was still aware of his surroundings, but was barely conscious. One of the men grabbed him by the hair and viciously pulled back to the point Davie Boy's back was arching.

"Get up, you stupid fuck." The man said.

Another man approached and tried to bring Davie Boy to his feet, but his legs didn't move off the ground.

"Fuck it," another man said. "This is a message on behalf of Dax Max."

The man pulled his leg up and stomped in the middle of Davie Boy's arched back. Davie Boy felt a crack and heard a snap, the air from his body left him and he lay motionless.

His eyes were still open and his body quivered as he struggled for air. He could see a pair of hands pick up one of the tire irons. At the corner of his eye, he could see the tire iron come down fast and hard toward his head. Everything flickered like a faulty TV screen. He saw red drown his eyes as he blacked out.

CHAPTER 65

Goodbye Brother

Liam's thoughts were on repeat as he stared at the casket that was still sitting above ground. His father stood beside him among multiple other people at the graveyard, most of which he hadn't seen or heard from in years; neither him nor his father were showing any emotion. The sorrow still lingered, but Liam was drained already by the many tears shed in the previous week. That night, seven days before, when he and his father had sat at the kitchen table waiting for the news about Sammy's whereabouts was the night he had deemed everything lost. The look on his father's face as the police stood on his door step was the first time he had seen any sort of love or caring from him in a very long time.

They weren't able to have their proper goodbyes. The last thing Liam said to his brother was that he was a retard. That ate him up to the point of feeling empty inside. The point-blank shot that Sammy took made it so they couldn't see his face one last time.

ROMA, with the exception of Davie Boy, stood among Liam's family and friends. They were all dressed in black suits and wearing sunglasses. They no longer looked like the same teenagers that met at the Creek daily. That day, in front of Sammy's grave, they had evolved into men, who now had an even greater purpose. Vengeance.

Two men in uniform, stood on the other side of the coffin, holding onto Liam and Sammy's mother. After the crime that she had committed, Liam was in disbelief that they would even consider allowing her to attend Sammy's funeral.

The casket that was engraved with the Star of David was lifted slowly and then gently lowered into a six-foot hole in the ground. The Rabbi who was conducting the ceremony recited some Hebrew prayers. When he finished, he turned to the crowd and said, "If anyone has some short words to say, now is the time."

Besides a few whimpers, they all stood in quietude for a few seconds before the Rabbi began again. Before he got any further, he was interrupted by Liam.

"My brother represented innocence. He didn't deserve this." Liam raised his head for the first time and glared in his mother's direction. "In fact, he didn't deserve any part of this life he was given. In a way, my brother was murdered twice."

Liam took a step back and now stood in the proximity to Christian who put his arm around him. They both turned their heads to a heavy breathing noise that was directly beside them. Braeden was sweating profusely and slightly swaying.

"Brah, I feel like I'mma be sick." He bent over trying to catch his breath.

The guest's eyes were all on the ground when they heard what Liam had to say. They all directed their attention toward the Rabbi when he started to recite the closing prayers.

Once the Rabbi concluded, everyone dispersed. Christian put both his arms around Liam and held him tightly. "We'll make this right," he whispered in Liam's ear.

Liam nodded as they released their embrace. "I know."

"I'm going to get the ball rolling, so I have to leave. I gotta meet someone," Christian said.

"That's cool, Chin, no worries. You hear anything about Davie Boy?"

"Get through this first, Li. We can talk later about that."

Liam tapped Christian on the back and Christian turned and hugged him again.

Christian and the rest of ROMA left the area to leave the immediate family alone. His father was down on one knee in front of the grave with his eyes closed. After a few seconds, he stood up and walked away.

Liam glared at his mother who stood with her two uniformed escorts. Tears were rolling down her face as she lifted her head, exchanging eye contact with Liam.

Her flooded eyes were accompanied by a partial smile, searching for Liam's approval. Liam didn't bat a lash. His mother passively absorbed the disdain that was projected from his face; with a slight nod, she brought her eyes back down to the grave.

He approached her and stood in front of her. "I'm surprised they let you out. Next thing, they'll probably give you an early release."

"I'll be in there a long time, my love."

"I never thought I'd see you again. I've been pretty bitter and angry for all these years. Sammy's death has put a few things in perspective for me."

"I'm not the person you think I am, baby. I love you so much, as I did your brother. I was sick. But I got better for my boys."

"Sick? That's interesting."

"I know there are a lot of things that need to be fixed."

"Fixed?"

"I'm happy you're at least talking to me. I'm so lonely. You are my little baby boy. We can make this work."

"I'm sorry, Ma. I think you misunderstood me. I just wanted you to know something before you were taken away again. The day they release you from those walls, I hope it's in a coffin. If and when that happens, *that* will be the day I set the hate I have for you free."

His mother's chin quivered and she turned her head away.

"One more thing. I told Sammy the truth about you. He died loathing your existence."

Liam turned to walk away. He hoped his words would echo in her head every day for the rest of her life.

CHAPTER 66

Three Million Reasons

A busy family restaurant downtown was the perfect atmosphere to diffuse a dangerous situation. Christian and Dax Max sat in the booth with their untouched beverages in front of them. Christian was hoping to make this meeting a quick one. Moreover, the only reason Dax Max was sitting there was because of Christian. His existence remained, because Christian allowed it to.

The big bag sharing the bench seat Christian was sitting on could possibly put an end to the simmering feud, or escalate it into an even bigger one. Christian crossed his hands and put them on the table.

"Here's how this is going to work. There's one hundred thousand in this bag. I'm going to get up and leave, and it's yours."

Dax chuckled. "You tryin' to dictate terms to me, little man?"

"Not trying."

"Not on my watch, you ain't."

"Dax, just take the money and we can peacefully go our separate ways. As for the drops, there's enough business to go around for everyone."

"The drops? Kid, you thinking you can get your hands on the pink powder?"

That statement made Christian realize that Dax Max had no clue about his connection with A.C. Brooklyn. He couldn't figure out why Russ wouldn't have told him. Christian instantly felt he had more leverage and control over the situation now. Dax's lack of knowledge could change everything.

"Listen Chinny, I ain't takin' that bag until every last dollar you owe is in it. I ain't just talkin' forty points either. I want all three million. After that, maybe you can live."

"I got six guys behind me that want to avenge Sammy's death."

"You think you and your little boys scare me?" Dax laughed. "Anyways, we had nothing to do with that."

"You underestimate me." Christian sat forward in his seat.

"Kid remember this. I will always be at least ten steps ahead of you. I knew how this shit was going to go down. So I already got a little surprise for you. Trust me, you're gonna love it."

"Right, I look forward to it." Christian picked up the bag and stood up to leave before Dax suddenly grabbed him by the wrist.

"Once you walk out of here, you know where this is gonna go, right?"

"Yeah, I know," Christian said.

"The next time we cross paths, Chinny, I'm sorry about what's gonna happen to you and your ROMA boys. Davie Boy was just a preview."

Christian ripped his wrist away from Dax's hand and stared down at him. "The next time we cross paths, Dax, you won't even see me coming."

CHAPTER 67

Three Million Mistakes

It was a long cab ride home from downtown. Christian hadn't been back to his place since the day he picked up his money. The cab pulled up in front of Christian's house and he was confused to see his gran's car still parked in the driveway. *Had she not left yet?*

He ran up to the car and saw that the trunk was partially opened; one of her suitcases leaned against the back of it. He opened the trunk wider and saw more of his gran's bags.

It was when he walked into the house that his gut feeling was confirmed; something wasn't right. The place was in a shambles. It appeared as though someone had rummaged through everything.

"Hello?"

Nobody answered.

Christian ran in and out of every room; all of them were torn apart. He picked up the phone and dialed Liam.

"Hello?"

"Li. You're home. Is everything OK at your house?"

"I guess. Why?"

"The money?"

"It's safe."

Christian looked at the counter and saw a yellow package. "I gotta go."

"What's wro—"

Christian hung up the phone and frantically opened the package that was labeled *Chinny.* It had a video tape in it. Beside the package, in a see-through plastic bag, was another video tape that was labeled *tape #2.*

He put the first tape in the VCR from the package and pressed play.

The first thing Christian saw were bushes and trees. Abruptly, a man in a mask came in front of the camera and started speaking.

"You don't know me. But I'm quite sure you know who I run with. You fucked with the wrong people. Here's the conditions. The whole purse, in three days."

The camera swung towards another man in a mask. Christian's heart dropped. The man held his gran with his arm around her neck. He held a gun to her head and she looked terrified.

The man behind the camera was laughing. *"Do it man, do it!"*

The man holding on to Christian's gran turned the gun around in his hand and started motioning the butt end toward her temple. He brought it close, then pulled it away, over and over as he laughed. Finally, he smashed it into the side of her head and threw her to the ground.

"Three million. Three days."

The tape cut out.

Christian was on the verge of vomiting. He stood up feeling helpless and started pacing. *Three days? Three days from when?* He didn't know when this tape was dropped off and there was no time stamp on it. This was the surprise Dax was talking about.

He quickly turned and looked down at the second tape. *Why was there a second tape?*

Christian ejected the first tape and slid the second one into the VCR.

Again, a man in a mask sat in front of the camera, but this time it was indoors. He recognized the voice. It was Dax Max.

"Chinny, Chinny, Chinny. So here's the thing. I didn't know you weren't going to be going home for quite some time. If I knew, I might have tried harder to get you the first tape. When you called me today to meet you, I realized you never saw the first tape we delivered to your house. That's a damn shame. This shit you're about to see was already done when you called me, anyway. The funny thing is, this tape that you are currently watching was delivered while me and you were meeting at the fucking coffee shop. If in the unlikely chance that you did pay up everything at our meeting…thanks…and just take the next part of this video as a life lesson."

The video cut to sometime earlier. Dax stood there in his mask and Christian's gran was on her knees. She was tied up with duct tape around her mouth. Her face was badly bruised and her clothes were askew.

"Whatcha think of granny?" Dax said to the man behind the camera.

The cameraman laughed and said, *"For a senior citizen, she was a decent ride."*

"She was, wasn't she? Dax said.

Dax removed the tape from her mouth and put a gun to the back of her head. *"You got anything to say to your grandson?"*

Tears were streaming down her face as she pushed out the words. *"Chrissy."* She swallowed deeply. *"Chrissy . . . you are . . . you are not one of them."*

Dax leaned down and put his face cheek to cheek with Gran. *"Three million dollars. It won't stop here, Chrissy. But you can make this end."*

Dax pushed Gran's head forward and fired a bullet into her skull.

The tape cut out.

PART 3

CHAPTER 68

Eviction

January 1997

Liam sat on the couch, which he now owned, while his father sat in the recliner. He finally had control over the biggest gift his grandpa gave them, their home. He didn't give his father any choice in the matter.

"So this is how it's going to be, son?"

"You got one hundred thousand over and above the mortgage, right in your pocket. You'll be fine."

"Yeah. I'll be fine." Liam's dad had a flask in his hand and a bag at his feet. A broken man sitting at the mercy of his only living son. He pulled out a cigarette and searched his pockets for a light. Liam reached into his own pocket, pulled out a lighter, and tossed it to him.

Liam pulled out a smoke too; after his father lit his, he tossed the lighter back to Liam.

"I know I wasn't a good father."

"Before or after Mom went to jail?"

"What do you mean by that?"

"Never mind. You *were* once a good father. Just not to me."

"Boy, I don't wanna argue. I'm sorry if that's how you feel. You're my only blood left. I never loved either of you boys more or less."

They both paused and smoked their cigarettes while Liam's dad took swigs from his flask. His father got up out of his seat, picked up his duffel bag and headed to the door. He dropped the bag at the entrance and turned around.

"You remember that fishing trip I took you boys on before your mom got arrested. That was my last good memory. I was thinking, how about you and me go back down there to the lake. This time of year, it won't be busy at all. We can forget all this shit for a couple days."

His father looked back down at his duffel bag and shoveled his flask into the inside pocket of his jacket. "Wish we could have done it again while Sammy was still here. We haven't even had our first beer together. What do you say?"

Liam looked away from his father. The mixed emotions in his body were overwhelming. The relationship he longed to have with his father in the previous years, at that moment, collided with the future, which didn't have one piece of his father in it. He was on the verge of letting down his guard and once again embracing the soft-hearted boy he used to be. A small part of him wanted to give in and take his father up on the offer. But a larger part of him dictated what he had to do.

Liam looked up at his father and shook his head. "Dad, you're too late. I waited a long time. But you're too late. I've always hated fishing anyways . . . and those stupid trips."

"Why do you hate me, son?"

"Why have you *always* hated me, Dad?"

Liam's father shrugged and bowed his head. "I've always loved you, boy." He picked up his duffel bag and walked out the door.

CHAPTER 69

Confined

It was a long, grueling four months that Davie Boy was forced to make his hospital room his home. He spent weeks in a coma, and the rest of the time he focused on rehabilitation, both mental and physical. He could have been killed, and the fact that he wasn't was Dax Max's big mistake. Maybe as much as it was Christian's mistake not killing Dax when he had the chance.

He may not have been able to walk away from the beating he took that day, but at least he was breathing on his own and could open his eyes. He pulled himself up in the bed by the metal triangle bar above him, and anticipated his discharge.

Despite it all, what really hurt—more than the broken bones—was the loss of his friend. He didn't get to say goodbye to Sammy at his funeral. Davie Boy loved him. The kid would be up at the Creek more often than anyone else. He just read comics and minded his own business. His situation was sad, but his innocence was a thing of beauty. While most people were poisoned by the hard truths of life, it was almost like Sammy was immune to them and as a result always saw the world through a child's eyes. When Davie Boy was alone with him, he would feel that same innocence momentarily. He longed for that, and Sammy gave it to him just by being Sammy.

Davie Boy was happy to finally be in his own clothes. His legs were in braces and his left arm was wrapped in a sling. All of that was nothing compared to the pain he felt every time he inhaled. They said there was nothing they could do about the broken ribs and it would take many months for them to fully heal. However, he resolved not to wear his pain outwardly. Davie Boy always prided himself in being a man's man.

"Hey, Davie." His nurse entered the room. She was a real hot one, too, and was the only high point of his stay. "Your friend is here."

Liam walked in behind her. "How you feelin'?"

"Just get me that there wheelchair and let's split."

Liam rolled Davie Boy through the hospital. He took in the smells and the same old sights of the hustle and bustle he was forced to see every day; hopefully one last time. He was more than anxious to go back to his normal life, but it was bitter sweet—he was leaving, but on wheels.

They reached the truck that Liam had recently purchased. He helped Davie Boy into the front seat and lifted his wheelchair into the truck bed.

Once driving, Liam turned to Davie Boy. "Any idea yet how long you're gonna be in that chair."

"My back's pretty messed up and I still can't feel shit from the waist down. Doc's can't guarantee I'm gonna get feeling back or walk properly . . . if I walk at all."

"Last time I saw you, you said—"

"Last time I didn't really know shit. Now it don't look too good. I did get some counseling, too. I learned I can't dwell on this here shit. I just have to adjust to a new way of living. It sucks, but I can't focus on it."

"Your folks know?"

"They called, but I didn't take it. So I dunno. Not even sure if they came back to town yet."

They pulled up in front of the trail leading to the Creek. Davie Boy grunted and groaned a little while Liam helped him out of the seat and into the wheelchair. Still, the minimal complaints didn't denote the high level of pain that was actually shooting through his body.

Davie Boy wheeled himself down the trail as Liam tried to keep up. He didn't want help and had something to prove; even if every bump was like a sword in his side.

Once they were at their spot they only saw a pile of ashes covering the fire pit. Where the tree house once was, there were only some odd pieces of wood nailed to the tree. The shed was partially intact, but most of it was dismantled and torn apart. That was the only portion of the Creek that wasn't destroyed at the hands of Davie Boy.

Davie Boy rolled himself to the fire pit. "It ain't fair."

Liam approached him and crouched down on one knee. He rested his arm on Davie Boy's chair.

"Your brother didn't deserve this here shit. I shoulda been there with him, Li."

"It's not your fault," Liam said.

Davie Boy turned to Liam. He didn't normally shed tears under any circumstances, but he couldn't hold them back. "It *is* my fault. I could have talked to him. We talked lots. I coulda got him home."

Liam put his arm around Davie Boy. "Don't do this to yourself."

Davie Boy rolled himself over to the tree that was etched with ROMA. "Almost every day he sat here . . . you ever think about if my brother Pete was still around, and if that there shit that went down with your mom and Sammy never happened? Where do you think we'd be today?"

"Yeah, Pete and Sammy were tight, just like you and me are tight."

"If we all just grew up like normal kids. If my parents were real parents, and your parents were real parents. Maybe we all would be walking down that there aisle like you did at graduation. Maybe we all would have a future. Now look at me. I'm a fucking gimp."

"Davie Boy . . ."

"I shouldn't have been such a little shit to Pete."

"Davie Boy . . . you can't—"

"Can't what, Li?" Davie Boy rolled his chair back and shoved his hands in his pockets. "I can't have regrets? I can't dream that things could have been different?"

"You're just torturing yourself."

Davie Boy continued to search each of his pockets frantically. "Do you got a fuckin' dart?"

"I don't have no smokes."

"Fuck." Davie Boy started to cry. He quickly wiped his eyes and continued. "What am I gonna do, man? I can't live this way. I wanna kill that fucker who put me here, but what am I supposed to do in this here chair?"

"Dax Max more than likely wants us dead too. Chin wants everyone to lay low. Things have been pretty quiet on both ends for quite some time."

"Calm before the storm, that's what this is, you know? Question is, who brings on that there storm?"

"I here ya, Davie Boy. Something's gotta give. What happened to Sammy can't go unanswered. Chin will have somethin' though. So, you're right, who *does* bring on the storm?"

"Let's hope it's Chinny. Catch all these fuckers off guard . . . and execute the lot of 'em."

"Amen to that."

"Just so you know, if ya don't wanna . . . I mean . . . I ain't takin' nothing away from you. But if ya don't wanna, I'll gladly be the one to blast the person who killed Sammy."

"When the time comes, and I can't pull that trigger—"

"If you can't, I guarantee you, I'll be the one that does."

CHAPTER 70

Propositions

ROMA were all supposed to be on the down low, but Christian didn't know if they actually were following that instruction. He definitely was, though. He hadn't received any calls or heard anything from Dax or his crew. While that was good for the time being, he knew it was only a matter of time. Four months of silence was an unusually long time.

A large tent was behind him, and multiple bags were strewn on the ground around it. There were some burnt logs that lay in the middle of some large rocks. He sat with his legs dangling over a cliff on A.C.'s island, watching the waves smash against the rocks as if they were crushing them; but the rocks stood their ground. Christian was unshaven and his formerly shaved head looked like a fuzzy mess. He never dreamed he could set foot on that island again, but there was nowhere else to go. He went against everything he had promised himself and hated going back to A.C. But this wasn't about pride or vendettas—it was about survival. If he was nowhere to be found, there would be less of a chance Dax would take any further action. But at the very least, Christian was only delaying it.

He heard footsteps crunching through the dried leaves. "You could say this isn't my business. But it actually is."

Christian turned and saw A.C standing behind him. "What do you want?"

"Christian. What do *you* want? I could take him out. I can make him disappear. It's not hard."

The beauty of his gran's face was burned in Christian's mind, and A.C.'s proposal would be so much easier than having to carry the burden on his own.

"No. I need more," Christian said.

"More?"

"You told me, if you lived that night, you would dedicate your life to redeeming yourself—for my mother."

"Christian. The man will kill you on sight."

"Supply ACB to me exclusively."

"You? You're not groomed for that kind of responsibility yet. Besides, what the hell do drugs and money matter anymore, after what he did to your grandmother?"

"It fucking matters, A.C.! I don't want to just kill him or have him killed. I want to take every ounce of pride and dignity from him first—just like he did my gran. I want chop him down to the lowest point of low, then gut him slowly while he screams for mercy and I taste his blood. Then, and only then, I will kill him."

"You have to control yourself, Christian. If you don't have control over your emotions, you're going to be the one who's gutted."

Christian shook his head and rose to his feet, still facing away from A.C. "I can handle the responsibility, if you give me what I want. You'll help me, I can get others to help me . . ."

"Can't do it, son. You know how much money that would cost me? You don't have the network to handle it. It's for your protection, too."

Christian turned and faced him. "I'm in trouble. I need this."

A.C pondered for a second, then slightly nodded his head and shrugged.

"It will only be temporary," Christian said. "Give me six months to establish what I know I can do. You can always put an end to it. Please."

"You're not getting it exclusively. But what I'll do is cut the life line to Russ Baxter's organization. You got three months. That's it. It will cost me a lot of money, kid. I will do this because I'm sticking to my word. That's the only reason."

"I can accept that. I won't disappoint you."

"Since I am going to do this, you need to lose your animosity toward me, for now, and hear me out."

Christian nodded.

"You want this role, you need to take on everything that goes with it. Everyone is your enemy when you're in control. Even your so-called friends. You aren't working at McDonalds as a manager, you're running the streets. You have to instill fear in the enemy. Especially the ones you label as your friend. You can't be a kid anymore, Christian. You want this, then you need to be ruthless."

Christian said nothing and took in A.C.'s words. He was in a very rare position that a lot of the guys in the underworld would have loved to be in—absorbing advice from the king himself. He wasn't even thinking about who this man actually was to him personally. At that moment, he was solely using A.C. for the role he played in this dangerous business.

"I need you to get it out of your mind that I'm backing you, even if I am," A.C. said. "That right there is a weakness. You'll be your own man, with my silent help in the background. Never throw out my name to strengthen your position. You don't just own the street. Anyone . . . friend or foe that crosses your path, you own them, too. Remember that."

***

The wheels were in motion and Christian strongly believed the pieces of the puzzle would fall into place. After the talk with A.C., Christian returned to BPI.

He now had the full support of A.C. Brooklyn, but it didn't just stop there. His next move was a very dangerous one in a dangerous area: Deer Park. By now there were people who knew the name Chinny and so he had to be careful.

He stood in front of a bar that was owned by the Indo Nation. He couldn't help but feel nervous because these guys didn't mess around. For all he knew, they would kill him the second they saw him.

When he entered, it was busy. He felt out of place because most of the patrons were of East Indian decent. He spotted the man he was there to talk to and approached his table.

Sonny the Money was what people called him. He was one of the top guys for the Indo Nation who had formed an alliance with their former arch enemies, The GN Soldiers. He wore a black beanie and his muscular physique bulged out of his tight, long-sleeved shirt. He repeatedly rubbed his hand down his evening shadow of a beard as he conversed with the men at his table. He looked up and spotted Christian approaching.

"What the hell? You have a death wish, partner?"

Christian knew his time was short so he just blurted out. "Your crew and the GN's have never had direct access to ACB."

Sonny stood up stunned and looked around at some of the guys that he was with. "You *do* have a death wish."

"What's your margin once it finally gets to you?"

"Are you suicidal, motherfucker? You come in my club and—"

"Now you're owned by The GN Soldiers. You let the GN's win."

Sonny placed his hand on the butt of the pistol protruding from the side of his pants. He was about to draw it, but paused when Christian spoke his next words.

"What if I could make it so that the Indo Nation was the main distributor of ACB, here on BPI? Direct from the source."

Sonny tilted his head to the side and slowly took his hand off the gun. "I'm listening."

"I got a business proposition for you."

***

It was really hard to pinpoint the exact time when things got this far. Going head-to-head with the biggest gangsters in the city wasn't what Christian ever intended. It was just how it turned out. This temporary fix was beginning to look more permanent.

He was reaching out to some individuals who may share a common interest. People who he felt he could use to get what he wanted. He had to pick and choose carefully, though. He still didn't trust anyone; and, more importantly, couldn't.

These hustlers either turned violent on sight, or they told you things they wanted you to hear and then stabbed you in the back, literally. It was just how it all worked, especially when you were coming up. Being that Christian was younger than a lot of his competition, he wasn't always taken seriously, but he still refused to be manipulated or taken advantage of.

Christian had one more piece of business. He had to make a phone call. He had a plan that could either work in his favor or be his demise. He had to take the risk because he had nothing to lose.

He was responsible for the murders of some high profile players. Even if he stood down, he would still face the consequences for his actions. He had to stand up and do what he could to try to conquer the backlash that was inevitable.

Russ Baxter's crew didn't just stop at the guys who were working under their new self-proclaimed leader; he had crews that branched out all over BPI, and also a large part of Stoneminster Falls.

The one thing that Christian knew was that a lot of these guys didn't take too kindly to the fact that Dax Max assumed the position he was in without any sort of discussion, so Christian could possibly leverage that and use it in his favour.

There was a man named Deevon Kelly who used to be connected very closely to Russ Baxter. He ran some crews back in Christian's hometown, Stoneminster Falls. If there was anyone who would hear Christian out, it would be a fellow mainlander.

Christian took a piece of paper out of his pocket and looked at the number scribbled on it. He dialed the payphone, not really knowing if Deevon would even talk to him.

"Yep," The voice on the other end said.

"I'm looking for Deevon Kelly."

"Who's this?"

"Chinny."

"Chinny? *The* Chinny, from BPI?"

"There's not many with my name."

"You gotta be jokin'."

"This Deevon?"

"Yeah it's Deevon. You made some dangerous enemies—me being one."

"Hear me out."

"What's there to hear, Chinny?"

"Where do you get ACB, Deevon?"

"Yeah . . . ok . . . this conversation is ending now," Deevon said.

"Dax's pipeline is done. I control it now."

"That's bullshit. How'd you get this number anyway?"

"Call my bluff then and you won't even touch the pink powder again, unless you are a junkie. But if you hear me out, you will own the distribution in Stoney."

"You got my attention, but I have a short attention span. Spill it."

"Dax Max is trying to take money that I earned. Dax Max killed someone very close to me. I'll be taking over BPI with or without you, one way or another. With you, we can dominate. And that is it."

"You wanna take out Dax?"

"Firstly, yes."

"Where do you want this to go down?" Deevon said.

"My connection owns an abandoned warehouse in a very remote area of the city. I'll get word to Dax that I want to set up a meeting there about the money. He'll have others there and probably want to end me."

"Let me sit on this. Call me in a couple days."

It was all a shot in the dark. He was disclosing information that could jeopardize everyone who was on his side. But it was a plan that made sense and one that could be a revolution, a new world order . . . an empire. Vengeance had taken him to a level he never thought would matter. But it did matter. He wasn't going to lose.

If he failed, he would be the reason that there could be seven graves, with each one of the ROMA member's names on them.

Explaining this all to Deevon was a challenge, especially over the phone. Russ told him once only ten percent of conversation was verbal. He was at a disadvantage not being able to see the other ninety percent.

CHAPTER 71

Set Her Free

After his conversation with Deevon, Christian made his way over to the park that was famous for its large duck pond, where Victoria finally agreed to meet him. He arrived early and found a bench to do some thinking to absorb everything he had been putting into motion. He was unsure if he was in over his head or not. After all, he was pretty new to this way of life. He hadn't even mentioned any of this plan to ROMA, but he intended to be pretty vague about it to them anyway. *Everyone is the enemy.* He took what A.C. said seriously. They were all in danger, so he knew he had to act fast.

Victoria appeared in the distance, calmly walking down the path. There was a time when he would have been ecstatic about this meeting, but today he dreaded it.

Victoria stood in front of Christian. She was wearing a pair of dark circular sunglasses and a silk scarf around her neck. Her stomach was bulging and she looked as beautiful as ever. She was always so classy. The feeling in his gut that used to be comforting was now painful.

She sat down beside him and Christian leaned forward, resting his elbows on his knees and his chin on his palms.

"You need to tell me what's going on, Christian."

"I can't."

"I agreed to get away. But I'm not going to Edwin's. I'm going home to my mom and dad's."

Christian felt he should have asked Victoria to leave town a couple of months ago, but he didn't know how to. But now that he was planning on bringing ROMA out of the woodwork, it was imperative that anyone close to him would not get caught in the line of fire.

"It won't be long." Christian ran his hand over his shaved head.

"Tell me, Chris. Why do I need to leave? I tried calling your gran, but she hasn't returned my calls. She was supposed to have moved here by now."

"Really? She was moving here?" Christian pondered for a second. "Oh. That was the surprise."

"Oh my God. You didn't even know that? She called me a couple days after I dropped her at your house. She told me you guys weren't talking, but didn't tell me why. What could you possibly do to make Gran not want to speak with you anymore?"

"I'm not getting into it, Vic."

"Not surprised. Anyways, I'm worried. She always returns my calls."

"She's on vacation because she wanted to get away for a while. But enough with the questions, Vic. Just trust me."

Victoria looked out at the water. There was a couple on the bench a few feet away; the man's arm was around the woman and they were both giggling.

"You've never contacted me even once to ask about the baby," Victoria said.

Christian pulled a cigarette out of his pack. "Guess I'm tired of being called an asshole and hung up on."

"If you don't want to be a part of our baby's life, I won't ask you for anything. I just need to know before she arrives."

"She?"

"Yes."

"Vic. You will both be taken care of, I promise."

Victoria went silent and glared at him. Her mouth quivered and her lips tightened. Christian was unable to see the full expression on her face because it was hidden behind her glasses. He reached over and gently removed her sunglasses. Her eyes were soaked and red.

"What's going on, Vic?"

"I loved you, Christian."

"Me too. I mean, I still do."

"I dunno. Maybe it was my fault. A two year age difference is a big one when you're young. I should have known better."

Christian rubbed his face from his forehead to his chin and looked down at the cement. "Maybe in time—"

"Don't." Victoria looked over at him and studied his face. "What do you do?"

"Do?"

"For a living. Be honest for once."

"I work for Edwin . . . on the island."

"Yeah right, and that's why I have to leave. Bullshit. I don't know who you are. Where did *my* Christian go?" Victoria got up, picked up her purse and began to walk away; she turned one last time. "Whatever happened between you and your gran, I hope you'll fix it. You shattered *her* heart, too."

The hurt on her face destroyed him. The last two people that were important to him in his life had been lost; one of them permanently. He had to do everything he could to bury it because he could not show any weakness. Russ Baxter had told him that love is a weakness. Since then, he had come to the conclusion that it was hate that would conquer his enemies.

CHAPTER 72

Loyalty

Dax Max smoked a cigar and sat at the desk his former boss used to sit at. Almost mirroring Russ Baxter, he had a scotch on the rocks in his hand and had his legs up on the desk, leaning back in his chair. He blew smoke rings, partially closed his eyes, and breathed deeply in through his nose that he had slightly raised to the ceiling. The muffled music of the club could be heard through his door and the sound got louder when someone opened it.

A man poked his head in. "You got a call."

"Who is it?"

"Deevon Kelly."

"Yeah? OK. Close the door behind you."

Dax removed his feet from the desk and sat forward. He picked up the phone and tapped the ashes from his cigar into an ashtray. "What up, D.K?"

"You got a problem. We need to talk about that boy, Chinny."

"What about him?"

"He called me. He's gunnin' for you and wants my help."

"Stupid fuckin' kid." Dax laughed. "I knew this would be comin'. I was plannin' something pretty soon anyway, so the timing's right."

"What do you want me to do?" Deevon said.

"He have a plan?"

"Yep."

"Then go along with it. Be his buddy."

"Then what?"

"You know. Maybe I'll jump on the ferry tomorrow and come your way. We can talk about our own plan then. Three million dollars says we need to get this shit done once and for all."

"What's in it for me?"

"Three percent?"

"Three? Nah, five points and I'll see you tomorrow."

"Done."

CHAPTER 73

Remorse

Braeden sat at the kitchen table in the upstairs of his house that was brightly lit by sunshine streaming through the window. The sunshine, however, wasn't what he wanted to bask in when it came to the mood he was in after all that had happened.

His nana sat on her single chair with her oxygen tank on the ground by her side, watching TV. She was lost in her own dark world of dementia.

Braeden got up from the kitchen table and approached Chloe's bedroom door, which was closed. He put his ear against it and could hear some soft music playing. He could also hear her finishing up a conversation with someone on the phone. He wasn't certain, but it sounded like she was talking about some boy.

He lightly tapped on the door.

"Come in."

Braeden opened the door and saw his little sister with cotton between her toes, painting her nails.

"You're growing up too fast, baby girl." Braeden sat down on the edge of the bed and put his hand on her shin.

"Whatever," Chloe said.

"Who's this dude you were talking about on the phone?"

"Braeden! You were eavesdropping?"

Braeden smiled and shook his head. "No, I just might have accidentally heard a small piece of your conversation. Just be careful of boys. We really suck, sometimes."

"I know, I know."

Chloe continued to paint her nails and Braeden's attention turned to a picture on her white and pink dresser. It was probably the last family picture that was taken with his parents, and it pained him to see where his life had gone since those days. They would be so disappointed in him.

"Let me tell you something, Chloe. If anything were to happen to me, you need to look out for yourself. I mean, Nana would probably have to be put in a home, and then you need to—"

Chloe immediately stopped painting her nails and her head darted up. "Is something wrong?"

"No, no. Nothing's wrong. I guess I been thinking about mom and dad lots. I mean you never know what can happen, you understand?"

"Yeah."

"So I just want to always be prepared. You're beautiful and you're so smart . . . damn, you started being smarter than me, years ago. Use all of that."

"Why are you all of a sudden saying this?" Chloe said.

"I just want to be able to say that I've actually taught you somethin'."

Chloe moved closer to Braeden, swung her legs off the bed so they were dangling down beside his, and put her arm around him. "You've taught me lots, Broskie."

Braeden chuckled. "Don't call me Broskie. Anyway, Chloe, always be a strong woman. Don't ever let anyone, especially any man, say you can't do somethin'. Anything a man can do, a woman can do. Sometimes . . . actually, most of the time, even better. Always hold your own against anything life throws at you. And be kind to people.

Even if they're strangers. You don't gotta give the change in your pocket to every homeless person who asks, but at least make eye contact with them when you turn them down. Love people before you judge them. Most importantly, love yourself. That's all I got."

"OK . . . Are you sure there's nothing wrong? You're starting to scare me a little."

"I just love you and will always worry about my little sister. There is nothing in this fuckin' world that I love more than you."

"Aw, Braeden." Chloe wrapped both her arms around him. "I love you too."

Braeden got up and made his way to the door. He didn't look at her again because he didn't want to reveal the tears that were forming in his eyes. "I'll let you get back to doing what you're doing . . . I'll see you later."

Once he left Chloe's room, he walked toward the basement door and opened it. Before walking down the stairs he glanced over at his nana.

"Nana, I'm going to head downstairs. Do you need anything?"

No response.

He let her be and made his way down to the basement.

On his coffee table was a pen and pad, and beside them lay a gun. He sat on the couch with his gaze affixed on the three items that lay among the other meaningless junk.

He leaned toward the coffee table and picked up the pen and pad, and did a quick skim of the short paragraph that was scribbled on the page. He signed his name at the bottom.

He put the pen and pad down and picked up the gun. He studied it as he held it closer, the barrel pointing at his face. He picked up a cushion and held it up against the side of his head and pressed the gun against the cushion. He closed his eyes and took a deep breath.

Who was he kidding? He was too scared to die, let alone blast himself in the head. He could if he wanted to, though, that was the point; for that one second he had control over his own destiny.

He was startled by the outside door of the basement swinging open. He quickly took the gun and placed it on the table, covering it up with the cushion.

"Where the hell have you been?" Jordy walked in with Jess and Kirt entering behind him.

"Braed. We been leaving messages," Jess said.

"I needed time."

"Time? We all feel shitty about Sammy, you need to get over it. It's our time now," Jordy said.

"What are you talking about, brah?"

"We're getting back at them tonight," Jess said.

"Getting back at who?" Braeden was feeling frazzled.

Jordy looked over at the answering machine beside the phone. There was a red light blinking. "You haven't even been checking the damn messages?"

"What's going on, Jord?"

"We're meeting up with Chinny tonight. Check the fricken messages, then be there."

The three of them left and Braeden looked down at the cushion. He could only assume that they thought Sammy was payback for Russ and Fiend. Those assholes deserved it, but this just wasn't sitting right. He knew what he had to do.

He took the gun from under the cushion, clicked the safety on and placed it in his pants, pulling his t-shirt over it. He ripped the paper off the pad, folded it, and buried it in his back pocket and started walking toward the entrance door. Standing just outside, he turned around and scanned his home, one more time. Everything happened because he refused to go to jail. But now, he had to right some wrongs, whether he was going to jail or not.

CHAPTER 74

Pest Control

Christian had his gran's car hoisted up on a car jack in the backyard. It was a big night, and he would do anything he could to ease his mind. Even something as minor as changing a car tire would help with the nerves that pulsated in his body.

He crouched down and jammed the tire iron into one of the bolts of the old tire and stepped on it to loosen it. He bent over and started to remove the bolt and felt a presence behind him. He looked up.

"Where have you been?" Christian said.

"There's somethin' I need to do, brah."

Christian stood up, leaving the tire iron connected to the bolt. He brushed his hands together to dust them off and pulled the tire iron off the bolt.

"What's on your mind, Braed? You haven't been answering calls."

"I can't live with this shit, Chin."

Christian pulled up two lawn chairs and sat down on one of them. He motioned for Braeden to take a seat.

"You're worrying me, Braed. You look like shit."

Braeden didn't sit, but he pulled a folded piece of paper out of his pocket. "You need to give this to Liam."

"What is it?"

"Read it." Braeden took a couple steps back.

Christian took the piece of paper, his eyes remaining on Braeden as he unfolded it.

Li, there ain't nothing I can say here that is going to bring your brother back. There ain't nothing I can say to make you forgive me. I'm sorry for what I did. You need to know the truth. I took your brother's life. Nobody else but me. I can give reasons but there ain't no point. There ain't no excuses. By the time you read this I'll be gone.

Braeden

Christian looked up with his eyes wide open. He rose to his feet and his hand tightened around the tire iron. He decided to place it on the ground, leaning against his chair. Braeden looked at him with tear-filled eyes.

"I'm at a loss for words?" Christian said.

"After this, I'm gonna go to the coppers and turn myself in."

Christian stood in silence. The blood drained from his face. He put his hand on his forehead and glanced down at the tire iron.

"Chin, I know you are about to lose your shit. Let it be. It was all me. I did it because I didn't want to go to jail . . . now I realize that's the very place where I belong."

Christian slowly raised his head. One of his closest friends, who had become like a brother, was now no better than his worst enemy. Betrayal was one of the most horrible acts that a brother could inflict on a sibling.

"Talk to me, Chin. You ain't gonna be implicated in anything."

"Implicated?" Christian said. "Implicated? You killed Sammy. You might have pulled the trigger, but I put the gun in your hand."

"Copper's will never know you were involved. I promise."

"Are you stupid? We're connected to multiple murders. We're involved in a massive distribution of narcotics. That alone could put us all away for life, and then some. They *will* connect the dots. They already are, for fuck sakes."

Braeden started to weep. Christian stood up and walked toward him, putting his hand on his shoulder. "Braed, no one needs to know about Sammy. What you want to do is the exact reason we agreed Sammy had to be eliminated."

Braeden didn't look up.

"I'll hang onto this letter," Christian said, why don't you go home and just think about this for one more night. You owe me this. You don't have to come to the thing tonight."

Braeden turned around and slowly began to leave. "Alright, Chin."

Christian took a partial sigh of relief, but Braeden stopped again, still facing away from Christian. Through his broken voice, he said, "I peddled a little pot in school. I never hurt nobody. I take care of Nana and my little sister every fuckin' day. I'm a good guy. I never asked for this. Somehow I need to make things—"

Braeden was cut off by the jarring blow of the tire iron. He immediately collapsed to the ground and fell to his hands and knees. Christian stood above him, raised the tire iron in the air, and brought it down again, connecting with the back of Braeden's cranium. The clinking sound of the blows was solid and abrupt. Braeden was bleeding from the back of his head and lay face down on the lawn beside Christian's car. Christian raised the tire iron one more time and contemplated crushing the side of Braeden's head for good measure, but stopped. Braeden lay motionless, yet Christian could see that he was still breathing.

Christian retrieved a tarp and threw it over the body of his good friend. He then ran into his house and picked up the phone, frantically dialing a number.

"Hello?"

"This is Chinny. I need you to do one more thing for me."

"Whatcha need?"

Christian explained the situation to the man on the other end of the line. The twenty thousand dollars Christian said he'd pay made it so there were no questions asked. He just needed to get the situation dealt with immediately.

When he thought nothing more could go wrong before the big meet that night, he heard a pounding at his front door. When he opened it he saw a man standing there. He was in plain clothes, but he flashed his badge.

"Christian Solomon, I'm Detective James Monty. You need to come down to the station."

"Am I being arrested?"

"Not yet. But I *could* place you under arrest. So I'd suggest you just come voluntarily."

With Braeden lying unconscious in the backyard, Christian decided to go without a fight.

CHAPTER 75

Mutual Friends

When they sat in the little interview room at the police station, the detective, who said nothing during the drive, just looked at Christian without asking him anything. It was nerve racking for Christian. What was worse, he didn't know if he was going to be let go in time for the meeting with Dax Max that night.

The detective finally broke his silence, "There's been a lot of shit going down lately. You seem to be the common denominator."

"Am I going to need a lawyer, detective?"

"You won't be needing a lawyer. You want a coffee or something?"

Christian looked up at the camera in the ceiling and tapped his fingers on the table.

"That's not on," Detective Monty said. "No one can hear us either."

"Why am I here?"

"Why don't you light up a cigarette? I can tell you're itching for one." The detective pulled out a piece of paper and listed off the names of everyone in ROMA.

"Those boys are under surveillance as we speak by some officers I've hand-picked. Only for the next hour or two. Everyone except Braeden Cunningham for . . . well, I think you know why."

Christian immediately pulled out a cigarette and lit it. He was astonished. How did he know about Braeden already? This was not good.

"Why am I here?"

"You have some friends in high places, don't you, kid?"

Christian shook his head.

"So do I. I think you and I have some mutual friends."

"Why am I here? And why are my friends being watched?"

The detective's cell phone rang and he answered it.

"Yep. OK. Thanks." The detective put the phone back in his suit jacket.

"You're here and your friends are being watched because you all needed a solid alibi. You're free to go now."

"I don't get it."

"You don't have to worry about Detective Ross Williams anymore."

CHAPTER 76

First Order of Business

The six of them were gathered once again around the fire pit, which very well could have been the last time. All of them were sober for once. They needed to be sharp and under their best judgment. None of them made eye contact with the other. They were hypnotized by the raging flames that flickered off each of their faces.

There were no words exchanged. Power enabled them. Vengeance lead them. Hatred devoured them.

There were brief questions that had arisen earlier about Braeden's absence. Christian passed it off by saying it was something they couldn't worry about right now if they wanted to accomplish the impossible.

The dark secret that only he and Braeden shared had to remain hidden. Sammy was dead. It was a hard decision, but it had to be done.

He had to get used to difficult decisions. There would be plenty more starting tonight.

Christian walked over to Davie Boy and all their eyes followed him. He looked down at him sitting in the wheel chair. "You know you can sit this one out."

"Not a chance." His arm was not in a sling anymore. He pulled out a semi-automatic pistol and tapped it against his left breast. "Sammy was just as much my brother as he was Liam's. Let's go kill this here motherfucker."

Without another word, Christian walked toward the entrance of the Creek and they all followed one by one, with Liam pushing Davie Boy in the wheelchair. They were soldiers on their way to combat.

***

They arrived at the warehouse and the parking lot was deserted. Weeds pushed their way through the cracked cement. A rusty, broken down wire fence surrounded the thick bushes and trees which gave the location perfect cover.

They stood in a semi-circle and Christian paced, turning in a circle and scanning the area in the distance.

"Right there." Christian pointed to a light that was flashing off and on in the woods.

"What's that?" Liam said.

"Our backup."

He had been extremely secretive about the plan and now a part of it was finally revealed. All the guys were motivated to succeed for common reasons. For Christian, though, it was Gran that was the only motivation to put Dax Max to sleep permanently. He knew this wasn't just about the money for his enemies either. Dax was coming there with the same intentions as his own. It would come down to who was smarter and quicker.

The sound of cars in the distance got louder. Not a soul came out there, so it could only have been who they were supposed to meet.

Two SUVs and one large van finally pulled into the parking lot and screeched to a stop a few feet away from where ROMA was congregating. All the doors opened and ten to twelve men started flooding out. They walked towards ROMA who were standing in a united front.

Dax, with his men behind him, came face to face with Christian. "You gotta be the stupidest motherfucker I know."

Christian didn't blink.

"I really thought there was more to you, Chinny. Do you get what's gonna happen to you and your little friends?"

Christian remained silent, his eyes not leaving Dax's.

It was then that there was rustling in the bushes, and what looked like another ten men started to emerge from the woods. They were heavily armed.

"Well, well," Dax said. He backed up and looked around, and, like Christian, did not show an ounce of emotion. He too wouldn't be intimidated. "What do we have here?"

The men stood behind ROMA and spread out.

Dax laughed. "Deevon Kelly."

"At your service." Deevon raised his shot gun and the rest of his crew followed. There was the clacking and ratcheting sounds of firearms as they all pointed their weapons—but not at Dax.

ROMA all turned around and were met by multiple barrels pointing at their faces.

"We're fucked, Chin," Liam said. "This is our backup?"

All of them put their hands up, with the exception of Christian. Dax pulled out a gun of his own and pointed it at Christian's head.

"This seems familiar," Dax said. "Isn't this the third time you're facing one of our guns?"

Dax started walking around, not taking his weapon off Christian. "So what did you think was gonna happen, kid? This ain't the movies."

Christian still said nothing. The rest of his guys followed his lead.

Dax walked toward Jordy Baxter. One of Deevon's guys had a shot gun an inch away from his head.

"You know, Chinny, I gotta hand it to you. You're smart, just inexperienced. Shit, if only you stuck by Russ. You coulda been somebody." Dax now stood nose to nose with Jordy and he spit in his face.

Jordy wiped off the spit with the back of his hand and Dax placed his handgun on Jordy's thigh. "It's too bad you chose the wrong brother." Dax pulled the trigger and Jordy fell to the ground, writhing in pain.

"Stand him up." Dax put the gun back in his belt.

"Yo, Dax," Deevon said. "Maybe we should take this inside."

Dax turned away from Jordy who was now being held up by two of his men. He quickly pulled a knife from his belt, spun around and plunged it into Jordy's other thigh. Jordy shrieked and then gasped as Dax wrenched the blade out of his leg.

Christian tried to advance, but was quickly restrained by Dax's crew.

Dax approached Christian and stood in front of him again. "Here's how this is going to work. We are going to go inside and tie you all up." Dax glanced at one of his guys who was holding an ax. The guy threw the ax and Dax caught it by the handle.

"You are going to watch me dismember Russ's little brother. Don't worry. I'll try my best to keep him alive as long as possible. Just so he don't miss the show."

Deevon and Dax's crew forced the ROMA boys to the entrance of the warehouse.

Dax pushed the door open and they all entered.

"I haven't decided yet if the rest of your executions are going to be quick or slow. I got all night, though. Don't you love the suspense?"

It was pitch-black in the warehouse and one of the men pulled out a flashlight.

"Somebody find a damn light switch." Dax said.

Suddenly, the door slammed. The hollow building that was now in blackness echoed. There were three loud clicks and the place was lit.

"Thank you." Dax said. But his appreciation was quickly turned to shock as he now saw what was standing in the dark of the now-lit warehouse. Surrounding them was a group of men that outnumbered all of them put together. Their skin was dark and there looks were fierce. They too were all pointing weapons. Standing among them was Sonny the Money.

Christian spoke up for the first time since Dax arrived. "I think you know them. But if you don't know, let me introduce you to the Indo Nation."

"Drop your weapons!" One of them yelled.

Dax didn't have a choice. There was no way he had a chance against this many men who were strategically arrayed against them.

Dax put his hands up. "OK, OK, take it easy. We can talk this out."

"Weapons!" The Indo yelled again.

Dax turned back to his crew and gave a downward motion with his hand. One by one they all complied. Deevon and his crew, however, didn't.

Dax looked back at Deevon. "D.K., weapons," he said softly.

Deevon and his crew still didn't drop their weapons, but Deevon swung his back, leaning it on his shoulder. He stepped over Jordy who was on the floor and walked past Dax's men. The Indo Nation didn't move a muscle. Deevon walked towards Sonny with no regard to the barrels that were trained on his skull. He stood directly in front of Sonny.

"Deevon, what the fuck are you doing?" Dax said.

Deevon turned his head, looking at Dax. "I really am sincerely sorry Dax. It's just that . . . our boy Chinny here had a better offer. So fuck your five percent."

Sonny chuckled. "Deevon fucking Kelly. . . I never thought I'd see the day." Sonny reached out his hand and Deevon reciprocated.

"What the fuck!?" Dax yelled.

Deevon looked at Dax and then right past him. He nodded to his crew who still had their weapons drawn. They advanced past ROMA; this time they forced Dax and his boys to the middle of the room.

Christian, weaponless, walked nonchalantly towards them. "Get on your knees."

All but Dax started to go down to the ground. "Not you guys," Christian instructed Dax's men. "Just him," he said, pointing at Dax.

"Fuck you!" Dax yelled.

Deevon hit Dax in the head with the butt of his shotgun. Dax fell to his hands and knees. The double barrel of Deevon's shotgun was now buried in Dax's skull.

Christian removed the knife from the side of Dax's belt. He held the tip that was still stained with Jordy's blood against his throat. With a swift motion, he cut the t-shirt Dax was wearing and ripped it off of him without putting a scratch on Dax's body.

Christian returned to where Jordy was lying and removed his own shirt. He threw both shirts at Jordy. "Here, tie your legs up with this."

Christian picked up the ax and resumed his position in front of Dax. The rest of ROMA were right behind him.

"What did you say you were going to do to my boy over there?" Christian pointed at Jordy.

"Chinny. . ." Dax said.

"Did my grandma ask you to spare her life, Dax?

There was no response.

"Beg for your life!" Christian yelled.

Dax, who was now in a sitting position on the ground, said, "Go fuck yourself."

"Beg for your life!" He jabbed the end of the ax handle into Dax's temple, knocking him onto his back.

"We need to hold him down." Christian said.

Deevon signaled a few of his guys.

"No, not them." Christian turned towards Liam, Jess and Kirt. "You guys."

Christian stood among many powerful men. Some of which had wanted him dead at one time. He looked down at Dax and everything seemed to be going in slow motion. A.C.'s words echoed in his head. *Everyone must fear you.* He understood what his father meant now. Then there was that odd time he went to a church, he remembered a preacher once saying: *fear the Lord our Savior.* He never understood those words until now. The fear of God. That same fear was what he had to instill in everyone that surrounded him. To instill fear, he had to be ruthless.

"Turn him on his stomach." Christian said.

The three of them obliged. Liam was resting his weight partially on Dax's back and legs. The other two had a hold of his arms.

"Don't do this, Chinny." Dax said.

"Hold his arm out, Jess."

"What? No, dude."

"Hold his fucking arm out!" Christian rested the ax on his shoulder.

Jess complied, gripping Dax's elbow joint as Christian stomped on the back of Dax's hand to keep it in place.

"Please don't." Dax said.

His plea gave Christian satisfaction. This was a high he hadn't felt before or imagined he could feel. He raised the ax over his head and swung it down as hard as he could on Dax's forearm.

Dax howled and Jess and Kirt pushed themselves away from Dax's body, horrified.

"Holy fuck!" Jess yelled

Dax's body shook with pain as his almost-severed arm raised up with the lower half dangling obscenely onto the ground. It was only connected by what looked like a tendon. Christian quickly fixed that with another hard stomp, ripping it completely from Dax's muscle.

Christian pulled his shoe from the growing pool of blood and scanned the room. Some faces stared coldly, while others were visibly shocked.

Christian addressed the group. "I don't know how many of you are going to be loyal. But I will make you rich men." Christian started to pace while he swung the ax by his side.

He directed his attention to the men that were with Dax. "I'm going to give you a choice. Join us, or leave now."

"We leave, we're dead." One of the men said.

"Not today you're not."

None of them moved. Christian wasn't giving them much of a choice. They had to take his word that they didn't get a bullet to the back of the head as they walked toward the door.

"There's a new order now. It's my order. Without me, you will just be peddling a little second-class dope . . . or get killed. With me, you will be part of an empire. If you're in, we aren't forming alliances. We are forming one group. We are all ROMA."

"What do you mean by that?" Sonny was the first to pipe up. "What the hell is ROMA?"

"You're looking at them." Christian gestured toward himself and his own guys as he walked back toward Dax.

"Don't worry. You're still the Indo Nation. But if you want to get paid, you're working under ROMA. Kirt, hold his other arm out."

"Fuck no, man," Kirt said. "I can't do this."

Christian gave Kirt and icy stare.

"OK. I'll do it," Kirt said.

Kirt stretched Dax's arm out, gripping the elbow exactly as Jess had, and Christian stomped his foot down on Dax's hand. It was not clear if Dax was even conscious. There was less of a fight from Dax this time and Christian raised the ax again. He brought it down on Dax's other forearm, this time severing it completely on the first try.

Dax was definitely conscious as he screamed loudly for the second time. He lifted his head, but it fell back and bounced off the concrete.

The dark puddle surrounding Dax's body threatened to become a surging lake as his open veins continuously pumped out more and more blood, warming the cold cement floor.

Christian straddled Dax's body which was face down on the ground. He grabbed his hair and forced his head up. He whispered in his ear. "Beg me to kill you now."

Dax was barely awake and was breathing slow and heavy.

"Beg me!" Christian repeated.

"P-please." His broken voice forced out his last word.

Christian rose to his feet and drew his gun. He glared down at Dax who lay almost lifeless, face down on the ground. The dead silence of the room was broken by the clicking sound of the revolver being cocked. Christian pulled the trigger. The reverberation of the loud blast was deafening. With one last stare at the mutilated mess, Christian spit on Dax's corpse and turned away.

CHAPTER 77

Last Order of Business

Christian looked at ROMA and they looked back at him with fear in their eyes. Jordy sat leaning against the wall by the entrance. The other four stood a short distance away from him.

Christian approached Sonny the Money.

"You're one sick fuck," Sonny said.

"Is he in the back?" Christian pointed to a door in the back corner of the warehouse.

"Yep. My boys left a blow torch up in there like you asked. You ain't gonna torture that boy any further now are ya?"

Christian ignored the question. "You can take everyone outta here."

"Look, I gotta tell ya." Sonny put his arm around Christian. "That shit you were talking about, ROMA or whatever. I'm not all in yet."

"Yet?"

"You prove you can do what you say you can do, I don't care what our name is."

"Then consider yourself ROMA."

Sonny signaled for his guys to leave and they all shuffled out. Christian approached Deevon.

"What do you want to do with them?" Deevon pointed at Dax's crew.

Christian looked over at them and pondered. "Take them with you. They're your problem now."

"Let me tell you something, Chinny. You don't come through after what we just did up in here today," Deevon pointed to some chains hanging from the ceiling. "I'm gonna hang you upside down from one of those, and skin you alive."

Christian snickered. "You don't gotta worry." He turned to rejoin the guys.

As Deevon exited the building he yelled out to Christian, "Pleasure doing business with you."

"Can we get out of here?" Liam said.

"It's not over." Christian put his hand on Liam's shoulder.

"How is it not over?" Liam said.

"I would have put the gun in your hand if it was Dax that was behind Sammy's murder."

Liam furrowed his brows and slowly shook his head.

"Dax had nothing to do with your brother." Christian pulled out the letter that Braeden showed him earlier in the day and handed it to Liam. "This is why Braeden isn't here."

Liam took the letter and opened it. The others, with the exception of Jordy, crowded around.

Liam took a few seconds to read it and then looked up. "No."

"Li, it's true," Christian said.

"How long have you know about this?"

"Found out today."

Liam rushed Christian and grabbed on to the scruff of his neck with both hands. "Where is he?"

"Calm down for a sec, Li." Christian said and Liam released him.

Davie Boy wheeled up to Christian. "Shit Chin, you should have told us this."

Christian signaled Jess and Kirt. "Help Jord. We have one last piece of business."

Christian picked up a gun, despite having one already in the back of his jeans. They all needed to embrace what he had done this day by using ruthless aggression to satisfy his vengeance and make his point. Tonight he was going to push the limits, just for the sake of exposing these guys to what they now were.

They all proceeded to the back of the warehouse. Kirt and Jess were holding up Jordy, almost dragging him along.

They opened the door and entered another room. They all surrounded Braeden who was tied up in a chair, with duct tape over his mouth.

He tried to speak, but his words were muffled.

"Holy shit, Chin," Jess said. "He's fucked up."

Braeden's head and face were soaked with blood. One of his eyes was swollen shut and there was blood clotting his nostrils. After Christian's brutal attack, someone else must have had some fun with him.

"This is our so-called comrade. He betrayed all of us. He took an innocent kid, who we all protected. Liam's brother. Our brother," Christian said.

Christian snatched the note from Liam, partially crumpled it, and threw it toward Braeden. Braeden looked down at it and looked back up directly at Liam with widened eyes. He continued to let out muffled cries through the duct tape.

Christian walked over to Liam and handed him the gun he'd picked up earlier and also removed the one from the back of his jeans.

"Avenge your brother," Christian said.

Liam looked at Christian and then at the gun with teary eyes.

Liam slowly raised the gun. His hand was shaking and his face was now soaked with a combination of sweat and tears. "How could you do this?" He whimpered.

Braeden was struggling to yell something through the tape. He started moving back and forth in his seat and the chair was rocking.

"Avenge your brother!" Christian demanded.

"He wants to say something." Liam said in a scratchy voice.

"Fuck him." Christian said.

"Take the tape off. I wanna hear what he has to say."

Christian's decision was a tough one. If he removed the tape, Braeden would more than likely out him for his involvement. If he refused, it might reveal he had something to hide.

"Fine." Christian decided he would take his chances. He walked over to Braeden and ripped the tape from his mouth.

Braeden's battered and bruised face was hardly recognizable. It was hard to believe that the man sitting before them was once the happy-go-lucky person they thought couldn't harm a fly.

"Li. . ." Braeden's voice was soft and weak.

"How could you, Braed? We were like—"

"Li. I'm sorry. Just listen," Braeden said.

"Tell me, Braed. Was he scared? Did he even know what the fuck was going on?" Tears ran down Liam's face.

"It wasn't just me, Liam."

Liam just glared at Braeden.

There was the blast of a gunshot. A bullet penetrated Braeden's gut and his body leaned forward, silencing him. He was moaning and the front of his white t-shirt was painted red. The barrel from Christian's gun was smoldering.

"Liam. It's time. Avenge your fucking brother!"

"I wasn't done talkin', Chin," Liam said.

Christian shook his head and walked over to the corner of the room behind Braeden to retrieve the blow torch Sonny said he left. He had a feeling this was going to be a challenge, so this was his backup plan. He wanted Liam to be the one to pull the trigger, so he needed something that would entice him.

He walked over and stood behind Braeden.

The white noise from the torch grabbed everyone's attention as Christian looked at Liam. "I'm going to prolong this until you decide to take care of your business." Christian held the blow torch toward Braeden as he continued to slouch in his seat.

Liam's finger was pressed firmly against the trigger.

"Just shoot 'em, Li," Davie Boy said. "Like he did Sammy."

The lit blow torch was brought closer to the back of Braeden's neck. For a second it got close enough that Braeden flinched.

"Fuck, Li. Just do it, for Christ fuckin' sakes!" Jess said.

The torch inched its way closer to Braeden again and Liam's eyes locked with Christian's. Christian couldn't tell if his eyes were playing tricks on him. The gun that Liam was supposed to be pointing at Braeden, looked as though it were pointed at him. He squinted and shifted his head forward. Then a gunshot went off.

Braeden's head snapped back and fell forwards. Everyone looked in the direction of Davie Boy who lowered his gun and placed it back beside him in his wheelchair.

Christian turned the blow torch off and threw it to the ground. He said nothing and walked over to Liam who had lowered his gun.

Christian ripped the gun from his hand and threw it into a corner. He turned and looked down at Braeden and then back toward the guys.

"We can't be cowards . . . *You* can't be cowards." Christian specifically looked at Liam.

"Do you have any idea what I've just built?" Christian started pacing. There was a lull in the room and all the guys stared at the ground, listening intently.

"Everything I said from the beginning has fallen right into our laps. And we have to continue to stand up by any means necessary. If someone harms us, we will harm them ten times over. If someone betrays us . . . we'll eliminate them. We will all live comfortably if we stick by what we stand for. All those men that stood out there, in that warehouse, now stand behind us. They are now owned by ROMA. They *are* ROMA. But us in this room, except Braeden, who was a traitor—we are the founders of this new order. The choices we've made tonight, we'll have to make again. Some will say it's wrong . . . I say it's standing up. When is it too far? It's *never* too far. It's not what we do . . . it's why we do it! No matter who stands behind us—all those men are just soldiers—they are just pawns that are an extension of the *new* ROMA. The brotherhood behind this group that we built stops right here, in this room. We are the leaders of the new ROMA. We are the force behind everything that happens here on out. We are blood. Inclusive of the kid that carved those letters on the tree that night, our fallen brother, Samuel Malachi. We are the original seven."

CHAPTER 78

Mixed Signals

It had been a long time since Christian had been in this area. He approached the high school in which he never spent much time. Walking through the courtyard brought him back to the day he cursed his mother for walking with him. The grass *was* pretty damn green.

Further ahead, Liam sat alone on a bench smoking a cigarette. Christian approached him and sat beside him.

"Thought you're not supposed to smoke on school grounds," Christian said, still facing forward.

"Thanks for coming."

They both sat there in silence. Christian lit a cigarette and Liam lit another.

"I was cleaning out some things in Sammy's room today. Look what I found." Liam handed Christian a folded piece of paper.

Christian opened it and laughed. "Shit. The Star of David poster. Fucking kid." They both shared a brief chuckle.

"Wasn't too far from here where you saved mine and Sammy's asses from our good friend, Jordy."

Liam took a long drag of his smoke, squinting from the sun shining on the side of his face. "You remember the first time we went to Russ's club and that dude started harassing that black guy, Chin? You stuck up for him and gave him a hundred bucks."

"Yep. It was the right thing to do."

"And this goddamn Star of David poster . . . that was the same day you stole my brother's bike back. That was also the right thing to do."

"You're going somewhere with this, aren't you, Li?"

"Back then you always did the right thing, Chin. All those things were the reason I thought you were the coolest kid on earth. That's the guy I met and looked up to. I really liked Christian."

"I'm still Christian."

"Sometimes I think we forget the whole reason why we came together as a group."

Christian pushed some ashes off his cigarette and leaned back against the bench. "You're telling me you're out. Is that what this is about?"

Liam ignored the question.

"You said that night in the warehouse, *it's not what we do, it's why we do it.*"

"The truth."

"Why do we do it then, Chin?"

"You need to find those answers yourself, Li."

"That's a cop out." Liam shook his head.

"What is it that you want me to say here, Liam?"

"*You* don't even know *why we do it.* You don't even remember what we were supposed to stand for. You preach it but you have no idea what the fuck you're talking about. When you first moved here, I think you did know. You always talked about rebelling at the injustices that you faced and we faced. We weren't gonna let the world beat us down, be it people or situations. We were supposed to take positive steps forward, even if it was with some questionable actions. But there's a fine line between questionable and . . . you know . . . what we do. Look at what we've done, who we've hurt and what we've lost. You have a daughter due any day, and you don't even talk to the mother of your child. You are working side by side with your father—a man you despise—and for what? Money?"

Christian turned his body toward Liam, waving his finger. "I have done everything I said I would do. I've accomplished everything I stand for. I won, Liam."

"What do you stand for, Chinny? What the hell do you stand for?"

"People change, Liam. Situations change. Goals change. I said from the beginning, I will go up against anything that life throws at me. For these last couple years I have, and I won. Now answer me this, Li, after all is said and done, who do you think would dare fuck with me now?"

"Fuck with you now? God . . . you're drunk on power. But you'd be nothing without . . . you know what, forget it. I'm done. I'm just gonna go." Liam rose to his feet.

"Find your answers, Liam. Then tell me where you stand." Christian leaned back on the bench, raising his head and blowing smoke in the air.

Liam turned and glared down at Christian who reciprocated the stare. "Braeden said he didn't act alone. He said it wasn't just him. The only answers that I need to find is the whole story behind what happened to my brother."

Christian stood up and flicked his cigarette to the side and stood face to face with Liam. They stared at each other for a few seconds.

Christian tilted his head slightly and glared deep into Liam's eyes. "Be careful, *brother* . . . you might not like the answers."

Liam's eyes widened for a moment and his face turned pale.

Christian continued, "What I mean is, I don't want to see you hurt so badly again. Sometimes it's just better to leave things be."

Liam slowly nodded with a blank stare on his face. "I'll see you, when I see you, Chin."

Liam left and Christian sat back down on the bench. In the distance there were five kids. Two of them looked like they were being harassed by the other three.

Christian got off the bench and started walking in their direction. "Hey!"

Three of the boys turned and spotted Christian walking toward them. Christian was able to hear one of them speak.

"Shit that looks like that dude they call Chinny." All three of them, without confirmation of their suspicion, sprinted away.

Christian approached the remaining two boys, who looked no more than fifteen or sixteen and were sitting on the ground against the wall.

"You OK?" Christian said.

"Yeah, we're fine."

"Let me tell you something. Next time some jerks like that pick on you, hit 'em here, then here." Christian pointed to his throat then his crotch.

"Are you really that Chinny guy?"

Christian gave half a grin. "My name's Christian. You just remember, it's always going to be this way, if you don't choose one day to stand up."

Author's Note

If you are reading this page, I want to thank you for coming along for this journey with me, taking the time to enter my mind and following it to the end; it means a lot. I hope you enjoyed it, or at least appreciate what I have done here.

For so many years I tried to write and complete something, but this was the first time I was able to accomplish that. The writing may not be up to par with writers who have been doing this for years, but it is still an accomplishment for me that I'm proud of.

I came up with The ROMA Seven in 2012 and only really started seriously writing it in 2015. It was one of many countless attempts to start and finish a story. Every other attempt I have ever made, I tried starting with outlines and this time I did something different—I just wrote the story from beginning to end, not knowing in advance of what direction it was taking me. I was happy with that strategy. I enjoyed living it as it played out.

I learnt a lot through this process and not just about writing. I've learnt about myself.

Christian Xavier Solomon, the leader of ROMA was an extension of myself. I never intended that. Don't get me wrong, I am nothing like him when it comes to how he made money or some of the drastic things he did. But in a very subtle way, there is a lot of me in his less drastic thought processes. I sat in a restaurant with my wife, Lori, on one of our date nights, and we discussed my book a little bit. I told her, Christian is ninety percent fictitious and ten percent real. That's probably not exactly true. I would say, in actuality it is more like ninety-seven percent fictitious and three percent real. Don't worry, I have never ran or even been a part of a criminal empire.

The story itself, although it is purely fiction, I enjoyed adding some incidents based on real life. Nothing major, but there are a few things I snuck in that had some truth to it. One example of this, was when Christian cooked eggs for Victoria, Miranda and Gran. He used soap instead of oil. My mother accidently did that when my sisters and I were kids and I was just a baby. She told me she felt so bad, because my sisters said the eggs tasted really funny and as a result didn't eat them. Me, on the other hand, not old enough yet to voice my opinion, gobbled them all up. Only moments after I chowed down, my mom realized her mistake. I guess sometimes life can be more interesting than fiction.

There is one thing I want to touch on, that I was questioned about, when it came to the story. Christian's reason for doing what he ended up doing. He preached from the beginning to the end that he wanted to stand up against everything that had previously beat him down. There were a couple times he chose not to do certain things and said: "That's not what I stand for." What did he stand for then? What was his purpose? And what was he actually standing up against? He was always pretty vague about why he made some of his choices and brought others a long for the ride. When he did give his reasons, they sounded more like excuses to justify his actions.

One of the last things he said to the group, was the tagline for the novel: "It's not what we do, it's why we do it." So I felt it was very fitting when Liam, in the last chapter, questioned him: "Why do we do it then, Chin?" Christian still didn't answer the question, because he just didn't know, himself, but he would never admit that.

While that may not be satisfying, or maybe it feels like a loose end that wasn't tied up—to me it's real. That's life. Many people, not all, walk around not knowing their purpose. They make impulsive, bad decisions, often fueled by their emotions. They don't really know why they are doing what they are doing, and just go with the flow. They find justification in their poor choices, and swear blind it is the right thing to do. Then when one poor choice leads to another, it's a snowball effect. As a result they find themselves in too deep.

In closing, I would like to thank you again and I hope that you will read my next project, which is the sequel to this one. It is being written as I write this and I have no idea when completion will be yet. Feel free to contact me at the below information, because I would love to hear your questions or feedback—negative or positive.

Richard L. Ross
rich.ross79@gmail.com
theromaseven.com

68381267R00219

Made in the USA
Charleston, SC
10 March 2017